Lunch with the Generals

'This story is about a man who falls in love with a woman many years younger than himself. He gives her, as an engagement present, a most precious gift. A gift that brings life where there is mere existence. Joy where there is suffering. Relief where there is guilt. It is the story of the man, the woman, the gift and the consequences of the gift. Consequences which result in the man hiding in a dark alley, an open razor in his hand. He intends to use it not as an act of violence but of love. Can you imagine the circumstances that could bring this about? How could such a thing possibly be an act of love or even construed that way? Truth does not have the convenience of fiction. Sometimes it is a cross too heavy to bear.

'My story comes in two parts... Listen well or you may prove too hasty in your conclusions. I will require your patience for many weeks if I am to do justice to those involved.'

The audience settled back in their chairs. The label had been read, the cork extracted. The story, having breathed, was now ready to flow. Nobody believed for a second that it would be true.

Lunch with the Generals

DEREK HANSEN

Mandarin

A Mandarin Paperback
LUNCH WITH THE GENERALS

First published in Great Britain 1994
by William Heinemann Ltd
and Mandarin Paperbacks
imprints of Reed Consumer Books Ltd
Michelin House, 81 Fulham Road, London SW3 6RB
and Auckland, Melbourne and Singapore

Copyright © Derek Hansen 1993
The author has asserted his moral rights

A CIP Catalogue record for this title
is available from the British Library
ISBN 0 7493 1765 5

Printed and bound in Great Britain
by Cox and Wyman Ltd, Reading, Berks

To Tom and Ethel

CONTENTS

Acknowledgements

Throughout the writing and editing of this book, I was continually surprised – and delighted – by the willingness of people to help me. I was never left wanting for reference material, photographs, expert advice or wise counsel.

Foremost among my helpers were Bryce Courtenay whose advice and introductions were invaluable; Louise Adler who taught me not to fear editors; Dr David Tiller at the Royal Prince Alfred Hospital; Brian Van Den Hurk and Maureen Santoso in Indonesia; Carol Lye, Nanette Morris, Alex Lyus and Alex Mills.

Special thanks to Mark Lees and Rob Kelly for help with the cover. And last – but by no means least – my patient researcher, tireless motivator and wife, Carole.

I owe them all.

FIRST THURSDAY

They met every Thursday at twelve-thirty, at the same restaurant and at the same table. Gancio always prepared them a special menu, which other diners would look upon with envy. Gancio came from the shores of Lake Como to open his restaurant in Leichhardt, the heart of Sydney's Italian community. But it was a journey with many detours. He owed his restaurant to one of the four men seated at the window table – Ramon, the tall one, the Argentinian whose turn it was to tell a story. Ramon had rescued Gancio from an endless succession of dead-end jobs. He'd found him in the pasta bar of a workingman's pub, where Gancio pumped out endless *bolognaise*, *marinara* and *matriciana* to an unappreciative clientele more interested in beer. Ramon had recognised his talent and an opportunity. Gancio's Giardino had quickly won a loyal following and generated sufficient profit to satisfy them both. Yet their partnership was a secret, Ramon insisted upon that. But that is why Gancio marinated little fish specially for them, or stuffed calamari, or baked capsicum for their entrée.

Ramon always arrived promptly. Gancio would watch for his taxi and escort him to the table. It was a courtesy not a necessity, even though Ramon was blind. He could find his way as surely as the sighted by following the carpet runner which, with one right

1

turn, led directly to his waiting friends. He was always over-dressed for the restaurant. He carried a silver-handled cane, and wore his Zegna suits with the easy comfort others wear t-shirts. His hair was elegantly streaked with grey, and he wore tinted glasses. Most women would say he was handsome and doubtless Ramon did all he could to encourage them.

'Ah . . . the last of the Mohicans.' Milos stood and formally shook Ramon's hand as Gancio guided him to his seat. Milos always rose to greet each of them as they arrived. The eldest by some ten years, he had assumed the role of unofficial chairman. Perhaps that's why he stood where the others were content to remain seated as they greeted each other. Or perhaps it was a demonstration of European courtesy. If so it was an affectation, for his feet had not touched European soil in more than forty years. Milos, having fought first the Germans and then the Russians, had decided his best interests lay in going as far from his native Hungary as a man could, and he had not felt the need to return.

'*Buon giorno*, Ramon. *Come sta?*'

'*Va bene*, thank you, Lucio.'

Short, fat, irrepressible Lucio came from Varese, also near Lake Como in the north of Italy. Gancio often disowned him because of the stories he told. Lucio always sat in the window seat so he was forced to look away from the young women eating pasta at the outside tables. His appetite for both women and food was prodigious. He maintained it was because he'd been obliged to share the first five years of his life with a war.

'First the Germans came and stole our women,' he claimed. 'Then the Americans. Friend or foe, both stole our food. I remember having to share a single strand of pasta with my elder brother. We'd each put an end in our mouth and when our mother gave the nod we'd both start sucking. We'd fight bitterly for each centimetre of pasta, but no matter how hard we fought we'd always end up kissing each other.' He had dedicated the remainder of his life to compensating for this early deprivation.

'G'day, Ramon.'

'Ah, Neil . . . did you take your trousers to my tailors?'

'Yup. They did a good job, but I made the mistake of letting them measure me for a suit.'

'They make very good suits.'

'They'd better. I told them I wanted to look like you, Ramon.'

'Thank you.'

'But without the stain on the tie.'

Ramon laughed. Neil was the only one who ever made jokes about his blindness. He seemed to enjoy niggling away at the flaws and idiosyncrasies in others. At the beginning, whenever Milos stood to greet anybody, Neil would whistle the national anthem. He kept doing it until Milos was no longer irritated by it. Neil was the only one among them who had been born in Australia. He was the youngest of them all, a fit forty-four year old. Neil was a property developer and had a property developer's suntan, pragmatism and taste. He wore a heavy gold chain around his neck like a badge of office, and his shirt was always open down to the third button so none could miss it. Neil never changed, whatever the state of the economy or his own personal finances. He rode the boom-bust cycle as if immune to its influence.

'You remember how we met four years ago?' Ramon began. Of course they did. How could they forget? But they knew better than to interrupt. Ramon was establishing his parameters, directing his listeners to a common viewpoint from which to begin his story.

'You arrived separately, three optimists each seeking a table for one on a Thursday afternoon. Gancio took pity on you and sat you at my table. I have been grateful to him ever since, for we discovered our common interest. But over these four years, what have you learned about me? What have I learned about you? Nothing.

'In this respect we are all typical Australian males. If one of you were dying of cancer, would you tell us? If one of you had decided to divorce your wife and run off with another woman half your age, would you tell us first? If you awoke one morning and discovered you were penniless, would you tell us? Neil, you know the answer to that better than any of us. You would rather slash your wrists than admit to being broke.'

'No you're wrong there. I'd probably throw myself under a Rolls-Royce. More my style.'

'Roller or razor, the point is made. What have we told each other about ourselves over the last four years? Nothing! If we were women we would know everything about each other by now. But no. We are men. And Australian machismo keeps the lid shut tight on our private affairs.

'Milos here has endeared us all to Hungary and shown us its people, its humour and its tragedies. Yet Milos has not once pulled the curtain wider on himself. My friend, what do we know about you? Like me you are retired and obviously not short of a dollar. I made my money in printing, you in rubbish.'

'Waste disposal,' interrupted Neil plaintively, with a near-perfect imitation of Milos' voice.

'You mean you have never sold landfill as prime real estate?' Milos always bit. The source of his wealth was a sensitive issue and therefore irresistible to Neil.

'Beyond that,' Ramon continued blithely, 'and the fact that you have a wife with whom you share our stories, what do we know about you? You reveal details of your life as unwillingly as a poker player reveals details of his hand. And you, Lucio, you fill our ears with your tales from Italian bedrooms and tell us nothing about yourself. It's enough for you that you make us laugh. But who are you really, behind all the boasts and bravado?'

'Who am I?' exclaimed Lucio indignantly. 'I have told you a hundred times! Are you deaf? I am a short, fat, bald Italian, at the peak of my sexual power. Women find me irresistible. Hundreds will testify to this under oath.'

'I'm sure you mean under duress, no?' Milos smiled his patient smile. 'Now let Ramon continue.'

'Our friend Neil constructs his stories with economy and simplicity, like a writer of short stories. But again reveals nothing of himself. The point is we sit here as friends yet we know nothing about each other, apart from what we reveal in the choice of stories we tell and the morality we apply. I am no exception. What do you know about me? Nothing other than what I've been prepared to reveal.'

'We know you like to play games, no? And I'm not talking about the games you play when you tell your stories. You have a callous streak, Ramon. Like just now. You deliberately set me up. You knew Neil could not resist the comment about rubbish and you knew I'd respond. With one casually dropped word you score points off both of us. It doesn't matter to me, but I don't know why you bother.'

'Oh come on, Milos, you are too sensitive. Where is the harm? You say I play games and I don't deny it. But don't we all? We have painted a picture of ourselves which we project to each other. That picture may be no more real than the stories we tell, yet it is a comfortable arrangement. Our private lives are our own and this leaves us free to enjoy each other's company in the roles we have each elected to play. That is why I hesitate to tell this story though it is my turn and my obligation. I do not wish to put our friendship in jeopardy. But this story burns to be told. It clouds my mind when I seek other subjects upon which to fabricate a tale. Unless it is told and dispensed with, I fear my ability to contribute at these lunches will be suffocated, and the day will come when I am no longer welcome. Yet I hesitate, for it is a true story and it trespasses upon my past. A past I do not care to remember.

'This story begins in my country, in the turmoil and troubles after Peron which resulted in my exile. Yet I may be considered the fortunate one. I lost my country and my heritage while others lost their lives. But I will not burden you with my misfortunes. There are parallels in this story but they are not for me to point out. They are yours to discover if you choose to look. I will draw the curtains no wider on my life. Nor will I encourage your speculation.

'This story is about a man who falls in love with a woman many years younger than himself. He gives her, as an engagement present, a most precious gift. A gift that brings life where there is mere existence. Joy where there is suffering. Relief where there is guilt. It is the story of the man, the woman, the gift and the consequences of the gift. Consequences which result in the man hiding in a dark alley, an open razor in his hand. He intends to use it not as an act of violence but of love. Can you imagine the circumstances that could bring this about? How could such a thing possibly be an act of love or even construed that way? Truth does not have the convenience of fiction. Sometimes it is a cross too heavy to bear.'

'Bravo,' said Lucio quietly.

'My story will come in two parts. The first deals with each of the main characters. You must come to know them well, to understand why they are the kind of people they are, and why they do the things they do. The second part depends on it, for it is the resolution. Listen well or you may prove too hasty in your conclusions. I will require your patience for many weeks if I am to do justice to those involved.'

The audience settled back in their chairs. The label had been read, the cork extracted. The story, having breathed, was now ready to flow. Nobody believed for a second that it would be true.

Chapter One

Buenos Aires, 1978

Roberto Sanguineti was six years old and small for his age. His family lived in an ornate colonial house in the 'little Italy' of Buenos Aires, La Boca. The house was large and needed repairs that neither landlord nor tenants felt disposed to make.

There were lots of places in this house for a small boy to hide without even going upstairs to the bedrooms. Roberto had tried them all. Tonight he'd found a special place because the restorers had failed to collect the table and eight balloon-back dining-chairs. The chairs were stacked one atop the other, and packed tightly into the recess beneath the stairs so that they wouldn't block the reception area. But chairs are one shape and stairs another, and Roberto knew that if he could wriggle his way through the forest of legs, there'd be a boy-sized space where the first steps formed a wedge with the floor.

Careful not to make a sound he began to worm his way through. Any moment now his father, Victor, would call him for dinner knowing full well that his son would be hiding. Roberto would tremble with anticipation as his father began to look for him. Roberto adored playing hide-and-seek with his father, and they'd played the game since he had first learned to walk. He couldn't wait to be found because that was the best part – his father finding him. Then for precious minutes he'd have his father all to himself, and they'd wrestle and tickle and laugh while his mother pretended to get angry with them both. They never tired of the game and Victor, who was often too busy with his work and his politics for such play, cherished these moments.

Roberto reached his little hideaway and pulled the rolled-up rug they stored there over him, so that only his eyes peeped out. He just knew his father would never find him. And his father never did.

Just as his mother called them to dinner, the soldiers burst through the front door and brought Roberto's world crashing down around him. He never played hide-and-seek with his father again.

Chapter Two

Roberto's mother, Rosa Angelica, was often blamed for the tragic events that took place because she had foolishly married the wrong man. But that is unfair and typical of Argentina where men are not allowed to be at fault. Besides, other women never missed the opportunity to be critical of Rosa. She was too popular with the men, too vivacious, too beautiful and, most unforgivable of all, too independent. Of course she was to blame.

As a child, Rosa was never out of trouble. She was brought up in the coastal resort district of San Isidro. The family home was neither old enough to be historic, nor modern enough to be comfortable. Her mother did her best to brighten up the old house by painting its stucco walls a pastel pink, knowing that it would fade in the sun and soften back to a more pleasing shade. It was not a small house but neither was it large. It was certainly not large enough to offer any escape from Rosa.

It wasn't that Rosa was wicked. It was just that she saw life as a boundless opportunity for fun and couldn't understand why others were so timid. Her family were devout Catholics and sometimes they would take Rosa and her four older sisters to the Cathedral of San Isidro. The cathedral wasn't particularly old, but it had a splendour and sense of grandeur which hinted at the majesty of heaven. Perhaps her parents hoped some of the reverence would rub off on Rosa, but they were always destined to be disappointed.

She would shock her parents and shame her sisters by letting go sneaky little smells, and giggling so none were left in doubt as to the source. Sex was never a mystery. It wasn't a subject her parents would allow to be discussed in the home but that was no impediment to her education. Nobody was quite sure how she acquired her knowledge, particularly the lurid details. But her sisters were never in doubt as to where they learned the facts of life. They learned from Rosa. And they learned never to leave Rosa alone within reach of their boyfriends.

Rosa couldn't help herself. She'd flirt outrageously with them, or sidle up to them and shock them to their souls, leaving their masculinity in tatters.

'I hope you're not planning to fuck my sister tonight,' she'd say innocently, 'because she's having her period.'

Or she'd say, 'Is your penis as big as Julio's? Bibiana likes a big penis. She says the little ones aren't worth bothering with.'

Sometimes the things she said found their way back to her humiliated sisters. She'd be beaten by her shocked parents, and dragged sobbing but unrepentant to her room.

Poor Rosa. She just couldn't bear the boredom of conformity, of life at a gentle trot when it was so much more thrilling to gallop. The nuns did their best, and made a fair job of educating her, although her free spirit and blatant sexuality must have sorely tested their faith.

Rosa's father gave up trying to understand her. He gave her an allowance instead. As soon as she was old enough he packed her off to the University of Buenos Aires, hoping that noble institution would put some sense into her where he had failed. It was a curious decision although, to be fair, his options were limited.

It was the time of violent conflict between students and the Peronist labour unions. Though most of the fighting took place in Cordoba, Corrientes and Rosario, the University of Buenos Aires had its own activists and underground movements, each infiltrated to some degree by the other and by the military. Even then, in the early seventies, political activism was a significant cause of death, though it was to get much worse later, under Rafael Videla and Galtieri.

The University of Buenos Aires spread its faculties throughout the city and had no campus. Even so, the students had chosen various places in Reconquista and La Boca which they made their own. Rosa's instincts led her straight to them.

When Rosa saw the social and political maelstrom to which her father had consigned her, she thought he had finally come to understand her and that this was his way of showing it. Tears of love welled in her eyes. She wrote him a long letter thanking him profusely and begging his forgiveness for her earlier excesses. Her letter oozed love and sincerity which pleased her father but left him totally confused.

It seemed that most students belonged to one faction or another, though the ones that interested Rosa weren't the kind to advertise their presence. For a while she flirted with the leftist Peronista, but her nose for the illicit and mysterious sniffed out the small and, she thought, extremist Trotskyite group, the People's Democratic Movement. Rosa thought that they'd be the most exciting to join because they were the most elusive. And membership, therefore, the most perilous.

She made enquiries, probably too many. When a soldier of the movement, a young woman dressed in battle fatigues, made contact with her, it may only have been to shut her up.

'Rosa Angelica,' the young revolutionary said as she ghosted up alongside her. 'We must talk. I am from the movement, I am instructed to bring you to the leader of our cell.'

'My God! Do I have to wear those appalling clothes?' asked Rosa.

Rosa was taken through a bizarre series of switch-backs and one-stop rides on the *colectivos* – the privately owned buses which swarm around the suburbs – in an attempt to shake off anyone bored enough to follow them. Finally, in the poorest part of San Telmo, she was led down chipped and broken steps to a dingy basement room.

It was cold, damp and smelled of cats. It screamed poverty and deprivation, and failed even to whisper excitement. Rosa was told to wait while her companion beat a complicated rhythm on a slatted timber door as a prelude to gaining entrance. She waited. And waited. After ten minutes of cats' piss and boredom, she was ready to head off and catch the first *colectivo* that happened to pass. But then the door opened once more and she was admitted.

She found herself facing an intense young man only a year or two older than herself. His ordinariness disappointed her – she had expected to meet a clone of Che Guevara. Yet he was not unattractive and he had the most piercing blue eyes she had ever seen. They stared at her, examined her minutely, and she had the disconcerting feeling that he could see through her clothes. She wished she'd worn a bra.

'Why do you wish to join our movement?' he asked abruptly.

'The poor are too poor. And the rich are too rich.'

Silence filled the room. Rosa hadn't really thought beyond that, and tried desperately to recall some of the more extreme slogans of the Peronist left.

'Go on.'

The blue eyes never wavered. Rosa realised with surprise that this man was genuinely interested to hear what she had to say.

'Aren't you going to introduce yourself?'

Rosa heard a sharp intake of breath from her escort. The man continued to stare at her as if nothing had been said. Then he smiled. Could anybody really be so gauche? The evidence stood before him. That is why he smiled.

'Forgive me. Sometimes we neglect common courtesies. Sometimes it is not wise to know the names of others. I am Victor.' He looked past Rosa to her keeper. 'Thank you, Lydia, you can leave now. Our newest candidate poses no threat.'

'Leader,' she responded, unable to disobey yet unwilling to go. But go she did.

'Now please continue,' said Victor. 'And please sit down.'

Rosa pulled the little bentwood chair across in front of his desk until she sat directly opposite him. She gazed around the tiny room as she stalled for time, hoping to find inspiration. But what inspiration could anyone find in a naked bulb dangling on a dangerously worn flex from a sagging, mould-spotted ceiling?

'The poor are too poor,' she repeated, 'and the rich too rich. Surely that is the crux of the matter. Solve that and you solve all of Argentina's problems.'

Victor nodded. If her answer was simplistic, it was also valid. Rosa was no intellectual giant, he saw that clearly. But doubtless she would respond to their teaching. Victor had the dedication and single-mindedness that makes martyrs of men. He was too ready to trust and too unwilling to suspect others of ulterior motives. His politics were not a product of a deprived upbringing, but of a well-educated mind that cried 'foul' in the face of injustice. He was an idealist, and for all his political sophistication, he was still an innocent. He was ill equipped to cope with a woman as formidable as Rosa.

He started to tell Rosa of their mission to create a better, more equitable Argentina, when she shifted position and crossed her legs. It was a nothing gesture yet it unsettled him. He told her about communising the *estancias*, the great cattle stations of the pampas, of the greed of their owners, and her lips moved as if she was about to speak. He spoke of the untapped oil and minerals beneath the wilderness of Patagonia and how exploration monies were dissipated by corruption, when she leaned forward and took his hand in hers. He was about to tell her of the natural gas resources of Tierra del Fuego, which were being senselessly burned off, when his mouth dried up and his words with it.

Victor never understood what she did or how she did it, but the prospect of a more equitable Argentina was quickly subordinated to the prospect of what Rosa offered. They made love there and then, upon the revolutionary desk, with Rosa astride him, skirts hoisted high. Victor's trousers never got past his knees. He reached his hands up inside her blouse to her bobbling breasts and hung on, it seemed, for dear life.

Whether or not Rosa really embraced the politics of the left is arguable. Some, like Lydia, claimed she'd only attend demonstrations that passed by her hairdresser, whereupon she'd slip in through the doors and keep her appointment.

Still, she stayed close to Victor and Victor stayed close to his mission. As it transpired, the People's Democratic Movement were extreme only in their beliefs, and moderate, even pacifist, in their actions. Once again, Rosa's impetuousness had let her down. She'd thought she was joining the Buenos Aires chapter of the hardcore People's Revolutionary Army, a militant and violent group which had the arms and audacity to take on the military in set-piece battles. It's as well she didn't. If the People's Revolutionary Army had allowed her to join, it would only have been to sacrifice her later. Argentinian politics is like that.

So Victor fell prey to Rosa, but Rosa was herself about to be preyed upon, by a fellow student called Jorge Luis Masot. He was the man Rosa should have married. Victor was just too serious and too responsible. Worst of all, where a girl like Rosa was concerned, too frugal. Committed leftists simply don't splash out and indulge in bourgeois pleasures. Rosa should have realised that.

At first there was the flush of new love made all the sweeter by the jealousy of Lydia and other bright-eyed hopefuls in the movement. They thought Rosa shallow and bitterly resented the fact that their leader had fallen for her. 'Anyone but Rosa,' they said in their anguish. 'Dear God, anyone but her.' There was also the thrill of being part of a big secret, of covert meetings, code words, subterfuge and intrigue.

But it was all a game to Rosa and she grew weary of it. There were lighter moments. Evenings spent debating over cheap red wine, while the problems of Argentina defined themselves with crystal clarity, and were resolved in wisdoms which evaporated with the morning sun.

Sometimes they went dancing, and tangoed to popular melodies doctored with revolutionary lyrics and sung in *lunfardo*, the half-Spanish/half-Italian slang of Buenos Aires. But the occasions were all too few. Rosa was a true *porteña*, and like all *porteños*, as residents of Buenos Aires are called, she lived for the night. For the clubs and the bars that rage till dawn. In her heart she heard the call of the *bandoneón*, the concertina-like instrument inseparable from the tango, not the call of a new order.

Rosa would have drifted away from the movement but for Victor. He loved her. Oh, yes! He loved her. Completely and utterly, without guile or condition. Poor Victor worshipped her, and in his innocence assumed she loved him equally. Rosa liked Victor, and she liked being loved. But she didn't love him. She was ready for the intervention of Jorge Luis Masot.

Chapter Three

Jorge Luis Masot was a child of privilege. He was born on the family *estancia* near Pergamino, in the humid pampas. He should have been born two hundred and fifty kilometres away in Buenos Aires, in the finest hospital attended by the most eminent doctors, but he had the presumption to arrive three weeks early. The birth was attended by a local doctor who smelled of whisky, and a midwife who was given to invoking God's saving grace at the slightest provocation. Fortunately for his mother, the child was in a hurry and the birth was as easy as any birth could be, where the only pain management is a whisky-flavoured exhortation to 'take a deep breath' and a prayer offered in the hushed tones of the last rites.

The pain and the indignity caused Jorge's mother to decide enough was enough, and so he became the last and youngest of four children, all boys. Perhaps if he'd been born a girl, his mother would have shown more interest, though it seems unlikely. Jorge was handed over to a nanny, as his brothers had been before him, and her first task was to wean him off the breast milk his mother expressed and onto cow's milk. Jorge couldn't know it at the time, but his mother would never take him in her arms again.

The family moved from the *estancia* to their home in Buenos Aires and back again, depending upon the season or the whim of

Jorge's mother. Of his two homes Jorge preferred the *estancia*, and most of the first five years of his life were spent there. The ranch house was palatial, as grand and stately as colonial architects and money could make it.

It was built within a perfect square, its four single-storey sides enclosing a courtyard which was grassed and cut by diagonal pathways. Each exterior wall had an entrance, flanked on either side by four shuttered windows. One entrance led from the driveway and this was the grandest, as its approach suggested it would be. The driveway, arrow straight, was guarded on either side of its half kilometre length by cypress trees. Another entrance led onto the sweeping lawns which surrounded the house. A third provided direct access to the inner courtyard past timbered gates that needed the combined strength of two men to move. The fourth led to an extension which would have dismayed the original architects had they still been alive.

It was a two-storey building which housed all the servants and a kitchen which would not have been out of place in a five-star hotel. It was Jorge's favourite part of the house because it was where his adoring nanny and all his friends lived.

His friends were the servants whose responsibilities included keeping the boys safe, entertained and out of the way. They taught Jorge to swim in the fifty-metre swimming pool, which nobody ever used except the boys and those servants fortunate enough to give them swimming lessons. They taught him to play tennis on the court made of pulverised reddish-brown stone and kept as immaculate as the gardens. They taught him to ride his pony, knowing that a fall would bring punishment or even their dismissal. So they taught him well, and breathed a sigh of relief when he displayed the same natural balance and athleticism as his brothers.

Jorge had everything a boy could ask for, except loving attentive parents. But what more could he expect, given that his father was one of the wealthiest and most powerful men in Argentina and his mother a leading socialite?

From the age of five, Jorge's time was spent at school in Buenos

Aires or holidaying at the *estancia*, or at the seaside resort of Mar del Plata. At various times he appeared to show promise as a swimmer, a tennis player, and, as fitting testimony to the effort that went into teaching him to ride, a polo player. But it was at schoolboy rugby that he excelled.

He made the school's first fifteen at the age of fourteen and one week. He was one of the youngest ever to be capped. Even more remarkably he won his promotion in the critical position of five-eighth.

Jorge was a natural. He could read a game as easily as others read books. He knew exactly when to unleash his backs, and when to turn the ball back into his forwards. He knew when to hold onto the ball, too, and this is what pleased the crowd. He had speed, a deceptive side-step off both feet, and a swerve and change of pace that left defenders looking leaden and foolish.

He also had an incentive to do better than any other boy on the field. One day he had used his skills to perfection. He broke the defensive line with sheer acceleration, dummied the cover defence, then side-stepped the fullback to score under the posts. He knew he'd done well. The cheers from the sideline and the back-slapping from his team-mates confirmed this. He looked for his coach. All players, from the great to the plodders, look to win the approval of their coach. There is no higher praise.

But on this day for the young Jorge there was. He recognised the figure standing next to the coach and applauding the try. It was his father. He could scarcely believe his eyes. His father was applauding him!

His father became a regular spectator at Jorge's games. What's more, his father seemed impressed by what he saw. Jorge would have happily kneed, gouged and stomped his own coach if he had thought that would increase his father's approval. He played every game as if the survival of the world depended on his efforts. At the end of each game, his father would nod to his son, shake hands with the coach, and disappear into his Mercedes with his minders. Jorge would glow with pride.

In his final year of school, as he prepared for university, a fellow student was kidnapped, ransomed and finally executed by a group purporting to be fund-raisers for the People's Revolutionary Army. Perhaps they were, but no one will ever know for sure, because they were comprehensively shot in the process of being arrested. Probably everybody in Argentina, bar the victims and their relatives, approved of the police action.

'Let that be a lesson,' they said righteously, without ever knowing at whom the lesson was aimed.

The event, quite understandably, brought the spoilt, indulged child abruptly into the real world. He did something neither he nor his brothers had ever done before. He rang his father in his office.

'I wondered if you would call,' his father said, and Jorge would never know whether he had or not. Nevertheless, it put him at his ease and made him feel special. He told his father about the boy who had been abducted.

'I am aware of this incident,' his father said. 'Now tell me, what has it taught you?'

Jorge thought for a moment, his brain racing, knowing his father would judge him on his response.

'I think your sons would do well to conceal the true identity of their father.'

'Yes. Go on.'

'Your sons would do well to be cautious with money and selective of their friends.'

'Yes. And . . . ?'

Jorge didn't know what to say next.

'Perhaps your sons should have bodyguards,' he blurted.

'All my sons have bodyguards.'

Jorge was dumbstruck. Who were they? He dared not ask, for if he was supposed to know his father would have already told him.

'There is one more thing my sons would do well to observe. Do not discuss your past. Never mention the family home in La Recoleta nor the *estancia*. Do not discuss your father's business either directly or indirectly. Do not discuss your friends. Your friends will be similarly instructed. Soon you will have your own apartment when you attend university. However, you will not go to Belgrano or St Andrews as you had planned. If these kidnappings continue, the private universities will be the first targets. It is too late for your brothers, but not for you. You will go to the University of Buenos Aires. There you will meet new people and widen your circle of acquaintances, and your past will lose its hold on you. Encourage this. You have done well to ring me and your answers show that your education has not been wasted. One more thing. Do not allow your socks to fall down around your rugby boots. It is undignified. Either endure the cramps or loosen your garters. Goodbye now.'

Jorge's father hung up, but even that failed to bring Jorge down from the clouds. He thought his father was the most wonderful man in the world. He couldn't recall his father ever speaking to him for so long before.

Three years would pass before he met Rosa. He spotted her in a student nightclub in Reconquista, and her sensuality reached across the crowd between them, igniting his nerve endings and turning his spine to jelly. Who knows what it is that one person sees that another misses? Why a glance can excite passions in one yet pass others by? Whatever Rosa did, it worked on Jorge. He began to stalk her, to hang out in places he knew she'd be. He'd follow her and spy on her. His head swam with her image. She consumed his thoughts. Nature had shaped her to attract a mate as surely as blossoms attract bees, and her particular blossom attracted Jorge.

She wasn't slim in the then fashionable Shrimpton mould. Her figure was far too full for the fashion gurus of the sixties, and nothing could conceal the majesty of her breasts or the outrageous curve of her hips. Jorge followed her to the cafeterias, and sat where he could watch her. She was animated and carefree, and unselfconscious in the way she'd play with strands of her long auburn hair. She drove Jorge mad.

But he was patient and he was calculating. He had confidence in his ability to win her. After all, he had charm, good looks, money and he was accustomed to getting whatever he wanted.

Like all good students, he did his homework. He found out her name, her attachments, and listened with interest to the malicious tales spread about her by her female colleagues. He liked what he heard. Jorge was no leftist and judged that Rosa wasn't either. Yet that appeared to be the key to her, for it was the predisposition of those who surrounded her. So he joined the movement, an extraordinary thing to do, given the extreme right-wing beliefs of his parents and his own near total lack of interest in politics.

He timed his entrance well. Rosa, fed up with Victor's austerity and endless commitments to the movement, welcomed the attentions of their newest member. Jorge had a lot to offer a girl like Rosa. He was handsome enough, and tall, with muscles well defined by hours in the gym and by college rugby. He was intelligent and money hadn't blunted his ambitions. He was one of those fortunates who seem able to cruise through life plucking the fruit but never troubling to water the tree.

Jorge knew he would steal Rosa from Victor, yet he was cautious. He didn't want her to run back to Victor, guilty and ashamed, the first time they made love. He waited till Victor was tied up in a factional debate before inviting Rosa to lunch. She accepted without hesitation.

The rains had eased and sun bathed the capital. Jorge took her to a cafe in Calle Lavalle, a boulevarde closed to traffic and therefore wide open to street musicians. It was lively and bustling, hardly the obvious choice of a sneaky seducer. But it was the right choice, exactly what Rosa needed, and a contrast to the austerity of life with Victor.

From the lunchtime cafeterias it was a short step to evening *confiterías* for coffee and pastries. From there, they gravitated to the pulsating tango clubs of San Telmo.

Jorge had charm and his charm hid his real intent. He didn't love Rosa any more than he had loved the other beautiful young women he took to bed. But he had a burning desire to sample her pleasures. He wanted to have her weep and moan beneath him. To subject her to his drives till both his mind and body snapped. Such were his fantasies. Such was his ego.

He was smooth. He listened with interest to her stories, flattered her wit, and never once failed to compliment her on her clothes, or the way she wore her hair. He was very observant. He was very attentive. He was very practised.

Inevitably, after yet another lunch during which they flirted shamelessly, they wound up on the Avenida Alveal, in Jorge's apartment. Once there, she rewarded him for his patience, and he took her to bed with the smug satisfaction of the true scoundrel. But she didn't lie back as Jorge had envisaged. She jumped on him. She wrestled him. She rode him. She bit him, she scratched him and she licked him. She never gave him a moment's rest. She was so enthusiastic and uninhibited that Jorge found he had little time to indulge his ego, lest a lapse in concentration cause Rosa to question his virility. She came at him and at him, and he loved every delicious moment until, finally, all he could raise was a white flag.

Over the next few weeks Rosa conquered Jorge. She over-whelmed him with her passion and infected him with her joy of life. Gone were the days when his interest in her was purely copulatory; now he felt a growing, deepening well of affection. He loved being with her, the energy that radiated from her, and her naïveté found the cracks in his civilised shell and penetrated to his very core. Yet he never asked her to share his apartment though it was large enough. Jorge was much too selfish for that.

When Victor finally accepted what all his friends had been trying to tell him, it was too late. He fell into a deep depression, the kind that only those who love blindly and foolishly ever know.

So Rosa had betrayed Victor. But she was young and that is the way of the young. Their affair was no more than a brief stopover on the road to maturity. Victor had expected too much and assumed too much. What she did was forgivable. What Jorge was about to do was not.

There was another witness to Jorge and Rosa's blossoming romance and his interest cast a shadow Jorge was unable to ignore.

At first, it was nothing. An irritating little cloud that briefly blocked the sun. But clouds have a way of gathering others to themselves until, one day, they grow and build into a great roiling mass, and unleash a tempest of destruction.

Jorge was approached on campus. To anyone watching, the encounter would have seemed innocent enough.

'Jorge Luis Masot,' the man said. 'An illustrious name in some circles. A name with certain attachments and obligations.'

'Who are you?' Jorge asked, angry, because he had taken considerable pains to conceal the identity of his family.

'Relax, I am a friend. I have an official interest in your well-being. Allow me to introduce myself. My name is Carlos.'

'Just Carlos?'

'Not much of a name to be sure, but adequate.'

The man irritated Jorge. He was a half-breed, a *mestizo*. His accent was coarse and provincial. Jorge suspected that he was in his father's employ one way or the other yet he showed no respect. In fact, his tone was mocking, even insolent. He was a big man, bull-necked, with powerful shoulders and chest; but it was his immense self-confidence which intimidated Jorge and inhibited his responses.

'Are you my bodyguard?'

'In a manner of speaking, I suppose I could be.' Carlos laughed. 'You have become a leftist, Jorge Luis Masot.'

It was a statement not a question, yet Jorge found himself unaccountably eager to explain. He dismissed the activities of the movement as childish, and boasted of his conquest of Rosa in the crude terms men reserve for such discussions. Plainly joining the movement had been an act of expediency.

'I suspected as much,' said Carlos evenly.

'Now I have my prize I think my membership will lapse.'

'No,' said Carlos. 'The People's Democratic Movement is a foolish affair and harmless enough. Still we like to keep an eye on things. Who joins, who the leaders are, what alliances are made, what they plan, what arms they may have. You know the sort of thing.'

Jorge did, and said he'd be happy to oblige, now knowing to whom Carlos answered. What did it matter? Jorge knew he'd never be trusted with any worthwhile intelligence and neither would Rosa. What harm could he do? It seemed such an inconsequential thing at the time, a variation in an increasingly silly game. Besides, he really had no choice in the matter. Only a fool went out of his way to make enemies in the military.

'You are a wise man, Jorge Luis Masot. I will see to it that your efforts are recognised.'

'Thank you.'

'I will also see to it that your initial indiscretion is erased from your record. I will be in touch.'

Chapter Four

For Rosa life suddenly revealed new pleasures and excitement. She knew Jorge was wealthy, though she never suspected quite how rich and powerful his family was. She did ask, for Rosa was not the sort of girl who would die wondering.

'You never mention your family,' she said. 'Have they disowned you? Did you make some poor girl pregnant that you shouldn't have?'

Jorge laughed.

'No, I did not make any girls pregnant, though God knows, I owe more to good luck than good shooting. And no, my family have not disowned me. At least, no more so than my brothers. We are not a close family. My parents are very busy, and we all have our own interests. When I marry they will come to my wedding. If I die before them they will come to my funeral. My father's secretary always sends me a card on my birthday. My father sends a boost to my bank account. It is the perfect arrangement.'

'Are they very rich?'

'Some would say so.'

'Are they very important?'

'Some would say so.'

'Are they related, are you related, to the newspaper Masots?'

'Yes,' he replied truthfully. 'But only distantly,' he lied.

Rosa simply accepted that Jorge was reasonably wealthy but no more so than his friends. They knew how to use their wealth for pleasure and entertainment. And that, as far as Rosa was concerned, was enough. There was always a lavish party somewhere, and often there would be photographers and famous people. Instead of the noisy student hangouts of the Reconquista she now frequented the elegant bars and restaurants of the Barrio Norte, and the Avenida Junin.

She watched Jorge play rugby though she hardly understood the game, and she watched his friends play polo which she understood even less. But both were followed by parties and they were events at which she starred.

Rosa became popular for the fun and irreverence she brought to such gatherings and the laughter that always seemed to surround her. She was in her element and Jorge encouraged her. He showed her off like a new toy.

Rosa's wardrobe expanded by the week. She only had to admire a dress or a blouse for Jorge to buy it for her. He was extraordinarily generous and sometimes Rosa felt a twinge of guilt at her excesses. She needn't have. She was Jorge's accessory and a reflection upon his taste. That is why he made sure she always dressed at least as well as he did.

Occasionally they would go slumming with her friends, to the bars of La Boca and Reconquista and occasionally, at Jorge's insistence, they would attend rallies and marches organised by the movement. Jorge took head counts at meetings and listened to the gossip. When Carlos rang, he duly reported what he'd learned. He couldn't imagine it being of any use to anybody. It didn't occur to him that Carlos might be training him, getting him used to the role of spy, recruiting him for more serious involvement at some later stage. Jorge would have reacted indignantly if anybody had called him naive. But that's exactly what he was.

Jorge and Rosa became inseparable. Still he would not let Rosa move in permanently to his apartment, though they virtually lived in each other's pockets. They played together, ate together, studied together and Rosa even adopted Jorge's exercise regime.

They would exercise naked, side by side, watching each other, competing with each other, all the time becoming more suggestive and blatant in their movements until their arousal demanded release. Then they would leap upon each other in a frenzy of love-making. Were two people ever more suited or happy together? Certainly Rosa was happy. Happier than she'd ever been. Happier than she'd ever be again.

Love can be likened to a match that flares too brightly when first struck, for often this match is the first to fail. So it was with Rosa and Jorge. For a year and a half they were as bound together as Siamese twins. But as Jorge completed his final year of study, the gaps began to appear.

It is the way of women in Argentina to give their rivals no peace. They flaunt their triumphs in ways too subtle for men to comprehend, yet too flagrantly for any woman to ignore. Rosa began to catch knowing looks and smug glances cast in her direction, suggesting that Jorge was also dipping into other honeypots. At least, that was Rosa's interpretation.

She confronted Jorge, fire in her eyes, flame on her cheeks, her voice strident. Jorge would simply brush aside her accusations. On occasions when her fury overran her brain he would hit her. The beginning of the end came when Rosa hit back, and Jorge put her to bed for a week, black and blue and bloodied.

Rosa could not forgive him. Their love-making, once a celebration of youth and athleticism, became mechanical. When they split up, each felt a sense of relief, and they separated painlessly with expressions of regret on both sides.

It was the behaviour of mature adults but, paradoxically, and with the benefit of hindsight, it served only to expose their immaturity. The fact is they never entirely let go of each other. The flame had burned too brightly to be extinguished altogether. Within each the pilot light still burned, ready to flare up at the slightest provocation.

The pain came later for Jorge. Many years passed before he really understood and came to appreciate what he had thrown away. But for Rosa the pain was almost immediate. She thought her life would return to its former carefree exuberance and for several days it did. But the fact is she had become dependent upon Jorge and had constructed her life around him. The realisation shocked her. She'd let go of her friends for his friends, and he had prior claim on their loyalty.

She didn't know who to talk to. She felt lost, displaced, unfocused. She was like the silver dorado which roam the South Atlantic Ocean. Unable to bear the emptiness of a world with no reference points, they congregate around flotsam, staying with it for thousands of kilometres or until it abandons them by sinking. Rosa needed something or someone she could attach herself to.

She stayed in bed when she should have attended lectures and tutorials. Her old girlfriends bubbled on a level Rosa could no longer reach and their company only depressed her more. Men rang her, but her libido had taken a holiday, and she read their best intentions as shallow opportunism. She thought of renewing contact with the movement, but both she and Jorge had allowed their involvement to lapse, despite his secret pledge to Carlos. Her interest in politics, never strong, was now almost nonexistent.

Besides, the increasing violence and number of political assassinations warned against further involvement. Only recently, the faithful Lydia, who had so gladly filled the void in Victor's life created by Rosa's defection to Jorge, had been dragged from her bed and left for dead in the gutter, having first been raped and brutally beaten. Popular opinion held that the right-wing Peronista were responsible, because Lydia had attacked them in a fiery speech. But it could have been any of a number of right-wing groups, because the People's Democratic Movement was now fair game for all. They had been thoroughly infiltrated, and their limited capacity to respond was well known.

Rosa felt that there was only one thing she could do, and the barriers of her pride began to crumble before the onslaught of her loneliness. She made her decision.

She rang her hairdresser and was fortunate to get a cancelled appointment. She ran a bath and was generous with the fragrant oils she added to it. She shaved her legs and rubbed lotion into every part of her body. She put on make-up, skilfully contriving to appear as though she were wearing none.

After some deliberation, she chose a simple white shift, provocatively short and tight-fitting. She put on gold hoop earrings and, around her neck, she hung a heavy chain of gold with a crucifix that nestled in the hollow between her breasts.

Before her hairdresser even laid a hand upon her she looked stunning. This was confirmed by the men she passed, in the sidewalk cafes and on the street corners. Their eyes locked on to her like radar, and they called out to her, and chrrrrrd to one another in appreciation.

Two hours later, she stood before the apartment door. She rang the bell. She was confident and devastatingly beautiful. She was as ready to conquer as any woman had ever been. But the door had no sooner opened than her poise evaporated and she dissolved in tears.

Is Rosa at fault because loneliness drove her back to the man who had loved her completely and unconditionally?

'That was her weakness,' people said, and that was why they came to blame her.

Victor picked her up on the rebound and it was unquestionably gratitude Rosa felt, not love. But how could she have anticipated the effect her actions would have on her life and the lives of those around her? Or on the lives of people she had never even met, thousands of kilometres away?

But what if she had been made of sterner stuff. What if she had not tripped at the first obstacle life had put in her path. What if she had retained confidence in her ability to pick and choose from the army of men who would gladly have been her suitors. What if she had taken any of the alternative paths open to her, if only she had looked. If, if, if! But the world is full of regrets, and hindsight is hollow wisdom. Rosa had chosen her path. Nothing could alter that.

* * *

In every story there are natural pauses, and this was one. They provide breathing space, giving listeners time to reflect upon what they have heard, and the storyteller time to collect his thoughts. Ramon eased back in his chair so Gancio could serve coffee.

'There is one more "if",' said Ramon and the others leaned forward expectantly. 'Milos, if you don't order Gancio's special grappa or at least a cognac, I will not continue with my story.'

Milos reacted in mock horror.

'Give me a chance, Ramon. You are your own worst enemy, no? I'm still in Argentina. How am I supposed to remember cognacs when you make me forget where I am? I must confess my thoughts had returned to Rosa's first meeting with Victor. I was a fly on the wall by Victor's desk.'

'Ha!' exploded Lucio. 'I was the desk.'

Their laughter reached Gancio at the bar. He heard them above the wheezing of his espresso machine. It pleased him greatly, for it reminded him of his home in Italy where men often met, as these four did, to laugh and enjoy each other's company.

Chapter Five

There comes a time when all men must begin to assume responsibility. That time had come for Jorge. He shut Rosa out of his mind and buried himself in his studies. He made plans for the future. As his final year at university drew to a close he rang his father to arrange a meeting. That is, he rang his father's secretary, Esther Teresa.

Esther had been his father's secretary for as long as Jorge could remember, and she greeted his call with more warmth and affection than he would have received from his own mother. Jorge suspected Esther was also his father's mistress, and she had developed an almost maternal interest in him and his brothers.

She made an appointment for him for half an hour the following week. It was only postponed twice before Jorge finally confronted his father. Jorge remembered how he had trembled in his father's presence, never daring to speak unless spoken to, and always addressing him as 'Sir'. How every Sunday after mass, his father would stand before him and his brothers and rebuke them for their transgressions, telling them exactly what was required of them in future. He was a hard and ruthless man yet he never raised a finger to his sons. He never had to. His hard eyes could strike with the force of hammer on anvil and his voice never knew a moment's doubt. It battered and hammered and pummelled the boys into compliance. Jorge maintained he could always tell when his father was at home somewhere in their vast mansion. He could feel the waves of power that emanated from him.

Now, as his father came forward to embrace him with the same impersonal elegance with which he would greet his business partners, Jorge once again felt the thrill of his presence. His father stepped back and took a long appraising look at his son. He was not displeased with what he saw.

'Come, sit down,' he instructed, leading the way to what he referred to as his informal area, as if anyone could relax in his presence. He pointed to a leather armchair which he wished Jorge to occupy. Jorge sat. His father took possession of the sofa, his arms spread expansively along the backrest in a gesture calculated to encourage conversation.

'So,' he began, 'you have decided.'

Jorge smiled to himself. No 'how are you?' because his father could see quite clearly how he was. Besides, he knew his father received regular reports on his progress and how he conducted his life. His father was a careful man.

'Wealth no longer guarantees power,' Jorge began. His father had wasted no time on pleasantries, neither would he. 'And without power there is no guarantee of retaining wealth. There are three pathways to power as I see it. The military, politics and the press. Of the three the press is the most stable.'

'What section of the press do you have in mind? Our interests, as you know, are varied.'

'Newspapers, of course. Argentina has over one hundred and fifty daily newspapers. To my knowledge, you have a controlling interest in at least twenty-three of the majors, four of these in the top ten by circulation. You are under-represented in the provinces and in the popular papers. There are opportunities for acquisition and consolidation of resources. Perhaps "opportunities" is the wrong word. These are not so much opportunities as necessities.'

Jorge could feel his father's eyes upon him, boring into his brain, trying to read his words even before he had spoken them.

'There are two reasons; one fact, one speculation. Firstly, the newspaper industry is on the verge of a technological revolution that will change it forever. Computers will take over from compositors and linotype—'

'I have read the reports. What is your second reason?'

Jorge had made a mistake, but it didn't slow him down or make him more cautious. His father's impatience was only the impatience of a listener anxious to know what happens next. Besides, the full flood of his ideas was upon him, and in this mode he was unstoppable. His brain raced ahead, fleshing out what moments before had been only skeletal.

'Speculation,' Jorge continued. 'The leftists are becoming too strong. Too militant. They will be crushed. It is only a question of time before the military seize power once more. I believe the press will face the most stringent censorship Argentina has ever known. Alliances will be tested.'

Jorge could sense his father's impatience and adjusted.

'This is what I propose. Your papers are all right-wing. This will stand you in good stead, come the coup. But when the Generals fall, as ultimately they must, you will be vulnerable. Your papers will be seen as opposed to democratic government. They will be fortunate if they survive the boycotts and purges. What's needed is balance, an equal number of moderate publications with liberal editors-in-chief. You may lose two or three who overstep editorial policy in their criticisms of the Generals. They will be dragged from their homes at night and become martyrs to the freedom of the press. Your press. And, of course, with your influence and a change of leadership, they can be rescued from imprisonment and reinstated as heroes.

'The point is, both right and moderate publications will be seen to issue from the same publishing house. Who, then, could argue that our reporting has not been balanced? That we have not done all we could to uphold the integrity of the press under a repressive regime?'

'Our? We? You see a role for yourself in my operations?' A smile spread across his father's face. 'You will have dinner with me tonight. There are some people I want you to meet. They will be interested in your views. They will be interested to meet our newest employee.'

He stood up. The interview was over.

Jorge was given the title of Deputy General Manager, New Business, and a one-third share in a secretary who would, of course, report back to his other mother, Esther Teresa. He was given a salary but that was incidental to his real income, his allowance.

Jorge knew that before he could change anything he had to know exactly what it was he was changing. His father gave him access to the files of each of their major newspapers, and files maintained by their intelligence gatherers on each of their major competitors. He soon realised that he had not outlined any new strategies to his father. It chastened him to recall how he'd left his father's office, flying high on the belief that he had given his father a whole new direction. Evidence to the contrary piled up in boxes all around him.

He uncovered a list of prime targets and a timetable for their acquisition. He found budgets and lists of key personnel, marked with asterisks to indicate who would be dispensed with and who would be retained. Yet he had reached the same conclusion on his own, unaided by an army of advisors. That is what had impressed his father.

Jorge visited each of the newspapers in turn. He took note of the type of presses they used, their capacity and any peculiarities in their production methods. He developed a map pinpointing the location of all their presses, the distribution areas and the roads and railways that linked them.

He read everything he could find on the new computer technology, but found it difficult to grasp. There were vast gaps in his knowledge and he was uncertain as to how to fill them. Others reported his weakness and his father had no tolerance for it.

Jorge was surprised one morning to find Esther Teresa waiting for him in his office.

'You are going to America,' she said. 'To New York. There is a job for you in the production department of the *New York Times*. You will get ink under your nails, you will get your hands dirty. In your free time you will go to night classes and learn about the application of computers. It has been arranged. Learn well, for when you return you will be responsible for installing this new technology, and restructuring our print facilities. We will be relying on you. Your tickets and everything you need are in this file.'

She stood and moved close to him. Then she kissed him in a way no mother ever kissed her son, pressing herself tightly against his body.

'Do well. Work hard. Your father has high hopes for you.'

This praise was not given lightly, Jorge knew, and the implications brought a surge of pride and satisfaction. Esther Teresa smiled once more and left his office without a trace of embarrassment.

'She is not mistress to my father,' Jorge thought with sudden understanding. 'She is mistress to his power.'

Jorge was away for five years. When he returned to Argentina in March 1977, the military regime of Rafael Videla was firmly in control. As Jorge had predicted, the left-wing Peronista had become too strong and were purged from office.

They were driven underground by the sheer weight and ferocity of anti-leftist violence. Political, union and student leaders became regular victims of the undercover Alianza Anticomunista Argentina, an outlawed organisation which most people believed was secretly funded by the military. Some secret.

For a while, the right-wing Peronista had held ascendancy. But when Juan Peron died, turning the presidency over to his wife Martinez de Peron, the worm turned. Rampant inflation and devaluation turned the populace against the rightists, and the left rose once more. As a new wave of violence broke out, the military stepped in, as it had in the past, and seized power.

Still this did not bring peace to the troubled country. If anything, the divisions deepened, with the junta determined to crush the left once and for all. Again the left went underground, but the Generals were relentless in their pursuit. Thousands of Argentinians were snatched from their homes to be tortured, imprisoned or executed. The police morgue became a charnel house.

The 'dirty war' had begun. Old alliances were tested and nobody dared criticise the regime in public. Humorists of the day claimed it was impossible for football teams to find players who were prepared to play on the left side of the field. Rugby teams no longer had left wingers, they had two right wings, one of whom was lost.

There was one voice, however, which did speak out. *La Voz del Pueblo* – the voice of the people. His diatribes against the policies of the regime and his cataloguing of their crimes and violations of human rights appeared in an underground newspaper, *Argentina Libre*. It was published, or at least suspected of being published, by a pro-democracy group of leftist radicals.

Possession of *Argentina Libre* was enough to brand anyone a sympathiser and land them in gaol. Yet it circulated widely, passed surreptitiously from hand to hand until a new issue superseded it. Those who had lost husbands, sons and daughters searched its pages for clues to their whereabouts, for sometimes *Argentina Libre* carried such information, gathered at God only knows what cost.

Sometimes the moderate legitimate newspapers carried entire extracts from the 'Voice', ostensibly reviling him but, in reality, carrying his message to those who had no opportunity to read it firsthand.

Occasionally, editors would be arrested for this indiscretion, and among them were editors from papers recently acquired by Jorge's father. The scenario Jorge had outlined five years earlier was becoming a reality.

Jorge himself was also under pressure. The peso, then the currency of Argentina, was hardening. Jorge's father was anxious for a decision on their new equipment so he could take advantage of favourable exchange rates. Jorge wanted to hold off until after Drupa 78, the largest trade exposition in the world, where the latest in print technology would be exhibited.

He had taken leave from the *New York Times* in 1974 to join his father's delegation and had been astonished by what he'd seen. He'd kept in touch with the companies he was most interested in, and received updates from them all. The investment was enormous, as was the responsibility. Naturally, Jorge wanted to be sure.

But his father was unrelenting in his demands. Jorge's days and nights were consumed by the enormity of his task. The playboy cruiser became a workaholic, driven by the awesome scrutiny of his father, and his desire to please him and win his approval.

Esther Teresa was often the conduit for his father's messages. She kept a watchful eye on his soul and tended to his body. Sometimes, when he was working late, she would lock his office door behind her, disrobe and leave him in no doubt as to what was expected of him. She demanded nothing in return except his discretion and, in truth, Jorge was grateful for the diversion.

Apart from Esther Teresa, his pleasures were few. He allowed himself a daily workout in the gym. And each night he would dine late but leisurely, enjoying whatever company there was, and the occasional one night stand that came of it.

His interest in politics was purely commercial, and limited to the bearing it had on papers within the group. He was unprepared when the phone rang and his past rose up to greet him.

It was Carlos, and Carlos suggested that they meet.

Chapter Six

Carlos nominated Los Locos, a small but expensive restaurant in the Port of Olivos. Jorge realised from the choice of venue that Carlos had risen in rank. He had no desire to meet him again but how could he refuse? In those dangerous times, a friend in the military, however dubious, was infinitely preferable to an enemy.

Jorge agreed to see Carlos. However, he was determined to leave him in no doubt that further meetings would not be welcomed. He would use his charm, his tact, and his debating skills, weaponry the crude provincial not only lacked, but would be powerless against. This is what Jorge believed when he set out for the meeting.

His taxi dropped him at Los Locos at ten that evening. His eyes noted, as they were intended to, the shiny black saloon parked thirty metres up the narrow street, two wheels on the pavement in defiance of the No Parking signs. The car's driver watched him arrive. He was uniformed, but Jorge had no idea what the uniform signified. He leaned, arms folded, against the passenger door. He looked like a bouncer from a seedy club, and if the military had not found a use for him, that is probably what he would have been.

Jorge shuddered. There was no denying that the situation was intimidating, even threatening. It was intended to be. Yet Jorge also found grim humour in it. He knew then that he would find

Carlos at the last table in the restaurant, his back to the wall, with an uninterrupted view of the entrance. He wasn't disappointed. He thought these machinations theatrical and pathetic, and that they revealed a lot about the man Carlos.

Carlos didn't bother to stand when Jorge approached, nor did he offer to shake his hand.

'You have done well, Jorge Luis Masot. There again, you are hardly a provincial buffoon like myself, without means or influence.'

Jorge had no ready response. He was good with words, but the situation was foreign to him. He had never been insulted so directly before. He did not have the vocabulary or the turn of phrase to respond in kind.

He would have had difficulty recognising Carlos if he had not been looking for him. Carlos had aged and hardened with age. His face bore the scars of his profession. Jorge shuddered. He would not like this face to appear on his doorstep at the dead of night.

'You have also done well.' Jorge willed his face to remain passive and his voice firm. 'Your family, or whatever it is you call it, have obviously looked after you as well. Who are they, by the way? Who are your masters now? The Alianza Anti-comunista? I can see how a man of your talents would do well in that organisation. Or do you report directly to the Generals?'

'We are all servants of the Generals, Jorge Luis. All wise men are.'

Again, the implied threat. Why did Carlos think he could insult him with such impunity? After all, Jorge was hardly unconnected and could certainly call on favours to bring him back into line. Yet Carlos seemed to totally disregard that possibility. What could he want from him? Jorge was unaware that he had anything to give.

Silence fell as they measured each other with their eyes, neither anxious to fill the void. When Carlos was ready, when they'd taken a longer look at each other, assessed each other's strengths and weaknesses and the value of their mutual dislike, Carlos would speak. Then Jorge would find out what all this was about.

'I have ordered *parrillada*,' Carlos said unexpectedly. 'I know you won't have eaten. It is not your custom to eat earlier. Unfortunately I cannot also supply you with a woman this time.'

So. Carlos had assigned someone to watch him. But why? The waiter interrupted Jorge's thoughts by bringing a steaming platter of charcoal-grilled beef chunks, kidney and liver, sausages and chicken giblets. He brought a bottle of strong red wine, which they cut to taste with soda water, as was the custom.

Carlos attacked the food in front of him as if he was frightened someone would take his plate away before he was finished. He ate noisily, and frequently used the nail of his thumb as a toothpick. He held his knife and fork the way a carpenter holds a hammer, and he operated them with the same subtlety.

Jorge had little appetite, and the sight of Carlos shovelling food into his mouth did nothing to encourage it. He thought Carlos should feed from a trough along with all the other pigs. Jorge wore these thoughts on his face with undisguised distaste.

Carlos looked up.

'Do my table manners upset you, Jorge Luis Masot? You must forgive me. We children of the provinces have little opportunity to acquire nice manners. We considered ourselves lucky to have a meal at all. I had three brothers and five sisters. Most were older than me. Meal times were a battle for survival.'

'It seems you survived.'

'Yes. And my table manners with me. I see no reason to change now. It is not easy to rise above humble beginnings, Jorge Luis. Tell me, how many of the men who work on your father's *estancia* have you taken to a restaurant like this? Five? Ten? None, maybe?'

Jorge said nothing. The answer was obvious.

'Sometimes I ask myself who is right and who is wrong. I look at you with your fine manners and I think, "How many men are there in Argentina like Jorge Luis Masot, who are born with everything including fine manners?" Not many, I think. But how many are there like me, born with nothing, not even nice manners? I think there are a lot more of us than there are of you, Jorge Luis Masot. So you tell me. Who is right? This is a democracy. Surely the majority is right?'

'You lose me when you speak of a democracy. The word has no place on your lips. Just as your manners have no place in this restaurant.'

Carlos stopped eating, the fork frozen in space en route to his mouth. Then he smiled.

'So the mouse has a bite after all.'

He finished the meal in silence, eating methodically until every scrap was accounted for.

'One more thing, Jorge Luis,' he said as he laid down his knife and fork. 'Where I came from it was considered bad manners to leave good food on the table. Not only that, it was suicidal.' Carlos laughed at his own joke.

He called the waiter over and ordered *yerba maté*, the Paraguayan tea made from a species of holly, in place of coffee. Jorge thought it was another theatrical gesture, calculated to underscore Carlos' peasant roots. To his surprise, the restaurant complied. Obviously, Carlos was a regular.

'I am a child of the Gran Chaco. I was brought up with *yerba maté*. I consider myself something of a expert.' He watched to see what Jorge would do.

'I will have coffee,' Jorge said, pushing his cup to the side.

'I will wager you have never in your life sampled *yerba maté*, yet you will not even try it.'

'You are right, Carlos. Neither have I sampled poverty, and I have no desire to try that either. I am happy with coffee and quite prepared to defend my ignorance.'

'I believe Rosa has acquired the taste,' Carlos said quietly. 'Her husband Victor introduced her to it. He is a very patriotic Argentinian.'

Jorge started at the mention of Rosa's name. For years, he had not trusted himself to think of her. When he was with other women, he would sometimes find himself unconsciously comparing them with Rosa, and immediately close off that forbidden part of his memory.

But Carlos had opened the door. Memories of her flooded back. The pilot flame within him flared at the sudden infusion of fuel. He could feel his cheeks flush. He was like a little boy caught with his pants down.

Carlos smiled. In the gloom of the restaurant, Carlos could not have seen the colour invade his cheeks. Yet he knew what effect her name would have on him, and he let Jorge know he knew.

Jorge felt anger and dismay as he yielded whatever advantage he'd aspired to. He cursed himself when his brain should instead have been looking for motive. Carlos did nothing that wasn't premeditated.

'You will renew your friendship.' An edge had crept into Carlos' voice. It was the voice of a man accustomed to giving instructions which were carried out without question.

'She has an appointment with her hairdresser tomorrow at three. You know where to go. You have picked her up from there often enough in the past.' Carlos made no effort to hide his triumph. If Jorge had carried a gun he would have used it then, pressing the barrel hard into the evil grinning face before him and extinguishing the smugness with one squeeze of the trigger. But he didn't have a gun. The only weapon he had left was the strength of his will and Carlos was about to dispossess him of that.

'And if I refuse?' Jorge asked through gritted teeth.

'You won't,' said Carlos with the certainty of a poker player dealt all the aces. 'You won't disappoint your father.'

Jorge's mind reeled. His father was involved? But the reality was that his father had many interests and who knows what favour was required. What error of judgement overlooked. He was being traded quid pro quo and there was nothing he could do about it. At least he now knew, or thought he knew, the source of Carlos' insufferable arrogance.

'I'll be in touch,' said Carlos as he got up to leave. He smiled once more, a smile loaded with the contempt victors reserve for opponents who fail to provide the opposition expected of them. Jorge was utterly humiliated.

'Enjoy your coffee, Jorge Luis Masot.'

Chapter Seven

'Rosa.'

She stopped dead in her tracks. She did not spin around to see who had called her. She recognised Jorge's voice immediately and it had triggered too many emotions for her reactions to be instinctive. Slowly she turned. She stared at him for the briefest of moments as if confirming his presence. Then her face lit up with the expression of uninhibited joy he had been hoping for.

'Jorge!' she cried. And then, 'You bastard!' She threw her arms around him and smothered him with kisses. Jorge could have sworn her tongue brushed his, but then it was gone, leaving him wondering.

'Jorge,' she said 'Oh, Jorge. You bastard. Why haven't you called me? How long have you been back?'

Her eyes raced over him, checking his hair, his lips, his eyes, the firmness of his chest, the flatness of his stomach against the reference she held in her head. Finally, her stock-taking was done.

'You look beautiful, Rosa. I'm glad you have let your hair grow. It suits you that way.'

Rosa glowed. This was typical Jorge. He always knew exactly what a woman wanted to hear.

'And you, Jorge, you look more handsome than ever. You are one of those men who improve with every passing year. You will

43

be the despair of the woman you marry.' She took his hand as a mother might take the hand of a child.

'Come,' she said, 'there is a new cafe and they have the most delicious cumquat tarts. I will allow myself one to celebrate. Jorge, you must tell me all about yourself. I want to know everything.'

But Jorge knew better. He would be the one doing the listening.

Rosa had married Victor shortly after Jorge had left for New York. They sent him a wedding invitation via his office, but Jorge had hurled it into the waste paper bin. He did not even grant them the courtesy of reply. Whether they married because Rosa fell pregnant, or whether they would have married anyway was immaterial. The mismatched couple had married and, to the curious, seemed as happy as any other couple.

Jorge wanted to know about Victor, what he was doing and what he had done to arouse Carlos' interest. The words had stuck in Jorge's brain. He could hear Carlos say them now, his voice heavy with irony. 'Her husband Victor is a very patriotic Argentinian.'

But Rosa only talked about herself and her son Roberto. She filled the air with words and her love for her child until she tired and urged Jorge to speak.

Jorge learned nothing from that first meeting and was glad. He was a reluctant and unenthusiastic spy. His deceit made him feel ashamed and disgusted with himself. But he had this to be grateful for. Carlos had thrown him and Rosa back together again.

He was in love with her. He had always been in love with her. Seeing her again had been like the warm breath of spring upon the hibernating beast. He felt alive once more. He wanted to go out and grab life with both hands and wring from it all the joy and rewards it could bring. He was in love. Yes! He admitted it to himself. In fact, he exulted in the knowledge. He was in love with the beautiful, wonderful, irrepressible Rosa, and he wanted her back.

He did not consider the realities of the situation. He did not ask, 'Does she want me back?' He knew only that he wanted her. He believed that he would do anything to get her back. Do anything. Risk anything. With all his heart, this is what he believed.

In the weeks that followed, Jorge saw Rosa as often as he could, but it was not as often as he would have liked. He was constrained by the demands of his work which, because it denied him access to Rosa, ceased to be the challenge his energies could feed upon, and took on the aspect of a burden.

When he was free to meet her, she would often be unavailable. She always had reasons. Roberto was sick. The repairman was coming. To Jorge, such reasons sounded trivial and unsatisfactory. He was impatient. He yearned to be with her. The pain of their break-up, which he had so successfully deferred, now took hold. It gnawed at him and distracted him and impeded him in his work. He would go to enormous lengths to make time so that he could see her. It angered him that she did not reciprocate.

Nevertheless, they did manage to meet, usually for lunch. Jorge would forget his frustrations and disappointments in the vibrance of her company. She would joke and gossip and tease and he would forget the other reason he was there. He learned nothing of use.

Within twenty-four hours of each meeting, Carlos would ring him. Despite Jorge's dislike of Carlos and his abhorrence of the role he was required to play, he would feel inadequate when he had nothing to report. To his disgust, he found himself wanting to please Carlos. He wanted to win Carlos' respect. He wanted to give Carlos information of a magnitude that would demand his gratitude. He wanted to put the upstart peasant in his place. If Carlos was disappointed with the lack of progress, he gave no indication.

'She will talk when your heads share the same pillow,' he'd say, and terminate the call with his grating, cynical laugh.

Ah, but if only their heads did share the same pillow!

Jorge courted Rosa, calling upon all his experience and skill. But Rosa deftly fielded his passes. She was not offended even when Jorge was too obvious. Men had always flirted with her and she enjoyed the game. But that was all it was. A game.

'I'm a happily married woman,' she'd say. 'Go away. Find another woman. There! She is beautiful. Go talk to her.'

But she enjoyed Jorge's compliments, and their flirting took them both back to younger, happier, days. Rosa had resolved not to have an affair with Jorge, or anyone else for that matter. She was happily married. She had a son to whom she was devoted. But she was not immune to Jorge's flattery, and gradually it exacted its toll.

She began making comparisons. She speculated on what life married to Jorge would have been like and compared it with her quiet, orderly life with Victor. Occasionally Victor would look up and find Rosa staring at him as if in a trance. But the honest, trusting man never thought to question why.

Rosa tried hard to see the good things about their marriage, and there was much to see that was good. Victor was a sympathetic husband and father, who loved his family and gave them as much time as he could.

Rosa was grateful for Victor's dedication to the family and loved him all the more for it. But this was not the life she was cut out to lead, however hard she tried. It was suburban. It was conventional. It was dull. In short, it was everything she wasn't. This was not the life for the little girl who had farted in the San Isidro cathedral, and questioned her sisters' boyfriends in minute detail about their genitalia. Still, she convinced herself that life with Victor was what she wanted, and that she was happy. Perhaps she would have been content to live with the lie if Jorge had not reappeared.

Rosa never asked Victor what he did when he left to keep his appointments. She never understood his work as a corporate lawyer, and he would no longer involve her in his politics beyond the small part she still insisted on playing. Even that caused friction between them and was the source of the few arguments they had. Naturally, it was in the one area where the true Rosa exerted herself. The People's Democratic Movement had long since disbanded, but the reason Rosa had joined them in the first place lived on.

'You are a mother now. You have responsibilities to your son. To me. You can no longer afford the luxury of involvement in politics. You are no longer in a position to take risks. You put us all in danger.' Victor's voice would rise in exasperation

Rosa would throw his own argument back in his face.

'You are a father now. You too have responsibilities. I will give up politics when you give up politics.'

They argued in circles and Rosa defiantly stood her ground. She'd watch, child-like in triumph, as her stubbornness drove her husband from the house, doors slamming behind him. And so Rosa, the vivacious, gregarious, frequenter of hairdressers and *confiterías*, continued to distribute copies of *Argentina Libre*. Who would suspect her? Certainly Jorge didn't.

'Where did you get this?' he exploded, when Rosa brazenly passed him a copy over lunch. *La Voz del Pueblo* had been particularly strident and his sources uncomfortably well informed. Everybody knew somebody who knew somebody who had been arrested for possession of the prohibited newspaper. Usually, they'd been beaten until blood and swelling blinded their eyes, and blood from their battered kidneys coloured their urine.

'Read it and pass it on. That's what everyone does. Or leave it on a chair for somebody else.' It amused Rosa to see Jorge panic. 'That's how I got mine.'

Jorge was horrified. How could she be so stupid? He felt sick. She was the reason Carlos had renewed his interest in Victor. She was implicated. And any information he gathered could only implicate her further.

'Rosa, this paper hasn't been read. Look at it. The pages are still crimped together from the guillotine.' He had become strident. He saw concern flash across her face and dropped his voice to a whisper. He grabbed her arm, so tightly it hurt.

'Rosa, are you still involved? Has Victor still got you doing his dirty work?'

'Relax, Jorge. And let go of my arm. Yes, if you want to know, I am still involved. But only slightly. To amuse myself. Every week I distribute a few copies. That is all.'

Jorge realised he could not withhold this information from Carlos. He was bound to reveal all that he learned. He had to keep faith, to keep up his side of the deal his father had struck. It was not the information that was important, for Carlos probably knew exactly what Rosa was up to. It was the fact that he reported it. How could Rosa have been so naive and foolish? But hadn't she always been that way? Jorge laid the copy of *Argentina Libre* on a nearby chair.

'And what of Victor?' he asked. 'Is he still committed to his mission?'

Rosa had given Jorge the opening he had been waiting for. He could not let it slip by. Perhaps he could make a deal with Carlos. If his information was good enough.

'Victor is still involved, as you would expect him to be. Which group, I am not sure and he won't say. He says it is better for me to know nothing of his other activities. It is safer that way.'

'Yet he still expects you to distribute *Argentina Libre*. There is nothing safe about that.'

'No, he is against it. We argue about that all the time. But I insist.'

Jorge understood immediately. Rosa was still a little girl playing her mischievous games in total disregard of the consequences.

'God help you, Rosa. It is only a matter of time before Victor is picked up. Informers are everywhere. Anyone will talk to save their own neck. Do you really think you will be spared when they come to your door? Do you really think you alone, in all Argentina, are immune to retribution?'

'Victor is no fool, Jorge. He would not put Roberto or me at risk. He loves us too much. Even more than his damned politics.' It was her turn to raise her voice and she glared at Jorge. But his words had sown doubts and brought to the surface fears she had tried not to face. She could no longer meet his eyes. She began to plead for reassurance.

'Victor is so careful. He works behind layers, behind filters. He has told me this. There is nothing to link him with this organisation or that. He has nothing to do with protests or demonstrations. He has nothing to do with violence. Like before in the movement, he fights only with his ideals and his pen.' She looked up once more. But if she was looking for reassurance, she found none. Jorge's face had become a hard, cold mask.

'Rosa, you have just defined somebody who is very senior. Why else would they go to so much trouble to protect him?'

Rosa burst into tears.

'Oh Jorge!' she cried 'What am I going to do?'

Jorge let her rest her head on his shoulder. He stroked her and comforted her and made soothing noises. At last, he was making progress.

Chapter Eight

Over the course of their next few meetings, Jorge played on Rosa's fears. Rosa, who was so often alone at home with her sleeping child, came to fear every squeal of brakes from the street outside. She froze when she heard a car pull up nearby. She began ringing Jorge at his office and at his apartment, seeking the comfort of his voice. But Jorge was master in this situation. The reassurance he gave was hollow, calculated to sound insincere, and her trepidation grew.

'You must stop distributing *Argentina Libre*,' he said, and she did. 'You must confront Victor. You are entitled to know what danger you face.'

Rosa hesitated. Victor had been adamant that she should never pry. But Jorge was relentless. He kept up his attack and gradually his persistence began to tell. In Jorge's mind a plan was developing that would honour his father's obligations to whomever was behind Carlos and, at the same time, win back Rosa.

'I am getting close,' he told Carlos, emboldened by the power of the information he knew would soon be his. 'But before I give you this information, I want a commitment from you. There is something I want in return.'

'I wonder what that could be?' Again Carlos mocked him, but the point had been made and Carlos could not ignore it.

* * *

Jorge was proved right. Informers were everywhere and nobody could be trusted to keep secrets when their testicles were being used as footballs.

In one devastating sweep, government forces raided the building where *Argentina Libre* was being printed and the homes of those who worked there. Many dissidents were killed in the firefight that took place and more than thirty were arrested. More arrests would follow as the interrogators and torturers applied their craft. The ranks of *los desaparecidos*, the disappeared ones, would swell.

The system of cut-outs and filters isolated Victor and he was spared. He did not find out about the raid until the following morning when Rosa found a note for Victor tucked among the still-warm brioche that was delivered to them.

Rosa screamed and Victor slapped her, suddenly and hard. She stood dumbstruck. Victor grabbed her by the shoulders and his blue eyes, now glacial, bored into hers.

'You are not a child, Rosa. Do not behave like one. We knew one day this might happen. It changes nothing. It is a tragedy for those who were caught and killed. But they cannot reach us through those who were arrested. Our systems make that impossible. They cannot reach us, so long as we don't panic. You must act as though nothing has happened. Because in the life of Señor and Señora Sanguineti, nothing has happened. Nothing! You understand? I love you and I love Roberto. I would not put you at risk. Don't you place us at risk either. Go about your day as normal. Now I must leave you. I must go to work as normal. As normal, Rosa, remember that.'

He kissed her, but when he went to move away, she held on.

'What are you in the organisation?' She hissed. 'Why are you so protected? What do you do? I am your wife. I have a right to know. I'm scared, Victor.'

Despite his outward control, Victor had been badly shaken. It caused him to say things he knew he shouldn't. He was about to make the biggest mistake of his life.

'Can't you guess?' he asked, his expression softening. 'What have you always done for me since the day we met?'

Rosa could think of many things, some which had nothing whatsoever to do with politics.

'Think, Rosa. You have always taken my words to the people.'

Rosa gasped. She saw herself as the headstrong girl handing out his pamphlets to students, and now leaving *Argentina Libre* on restaurant chairs.

'*La Voz del Pueblo?* No. No! Tell me it isn't true!' Her eyes begged for a denial, but Victor's soft, sad smile held firm.

'I must go,' he said. 'Please, Rosa, there is nothing to fear. Just go about your life as normal.'

Then he was gone. But how could she go about her life as normal? Her life had changed forever. She'd just discovered that her husband was the most wanted man in Argentina.

Roberto was anxious to get to school. Rosa let him go with his friend, for once not insisting that he eat breakfast. With the house empty, with no reason to pretend, Rosa broke down and cried. She cried for an hour, sitting alone in the kitchen. Tears of despair, hopelessness and fear coursed down her cheeks. How could Victor do this to them?

She began to hate. She hated Victor's politics, all politics, and she hated his mission. But she didn't hate him. She hated the position Victor had put them in. The more she thought about it, the more obvious the solution seemed. Victor would have to give up politics and let someone else be *La Voz del Pueblo*. She would give Victor an ultimatum. His politics or his family. He would have to decide. She would make him decide. But in her heart she wasn't ready to make a stand. She was helpless. A fresh outpouring of tears testified to that.

* * *

Jorge could tell she'd been crying. She wore dark glasses though the day was overcast and rain was imminent. She kept them on even in the restaurant, but Jorge had seen that her eyes were swollen. She was distracted and had no appetite. Jorge sat quietly, biding his time. She wanted to speak, but didn't know how to begin. She wanted to tell someone, to share the burden, but didn't dare.

'Come,' Jorge said eventually. 'There is no point in staying here. I can see you have a lot on your mind. I suspect they are things that can only be said in private. My apartment is nearby. We can go there.'

Jorge paid for the drink he'd had and left a generous tip. A taxi took them to his apartment. As soon as the door closed behind them, Rosa began weeping. Jorge put his arm around her and comforted her. He spoke to her as if she were a child. Still she wept. He took her in both arms and she sobbed as though her heart would burst. He patted her back. He stroked her hair. He kissed her. And when she didn't object, he kissed her again. And again. Not lightly, not as a friend, but as a lover. This time she responded. Their kissing became urgent and desperate. Then she was upon him as the confusion of her rioting emotions sought release in passion.

Her tongue darted inside his mouth and she could feel him pressing hard against her. She wanted him more than she'd ever wanted anyone in her life. She kissed him and kissed him and wouldn't let go. Her skirt fell away. His questing fingers unbuttoned her blouse. Her passion was in full flood and the dam ached to burst. His hands were on her buttocks as he stripped off her bikini briefs. Then she took him inside her in one great shuddering gasp.

For a while, the frenzy of their love-making freed her from the pain and desperation of the reality she could not face. Then she told Jorge everything. Carlos was right. Their heads shared a pillow and she told him more than he had ever hoped to hear. Victor's life was in his hands. He had the information he needed to force a deal with Carlos. And what information! He could already see the admiration on Carlos' face. He could already taste his triumph. Jorge wanted to shout with joy but he forced his attention back to Rosa. He would have to handle her carefully. It was one thing to make love, another thing entirely to make a commitment. Rosa had to want to come back to him.

'You must leave Victor,' he said. 'You must take Roberto and leave him now. Now! While you still have a chance. I will find a place for you and protect you. I will get you and Roberto to a safe place, away from Argentina. I am right and you know it. You must trust me.'

'I can't. He needs me. He is my husband and he is a good man. I cannot abandon him.' Rosa clung to Jorge, secure in the protection of his body. 'I will talk to him. I will make him give up his writing. Maybe we should all leave Argentina.'

'You think the Generals have short memories? You think they forgive so easily?' Jorge got up with apparent disgust. He left Rosa lying on the bed, naked and vulnerable. She held out her arms to him but he ignored her.

'Victor is the most wanted man in Argentina. They will not rest until they have him. And, Rosa, they will take you with them. And they will take Roberto. If not yourself, Rosa, think of little Roberto.'

Rosa began to cry once more. Jorge ached to take her in his arms, but he didn't. He left her lying exposed and alone on his bed.

'Leave him, Rosa,' he urged. 'You have no choice. You must leave him.' He walked out of the room.

Rosa didn't leave Victor. She argued with him and she ran crying to Jorge. She sought solace in his arms. Still she would not leave Victor and the home they had made together. As the nights passed and the soldiers did not come, they returned to the old, familiar patterns of their lives.

Jorge grew impatient, Carlos more so.

'Where is the information you promised?' he demanded. 'Your father, too, grows impatient. Other matters are involved.'

'I will know soon,' Jorge equivocated. 'These things cannot be rushed. You are a professional, surely you know that?'

But Carlos was unimpressed by Jorge's rhetoric.

'Give me a number where I can reach you,' Jorge asked.

'Sometimes I wonder if you are really so stupid.' Carlos rang off.

Jorge was getting desperate. He knew if he pushed Rosa any harder she would turn on him. He couldn't risk that happening. He had to secure his position as her only true friend. She had to believe he wanted only what was best for her.

But time was running out. Jorge could not believe he was the only source being used to trap Victor. Perhaps others would discover Victor's secret, before he could trade it in return for Rosa and Roberto's safety. The consequences then were unthinkable.

Jorge had another problem. Drupa 78, the printing exposition in Dusseldorf, was less than three weeks away. It would take him out of the country for a month, and demand every second of his time for the following twelve. He had to act.

He took a taxi to his father's headquarters and went to see Esther Teresa.

'I need funds transferred to my New York account,' he said and gave her the details. She showed no surprise at the amount.

'Sit down,' she said, and a sigh came from deep within her. She reached across her desk and took his hands. She held them silently, as if in prayer, before speaking.

'It is a dangerous game you play, Jorge Luis. There are no friends in this game, no allies, just shifting alliances. Every one, even you, is expendable. This is not a time for heroics. Just to survive is enough.'

So Esther Teresa also knew. Who else, Jorge wondered? The stakes kept doubling, and the longer the game lasted, the greater the risks became.

'I have no choice, Esther Teresa. I did not seek involvement in this thing. But I must also do what is best for me. It is my life. No one else can live it for me.'

'They can, Jorge. Sometimes it is better to let them.' Her eyes pleaded a cause she hoped was not lost. 'We must all make sacrifices. Sometimes the sacrifices seem too much. But the head must rule the heart. Take care, Jorge. Weigh every action carefully.'

She watched Jorge leave. Then picked up the phone to his father's office.

When Carlos rang again, Jorge was curt with him.

'We must talk,' he said. 'This time I will try the *yerba maté*.' He hung up.

After almost two months of silence, the Voice of the People was once more raised in protest. He listed the names of those who gave their lives in the raid on *Argentina Libre*, and those who had simply disappeared.

'The Voice of the People cannot be silenced,' he raged, 'while people are still free to dream. Of justice. Of equality. Of a society both fair and free. While a single Argentinian is denied the right to his own opinion, to the freedom to express it, then the Voice of the People shall be heard. While a single Argentinian is held in poverty by the greed of the few, then the Voice of the People shall be heard.

'My voice may be extinguished by a single bullet, but others will take my place and cry out in the name of justice. And others will take their place, and still others theirs. This voice will not be silenced.'

Argentina Libre began appearing in cafeterias, bars and public places as before. Every Thursday, ordinary men and women risked their lives distributing copies, leaving the damning trail of evidence behind them.

By normal standards *Argentina Libre* wasn't much of a newspaper. The quality was poor and it was pathetically thin. But it did adhere to the principle that readers of newspapers are creatures of habit. Dailies must arrive daily and morning papers in the morning, always at the same time or earlier. *Argentina Libre* was a

Thursday newspaper. That is when people looked for it and expected to find it. That is also what made it easy to catch distributors.

When Jorge arrived at Los Locos, the car, the driver and Carlos were already in place. However, neither Jorge nor Carlos were in a mood to eat. They settled for the wine and soda water.

'So,' Carlos began, 'you have brought me here to tell me you want indemnity for the adulterous slut.'

'It is a small enough thing to ask, considering the information I bring.'

Carlos laughed.

'What could you possibly tell me that I don't already know?'

For an instant Jorge felt panic rise. But of course Carlos couldn't know or else he would have acted. Jorge looked at the sneering face across the table. Patience. He would put the peasant in his place soon enough.

'First your guarantee of indemnity. For Rosa and her child.'

'What do you want? The boy scout's oath? Shall I cross my heart?'

Jorge let him play.

'Okay. You have it.' Carlos smiled benignly. 'What's one whore more or less for my men? They have enough to amuse themselves already.' His eyes hardened. 'Now you keep your side of the bargain.'

'Victor Gustavo Sanguineti is *La Voz del Pueblo*.'

Carlos froze. The smile vanished.

'You are certain of this?'

It was Jorge's turn to show contempt.

'Just make sure you keep your end of the deal.' Jorge stood and turned to leave the restaurant.

'Sit down!' roared Carlos. And Jorge did, as surely as if his father had spoken.

They planned the raid for Tuesday evening at dinner time, when they knew both parents and child would be home. Victor, they reasoned, would be up against the deadline for his story for *Argentina Libre*. There was a chance they might find some evidence of it in his home. Some thoughts, perhaps. Some revisions. Proof wasn't necessary for conviction for there would be no trial. But it would convince Carlos' superiors that he had indeed got his man.

For Jorge, the days leading up to the raid were full of doubts and self-recrimination. After all, hadn't he just condemned Victor to the most horrible fate? To torture and, ultimately, to death. Yet it was necessary, he reasoned, made necessary by his obligations to his father. And what about Rosa? He was reasonably sure she would come to him first, but not certain. There were many things he'd wished he'd handled differently. But she'd been so reluctant to act. She'd forced his hand.

He decided to take Rosa and Roberto with him to Dusseldorf, but he wasn't convinced that Carlos would allow them to leave the country. He arranged for a light aircraft to fly them over the border to Paraguay, where they could fly to the United States and then on to Europe. He asked for permission for one of his father's minders to accompany them, to handle the bribes and pay-offs.

He threw himself into his work, hoping that would occupy his mind. The tension would build until it made him physically ill. Then he would return to his work, and the cycle would begin again. Rosa rang him, anxious to meet, but he pleaded pressure of work and put her off. He could not face her over lunch, knowing what was about to happen, knowing what he had done.

Tuesday dawned wet and overcast. The clouds swept in over the River Plate and dumped their load on the city. Jorge was filled with foreboding. Things went wrong right from the beginning. Jorge had decided to stay at his office till either Rosa or Carlos rang, and confirmed that the terrible thing had been done. But this was not to be.

His secretary rang. While she was announcing his visitor, Carlos strode into his office. Two thugs accompanied him.

'I have decided to let you share our moment of triumph, Jorge Luis,' he said. 'You will accompany us.'

Jorge swallowed hard. This was not in the plan. Rosa would know he was involved.

'No!' he said. 'That would ruin everything.'

'Do you want the whore or not?'

What could Jorge do? He had no choice. He collected his raincoat. The two goons grinned at one another. They would have carried him out bodily if he had resisted.

As their car sped towards La Boca, Jorge tried to think of ways to save the situation. He could tell Rosa that his father had heard of the impending arrest and alerted him. He had interceded on her behalf. He had come to make sure neither she nor Roberto were harmed. He might get away with it if he could get her and the child out of the house quickly enough.

As soon as their car pulled up outside the house, the waiting soldiers rushed in. Jorge heard the door burst open. He heard Rosa scream. Then Carlos took his arm and led him inside.

'Jorge! What have you done?'

Rosa's eyes were wide with horror and disbelief. Her accusation hung in the air. Soldiers held her and Victor immobile, pinning their arms behind their backs. Rosa's eyes never left Jorge, even as they bound tape around her mouth. He burned with shame. He knew then that no explanation would ever be good enough. Soldiers came in from the study with slips of paper and notes. *La Voz del Pueblo* had been careless, not that it changed anything. Victor was as good as dead. At least he could save Rosa and the boy. The boy! Roberto! Where was he? His eyes flicked around the room and caught Victor's. His eyes held Jorge's, silently pleading, 'Spare the boy.'

'So. How do you feel now, Jorge Luis Masot?'

Jorge's mind raced. What was Carlos doing! The room was filled with soldiers, all of whom would boast of the capture of *La Voz*.

'Well, what do you say, Jorge Luis Masot?' Carlos taunted him, drawing out each syllable of his name.

'We have an arrangement.'

'So we do, so we do . . .' Carlos seemed pensive for a moment. 'I keep my word. I give her to you. Go ahead, take her.' He nodded to the two soldiers holding Rosa. They picked her up and slammed her down hard on her back, on the dining-table the restorers had failed to collect. They pulled up her skirt and tore away her panties. They spread her legs wide.

'See?' said Carlos genially. 'I give her to you. And afterwards, I give her to my men. Did you really think I would let her go free? This whore who has been distributing illegal publications for the last four years? What's wrong with you, Jorge Luis Masot,' he taunted, 'aren't you man enough to take her? Don't you have the balls to do it in front of her husband, instead of behind his back?'

Any hope Jorge had now vanished in the face of Carlos' treachery. He looked at Rosa, spreadeagled before him, and his eyes fell. There, suddenly, he saw a small face staring back at him. Two eyes so wide and filled with unimaginable terror. The boy! The boy was hiding under the stairs. His head spun but he forced his face to remain unaffected. He turned away and there was Victor. Victor knew. Victor willed him not to betray his son.

'Well, Jorge Luis Masot, shall I show you how?' Carlos advanced on Rosa, unbuttoning his fly. Jorge could take no more. He turned and ran. The soldiers laughed at him as he ran past them down the stone steps and out onto the street. He ran and ran. But could he ever outrun his guilt? Could he ever outrun the horror of his betrayal?

Ramon's voice had diminished to a whisper, then ceased altogether. His friends, still bound up in the story, let the silence hang over them. When their eyes finally sought out Ramon they found him lost somewhere within himself as if, in his story, he was reliving his past.

They exchanged looks with one another, embarrassed but also concerned. They waited for Ramon to gather himself together. Neil was first to speak.

'Nice fella, that Jorge. Friend of yours?'

'Oh Jesus, Neil . . .'

'It's all right, Milos. We all know what Neil is like. My apologies. Sometimes the storyteller gets more wrapped up in his story than his audience.'

'Are you sure you're all right?'

'Yes.'

'Of course he's all right. He's just stringing us along. Dramatic effect. Game playing, what you're always on about.'

'Sometimes, Neil, you overplay the insensitive property developer.' Milos turned to Ramon. 'You said earlier this story trespassed on your past. Did a lot of this sort of thing go on? Were you . . . ?'

'Was I involved? Milos, all of Argentina was involved.'

'What would have happened to Victor and Rosa?' Neil always asked where others were content to wonder.

'Who knows?' Ramon spoke slowly. 'Unspeakable things happened. There were over three hundred clandestine detention centres. They may have witnessed each other's death.'

'Holy Mother! How much of this story is true?'

'All of it, Lucio.'

'Ha! What did you expect him to say?' Neil shook his head at Lucio's naïveté. 'He always says his stories are true. This time he has drawn on his past, that's for sure. An unfortunate past, too. Ramon has drawn on many facets of his life. Like Jorge, Ramon also has ink under his fingernails. We know that. But beyond that we're really no wiser. Were there atrocities in Argentina? Of course there were. They go on in every war. Besides, we've already read stories about them in the papers. But you know better than to take Ramon at face value. Yeah, he looks genuinely tired but it could just as easily be one of his little games. A game to add credibility, to sucker us along. What do you reckon, Milos?'

'Maybe . . . but I'm inclined to give Ramon the benefit of the doubt. The story so far rings true and the way he's telling it suggests he was pretty close to what happened. Uncomfortably close, in fact. Close enough to feel some distress in reliving it. I don't think you're playing a game with us, Ramon. Not yet anyway. If you are, it's unforgivable.'

'Two-one against. Okay, everybody, the story is true. If so, why did you base Jorge on yourself, Ramon?'

'Jesus, Neil. Give him a break.'

'What's the problem? If you and Milos are right, Lucio, and I'm wrong, then it's a fair question.'

'It's not the question, it's your attitude.'

'Look, the man Ramon has described sounds very much like how I imagine he would have been as a young man. Impeccably mannered and a snappy dresser.'

'With or without the stain on his tie?' Humour is all a question of timing and Lucio had timed his interjection perfectly. The moment Milos and Ramon laughed, Neil lost the momentum he'd been gathering. The mood around the table lightened considerably.

'Coffee,' called Milos. 'And grappa. And do us all a favour, Neil. Back off a bit.'

Gancio was there with the tray, seemingly in seconds. He looked hard at Ramon and was relieved to see the colour back in his face.

'I don't understand why Carlos set Jorge up.' Neil was nothing if not persistent. 'Jorge's father was a powerful man. Someone who could harm Carlos' career. Why would he go out of his way to provoke him? He must have known that one day Jorge's father would want revenge.'

'I will answer that.' Ramon had recovered some of his poise. 'I have not quite finished telling the story for today. There could be several reasons. Perhaps Carlos had no choice. Perhaps the people he worked for wanted to undermine Jorge's father. Think about it. He would be publicly exposed for having a son involved with leftist revolutionaries. You can imagine how well that would go down with the Generals. Then again, Carlos might simply have resented Jorge and his privileges. If that's the case, Carlos probably thought the people he worked for were powerful enough to protect him. Without knowing all the facts, how could anyone be certain of his motives? Not having lived through it, you'd find it hard to comprehend how arrogant the military were in those days, how absolute their power. Of course Carlos, a dirt-poor, peasant *mestizo*, was the antithesis of Jorge. Imagine how much he must have hated and envied the privilege Jorge was born into. Perhaps it's as simple as that. Perhaps he betrayed Jorge and his father out of sheer spite and arrogance. Why not? The irony is, of all the characters I have introduced to you, Carlos had the best credentials to be the true revolutionary. Yet he found himself on the other side.'

'He also had the credentials to be a true fascist, no? A man in his position might easily prefer to wear the boot than bear the brunt of it. That's clearly the decision Carlos made. Don't give me any bleeding-heart philosophy, please.'

'Milos, I have to believe there is more to it than that. Sure, Carlos had a choice, but what were the influences on his choice? You condemn him too readily. Isn't it fate that determines whether people act for or against humanity? Victor was a martyr, Carlos a murderer. If they'd swapped mothers wouldn't their subsequent roles also be reversed?'

Milos shrugged. He felt he'd made his point.

'Now, Neil, have I answered your question adequately?'

'No, but that'll do for now. There'll be other opportunities.'

'What happened to Jorge?' asked Lucio. 'You know, after he ran from the house.'

'That's too big a question to answer now.' Ramon smiled despite his tiredness. 'You will find that out over the next few weeks. But I will tell you this much. Like I said, I have yet to finish today's story. Just make sure Neil keeps his mouth closed for the next couple of minutes.'

Jorge ran. He ran to his father's office. He had nowhere else to go. He told his father what had happened.

'Jorge Luis Masot is dead,' his father said. 'Carlos has seen to that. By tomorrow everyone in Buenos Aires will know the name of the man who betrayed *La Voz del Pueblo*. Our plane will fly you to Chile. After that you are on your own.' He handed Jorge a packet containing his new life.

Jorge looked at his father. 'I have failed you. I am sorry.'

'I regret I had to involve you. Under the circumstances I had no alternative. Carlos was not my choice. Indeed I had no choice.' This admission left Jorge wondering what his father could possibly have done that others could exert their will over his. 'Esther Teresa informs me that you have funds. Goodbye, my son. Do not contact me again. Even I cannot guarantee loyalties.'

'And Carlos?'

'It seems Carlos has begun to believe his own reputation,' his father said grimly. 'I don't know why he chose to destroy you as well. Perhaps someone also wants to discredit me. These men we deal with are without honour. Your name was never to be mentioned. I had agreement on that. He has betrayed me in betraying you. He will become a powerful man as a result of capturing *La Voz*. But he will not be beyond my reach.'

His father kissed him perfunctorily. Jorge turned and walked away. He paused as he passed Esther Teresa but she did not bother to look up. Why should she? Jorge Luis Masot had ceased to exist.

SECOND THURSDAY

Gancio had risen early and gone himself to Flemington Markets instead of sending the woman who helped him in the kitchen. He liked to joke and trade insults with his fellow Italians who were the growers. They'd look at his spreading waistline and accuse him of eating half the food he cooked. Still, they liked the big restaurateur and went out of their way to point out the best produce. The four friends were the main beneficiaries of Gancio's dawn labours, though none who dined at his restaurant that day would have cause to complain. He went with an open mind and returned with baskets full of aubergines and zucchini, big red capsicums and rockmelons.

Gancio liked to serve a variety of little dishes even though it kept him running to and from the kitchen. He brought the four friends prosciutto on melon. Then strips of capsicum, which he had roasted, peeled and marinated in olive oil, garlic, vinegar and ground black pepper. It was a favourite of Ramon's. Salami and olives followed. Then thinly sliced bocconcini with tomato and basil to cleanse the palate before his speciality, *frittata a la verdura*, which transformed the aubergines and zucchini into a dish Lucio claimed was worth dying for. They declined second helpings but could not say no to the tiramasu which Gancio had made specially for their dessert.

'After such a meal, I cannot take you back to Argentina,' Ramon began. 'It would depress me and perhaps you as well. It would not do justice to the mood Gancio has created with his culinary masterpieces. I think it is time I introduced you to Jan Van der Meer. He is a delightful man. However, you will meet him first as a nineteen year old, on the verge of the greatest adventure of his life. The year is 1949 and, like many young men in those post-war years – like Milos here – he could find no reason to stay on in Europe.'

'Already I miss Rosa,' said Lucio. 'Tell me, will there be other women like her?'

'Sometimes, Lucio, you are a perfect arse.' Milos was angry. Storytelling was a serious matter to him, not just its content but also its style and technique. Ramon had begun to build a mood and set the scene for a change of pace. Now he would have to do it all over again and it was never the same.

But Ramon did not seem to mind.

Chapter Nine

Jan Van der Meer was nineteen years old and a touch under two metres tall. His body had not yet filled out to fit his frame, and he still had the raw-boned look of the adolescent as he picked his way along the steaming Singapore docks.

A blast from a ship's horn caused him to pause and look out to sea, searching for its origin. He found it quickly enough, and the empty feeling of loss washed back over him. It was the Shaw Saville liner *Arawa*, his home for the past four weeks, now steadily gaining speed as it turned for the voyage to distant Europe. On board were the only friends he had for a thousand kilometres. Perhaps for ten thousand kilometres.

He swallowed nervously. What had begun as a great adventure in Amsterdam had now taken on an entirely different complexion, its conclusion uncertain to say the least.

Would he still be welcome? He had asked himself this question a thousand times and was still no closer to an answer. Would they accept him? Could they begin again, as before? Or was the whole escapade the childish folly his mother had said it was?

The hard part of his journey had begun. There were no friendly booking agents here to get him where he wanted to go. At least, not for the money he was prepared to pay.

He looked around the bustling quay at the Chinese, as they shouted and cursed each other in Hokkien, pausing only to clear their nose or throats onto the timber decking. There was not another white face to be seen. Yet it was not a situation he felt uncomfortable with. In fact he felt a sense of belonging in this chaotic and alien world.

His eyes registered the flat, bland faces of the Chinese, but they were not who he was looking for. He could not speak a word of their language nor they his. He took a long swallow of tepid water from his army surplus canteen. That was one of the few good things to come from the war. There was plenty of cheap gear for a young man bent on adventure. His khaki shirts and shorts were army surplus, as was his rucksack, sleeping bag and tin cup, plate and eating utensils. He also carried a rather brutal commando knife, for no other reason than the reassurance it gave him. The broad-brimmed hat that covered his closely cropped blond hair, and the sturdy sandals on his feet, had been his father's.

He walked on, taking care not to block the way of the coolies, bent double under their loads. In this part of the docks there were no cranes or slings, and the contents of boats were carried out on the backs of men. He politely gave them right of way even though he knew they would have deferred to him. Their job was hard enough. He would not make it any harder.

He saw a group of men who weren't working and knew he'd found what he was looking for. The men squatted patiently, back on their heels, protected from the hot August sun by an ancient canvas sheet which they'd strung up between two poles. They were smoking cigarettes they'd rolled themselves using strips of newspaper.

'*Selamat pagi*,' Jan said. 'Good morning.'

'*Pagi*,' the Malays replied, surprised to find this tall young Dutchman among them. And doubly surprised to find he spoke Bahasa.

'The day is very warm. You are wise men to make this shelter.'

The men nodded and smiled. Jan knew it was bad manners to get straight down to business. Besides he was in no great hurry, and his Bahasa was more than a little rusty. He welcomed the chance to get some practice.

'I am Abdul Malik,' said the man who was their leader. 'These men are my crew. There is room. Please sit with us.'

'Thank you,' said Jan. 'I am Jan Van der Meer.' He extended his hand and shook hands with each man in turn.

'Would you like a cigarette?' asked the leader.

'No, thank you, You are very kind. But my mother insists I am too young to smoke.'

The men laughed and rocked back on their heels. As if this giant would take notice of his mother.

'So why has this young man – who may not yet smoke – come to Singapore?'

'I have come for two reasons,' said Jan. 'The first is to find the grave of my father. He was shot by the Japanese.'

The Malays all turned their eyes to the ground. In sympathy? Or in memory of their own losses suffered during those bitter years? Jan didn't know and it didn't matter. But he found their simple gesture touching.

'The second reason is to return to the place of my birth. The island of Java.'

The men looked at him. They wondered what twists of fate could have made Java the birthplace of this blond giant. They also wondered if that made him their enemy.

'Java!' Abdul Malik spat onto the dusty ground. 'How will you go there?'

'I don't know. I seek advice. Perhaps you can help?'

'Your country has abandoned the East Indies. Do you not know this? East Indies is now the United States of Indonesia. Sukarno is President. We hear this on the wireless. Sukarno is bad man. You see. Soon he throw out all the Dutchmen. Soon he steal all your property. Soon he make trouble for us. He try to make Malaya belong to Indonesia. And Singapore. No Malay boat will take you there.'

The crew murmured agreement.

Jan was stunned. He was aware of Sukarno's ambitions, and had known what the political situation would be before he left Amsterdam. At least he thought he'd known. He knew one day Holland would have to relinquish sovereignty, but he'd thought that day was years off. What would happen now? Would this change things? Would he still have friends there? Sitting with these Malay seamen, he was assailed by doubts. Perhaps the past was lost forever, gone with his childhood.

The Malays watched him, wondering whether their leader's words had changed the young man's mind. Finally the leader sought the answer to the question they all wanted to hear.

'Why do you go there? Why take any boat there? You will not be welcome any more. They have fought your people and they have beaten them. They are arrogant with victory and their new independence. They have no love for you. Why go?'

'In truth I don't know. I hear your words and I am grateful for them. But there is only one way I can find out if I am still welcome. I must go there.'

The Malays rolled their eyes and accepted that it was his fate to pursue his journey.

'Then go with God,' said the captain kindly. 'We cannot help you. Perhaps you can find another boat that will take you.'

'I have one thought,' said Jan. 'Again, you may be able to help me. When I was a child my father spoke of the Bugis men and their powerful schooners . . .'

'Ha!' spat the captain once more. 'Bugis men are pirates.'

The Buginese had settled in South Sulawesi more than a thousand years earlier. They were legendary seafarers and shipbuilders, and there was not a stretch of shore for a thousand kilometres that had not been subject to their influence.

'But if there are Bugis schooners in port, perhaps one of them will take me to Java.'

Abdul Malik looked over the boy-man carefully, taking stock of his clothes and his rucksack.

'My young friend,' he said, 'be warned. There are none so poor that the Bugis men will not rob them. A man with nothing at all to steal they rob of his life. But if that is your choice . . . ?'

Jan nodded.

'Then yes, there are Bugis schooners in port. They bring timber from Kalimantan. Keep walking this way and you will find them. Good luck, my friend.'

Jan stood and shook hands once more with Abdul Malik.

'You are a good man, Abdul Malik. *Selamat tinggal.*'

'*Selamat jalan,*' they responded. 'Goodbye and have a safe journey.'

They watched the young man until he was out of sight.

'Rather him than me,' said Abdul Malik, and they all laughed.

'*Selamat siang,*' Jan called from the foot of the plank that linked the schooner with the shore. 'May I come aboard?'

'*Selamat siang,*' the skipper called back. 'Yes, Tuan, you are welcome aboard my boat.' He held his hand flat, palm down, and gestured with his fingers. Jan smiled. It was a way of beckoning he had not seen for years.

The Bugis schooner was banana-shaped and more like a Chinese junk than a schooner. Its massive high prow swept down to a broad-beamed waist, then back up to a high, overhanging stern. The wheelhouse was not much more than a two-roomed shack in which the crew ate, slept and lived together. Behind it was a weathered timber awning beneath which the crew sat on their haunches, awaiting their visitor. There were five of them, all tough and weathered like their boat.

The captain introduced himself as Andi Sose, and invited Jan to squat down with them. Jan felt the ache and soreness of muscles that had grown unaccustomed to this position. It had never troubled him as a child.

He looked around the circle of men as calmly as he could, trying to divine their true nature. He would never describe their expressions as friendly but, with only one exception, they lacked hostility. The exception was the largest of the Bugis men, a man whose arms had the girth of other men's legs. At least that is how it seemed to Jan. A scar as thick as rope divided his face into two uneven parts, and whatever had caused it had also robbed him of his right eye. Jan hoped the malice he read in this man's face was a result of his disfigurement, and not a reflection of the mind behind it.

He exchanged cautious pleasantries while the Bugis men wondered what fates had brought this man to them. In due course, the captain politely enquired as to the reason for the visit. He picked the reason most likely.

'Do you have cargo for us?' he asked.

'In a manner of speaking, yes.'

The crew smiled. Cargo meant wages.

'But it is an insignificant cargo which will not bring you riches. The cargo is myself. Can you take me to Java?'

The Bugis men looked at Jan in amazement.

'Has no one told you, young man? Bugis men are thieves and pirates. They cannot be trusted. This man here,' the captain pointed to the man with one eye, 'he is the biggest pirate of all.'

The crew laughed. Jan joined in. He thought that was the best thing to do.

'Yes. I was told that Bugis men are pirates. But the men who told me were Malays. Perhaps they envy the power of your boats and the skills of your crew.'

The captain was delighted with this answer. But he was not yet finished with Jan.

'Do you not know that for two centuries Bugis pirates plundered the boats of the Dutch East Indies?'

'Yes. And the boats of the English,' Jan replied. 'You frightened the English so much, your name has now become part of their language. They call you the bogey men. They tell their children to behave or the bogey men will come and get them.'

The captain laughed uproariously. He liked this confident young Dutchman. All but 'One-Eye' followed his lead. He just scowled. His malevolent gaze never left Jan.

'Perhaps the English are wiser than the Dutch?' suggested the captain.

'Perhaps the Dutch are braver than the English,' countered Jan.

Again the Bugis men laughed. But now it was time for the captain to be serious.

'Yes we can take you to Java. But if we agree to take you to Java, what makes you think you will be welcome there?'

'I was born there,' said Jan. 'My family have a tea plantation on the slopes of Tengkuban Prahu, near Bandung. I grew up there until the age of nine. I have many friends in the kampongs. They will not have forgotten me. I ran with the children of the village who were my age. We stole mangoes together. And mangosteens, pineapples and snake fruit. We took the eggs from kampong chickens and boiled them in the hot pools of Tengkuban Prahu. I have sat with them at the feet of the elders and learned their customs and history. Like the village children I was raised practising *rukun*, *gotong royong* and *sopan-santun* – harmony, mutual help and manners. My skin is white. Everyone can see that. But my heart belongs in Java, among the Sundanese people.'

Jan could see that the captain was moved.

'Times change,' he said sadly. 'First the Dutch destroyed our empire and scattered our people. Now it is your turn to feel the sting of new masters. Things are no longer as they were. Your friends may now be your enemies. You may not be welcome in your own home. They will take your land from you. That is the way it is now.'

'My father was a good man,' said Jan. 'He was a fair man. This gives me cause for hope. Also, he was not deaf. When the drums of nationalism began to beat he was first to hear them. He did something quite extraordinary. Something you will understand and appreciate. He could see the time coming when the Dutch would be forced to leave the East Indies, and he thought the war in Europe might be the catalyst. He knew that he and the other colonisers would lose everything they owned. He loved Java, and the tea plantation was his life. He started thinking of ways that he could make sure he had something to return to after the war.

'He called the elders from all the villages around his estate to a meeting. He suggested they form a cooperative and that the cooperative become his junior partner. He explained how each village would share in the rewards of their labour according to their contribution. He gave them thirty percent, and a good idea of what they could expect to receive in a good year. The elders went away and in their mosques gave thanks to Allah for this good man.'

The Buginese men nodded. They understood the generosity of this for they too were part of a cooperative. The owners of their boat lived in their home port of Ujung Pandang in South Sulawesi, which the Dutch had known as Makassar. They took eighty percent of the profits. The remainder was divided up among the crew according to contribution and seniority.

'Of course the Europeans could not understand what he had done and despised him for it. But he would not change his mind. He had a deed drawn up in Jakarta, and gave it to the cooperative.

'So you see. The people who work on the plantation are joint owners with us. There is a good chance that we will keep our lands. The government may steal from the Dutch but surely they will not steal from their own people?'

The captain considered Jan's words.

'He was a good man, your father. It is a pity he is not with you.'

'My father was killed by the Japanese. His grave is somewhere here in Singapore. Before I can go to Java I must try to find it. My mother and I were in Holland on holiday when the war broke out. My father stayed on to produce rubber for the war effort. He fled to Singapore after Pearl Harbor. All we have are his letters.'

'I hope you find your father's grave. Perhaps we can take you to Jakarta. But as you can see, we are poor people and we cannot take you for nothing.'

'I am willing to pay,' said Jan, elated that the negotiations had begun. He could feel the excitement mounting within him. Soon he would be on his way. Even better, soon he would be able to stand and stretch his aching thighs and calf muscles. But business first. 'The question is, how much money do you ask?'

'Three thousand rupiah,' said the captain after what appeared to be considerable thought.

'Captain, you misunderstand me. I do not wish to buy your boat.'

The crew laughed. The captain nodded graciously.

'Fortunately we like you. That is what we would normally charge. But you are a friend. You will have to work as one of the crew, you understand. Fifteen hundred.'

'I would be honoured to work as one of your crew on your fine boat,' Jan countered. 'Five hundred.'

'Alas, there are not enough hours in the day for you to work to repay me. One thousand.'

'Seven hundred and fifty is all I have,' said Jan.

'Then it is agreed. You will pay seven-fifty. Then you can sleep in peace at night, knowing the terrible Bugis men will not come and steal your money.'

Jan could see the sense of that. He laughed along with the crew and the deal was done. One-Eye turned and spat over the railing.

Jan's elation at finding a boat to take him to Java was tempered by disappointment. He did not find his father's grave nor was he encouraged to believe it would ever be found. He began his search at the Netherlands Embassy. They were expecting him, but they could give him no more information than they already had in their correspondence with him. Once more they told him the circumstances of his father's death as far as they could ascertain.

He had been rounded up with several other Europeans. The Japanese had separated the men from the women and marched them away towards the prison at Changi. Along the route they passed a building site where some Japanese soldiers had captured a group of Malays or Javanese – no one was exactly sure – and were executing them. There were women and children among the men who were also being shot. Again no one is sure why. Their bodies were thrown into the trenches and pits which had been dug for foundations.

Jan's father saw this outrage and reacted instinctively. He broke free from the column and ran over to remonstrate with the Japanese officer in charge. The officer withdrew a pistol from his belt and shot him dead without a word. The executions continued uninterrupted.

Given the circumstances, his father's body was probably buried along with the bodies of the other victims, somewhere on that building site. Nobody could be sure. And nobody was even sure where the building site was.

There are no soft edges to news of this kind. Tone of voice can show sympathy and understanding. But there is no point in promoting false hope. Jan was lucky, they said, because at least he knew what had happened. Others were less fortunate. Their loved ones had simply disappeared, lost without trace. His father had acted rashly but there could be nothing but respect for his courage. That was small consolation, but consolation nonetheless.

They offered him one glimmer of hope. Sometimes the Malays returned to claim their dead when the Japanese moved on. There were many confirmed instances of this happening. If they had, they may also have taken Jan's father's body with them, and buried him with the honour due to one who had tried to help their kind. Perhaps if Jan asked around the Malay quarter he might find someone who recalled the incident.

Jan knew from the beginning it was a long shot. But he owed it to his mother and his father's memory to give it a try. He thanked the embassy staff for their help and, before he left, confirmed that the money he'd sent on ahead would be waiting for him at the embassy in Jakarta.

For three days he walked the streets around the dock area, returning to the boat each evening to sleep. He had no fear of his Bugis crew mates nor of One-Eye, for if they planned any treachery, that would come later when they were at sea, beyond the reach of the law. The three days were not entirely fruitless though, in the final analysis, the fruit was poor.

Jan concentrated on speaking to the older Malays who no longer gave up their days to the slog of hard labour. With little else to do, they had become the repositories of knowledge for their people.

They were eager to help, and tried hard to recall that particular execution.

Those who claimed to remember it were unreliable and the people they called to corroborate their story even more so. The building site where the executions occurred was variously placed from one end of the island to the other, and the execution from the days immediately following the invasion to six months afterwards. Nobody could recall if the dead were claimed. Nobody knew what had happened to his father. Jan's father was not the only European civilian shot by the Japanese. Nor were the circumstances unique. There were many unsung heroes. On the evening of the third day of his search he put his father's memory to rest in a long and loving letter to his mother.

They sailed the next day.

Chapter Ten

The depression Jan felt lifted the moment they put to sea. He was relieved to be away from the stale, suffocating air of the overcrowded island. He stood on the bow, arms spread to the freshening breeze, eager to help out in his new role of crew but entirely ignorant as to how he might do so. In truth there was little for him to do, and he would have only got in the way.

They cleared port under the power of their small motor, then set the sails upon the two masts. The sails were not the pristine white Jan was expecting, but dyed dark brown. They caught the wind and the schooner surged forward. Jan was elated. Their twelve hundred kilometre journey would take them around eight days, as they set course first towards Pontianak, on the island Jan knew as Borneo and the Buginese called Kalimantan. Then they would swing south, through the Karimata Strait to the Java Sea, and the port of Jakarta.

Perhaps the elation Jan felt is shared by all sailors when they leave port for the wide expanses and freedom of the ocean, for once clear of the harbour the Buginese broke into cheerful song.

Jan stood in the point of the bow and watched the flying fish scatter before them, marvelling at the distances they flew before diving back beneath the waves. He watched the sky grow steadily more blue as the land fell away behind them and, with it, the humidity that had sapped his strength. But as the sky cleared, the tropical sun grew more intense, and not even the sea breeze could cool him adequately. He turned to find the Buginese had already taken shelter. He decided to join them.

'After so much hard work you must have an appetite.' The captain's voice came to him from a dark corner of the cabin. 'Sit down. We are preparing our meal.'

Jan threw his hat down upon his pack and slowly his eyes adjusted to the gloom within the cabin. He saw the youngest of the Bugis men heating oil in a wok over a paraffin burner. He watched as the lad, roughly his own age, threw in a handful of fresh chillies. His eyes watered as he felt the bite of their fumes. The young cook added pieces of fish and vegetables and a palm full of salt.

When the meal was ready, the cook took a pot of rice off a second burner and spooned the contents into bowls. With dismay, Jan counted the bowls and saw that there were only five. Someone would miss out, either he or the helmsman, and he couldn't imagine the helmsman missing out.

'We have only five bowls,' said the captain reading his mind. The men laughed, for this was a scenario they had planned. 'My nephew the cook will eat from the rice pot.'

They passed Jan a bowl, now steaming with fish and vegetables.

'No. I will not eat this,' said Jan, with as much authority as he could muster. The cabin fell silent and they looked at him, wondering at his madness.

Jan looked around at the men. 'Why should I take this bowl from the cook who has worked so hard, when I have a bowl of my own?' He reached into his rucksack and pulled out his enamel war surplus plate.

'Besides,' he said, with the satisfied grin of one who has turned the joke back on the jokers, 'my bowl is bigger.'

'We must watch this man,' said the captain gleefully, 'His mouth is quick and his mind is quicker.'

Jan passed his bowl over to the cook to be filled with the fiery concoction, secure in the knowledge that no virulent organism could possibly survive the salt and the chillies. He waited to see how the crew ate their meal. Each man produced his own spoon, so Jan did likewise, not wishing to upstage them with his knife and fork. Besides, the fish was well cooked and fell apart easily. Jan reached inside his rucksack once more for his canteen, and drank from it. He did not offer it around, because he knew the Bugis men had a large barrel of fresh water from which they regularly helped themselves.

He put his canteen back inside his rucksack, aware now that One-Eye was watching him closely. He turned to meet his gaze and realised his error. One-Eye wasn't looking at him. He was focused squarely on his rucksack, and Jan could imagine him speculating as to what other treasures might be inside it.

'It is time now for our guest to earn his meal.' The captain's voice snatched Jan from his thoughts. 'You will steer for us while we sleep. Tonight while you sleep, one of us will steer. Come with me.'

Jan followed the captain into the adjoining shack which was flatteringly referred to as the wheelhouse. Its forward windows were tightly shut and their frames so often painted over, they were destined never to reopen. The only ventilation came from portholes on either side wall, their heavy frames fastened back to admit what breeze they could. The air inside was stifling and Jan could feel the sweat begin to flow from every pore in his body.

'Keep on this heading,' said the captain as the helmsman handed Jan the wheel. 'If the wind changes direction, you wake me. Okay?'

Jan took the wheel and felt the breeze die away almost at the same instant, as the captain surely knew it would. He heard a laugh from the adjoining cabin. What good was his quick mouth and even quicker mind now? He realised he hadn't really been given the responsibility of steering the ship, but of minding it through the hot afternoon watch. He groaned but he had no choice. He had agreed to share the work and this was probably the only work he was qualified to do. All he had to do was stay awake. And with the heat of the wheelhouse and a huge meal in his belly, that would be no easy task.

He thought he would amuse himself by watching the flying fish, but they kept to the depths, preferring the risk of rampaging tuna to flight in the torpid air. The sea turned slate grey and heaved ponderously, with the heavy effort of a dying man struggling for breath. Jan searched the sky for clouds but there were none. His eyelids grew heavy and he yearned to rest them, if only for a moment. He snapped awake. How long had he slept? Hours? Minutes? Seconds? He looked around him, nerves jangled, his brain screaming for more of the brief comfort it had found. He realised with a mixture of relief and dismay that he'd only nodded off for the briefest of moments. But only a fool fails to heed such warnings.

He waited till the snoring from the aft cabin indicated that all were asleep, before tiptoeing to his rucksack for his canteen, a pen and notepaper. For the remaining three hours of his watch he wrote a letter to his mother, challenging his mind to recall every little incident and detail since their departure that morning. It didn't matter that his mother would never read the letter because he had no intention of sending it. As he read over it, and re-read it, he had to admit it was probably the most boring letter anyone had ever written. Still, it had served its purpose. As the breeze freshened late in the day, the captain found his apprentice helmsman weary, but wide awake.

Jan should have taken the opportunity to grab some sleep but all he could think of was cooling down. He decided to return to his favourite position at the point of the bow where the cooling wind and spray could wash over him. He looked for his hat. It wasn't on his rucksack. It wasn't on the floor. On his way forward he noticed One-Eye wearing it. One-Eye scowled, as if daring Jan to reclaim it.

'It's only a hat,' Jan told himself.

Night fell, and they finished off the cold rice and fish by the light of oil lamps. In that flickering half-light, One-Eye looked more sinister than ever. The heat and fresh air had taken its toll on Jan, and again he fought off sleep. But he was determined not to fall asleep before One-Eye. He went back out and lay down on the timber decking.

Planets as big as footballs swung from one side of the mast to the other, as if on an inverted pendulum. Around him in the blackness, the vast reaches of the ocean merged with the infinite sweep of the universe. The boat rocked gently. The stars swam in dizzying patterns. And sleep beckoned.

Jan dragged himself to his feet and made his way to the cabin. His hat was back where he had left it, but he couldn't have cared less. He lay down with his head pillowed on his rucksack and surrendered instantly. He slept the sleep of the innocent, profound, healing and regenerative. He would have slept soundly till dawn, if the hand moving around inside his rucksack had not tripped an alarm in his brain and dragged him from his slumbers.

He awoke disoriented, but immediately sensed a presence above him, invisible in the near total black. He felt the groping hand search out his commando knife, and made a grab for the arm. He threw his weight sideways against the intruder. But his force was met with another, even greater, and he was pushed onto his back.

A hand took hold of his throat and squeezed. He could feel his windpipe and the arteries in his neck caving in under the pressure. He wanted to cry out but no sound came. In desperation he grabbed the hand at his throat, but even with two hands he could not budge it. Then his head seemed to explode as a fist clubbed into the side of his face. He kicked upwards with his knee, a final act of defiance against the certainty of his death, and heard a sharp cry of pain. He kicked again as blackness enveloped him. He felt the hand around his neck loosen its grip, and then there was shouting.

His head pounded and his breath rasped in his throat. He heard tins fall and bottles break, and men cry out in agony. But it meant little to him. There were only his choking sobs as he fought for breath, and the skull-splitting pounding inside his head. He gagged and vomited, the bile and his partially digested dinner stung his throat, yet somehow helped him regain his grasp on reality. He sensed light and opened his eyes.

The captain knelt over him, examining him with the help of a paraffin lamp.

'Ah. So our guest still lives. Do not worry, that dog will trouble you no more.'

Someone was helping him up into a sitting position. He felt himself being lifted as easily as a baby. He turned to his benefactor and gazed into a face burning with hate and malice. He recoiled instinctively, unable to help himself.

'Do not worry, my friend,' soothed the captain, 'that dog will not trouble anybody any more. He has gone from us. He is swimming to Java.'

One-Eye gently propped Jan up against the wall of the cabin and handed him his canteen.

'He was not a regular member of my crew,' continued the captain evenly. 'He was not even my nephew. He was the son of the man my sister married. He was always trouble. I only took him on to oblige my sister. It was always going to end this way. The sea is a hard life. Men are always being lost overboard. Ha! He was not even a good cook.'

The incident was never mentioned again. At meal times five bowls were put out, and Jan's enamel plate was not called upon again. Life aboard slipped easily back into its timeless routine. Jan volunteered himself for the afternoon watch but, as it turned out, it was a hollow gesture.

Perhaps it was the warm fellowship of the Buginese that made him careless. Or the relief he felt in the knowledge that he could now trust them absolutely. He shared their food, and now that he had exhausted his canteen, he shared their water. Perhaps he thought their water was safe enough to drink unboiled. But before lunchtime of the second day at sea, the hot iron fist took hold of his stomach and squeezed.

At first the crew had laughed when he made a dash for the hole in the planking of the overhanging stern which acted as a toilet. But his visits became so frequent that he discarded his khaki shorts and took to wrapping a sarong around his waist. He learned to use his left hand, like a good Muslim should, in the absence of any alternative. His stomach continually cramped with pain, and the constant scouring inflamed his anus which was further irritated by the chillies he had eaten.

Loss of fluid was his main concern. He was sweating profusely. He was aware of the pain in the back of his head which warned of dehydration. He begged the captain to boil up some water, which he did. When it cooled, the captain filled Jan's canteen and placed it by his side.

'You must sip this water,' he said to Jan. 'Little by little, all of the time, you sip this water. Day and night. Tomorrow morning, eat one of these. Then later, eat another one. They will help your stomach.'

He gave Jan some salak, fig-shaped fruit with scaly, snake-like skin. Jan knew immediately what they were. On Java, they had eaten these snake fruit to settle their stomachs, but he doubted whether they'd be strong enough to stem this rampaging diarrhoea.

For three days he lay on the aft deck doing penance for his arrogance, while the Buginese tended to his needs and teased him mercilessly.

'Is this how you repay our kindness?' they asked. 'Is this the work you promised us? You steal this passage from us. Tell us now, who is the pirate?'

Despite his discomfort, Jan couldn't help laughing, and their chiding helped to pass the days. On the fifth day, Jan added a little fish to the brown rice they gave him to eat and announced that he was strong enough to work. They gave him back his mid-afternoon watch and a course to steer, and retired to the shade for a sleep.

For the first time in days, Jan felt truly alive. He believed he was the luckiest man in the world. For once the breeze held, and he could feel the boat beneath him, under his control, surge and roll with the waves. He watched the flying fish scatter before them and glide for hundreds of metres. He watched as they were attacked by marauding schools of yellowfin tuna, which would launch their bodies clear of the water in the frenzy of the hunt. How many of his friends had seen sights to compare with this?

He forgot about his days of suffering and the treachery of the young cook, and he closed his mind to the nagging uncertainties of his return. For three days he became a Bugis seafarer making the return run to Kalimantan for more timber, revelling in the spriteliness of their under-ballasted vessel.

When they finally reached Jakarta and parted company, Jan was genuinely saddened. He wanted to give the captain a gift. He had nothing to give except his commando knife, so he gave him that. The captain was delighted. At last the knife had an owner who had use for it.

'Thank you, Pak,' he said. 'We have seen this knife in your bag and wondered why such a man would carry such a knife.'

So they too had searched his bag. Jan had suspected as much.

'I was scared,' said Jan. 'Scared that I might get carried away by Bugis pirates.'

'Go with God,' said the captain. 'May your dead father's wish be granted. May you find yourself among friends.'

'Go with God, also,' said Jan. 'Perhaps, Pak Andi, one day we will meet again. Insh' Allah, with luck.'

He shook hands with the captain and each of the crew in turn, until he came to the man whose face would never again show the kindness and friendliness within him.

'My friend, you saved my life. I wish I had something to give you worthy of the debt.' On the spur of the moment, Jan took off the hat that had been his father's and placed it on One-Eye's head.

One-Eye scowled with pleasure.

Chapter Eleven

Jan hired a bicycle-powered becak to carry him to the Netherlands Embassy. The people in the crowded streets seemed unchanged. Whenever he smiled his smiles were returned. If they resented his being there they hid their feelings well. Jan began to relax. If he was welcome in Jakarta, would he not also be welcome in Tengkuban Prahu? His confidence grew.

As the distance and heat began to tell on his driver, he called out to him.

'It is too hot and I am in no hurry. Let us rest and take some tea.'

The driver nodded gratefully, and pedalled over to the side of the road where a stunted tree offered a little shade. They left their becak and walked over to a tiny shop, no bigger than a packing case. Perhaps it had once been one.

Jan ordered cold tea for his driver and bottled mineral water for himself. He felt buoyant despite the heat, and turned to the shopkeeper to make light conversation.

'It is good to return to Java,' he said, anticipating polite enquiry from the shopkeeper. Instead he slammed Jan's mineral water down on the counter in front of him. Jan was taken completely by surprise. Then he noticed all the posters and stickers fixed to the walls, proclaiming *merdeka* or freedom, which was the rallying call for independence.

'Go away,' said the shopkeeper angrily. 'Can you not see? You are not welcome here. Go home!'

A crowd began to gather around them, but Jan could not gauge from their deadpan faces whether they were hostile or otherwise.

'*Ma'af*,' said Jan. 'I'm sorry. Please excuse me. How much do I owe you for the drinks?'

Before the shopkeeper could reply, Jan's driver began to abuse and berate him for his rudeness. The crowd joined in, taking sides as the debate became heated. This was the last thing Jan wanted. More and more people joined in, some just curious, others to push their cause. Jan drew himself up to his full height, put two fingers in his mouth, and blew the loudest, most piercing whistle of his life. The Javanese stopped and looked at him in amazement. Jan seized his opportunity.

'Please,' he cried. 'No good will come from arguing. Some of you see me as your enemy. Some of you see me as your friend. This is good. This is how it should be. That is what *merdeka* is all about. It is your freedom to think of me as you will. Each of you is free to have his own opinion and to respect the opinion of others. That is *merdeka*. This man wants me to leave so I will leave. I will pay for our drinks and leave. I hope one day he will come to see me as his friend.'

Jan paid the shopkeeper and walked away to the becak with his driver.

'*Selamat jalan*,' called a friendly voice which was immediately echoed by others. 'Goodbye.'

'*Selamat tinggal*,' Jan responded, and made an exaggerated bow. Even the shopkeeper laughed. Jan realised he would have to be more careful. It was hard to believe that these people could turn against him. But hadn't Hitler just shown the world what the politics of nationalism could do?

Jan reached the embassy without further incident, and dug deeply into his diminishing store of rupiahs to pay his driver the amount they'd agreed and a little extra besides. The driver thanked Jan profusely and pedalled off to find some shade where he could sleep.

The embassy staff gave Jan the welcome of the prodigal son. They urged him to stay for lunch and pressed him to tell the story of his journey so far. Jan did so, in great detail, and they hung on every word. They plied him with beer to sustain his tongue, and gradually the alcohol, the heat, and the comfort of company of his own kind began to tell on him.

But by then he'd earned his rest, and the embassy staff went back to work with a new perspective on Bugis men.

Jan spent the night at the home of one of the secretaries, and for the first time in a fortnight, slept in a bed. He had to be shaken awake in the morning to be driven to the station in time to catch the train to Bandung. His pockets were filled once more with rupiah, though he'd been cautious enough to leave the bulk of his money at the embassy.

The train was not crowded and Jan found a seat by himself. For once he did not feel like talking. The staff at the embassy had warned him not to get his hopes up too high.

'The vast majority of Indonesians are no better off with independence,' they cautioned him. 'Most of the wealth and property is still in Dutch hands. But for how long nobody knows. If the communists become too strong, Sukarno will use them to nationalise all the industry and property. If the military become strong enough, there will be a coup, and they will just walk in and take everything. The future here is very uncertain. Perhaps your unique arrangement will prove your salvation. Perhaps your father was a visionary. But, Jan, a wise man would not bank on it.'

Jan was filled with trepidation. He felt dispirited and out of his depth. He felt he had been a fool to think he could just come back and find everything as it was. There was no way he or his mother could ever raise enough money to buy back the plantation, even if it was possible to buy it. They were looking to the plantation to support them.

For the full six-hour journey, he gazed out of the window and avoided the eyes of the people who had joined him in the carriage. When the train stopped he was last out. He stood among the milling crowd on the platform pondering his next move. He saw only one other white face as it emerged from the first-class carriage. It belonged to a middle-aged man with what Jan believed to be the unmistakable attitude of the English. He was tall and slim, with a clipped moustache and aloof manner. And he had a Sundanese woman with him who appeared to be his wife. This was confirmed when a young girl appeared and took the Englishman's hand. Already she was a beauty, this child of two cultures. Jan was captivated by her. He watched her until she left then slowly gathered up his own bags, reluctant to make the move that would decide his fate.

His becak driver knew of the bus that went to Tengkuban Prahu, and took him to meet it. In his heart Jan hoped he'd missed it, but the waiting crowd told him otherwise. He paid off his driver and took his place in the queue. People stared at him curiously. Some smiled hesitantly. But Jan was unsure whether to engage them in conversation or not. He did not want to spark another debate on whether he was welcome.

Bandung had been an administrative centre for the Dutch, and they'd left a legacy of museums, cultural centres, a university, art deco buildings, and gracious living. But what other legacies had they left behind? The young Sukarno began his political career in Bandung, and the cries of *merdeka* had rung as loudly here as anywhere else in Java.

Jan took his place on the ancient bus. The springs sagged and the shock absorbers were nonexistent. He had only thirty or so kilometres to travel but they would not be easy. The other passengers had left him a double seat all to himself. Again, their motive was not clear. Was it deference to his skin, a hangover from the colonial days? Or something more sinister? The bus stopped to take on more passengers, among them a young woman struggling with odd-shaped bundles and carrying a child on her hip. The place beside Jan was the only remaining seat yet she did not take it. Jan could not allow this. She had more right to sit than he. So he stood.

'Please sister,' he said. 'You must sit. If you wish, I will stand.'

The woman turned away in embarrassment. Other passengers stared at him.

'Please,' he said again.

A young man about Jan's own age stood. 'I will share the seat with the stranger,' he said.

The man came and sat next to Jan without exchanging a glance. The woman gratefully took his seat. Conversations which had faltered began again, and Jan was temporarily forgotten.

As the bus laboured up the hill north-west from Bandung, the young man turned towards Jan and spoke to him shyly.

'It is not usual to find Europeans on this bus.'

Jan grunted.

'It is not usual to find Europeans on any bus in Java.'

Jan smiled. The young man was obviously playing with him.

'Are you going to see our mountain, Tengkuban Prahu?'

'No,' Jan replied. 'I am going only as far as the road to Ciater.'

'You have friends there?'

'Perhaps.'

'You have business there?'

'Perhaps.'

'Life is full of uncertainties, my friend,' said the young man. 'But it seems God has given you more than your share.'

Jan laughed despite himself.

'And you are certain of the path your life takes?' Jan asked.

'My path takes me to Lembang. To my wife and her parents and my son. Once I lived on Tengkuban Prahu, but I married this woman from Lembang. Her parents are old and they have no sons to work their land. Their land is now mine. It is a fortunate marriage. The path of my life is certain, God willing.'

'You are indeed fortunate,' responded Jan. 'Merciful God has been kind to you.'

His companion looked at him in surprise. 'You are of the faith?'

Jan shook his head and smiled. He turned to look out of the window to discourage further conversation. He was in no mood for it.

After what seemed like hours in the boiling heat of the crowded bus, they wheezed and spluttered into Lembang. The young man stood to leave and, to Jan's surprise, offered Jan his hand. As Jan shook it, the young man leaned towards him and whispered.

'You are free to steal the eggs from my chickens, my friend.'

Jan looked up at the young man, surprised and confused. But he just laughed and climbed down off the bus.

Twenty minutes later Jan stood on the road to Ciater, with just a four kilometre walk ahead of him to the place of his childhood. Already the sun was racing towards its nightly retreat behind the mountain. He walked briskly. Come what may, by nightfall he would know where he stood. He reached the eastern boundary of the plantation.

There were some weeds between the bushes, more than his father would ever have allowed, but they were hardly rampant. He looked along the line of the boundary to places where the surrounding forest was beginning to encroach. It was not significant, but his father would never have allowed that either. Given the chance neither would he.

He turned into the driveway, heart pounding, but that had nothing to do with the heat. He walked on towards the house. The shutters were closed but, as far as he could tell, looked in fair condition. Perhaps it was as his father had left it. But how could it be? He walked on, unannounced and uncertain of his welcome.

But the young man on the bus had recognised him, and the bush telegraph works as efficiently in Java as it does anywhere else in the world. It is faster by far than an ancient, wheezing bus.

The boy who had run with the children of the village, and stolen mangoes and mangosteens, and eggs to boil in the thermal pools, had not been forgotten. Nor had his father, now revered for his foresight. Had he not been the first to remove the colonial yoke, and acknowledge their claim to their own lands? The dark familiar faces of his childhood poured forth from the enveloping green, eyes streaming, his name singing on their lips.

They surrounded him and showered him with petals, and carried him in their throng to his house. Proudly, they threw open the doors and shutters, and told him how they had patiently waited for the return of the Van der Meers. In eight years not a day had passed without the house being aired and the floors swept. Jan's misty eyes saw the truth of this and he was overwhelmed by relief and gratitude. They brought him tea and sweet cakes, and sat down to hear his story. His father's agreement had been honoured. Jan could not imagine a finer legacy.

Chapter Twelve

Jan did not grab the reins and impose his will, exercising the superiority most Europeans assumed was theirs. Had he done so it is unlikely that anyone would have opposed him, at least not directly, because Jan was a giant among the diminutive Sundanese. His size intimidated them.

But Bapak Jan, or Pak Jan, as they called him, formally according him the honorific of 'father' appropriate to his position as head of the estate, had already determined to run the plantation the Indonesian way. After all, they were his partners and had operated well enough without him.

He took his time and saw how things were done, then formed a council with himself at the head. He ruled by consensus, aiming to guide them into a western way of doing business rather than dictate to them. His thoughtfulness marked him as a worthy successor to his father, and the estate steadily reverted to its former prosperity, although the profits were now shared more equitably.

The following year and each year thereafter, Jan returned to Europe on the fledgling Dutch airline KLM, to sign up buyers for his tea, and to see his mother. She was in her early sixties and arthritis had become her constant companion. Her doctors suggested a warmer climate but she wouldn't hear of it. She steadfastly maintained she would rather suffer the bitter cold of a northern winter than once again endure the claustrophobic heat of Java. She never returned.

It was on these visits that Jan discovered the potential for another enterprise. He obliged friends by bringing with him as gifts the Indonesian artifacts they requested. As the number of requests grew and Europeans discovered a taste for primitive art, he found he was shipping in commercial quantities. In this way he began a small but lucrative trade.

He leased a small shop on the Prinsegracht canal near Vyzelstraat to sell his artifacts and installed his mother as manager. She needed something to occupy both her mind and her time. But more than that, she was a very independent woman and a reluctant recipient of Jan's charity. She also understood the value of the artifacts better than Jan and marked up his prices outrageously. Yet she sold everything Jan brought and began to take orders from customers for Jan to fill. Gradually she took the initiative and, with it, the running of the business. The shop's reputation and clientele steadily grew.

His mother hired a young assistant, for there were days when her arthritis held her prisoner in her bed. But whenever possible she would make the trip into her little shop. It had begun as a much needed interest, but in her remaining years it became her life.

Whether Jan opened the shop as an act of kindness to his lonely mother or as the astute act of a visionary, is immaterial. Whatever his motives, the day was coming when he would be grateful indeed for that little shop in Amsterdam.

In Indonesia the political scene was as chaotic and volatile as the embassy had suggested it would be. Coalition governments came and went with the seasons, as one Muslim group sought ascendancy over the other, and over the socialists and communist PKI. Revolts in the outer islands and West Sumatra against the Javanese Government were abruptly suppressed by the military.

In 1957, Sukarno made his move towards a totalitarian regime with himself installed at the head. He proposed a village system of consultation and consensus but, in effect, set about creating a vehicle from which to impose his will. At the end of that year, following a dispute with the Dutch over the future of Irian Barat, now Irian Jaya, he ordered the seizure of Dutch property.

Once again, the people of the villages stood by Jan and the unique arrangement they had made with his father

Ten years from the day Jan made his tear-filled return to the slopes of Tengkuban Prahu, he met Melita and fell utterly and hopelessly in love.

He was invited to a rijstaffel banquet at the exquisite art deco Savoy Homann to celebrate the birthday of an expatriate friend. Whether by accident or design, for good-intentioned people were always trying to marry him off, he was given a seat next to the most stunning woman he had ever seen.

The beautiful child he had first spotted on the platform of the Bandung station was now a woman. Her skin was an exotic, coppery-olive, owing as much to her British father as her Sundanese mother, and was as delicate and translucent as a baby's. She was dressed simply, European style, in a full-length white evening dress. Her only jewellery was an antique silver-lace comb. It was both decorative and functional for, let loose, her jet black hair would cascade over her shoulders and down to her tiny waist. The comb held her hair clear of her face so her big European eyes, smiling from her fine featured Sundanese face, could work their magic.

Jan was not inexperienced. He knew women were as attracted to him as he was to them, and he'd had numerous affairs. But in the presence of this exquisite jewel of two cultures, he found himself tongue-tied.

His attempts at conversation broke down into stumbling, stuttering inanities. He hoped he saw encouragement in those astonishing eyes, but it could have been the glint of amusement. He tried to eat the delicacies that were placed before him but his fingers had turned into thumbs and he could only pick at them. Every course became an obstacle to be negotiated. He wound the mee goreng onto his fork as he always had but it would not stay there. It slid back onto his plate and every little splash threatened the pristine white dress of the angel alongside. He did not trust his voice sufficiently to apologise to her.

At any event she abandoned him at the first opportunity, leaving him feeling empty and as hollow as an old, dried up coconut. She smiled as she left him though, and in that kind gesture he tried to read cause for hope.

For two weeks he moped about the estate, irritable and uncommunicative. He complained about food he'd normally devour with relish, and spent hours every evening soaking alone in the hot thermal pools at Ciater.

Often they'd find him sitting alone by the monkey forest, silent and still, watching the monkeys go about their business. The monkey forest was on Jan's estate, and both Jan and his father before him insisted that the monkeys be allowed to live their lives unmolested.

Left to themselves the council would soon have turned the land over to the production of tea, but they respected Jan's wishes and the small monkey community was left in peace. On the crowded island of Java, the monkey forest afforded solitude and that was precisely what Jan wanted.

Nobody was offended by Jan's ill temper. They knew the symptoms well. His staff engaged in endless speculation as to who might be both cause and cure. The women in distant lines on the hillside, identified by the sun-bleached pink, blue and saffron scarves they wore around their coolie hats, would enthusiastically discuss his prospects as they filled their hessian bags with tea leaves.

'A love so big could not go unnoticed,' they reasoned. 'We will soon see who the new mistress is.'

'A wise woman makes her man wait,' argued others. 'It

strengthens his love and concentrates his resolve so in later years it is not easily swayed.'

'I always make my husband wait,' commented another mischievously. 'It certainly strengthens his love and that is not easily swayed either.'

The women laughed and they filled in their days this way, forgetful of the back-breaking grind of their job.

The women were right, of course. Melita – or Lita as she preferred to be called – was perfectly aware of the effect she'd had on Jan and was anxious for their next encounter. She was not concerned that she may have discouraged him. Women discuss these matters and all agreed she had timed her exit to perfection. Still she grew impatient, a reaction she put down to her European blood. Her Sundanese mother laughed and counselled her gently.

'Stay calm, *car ayu*. He will come running to you. It is for men to make fools of themselves at such times, not women. And your young man is not yet finished with being foolish.'

Jan was in a quandary. He wanted to pour out his heart in letters to her, but thought it presumptuous. His pride would not allow him to ring a mutual friend to intercede. He was too proud to declare his love even in confidence, in case it was spurned. But what confidentiality could there be in a small and isolated expatriate community? Confined to his estate Jan was unaware that friendly forces were already at work on his behalf.

A dinner party was arranged with Jan sitting as far from Lita as the table would allow so that he might accustom himself to her presence and avoid a repeat of his previous performance. The hosts sat them both on the same side so that their eyes could not accidentally meet and cause embarrassment. But their good intentions back-fired.

Jan could not help himself. He would constantly lean across the table to reach for some fruit chutney or fiery pickle, and every time he did so his eyes would search out Lita. Do women with Lita's colouring blush? Of course they do! Invariably somebody came to the poor girl's rescue by directing a question or comment towards Jan, demanding his attention. Yet he persisted. Nobody ever used more salt, pepper, desiccated coconut, pickle, chutney or relish. And every time somebody was forced to offer a distraction. Couldn't he see that after dinner, there would be ample opportunity for two young people to get together and talk if they were so inclined?

Lita knew then that this big man she had chosen would always be a child before the rush of his emotions and that he would need her strengths. Any doubts she may have had about the future course of her life vanished at that moment. She made up her mind. She would be his wife.

The courtship was old-fashioned and romantic. Their love for each other grew until it was almost tangible, and the matchmakers fair wept to see their handiwork. Jan and Lita did not make love until their wedding night, when they took each other in a floodtide of passion.

They conceived twins that night – two sons, Thomas and Pieter – which caused Jan to boast jokingly of his virility. But, more accurately, it was fitting testimony to the fecundity of the amazing island of Java.

They say in Java that if you drop a box of matches you will return next year to a forest. Two and three times a year, Java wears a vivid emerald carpet as its rice crops ripen. And the fabulously rich volcanic soil gives rise to a profusion of vegetables and fruits all year round. Into this Garden of Eden Jan and Lita brought three children. The two boys, and then an angel they called Annemieke.

She was born on March 27, 1966, and while bigots and those opposed to inter-racial marriage still number in the majority, none would ever begrudge the union that produced Annemieke Van der Meer.

Ramon finished speaking. Gancio watched for Milos to signal that it was time for intermission. He reached for the cups.

'What are you doing to us?' asked Neil. 'One day you tell us a horror story and now you tell us this. Barbara Cartland would be proud of you.'

'Why are you always so impatient, Neil? Don't you think it is important to know where people are coming from? It helps explain why they are who they are, why they do the things they do. We are all products of our upbringing – even you – and I shudder to think what yours must have been like.'

'Agghhh . . .' Neil clutched his chest as if mortally wounded.

'Ramon . . .'

'It's okay, Milos, he knows I'm being facetious and it takes a lot more than that to offend him. His hide rivals that of a rhinoceros. You're not offended, are you, Neil?'

'Yes, I bloody am,' said Neil evenly.

'Then I take it all back.'

'You can't do that. That's one thing you can never do.'

'Milos, what are you going on about?'

'There are three things, Ramon, that can never be taken back, no? The arrow in flight, the spoken word . . .'

'And?'

'. . . and anything bought in a sale.'

The four men broke into easy laughter.

'I think you got this story in a sale,' said Lucio. 'Your story today does not have the drama and tension of last week's. I miss Rosa, Jorge and Carlos.'

'What if I was to tell you that Jan went mad one day, butchered his wife and children and flushed them down the lavatory? Would that make him more interesting? Is that what you want to hear?'

'Don't be absurd, Ramon. The fact is the people you told us about last week were all flawed,' cut in Milos. 'It's the flaws and faults and weaknesses in people that make them interesting, no? Jan bores me too. He is just too nice. His story is too nice. I don't like nice people, present company excepted of course.'

'You're quite right, Milos. People don't have to be extreme to be interesting. But you're making assumptions because Jan, too, is

99

flawed. You just haven't yet discovered his weakness. Perhaps his story is too nice, as you put it. But you may look back and envy the peace and pleasantness of this afternoon. It won't last. Happiness never does. The story is moving towards its inevitable climax, and Jan Van der Meer is about to learn just how fragile happiness can be.' His voice took on a startling intensity. 'Perhaps my life has been harder than yours. In the bad years I learned to grab the good times while they lasted and be grateful for them. It's a lesson you should heed.'

'Jesus, Ramon.' Neil began to chuckle. 'I know this is another of your little tricks, but you're not usually so obvious. That wasn't up to your usual calculating standard at all.'

Gancio brought their coffee. He looked around the table that usually sparkled with energy.

'What's the matter?' he asked.

'Your friend here is accused of being too nice. Of giving us Barbara Cartland when what we want is something with a little more meat.'

'Neil is right,' said Lucio. 'We need spice and excitement. We need a little bit of what Rosa gave to Victor. Let me tell you this story while we have our coffee. It is a true story. It happened to me just last week. Look at me. What do you see? Answer truthfully.'

'A short, fat, balding Italian,' said Neil.

'Why does he have to be Italian?' moaned Gancio theatrically. But now they were all caught up in Lucio's diversion.

'You think it is easy to be short, fat and bald? Short and fat is a problem, but that's okay, I can handle that. Bald is something else. For some reason women like to pat bald men on the head. You tell them a joke, they laugh and pat you on the head. You do them a favour, and they pat you on the head like a good dog. Or sometimes they kiss you on the head. I can't tell you how humiliating this is for a sexual Olympian like myself.

'So sometimes, I confess to you, when I am sure nobody I know will see me I wear a toupee. No! Don't laugh, it's true! Stop it. Why do you want to hurt my feelings? God – who everyone knows is Italian – is not always fair. He didn't give me the gifts he gave to

Gancio even though we were almost neighbours. I am not tall and dark and handsome like he is, and I don't have his wonderful head of hair. I would give my right testicle for hair like that. Instead I have to pretend. Please, don't laugh. This is a true story. I am lifting the veil on my secret life and you laugh at me.

'I'll tell you something else. My toupee is a bit salt and pepper because I don't want to cheat too much and lie about my age. But when I wear it, I swear to you, I feel tall and slim. It gives me confidence to talk to tall elegant women. I don't know what it is about short, fat, bald Italians, but we love tall, elegant, beautiful women.'

'Lucio, we all love tall, elegant, beautiful women,' cut in Milos. 'Even us well-preserved Hungarians of average height.'

'I met such a woman,' he continued, ignoring Milos, 'I told you about her. The florist. She owns the shop. I'd met her three times before and always with my toupee. I suggested dinner, she accepted. She suggested her place, I accepted. So she ordered two dozen oysters for dessert. It was ridiculous of course. I could hardly look at the waiter who brought them. But that's the kind of woman she is. Unpredictable, imaginative – you know – what's the word?'

'Vulgar?' volunteered Milos.

'No! Artistic. Not vulgar, she is artistic. So we went back to her apartment. Very nice. Many beautiful things. But by then we could not keep our hands off each other. I jumped on the bed. "No!" she says, "Wait. Not on the covers." So she pulled back the covers. She pulled back the sheet. Pure top quality cotton trimmed with damask. Pillowslips the same. Beautiful. We leaped back on the bed and my thing was so hard and straight I swear I nearly vaulted right over it. I thought I would give her engine one last tune-up by an Italian expert, when she just grabbed it and shoved it in. We went at it like eighteen year olds. Like Jorge and Rosa. The harder I pushed the harder she pulled. I pulled backwards, she thrust upwards. She was one greedy lady. It became a race to finish first and in the end it was a photo finish. I collapsed. I wanted to lay there forever in her honeypot, head pillowed on her breasts, savouring every delicious moment, reloading the gun for a second assault. Suddenly she killed me stone dead. Just like that.

'"Damn," she says, "I can't reach the tissues. You don't mind do you?" Then do you know what she did? Unbelievable! She pulled off my toupee and used it to mop her crotch!'

The other diners wondered what joke could make five men explode with laughter and send Gancio back to his kitchen with tears streaming down his cheeks.

They finished their coffee and Ramon prepared to return to his story.

'If I had a daughter,' he said wistfully, 'I would want her to be like dear, sweet Annemieke.'

The others gave Ramon their full attention and watched him closely. It was not always what Ramon said that was important, but the manner of the telling. Was this gentle wistfulness another of his ploys? If so, what was he trying to tell them? If not, what did it reveal?

'Annemieke was a little angel. Even as a baby her beauty, serenity and the sheer joy she drew from life touched all who knew her. It is often said of such children that they are too good for this world and that is the reason given when the gods take them back before their lives have barely begun. Annemieke Van der Meer was more fortunate, though there would be times when it seemed death may have been a greater kindness.'

Chapter Thirteen

From the day she was born everybody loved Annemieke, even her rampaging brothers, Thomas and Pieter. People drew a pleasure from holding her that they found difficult to explain.

The servants vied with one another for the privilege of carrying her, as they carried their own young, in a sling strung around their shoulder. But even then, Annemieke had her favourite. Her name was Levi and she was only twelve. Her job was to help the older women but more and more she came to be the baby Annemieke's special minder. Annemieke would not go to sleep in the afternoon unless Levi was there to lay down beside her and stroke her hair.

Jan and Lita could not have been happier. The twins were already nearly as big as boys twice their age and had twice their energy. Their world was a wonderland, a gigantic playground that held no terrors for them. Even at the age of five they would run off to the villages to play with their Sundanese friends. Yet they still managed to wear Lita out, and she was always grateful when Levi finished her morning school and came to help her with Annemieke.

Jan adored all his children and the twins often went with him when he did his rounds of the estate in his Land Rover. But Annemieke was his weakness. He would crouch over her tiny crib, shake her rattles and talk baby talk until Lita would laugh and say she hardly knew who was the greater child. On the rare occasions that Annemieke was upset or in the grip of some childhood fever, Jan would become as helpless as a baby and mope around the house. He always wore his emotions for the world to see. Lita maintained she had four children. Three that she had given birth to and one she'd married.

Fortunately for Jan, Annemieke was rarely sick and hardly ever cried. What was there for her to cry about? She was born into paradise and a loving family. When she was old enough to walk, and the twins were at school, she took their place in the Land Rover when Jan did his rounds. Levi always accompanied Annemieke on these outings to watch over her.

Wherever they went, people would gather around the tiny child to marvel at her blonde hair, her big blue eyes and skin of softest olive. She'd wander into the homes of the villagers and climb on knees and everyone she touched felt somehow blessed. They called her *adik*, little sister, and there was not a home where little sister was not welcome.

But angels are not necessarily always meek and mild. From the very beginning, Annemieke stood up for herself. If the boys needed a ball and took hers, she would go after them until she had it back. If, on the other hand, they asked if they could borrow it, she would give them the ball without hesitation. When the boys fought she would come to the rescue and throw herself upon whichever brother was winning. She'd push and pull hair and pummel their backs and arms until they'd stop fighting. It got so that whenever Tom or Pieter was copping a hiding from the other he'd call out to Annemieke for help. And she would come without hesitation, fists flying. It was ludicrous, of course, the baby Annemieke trying to do battle with the giants who were her brothers. But it would force them to cease hostilities as, inevitably, they cracked up with laughter. Naturally, stories of how Annemieke tamed her wild brothers would make their way back to the people of the villages via the servants, and they adored their little sister all the more.

Whenever she came to visit them the men would hold the flat of their hands towards her, and encourage her to punch it as hard as she could. Annemieke always obliged them, and the men would pretend to reel back with the force. They showed her how to make a proper fist, how to set her feet, and how to put her weight into each punch.

'This is how you will keep your brothers under control,' they said, 'and one day your husband.'

Annemieke loved this game and she would run up to the men shouting, 'Hold out hand! Hold out hand!'

One day when Tom and Pieter were playing soccer with the village boys, their rough and tumble play became a little too rough and escalated into a fight. It was nothing more than a normal playground incident where tempers are inflamed, the issue resolved by the superior force, and play resumed as normal. But on this occasion, the twins had chosen opponents who were at least three years older with muscles that had hardened with their greater maturity. The twins realised their mistake but pride demanded that they give a good account of themselves. They traded punches before moving in close to try and wrestle their opponents to the ground. They overlooked the fact that Annemieke was acting ball boy behind their goal. They never considered her or her likely reaction.

Annemieke could see that Tom and Pieter were in for a hiding, and couldn't stand by and let that happen. She rushed to their help as fast as her little legs could carry her. One of the village boys felt a punch strike his backside and threw his fist blindly behind him. It caught Annemieke on the side of her head and she dropped like a stone. The combatants heard their audience cry out and stopped to see what had happened.

'Annemieke!' Tom cried and rushed to her side.

The boy who had hit her was devastated.

'I'm sorry. I did not know it was little sister,' he protested.

'My dad will kill you for this!' Pieter hissed, and the poor boy from the village suddenly realised the full extent of the trouble he was in.

'I'm sorry,' he said again. He bent down over Annemieke who, with Tom's help was sitting up. 'I am sorry little sister. I didn't mean to hit you.'

Annemieke looked up through her tears at the boy who had hit her so unbelievably hard.

'Hold out hand!' she ordered.

She staggered to her feet. The boy held out his hand. He had no idea why. Annemieke set her feet as she'd been taught and punched his hand with all her might.

Of course the boy wasn't hurt. He reeled back from surprise then had the wit to fall over and pretend to be hurt. It still took the audience a second or two to catch up before someone laughed. They all laughed. Tom and Pieter swelled with pride at her courage and hugged her. They let the boy who had hit her pick her up and hold her, so he could wipe away her tears and once more say sorry.

That night the story swept the villages, and nobody laughed more than the men who had taught her how to punch.

Annemieke was going on three when the Netherlands Embassy rang. Jan was in his study writing up his accounts.

'There is a man here who wishes to speak with you,' the Secretary said. 'He will not go away.'

Jan was impatient. He was always impatient when he worked on his accounts. Paperwork bored him, yet his sense of discipline forced him to keep his books up to date.

'Who is it?' he demanded.

'The man calls himself Andi Sose.'

'Never heard of him. The name means nothing to me.'

'He says he is your friend and that he saved your life.'

'Saved my life? How? What does he do, this man?'

'He said to tell you that he is a Bugis pirate. He said . . .'

But Jan no longer listened. His mind raced back to his voyage on board the pinisi, to his friend the captain, to the unfortunate One-Eye and the treachery of the cook. To the debt he still owed.

'Jan? Jan? Are you there?'

'Yes, I am here. Would you please let me speak to the captain?'

'Pak Jan?' His voice was tentative, but Jan recognised it immediately and felt a flood of shame.

'My friend, forgive me, it has been too long.'

'There is nothing to forgive, Bapak. It seems that God and your father's wisdom have stood by you. This makes me very happy. You keep in good health?'

Jan exchanged patient pleasantries with Andi Sose and the more he listened the more he became aware of a hesitation in his voice that had nothing to with his unfamiliarity with the phone. His old friend was in trouble and needed his help. But offering help was a matter of extreme delicacy, given the formidable pride of the Bugis. It was not something that could be done over the phone.

'I would like you to come and visit me and meet my family,' Jan said. 'We have many years to talk about. Let me speak once more with the Secretary.'

Jan guessed rightly that Andi was penniless. He arranged for the Secretary to advance the old man enough money for the train to Bandung, for new shoes and clothes, and for meals along the way. He hung up and gazed out of the window at Annemieke trying to climb on the back of the old black labrador bitch. He wondered what on earth he could do with an old Buginese pirate on a tea plantation in the middle of West Java.

'They sold my ship from beneath me.' Andi seemed philosophical about this and appeared to harbour no grudge towards the owners. He was not the first skipper to be dismissed this way. Sometimes the captain and his crew were lucky and were transferred along with their boat to the new owners, accepting whatever wages and incentives were offered. Andi had been a good captain and his pinisi had always been profitable. He hoped that fate would allow him to stay with his boat until he could no longer sail. But fate is no more a bound servant of the deserving than it is of any other mortal.

Jan had had no difficulty picking Andi out from the crowd on the station platform. Self-confidence is firmly inscribed in the genetic code of the Bugis, and for centuries the people of the archipelago knew them as men to fear. The crowd parted before him as he strode in his rolling seaman's gait towards Jan. He'd grown a drooping moustache, and hunger had robbed his bones of their meat and left his cheeks hollow. Yet his face was as familiar to Jan as it had been almost twenty years earlier.

'The agent for the company paid us the money we were owed and I said goodbye to my home of forty years. The new crew was waiting on the dock. We left with just our clothes. Of course we looked for other ships who would hire us. But nobody hires Bugis except Bugis. And why would Bugis come to Jakarta to hire crew? The men looked to me as their captain to help them find a boat. It took time, but we walked the docks every day, looking for pinisi that had lost men overboard. Gradually I found ships for all my men until only Daeng – the man you called One-Eye – and myself were left.

'One day a pinisi came in and I recognised the captain. He was a man I knew well, a good man. He had a full crew but he was prepared to take on one of us. Pak Jan, only God and myself know how much my heart craved to join this ship. But how could I take this work and leave my friend Daeng behind? Who would hire this man whose face was split in two, who could no longer speak? Who would hire a man with one eye over a man with two? I could not leave Daeng alone ashore. He hated and feared dry land and was only happy with the sea beneath him. Only my friend, the captain, would take him. So be it, I thought. Let them take him!'

Jan could not look at his friend, fearing to see the tears of a beaten man. But Andi still had the capacity to surprise.

'Daeng was overjoyed and his joy reached out to me. A man does not have to speak to show his appreciation, my friend. I knew then, as God also knows, that I did the right thing. It was my chance to return the loyalty Daeng had shown me and I had not flinched. Bugis men are proud men, Pak, and I was very proud.'

It was true. Even now, Jan observed, the memory of the event caused Andi's chest to swell and his chin to rise. Tears were not easily drawn from this man.

'One year had passed. Now I was alone. I watched the pinisi come and go and wished with all my heart that I could go with them. I would have gone as cook, as forward hand, as helmsman. I would have gone as cabin boy. But captains of ships are not eager to hire other captains and this is easy to understand. And nobody came to Jakarta to hire a captain. Then one day I saw you, Pak. You came down to the docks and took away a cargo. You had changed, but not so much that this old captain could not recognise you. One month ago, correct?'

'You are quite correct. I went to collect some artifacts from Kalimantan. Why did you not speak to me then?'

'Pak, I was in clothes unfit for any man to wear. I was not clean. I relied on the generosity of visiting ships for my meals and for what clothes they could spare. Perhaps this is one reason why your embassy was unwilling to admit me. I could not approach you as a beggar. What would you have thought of me then?'

Jan smiled. Even if he had not recognised his friend on the platform at Bandung, he could not have missed him. He had stood out like a bride among prostitutes in his brand new trousers, shiny sandals and shirt that still bore the creases from the packaging. Andi had waited until the train had drawn into the station before he had changed.

'One day a long time ago you offered me a job on your pinisi which I was glad to accept.' Jan took his time to make sure he expressed himself correctly. 'Perhaps, in return, you will do me the honour of accepting my offer of work on my plantation?'

'I accept with gratitude but conditionally. I must warn you, Pak, my intention is to work my way home to Ujung Pandang, to the pandanus cape. Perhaps there I will find my ship. Is that acceptable?'

Jan had to smile once more. Andi Sose was letting Jan know that he would not impose for one second longer than was necessary.

'Very acceptable,' Jan said, and took his friend's hand to close the deal. Just what Andi would do was a total mystery to him. But he knew a man could not be captain of a pinisi for forty years without acquiring some skills which would be useful, even to a tea plantation owner.

Jan was right. Andi had a way with engines and machinery that came from years of breathing life into exhausted diesels, keeping his boat afloat and crew alive in waters that were regularly swept by tropical cyclones. He repaired the Land Rover, the village trucks, broken bicycles, leaky pumps, the washing machine and refrigerator. He kept the generator working so well they became accustomed to it not breaking down during meal times.

They gave Andi a one-room house of his own behind the servants' quarters. But in the evenings he would stroll around to the main house, sit on a chair on the verandah, and tell seafaring stories to the boys when they were home and to Annemieke when they weren't. Annemieke was absolutely fascinated by the old captain. She'd hang off his moustache until her grip on his whiskers was all that supported her, giggling helplessly while he just laughed. When she tried to poke her fingers in his eyes he'd tickle her until she begged him to stop. It seemed that he would let her do anything to him. One day, in the excitement of the game, she punched him to see what would happen. He smacked her. She hadn't known that men had places that little girls shouldn't punch. This was a revelation to Annemieke. The smack was genuine and it hurt. Yet she understood that she had upset her new friend and what she had done wasn't funny. Andi walked away before she could say she was sorry.

Levi witnessed the smack and horrified word spread among the servants until it reached Lita.

'About time!' she said.

That night Annemieke went missing. After a frantic search Jan found her in Andi's hut, curled up asleep on the floor next to her new friend. How else does a three year old say sorry? Jan gently picked her up and returned her to her bed. He smiled as he thought of the old sea captain asleep on the floor, his clothes neatly folded on the bed. He realised Andi had never known the feel of a soft western bed and was too old to change his ways.

Like her brothers, Annemieke had no fear of animals. But she had an advantage over the twins which the people in the villages would discuss at length. Animals had no fear of her. She was calm and serene and seemingly unintimidating so animals trusted her. Dogs could not resist rubbing up against her and she let them, even the mangy, scrawny dogs that hung around the villages. Cats trotted up to her to be patted and pampered. She even charmed the normally shy birds out of the trees to feed them bread soaked in honey and water.

The villagers would shake their heads in wonder to see her sitting on the lawn surrounded by dozens of brightly coloured birds. For centuries birds had been a supplement to their diet, and they were as wary of human contact as any birds could be. The villagers went home to their tiny houses and made feeding troughs, which they fixed on top of long bamboo poles so the birds could feed safely. They set them in the grass at the side of the house where Annemieke sat and soon the gardens were filled with birdsong from dawn till dusk. This was the idyllic world in which Annemieke spent her early years.

But there was a void in her day. When her father did the morning rounds of the plantation, her brothers and Levi were at school and her mother busy with housework, she was alone. Her new friend Andi helped fill the gap.

When the village dogs came down to pay their respects, Andi tied tin cans on a piece of string, made a noose and showed Annemieke how to slip it over a dog's tail and pull it tight. Annemieke was so stunned by the simplicity and potential of the scheme, she wondered why she hadn't thought of it before. The dogs trotted up to her full of trust, to rub up against her legs, have her pull their ears, and try to climb on their backs. They were totally unsuspecting until, suddenly, they became aware of the noisy extensions to their tails. What did the dogs do? Those with cans attached tried to outrun them. Those that had escaped the noose chased the cans. Dog chased dog until dog turned on dog, and the cans got dislodged in the ensuing brawl.

Annemieke fell on the ground helpless with laughter. Andi grinned, cleaned up the debris, and explained to her mother how the village dogs had stolen some garbage and then fought over it. Lita didn't believe a word of his explanation and Andi didn't expect her to.

Andi taught little sister how to catch butterflies without damaging their wings, and taught all three of the children how to make baskets and fish traps from the leaves of palms. In return the children gave him company and Annemieke, who had the most to be grateful for, stole biscuits for him to feed his sweet tooth.

'Only two,' he'd tell her, and pretend to get angry when she brought him three.

Andi spoke Bahasa to Annemieke, and she spoke Bahasa and English to him. Andi already spoke a little English and was keen to learn more. Often Jan would return home for lunch to find Annemieke giving the old sea captain English lessons, and almost crying with laughter every time he got a word wrong. Occasionally Jan would feel envious of their relationship. But once Jan appeared on the scene Andi withdrew and returned to work. He knew better than to come between a father and his child, and Annemieke learned not to protest when he left. Jan had no cause to be anything but grateful for the attention Andi gave his daughter. Indeed, he had reason to bless the day the old man came back into his life.

Of course most parents of small children are reluctant to let them out of their sight for long, and Jan and Lita were no exception. But they soon discovered that whenever Annemieke was out of their sight she was invariably in someone else's. So they let her wander. Why wouldn't they? Besides, there was always Andi riding shotgun in the morning, and Levi in the afternoon.

Jan liked the fuss everyone made of Annemieke and he loved the little face looking up at him with eyes full of trust and wonder.

Sometimes in the afternoons, he would get impatient waiting for Levi to finish her chores, and he'd grab his daughter and take off without her. Lita would scold him for it but nothing she said could make him change his ways.

So when Annemieke wandered off by herself at the age of three, away from the women picking tea, Jan had nobody to blame but himself. At first they didn't realise she was missing. The women always worked faster when the boss was around and put aside their squabbles. Of course they stopped to greet Annemieke and play with her when she first arrived. But it didn't take them long to figure out that Jan was in one of his serious moods and they reacted accordingly.

Everyone assumed that someone else was looking after little sister, so when Jan prepared to leave no one was particularly concerned when Annemieke wasn't produced immediately. When all the ladies were accounted for there was still no cause for alarm.

'Little sister sleeps,' they called out, and retraced their steps, looking in the shade of the tea bushes. But as time passed and they still couldn't find her Jan began to panic.

There are deviates in Indonesia just as there are in every country and society. There are those who prefer little children for their pleasures. There are snakes and wild pigs, and desperate, starving dogs. There are steep gullies eroded by flash flooding, and countless streams that a child could drown in. All these thoughts took possession of Jan's mind.

'Find my child!' he bellowed. 'Stop what you're doing and find my child.'

He sent some women off searching in different directions, others he sent for reinforcements. One he sent home to fetch Andi.

Annemieke wondered where all the people had gone. She wasn't frightened to be alone, because there had never been anything to frighten her. Besides, she wasn't alone. She had butterflies. Brown ones and blue ones, and lovely yellow and white ones. She wanted to look at them more closely, but they flittered away, always just beyond her grasp. She called to the birds high up in the canopy but they didn't hear her. No matter. There were more butterflies and they led her deeper into the cool of the forest. The hill sloped away to a gully with a tinkling stream. Annemieke headed towards the sound, growing tired as she negotiated the creeper vines, and climbed over the spreading roots of the banyans. Then she spotted the cutest little playmate she'd ever seen.

'Baby,' she said.

Jan stood by his Land Rover alone with his fears, as the women's shouts and calls grew dim. He tried to think how far she could have gone. But how long had she been missing? Did she go up hill or down? He thought of fetching Lita but he didn't know what he could possibly say to her. He couldn't face her. Not yet.

It didn't take long for reinforcements to arrive, but all the while his darling Annemieke could be getting further and further away. Many of the new arrivals were men, and it was their way to discuss possibilities and formulate a plan before rushing off in different directions. Jan was nearly beside himself with impatience. But he'd never raised his voice to the men before, and he would not start now.

'If she stays among the tea we will find her soon enough,' they reasoned. 'If she has fallen down and hurt herself again we will find her. If there was a dog that would attack her we would know of this dog and we do not. If a snake has found her then we can do nothing. That is God's will. If there was one among us who would harm her we would know of him and we do not. If there was a stranger among us we would know of him also and we do not. If she has reached the forest that will be difficult, for there are many places in the forest that can hide a child. Therefore we should concentrate our search on the forest while it is still light.'

The men ran off and Jan was again left to himself. He climbed as high as he could to where the tea reached the tree line, where he could watch the women as they combed the hillside. The thought of losing Annemieke was unbearable.

He saw two figures rushing towards him from the homestead. His heart sank. It must be Lita and Andi. But as he watched with growing trepidation, he realised the female was too small. It was Levi. She rushed up to Jan and threw her arms around him sobbing pitifully.

'Levi, I want you to help. Go as far across the hill as you can till you see the men. Try and keep me in sight. Signal me if they find little sister.'

'Yes, Pak Jan,' she sobbed, grateful to be needed.

'Andi, go find the men in the forest. Help them find my child!'

'As you say, Pak.' The old man took off with purpose.

By Jan's reckoning an hour and a half had passed since Annemieke had wandered off when Levi called him. He raced down the hill to his Land Rover, and drove along the track towards her.

'The men signal,' she said as she climbed in. 'By the monkey forest.'

Jan's heart leapt into his mouth. He couldn't imagine how she'd got so far. Perhaps she'd seen a monkey scavenging for food the women had left behind and followed it. But that seemed unlikely because the monkeys generally kept to their own territory. Whatever the reason Jan could hardly imagine a worse place for her to go.

The men obviously thought the same. They sent a boy to stop the Land Rover before it got too close and caused alarm. They knew what monkeys could do to a child, particularly a child who loved animals and might try to play with one of their babies. Perhaps they had already. Jan dreaded what the boy might say.

'How is she? Have you found her?'

'Yes, Pak Jan, we have found her. She is with the monkeys, Pak. We dare go no closer.'

'But is she all right?'

'She is not frightened, Pak, so the monkeys have not attacked her.'

'Yet,' thought Jan grimly. There would be little hope for his daughter if they did.

The men silently led him as far into the forest as they were prepared to go. There was Annemieke. She was surrounded by monkeys, some posturing, some merely curious. He could hear her tinkling laugh. Little monkeys reached out to her and dashed away as soon as she moved. She clapped her hands and sent them all scurrying. But they always came back, and it was always the biggest and most aggressive that came back first.

Jan did not carry a gun but that was what he needed. Just to scare the monkeys away. Just to give them time to rush in and rescue her.

'We must go closer,' whispered Jan.

'No, Pak Jan, that will alarm them.'

'We must do something!'

'We must wait, Pak Jan. Little sister walked into their home. Little sister will walk out again if God wills it.'

Jan watched and his fear grew. The biggest monkey was now becoming aggressive, and they lay watching helplessly as he faked attacks only to retreat at the last moment.

Annemieke had stopped laughing. This monkey alarmed her. She stood up and the big ginger monkey began to shriek and beat its chest. Annemieke started to cry, they could hear her quite clearly. Hands grabbed hold of Jan and held him still.

Two females dropped down beside the ginger monkey and started to bare their teeth and shriek at him. The big monkey slowly backed away. But not far enough for Jan's comfort. Annemieke stopped crying to watch. One of the females had a tiny baby on its back.

'Baby!' she said.

'Please don't!' sobbed Jan under his breath.

As they watched, the big male suddenly charged the female with the baby, knocking it over and sending the baby flying. The female bared its teeth and cringed, its baby crying out in fear.

'Bad monkey. Go way, bad monkey.' Annemieke stepped forward, her fist clenched.

The big male turned to face this unexpected challenge with eyes blazing.

'No, Annemieke!' One of the villagers clapped his hand over Jan's mouth to muffle his voice. To scare the monkeys now would be disastrous.

'Little sister,' called a voice, below and away to their right, quietly, soothingly, a voice that carried with the softness of a breeze weaving in and around the banyans and giant figs.

Annemieke dropped her hands and turned towards the woods that whispered her name. She looked back at the baby monkey and held her arms out.

'Little sister,' came the voice once more, and again she turned. The monkeys fell silent, not alarmed but cautious.

They heard it again, the prayer-soft sound. The whispering of trees, of flowers calling to each other when no human ear is listening.

'Little sister,' it whispered. 'It's time to come home.'

'Bye-bye,' said Annemieke to the monkeys, and slowly climbed over the spreading roots of the banyan trees. The monkeys watched her go, then forgot her. When the men judged Annemieke was safe, they stood.

'Daddy!' cried Annemieke. 'Come and see. Me found monkeys!'

The men laughed but Jan was too choked up. He ran to Annemieke and scooped her up, holding her tight, his mind still racing with thoughts of what might have been.

To his surprise, Levi showed no concern at all and joked with the men. They all laughed and patted Andi on the back when he climbed up from his hiding place below them. It was Andi who had called to Annemieke. He demonstrated the voice he had used, over and over, until everybody was helplessly convulsed with laughter. Jan began to laugh and so did Annemieke. Why not? What might have been didn't happen. What useful purpose could be served by dwelling on it? Jan was no stranger to this simple wisdom but the western part of him needed reminding.

When the story was retold, the women of the village scoffed at any suggestion that the monkeys might have hurt Annemieke.

'Why would they hurt little sister?' they asked. 'They would feel honoured by her presence. Are you insensitive? Can you not feel the peace she brings? Ah, men! Monkeys are smarter. Little sister knew they would not harm her. Did not the females protect our little sister?'

Jan was happy to humour the women. He wanted to believe his little angel could walk into the lion's den and emerge unscathed. But in his heart he knew he was once more in the debt of the old Bugis pirate.

If Jan was indulgent towards Annemieke, he was equally indulgent towards the two boys who ran wild from the day they could walk. He was determined to allow them the freedom he'd enjoyed as a child. But in a community where they ran as nominal Christians among children from devout Muslim families, order and discipline came as a natural part of their lives.

They learned to honour and respect the traditions and beliefs of their friends and elders. In this way they acquired awareness and tolerance of others, and a set of values that would stand them in good stead all their lives.

All three children grew up speaking the local Sundanese dialect, Bahasa Indonesia, Dutch and English. At Jan's insistence, they learned Indonesian history and geography. As Jan gathered stock for his little shop in Amsterdam, they learned about Indonesian art and artifacts: primitive carvings and weaponry from Kalimantan and Irian Jaya; antique silver and jewellery from Yogjakarta; paintings and wood carvings from Bali; beadwork from the Dayak tribesmen; and exquisite batik and ikat from all over the archipelago.

At night Jan and Lita would put the children to bed with tales of princes and princesses, monkey warriors and evil sorcerers. There was one story Annemieke loved above all others and she would beg her parents to tell it over and over. It was the story of how the

Minangkabau people got their name and the hero was a buffalo calf. Lita made a little cloth calf for Annemieke which became her favourite possession.

Chapter Fourteen

Such happiness could not last. It would be wrong to think that their lives on Tengkuban Prahu were quarantined from the trials which affect other mortals. They had their ups and downs. Some years were good but others were too dry or too wet. But they always salvaged something from their crop though at times they were lucky to break even. But that is the lot of farmers the world over and, all things considered, the good far outweighed the bad and they were happy.

When the boys were old enough Jan sent them to boarding school in Bandung. He would drive in and bring them home for weekends whenever he could. That is how Jan became aware of the changes that were taking place. With the same foresight his father had displayed, he realised their days in Java were numbered.

For five years, Sukarno propped up his power base and his 'Guided Democracy' by maintaining a delicate balance between the army and the PKI. On September 30, 1965, Sukarno directed his Presidential Guard to assassinate the Generals headquartered at Halim Air Base, whom he suspected of plotting to overthrow him. General Suharto, then commander of the army's strategic reserve, saw his opportunity and used the attempted coup to gather power to himself. By evening he was in control.

The military blamed the communists for the attempted coup. The army turned on the PKI, and neighbour turned against neighbour. More than half a million communists were dragged from their homes and executed or imprisoned. With the elimination of the PKI, the delicate balance Sukarno had used to maintain his authority was lost. He came under increasing pressure from General Suharto, who took over the presidency in March 1968. Sukarno was placed under house arrest until his death in 1970.

Throughout it all, Jan tried to keep himself and the villages apart from politics, and to a fair degree he succeeded. His unique arrangement with the villagers was an anomaly which was barely tolerated. Jan was well aware that the slightest indiscretion could result in the appropriation of his property by the State.

Jan welcomed President Suharto's rise to power for he brought economic reform, stability, and foreign investment laws which guaranteed Jan's partnership in the tea plantation. But the policies which were his salvation were also, paradoxically, his undoing. His family would not now be forced out at gunpoint but by something more insidious – progress.

On the eve of war, when Jan had been sent home to Holland, Bandung was known as the Paris of Java. Because of its altitude, some seven hundred metres above sea level, it was spared the worst of the tropical sun. The Dutch made Bandung their administrative centre and built broad, shady boulevards, large, elegant homes that caught the cool breezes, and established a university and hospital. The population was then a modest hundred and fifty thousand.

But now Bandung was falling victim to the government's relentless drive towards industrialisation, and the haze which built up during the heat of the day was discoloured by pollution. The population swelled as villagers left their crowded land for the excitement and illusory affluence of the city.

Beautiful boulevards like Jalan Asia-Afrika, once the domain of horse-drawn carriages and bicycle-powered becaks, now suffocated under the onslaught of car and motorbike. Sewers choked and drains flooded and people lived in squalor. Some inevitably rose above their neighbours to occupy the homes vacated by the Europeans. But they had no tradition of dense urban living and did little to control the spread of rubbish and filth.

Jan began to see evidence of this everywhere he went. Indonesians had always wrapped their foodstuffs and goods in leaves or baskets which they would abandon in piles outside their villages to rot and return to the soil. Now the wrappers they abandoned were plastic and foil, and they littered the countryside. Rivers, from which villagers drew their water and in which they bathed, now ran with industrial effluent. It could only get worse. Before long, Jan realised, paradise would be lost forever.

There was another problem which he and Lita discussed incessantly. They were anxious for their children to have the best possible education. They had to concede Bandung was only a stop-gap measure, a deferral of a decision neither wanted to make. They considered sending the children back to Europe, but neither could bear to be parted from them for any length of time. Jan thought of uprooting and returning to Amsterdam but in his heart he knew he could not endure the climate or the city life. Besides, how could he ask his children to surrender the rolling hills of Tengkuban Prahu for cobblestones, and parks where it was forbidden to walk on the grass? Jan had a decision to make and it could no longer be postponed.

He took off for Europe. He had another consignment of artifacts for his shop and for dealers in France and Germany. But he had another reason for going. He would need money if they were to leave Java and set up in another country. The plantation had been good to them and they had lived well, but it had not made them wealthy. He needed money to buy a home and time to sort out his future. He hoped the little shop in Amsterdam would provide the help he needed.

Age and arthritis kept his mother confined to her apartment

now, but she maintained a keen interest in the business. She rang the shop every day and kept a sharp eye on the accounts. Only when new pieces arrived and her knowledge was needed for pricing would she venture out. She'd make a day of it and take the staff of two out to a restaurant that night. It was one of the few times she ever relaxed the purse strings.

She had the caution of the elderly who have known hard times and fear their return. Money gave her security, and she hoarded it away in banks. Every year she gave her staff a generous bonus which reflected their efforts and the results of the year's trading. The rest of the profits went straight into the bank.

She lived frugally for her needs were few. Apart from her medical bills, her only other significant expense was the neighbour she paid to clean and make her meals. The neighbour, not many years younger than herself, would gladly have helped out just for the company they gave each other. But Jan's mother was not the kind to be beholden to any other human being. When Jan told her of their need to leave Java and asked to see the accounts, she easily guessed his motives.

'How much do you need?' she asked him.

'I cannot sell Tengkuban Prahu,' he replied. 'Who would buy it with the arrangement we have with our friends in the villages? We have them to think of.'

'How much do you need?' she asked again, and Jan was dismayed to see that she appeared to be enjoying his discomfort.

'I plan to assign forty-nine per cent to the council. I will retain control and meet with them three or four times a year. It will provide a reasonable income but no capital.'

'How much do you need?' she asked again, softly.

'It's hard to know exactly. Between one and two hundred thousand US dollars.' Jan could not meet her eyes. He felt ashamed.

She laughed and wrote him a cheque for two hundred thousand dollars. Jan was speechless.

'You are just like your father. In thirteen years you have not once asked to see the books of your own shop. You have taken no salary and no dividends. I know you take a small profit from your costs and the price the shop reimburses you for stock. But that only serves to convince me of one thing. You have no more head for business than your father. You should let Lita manage your finances just as I managed his.'

'Mother, I don't know what to say. How can I ever thank you?'

'It's your own money. It's your shop. Besides there is more than enough left to cover my needs.'

He looked at his mother, now tiny with age and bent with arthritis. He kissed her.

'One more thing, Jan. I am grooming Anke to be my successor. No, don't say anything. I am getting old and it is becoming increasingly difficult for me to do my job. Anke is a good girl. She gets better every day and she learns quickly. You must arrange for her to become your partner. She deserves it and she will be good for you.'

'Why am I so lucky?' he asked her. 'To have you for a mother, a perfect family of my own, and to have lived the life I have.'

'It may not always be this way, Jan. If you understand that now you will find things easier to cope with when the tide turns.'

'I understand, Mother,' he said, but of course he didn't. How could he?

He chose the occasion of Annemieke's fifth birthday to announce his decision.

Annemieke had asked if she could celebrate her birthday near a thermal pool high up on the mountain where they could boil and decorate eggs. People came from all the local kampongs, bringing brightly coloured, over-sweet cakes to add to the traditional birthday fare. They cooked satays and rice, and the children played games and filled up on coloured cordials. They brought Annemieke little presents they'd made painstakingly over the preceding weeks. Nobody had any inkling that the day would be anything other than a celebration.

Jan rose to his feet and stood before everything he loved in the world.

'I have an announcement to make,' he said, speaking in the local dialect so all could understand, 'and it is one that causes me more pain than you will ever know.'

The mountain fell silent. Lita took Annemieke from Levi and gazed at her husband, her face expressionless. They had discussed their options but he'd given no indication that he'd reached a decision.

'The time has come for the Van der Meers to leave our home on Tengkuban Prahu, to leave Java.'

The news, so unexpected and unwelcome, brought a gasp that set birds to flight and sent lizards scurrying.

'I have decided that we will move to Australia where my children will go to school. We will keep our home here and visit whenever we can. We will never forget you. Our hearts will always be here on Tengkuban Prahu.'

Jan was deliberately brief for he feared his voice would betray him. The lump swelled in his throat and he felt an overwhelming sadness. He stood gazing down over hillsides dark green with tea, and splashed burnt red where erosion had bared the soil. He looked over land which for seventy years the Van der Meers had been glad to call home. He did not move.

Tears began to glisten in Lita's eyes and flow down her cheeks. Annemieke looked at her mother's tears, so seldom seen, and cried too. But it was Levi who gave voice to their common grief. Her sorrow echoed around the hills and forests to be taken up by the villagers. Soon the mountainside was awash with tears.

It took them six months to tidy up their affairs and leave Tengkuban Prahu. Each village took it upon themselves to formally farewell the family so their sadness at leaving became drawn out and wearying. Andi Sose was the last to make his farewells.

'The sea calls me,' he said. 'It is time to return to my people in Ujung Pandang.'

'Goodbye, my friend,' said Jan, and threw his arms around the old man to whom he owed so much. 'I will look for you whenever I visit the pandanus cape.'

'Ask for me at the Pantere Anchorage or Prahu Harbour. If I am not at sea that is where you will find me.' He turned to Lita. 'Take care of him, *Nyonya*, sometimes his heart is too big for his brain.'

The old pirate shook hands with both boys, and turned to Annemieke. He reached into his pocket and slowly pulled out a silver chain. Annemieke's eyes widened. There was something on the end of it but she didn't have time to see it properly before he slipped the chain over her head and around her neck. She took the little pendant in her hand and examined it. It was a tiny monkey beaten out of silver.

'I have made this for you, little sister. I taught myself this skill in the long hours at sea.' He looked up to Jan and Lita. 'We don't always have foolish young Dutchmen, strong in the head and weak in the bowels, to amuse us. And life is dull now that we are no longer pirates.'

Annemieke hadn't really thought ahead to life without her friend. She could hardly remember a time when he wasn't around to play with her. She thought of him as family. Now she was going away. Now he was going away. A great sob built up inside her and burst from her throat. She threw her arms around the old man's neck and drenched his collar with her tears. Andi gently pulled her arms apart and held her in front of him so that she was forced to look into his eyes.

'Don't go away!' she pleaded.

'But I am not leaving you, little sister. Whenever you wear this silver chain you will think of me and I will be with you. That is why I made it. This chain joins us. We will always be together.'

The Van der Meers arrived in Sydney seven years before the tall

Argentinian who now called himself Eduardo Remigio Gallegos, but their paths were destined to cross.

The Van der Meers found the northern beaches irresistible. The boys who had spent their lives in a sea of green now discovered the sea of blue. They threw themselves into the surf with joyful abandon to be hauled ashore by lifeguards whenever their enthusiasm outstripped their competence.

The children also discovered sunburn. In Java they had always worn shirts and hats. Everyone did. Now their noses peeled and their backs blistered. But it wasn't the pain of their burns that taught them the wisdom of sunscreens. It was being confined to the shade while they watched their new friends tearing the waves apart. That is what hurt most.

Lita followed the Javanese custom and kept out of the sun. She encouraged Annemieke to do the same. Annemieke always wore a broad-brimmed beach hat and a t-shirt over her bathing costume when she swam. She clung to Lita, and Lita clung to the shade.

It is said that children adapt more readily than adults to any change in circumstance and the boys were proof of that. But Annemieke became listless and clingy. She was easily upset. She missed Andi and she missed Levi and the other house girls. She missed the friendly, dark faces. She missed the world which had seemingly had her at its centre. She never took off the silver monkey Andi had made for her and Mong, her ragged little Minangkabau calf, was her constant companion and comfort. Every day she would ask Jan when they were going home.

But Jan had another home in mind. Property prices had slumped following the nickel boom that had put Poseidon on the front pages of newspapers around the world. He had his eye on a large, rambling, Federation-style house in Mosman on Sydney's lower North Shore. The house had views to Middle Harbour but, surrounded by box gums and jacarandas, it also gave them a privacy that people unaccustomed to neighbours must have. It was close to the city without being suffocated by it. And close enough to the beach to satisfy the boys. It was also close to schools, which the boys noted with mounting dismay.

Jan bought the house and their lives soon settled into a new routine. Annemieke still pined for her home on Tengkuban Prahu but gradually succumbed to the many diversions Sydney had to offer. She became a regular at Taronga Park Zoo, and made friends with the big, sad-eyed orangutans and skittering monkeys. She discovered the cinemas and toy shops. And she discovered 'Sesame Street', 'Play School' and 'Humphrey Bear'. One day she discovered she was happy and her song reached into every corner and crevice of the old house. Jan and Lita looked at their youngest child and smiled. When she tied a string of cans to the tail of the next door neighbour's dog, any lingering doubts they'd had about their move vanished.

But as their new life began, another ended. Jan's mother finally succumbed to age, arthritis and the bitter northern winter. Jan was distraught. He flew to Holland immediately.

His mother was cremated on a bleak, joyless, wintry day that reduced the world to monochrome. He thought his mother deserved better, and his opinion was shared by the small gathering that attended the short service: her few friends and neighbours; her staff from the shop; her doctor; and the bank manager who had been her friend and business advisor. It was a humble gathering. But at least there were mourners, and those who mourned her passing were genuine. She had fared better than her husband.

Before Jan could return to his family in Australia, he had first to attend to business. He called into the shop to see Anke.

He made Anke a proposition whereby she purchased a twenty percent holding at a value far below the real worth of the business. Then he provided her with the incentive that would make the partnership work. He set profit targets based on previous results. Profits would be split fifty-fifty and, on a points basis, increased her entitlement to purchase more shares. It was a good deal for both parties, and it guaranteed Jan a stable source of income for years to come.

Jan would have liked to claim that he had thought of the proposal himself. He hadn't. It was the last gift he ever received from his mother, the details handed to him by her solicitor along with her will. He suspected she had also discussed the proposal with Anke, for she showed no surprise and accepted without condition.

He also visited the people who bought his tea. It was the last time he would do so on a business basis. Jan had discovered that Australia was a nation of tea drinkers and he had found a ready market for his medium quality black tea, which was an essential part of the blends Australians preferred. Now he had to advise his European customers to buy elsewhere.

He returned to Australia with his mother's ashes sealed in a tiny pewter urn. He wished with all his heart that they had shared more time together, but they had both made their choice.

Chapter Fifteen

Annemieke was thirteen years old when her father finally gave in to her.

'It can be your birthday present,' he said.

'I love you!' she cried, threw her arms around him, and ran off to tell her mother. 'Mum! Mum! Guess what? Dad says I can come with you to Tengkuban Prahu. I can't wait!'

Her happiness filled the house. And the two boys for once didn't complain about the interruption to their studies. Not even Pieter, who had become uncharacteristically short-tempered, under pressure to perform well in his Higher School Certificate.

'You're spoilt,' he said, smothering his sister in a huge bear-like hug. 'Take plenty of pictures because that's where Tom and I are going as soon as we finish HSC. Now let me study or I'll never get to university.'

That night Annemieke made her father tell the story of his return to Tengkuban Prahu after the war. Annemieke knew the story by heart. When Jan reached the part where the village people came to meet him, eyes streaming with joy, Annemieke glowed and wondered what her own reception would be like.

The little girl who, unlike her brothers, had always been small for her age, was finally beginning to grow tall. Her legs had grown so long they seemed to have a mind of their own and flopped as helplessly as a newborn foal's. Her long fair hair fell mid-way to her waist in a cascade of honey and sunshine. Her pale olive skin glowed with health and vitality.

She had boyfriends with whom she'd go to movies, ice skating and to parties. No matter how well supervised they were, teenagers who want to can always find the opportunity for a little petting. Even so Annemieke was careful about how far she would let her boyfriends go. When she overheard one boy at school boasting to his friends that he had gone a lot further with her than she'd ever allow, she didn't ask him to 'hold out hand'. She clenched her fist, set her feet and punched him in the nose with all her weight and force. She demanded an apology right then and there in front of everybody and got it. Her friends developed a sudden new respect for her. Annemieke was one girl who would never have to ask her brothers to uphold her honour.

The girls in Annemieke's class envied her beauty but they didn't resent her for it. She was always the first to point out the most attractive features of others. If Annemieke said someone had nice eyes or beautiful skin, her comments were accepted as gospel, and the recipients of these compliments loved her for it. She was kind, generous and sensitive. And just as the servants had vied for the honour of holding her when she was a baby, so her school friends now vied for her attentions.

Annemieke gave the lie to the argument that beauty is only skin deep. Her beauty also came from within and none could fail to recognise it. She had never stopped writing to the servant girls and the little village girls who had been her playmates, though the replies were becoming fewer as the years passed and more and more of them got married.

Now she wrote to everyone she knew to tell them she was finally coming back to visit as she had so often promised. In her mind she saw her return as a replay of her father's. During her first years at school, she was often made aware of the fact that she was different. Her friends teased her because of her funny accent and her olive colouring set her apart from them. It had hurt Annemieke to feel that she didn't quite belong so she'd compensated by turning Java into a fantasy land where the sun always shone, and beautiful birds and butterflies filled the air. The more she thought about Tengkuban Prahu the more she came to love it. Her affection was so deep and heart-felt she couldn't conceive of it not being reciprocated. And if that was the case, why wouldn't the villagers welcome her back the same way they'd welcomed Jan?

As the day of departure drew closer, she practised her Bahasa Indonesia and the traditional greetings and expressions of gratitude in the local dialect. She bought gifts to take with her. As her excitement grew, Jan realised he would have to take precautions to make sure everything turned out the way Annemieke had convinced herself it would. He took on the role of stage manager.

At every step of their journey he called Tengkuban Prahu to update them on their likely arrival time. He made his final call from the Rindu Alam restaurant on top of the pass at Puncak less than two hours from the plantation.

'All is ready, Pak Jan,' they assured him.

Even so, Jan and Lita were staggered by the scene which awaited them at Tengkuban Prahu.

Indonesians love a celebration. They probably have more festivals than any other nation on earth. These festivals are not purely for pleasure. Originally, they were the means by which a people who were largely illiterate passed on their history and culture, reinforced traditions, and maintained order in their lives. As education spread through the villages and all the islands, the festivals became more celebratory, an opportunity for people to dress up, make social contact, and to feast until their bellies groaned.

The Council who now ran the estate decreed that the return of Annemieke warranted such a celebration. They saw Jan regularly and Lita once a year when she came to visit her parents. Annemieke, the blonde child of Tengkuban Prahu, was obviously special to them. But both Jan and Lita knew the reception was calculated to honour them all.

Annemieke was oblivious to any such subtleties. All she had

eyes for was the cheering, waving crowd of once familiar faces, and the banner which straddled the driveway between the tallest palms proclaiming in a delightful confusion of two languages, 'Welkom home Annemieke'.

The members of the Council stood in self-conscious formality on the steps of the house. But as the car pulled to a halt, Annemieke saw Levi, now a mother herself with a baby on her hip, and her carefully rehearsed greetings evaporated. With eyes awash, she dashed from the car to embrace her sister, and the blonde-haired girl was quickly swallowed up in a dark sea of smiling faces.

The next few days were among the happiest of Annemieke's life. Her friends and playmates were now strangers to her, painfully shy and self-conscious in her presence. But Annemieke charmed them with her honesty and easy manner, and her lack of guile encouraged them to be more forthcoming. Her gifts were a huge success that helped build bridges. She still spoke a little of their language, but with the most comical accent they had ever heard. They began to mimic her, not unkindly, and roll around with laughter whenever she spoke.

Jan and Lita let Annemieke rediscover her childhood at her own pace, and watched delightedly as her Sundanese blood rose like sap in spring. She relearned the customs, the courtesies and the songs that had slipped away over the years.

The villagers told her the story of her visit to the monkey forest though now the story had grown to become a legend which she scarcely recognised. And they read special significance in the silver monkey she still wore around her neck.

'You must visit them once more,' the villagers insisted, anxious to see the legend with their own eyes. Mother monkeys would come down from the trees to offer their young to Annemieke for her blessing. The males would form a guard of honour to see that no harm befell her.

Annemieke knew she could not charm the monkeys from the

trees, though the supposed eye-witness accounts she heard confused her. She knew she had no special powers. The monkeys at Taronga Park liked her only for the peanuts she brought them. Still she liked the little creatures, and agreed to accompany the villagers to a spot where they could observe the monkeys without disturbing them.

Of course the entire village wanted to join the expedition and witness the miracles for themselves. So the chances of getting near the monkeys unobserved were negligible. Indeed, they had no sooner entered the forest when the monkeys set up cries of alarm.

'See?' the women cried. 'See how the monkeys sense her presence. Already they are shouting their welcome.'

Annemieke looked at the men who had accompanied them and they grinned back at this outrageous assertion. But such is the way legends are born and this one was harmless enough.

'I will go forward with three men,' said Annemieke. 'You must all keep perfectly still.'

The women chose their vantage points and settled down to watch. Annemieke and her three companions crept forward until she also told them to wait. She went on over the same spreading roots she had climbed as a child, past the same great banyans. She stopped short and sat down.

She sat very still for a long time. The monkeys grew curious. Slowly the adults came down from the heights to watch her. She pulled a bag of peanuts from her pocket, cracked the shells and ate a couple. The monkeys showed more interest. Monkeys the world over know what peanuts are and Annemieke was making them hungry. They came down from the lower branches to sit on the ground, firstly the males, then the females. Annemieke noticed the ones which were carrying young. She wondered if the village people would be satisfied now and decided that they probably wouldn't.

These monkeys were wild animals and not accustomed to human contact. Yet she felt that if she remained calm, they would not harm her. Slowly she rose from the tree root she was sitting on. The monkeys grew tense and watched her carefully. She never looked at them. She stared straight at the root in front of her, reached into her bag, and began to line peanuts up along the length of it. She put down nearly thirty peanuts this way, all with deliberate slowness. Then she eased her way back to the root she'd chosen to sit on.

Two metres separated her from her makeshift table. With great caution and a couple of false starts, the monkeys advanced towards her. The bravest snatched a peanut and raced away in retreat. The others saw that no harm came to it and crept closer. The males came first. Dashing in then skipping away with their prize. But one or two stayed and began to work their way down the line of nuts.

At last a female with a tiny infant on its back had the courage to come to the table. But there were no peanuts left where she was. Annemieke rose slowly, and reaching as far forward as she could, held a peanut out to the mother. The mother hesitated, torn between the desire for the peanut and the urge to run. Greed overcame fear and she reached out and grabbed the peanut. She darted away out of range and ate it. She looked up. Annemieke was still there with another peanut in her hand. She came forward again and took the offered nut, but this time did not retreat. She took another and another until Annemieke had exhausted her supply.

The monkeys watched her carefully. How would they react when they realised there were no more nuts? Annemieke knew they could turn nasty.

They crept closer and Annemieke could not decide what to do. She glanced over her shoulder to where the men were hidden. They stood up. That's all it took.

The monkeys fled back to their trees. Annemieke rose and silently watched them go. The show was over and she knew she'd done well. In her mind she could already hear the village mothers telling this story to their children as they put them to bed.

When she told Jan and Lita about her adventure, they were proud of her bravery. And delighted that their child had the wisdom to allow her friends in the village their legends.

'It will become another story,' Jan said. 'Soon the story of Annemieke and the monkeys will become as well known as the story of how the Minangkabau got their name.'

Annemieke blushed, embarrassed. Her parents had seen through her. She'd desperately wanted to leave her mark on this land which claimed her as its own. That was the real reason she'd gone back.

Chapter Sixteen

Once again, Annemieke climbed the slopes of Tengkuban Prahu to boil eggs in its thermal pools, and walk around the sulphurous rim of its smouldering crater. She never thought of Tengkuban Prahu as a volcano. The mountain had always been a friend to her when she was a child, a favourite place for picnics and adventures. She never thought to fear any of Indonesia's volcanoes. They had given her no cause to.

'Indonesia has more than seventy active volcanoes,' Jan told her as the two of them soaked in the hot springs of Ciater. Jan never missed an opportunity to give history lessons. Australia was now his home but not yet home to his heart. 'The islands of Indonesia are among the youngest in the world. Only fifteen million years old. In a sense this country is still being born.'

The idea of being present at the birth of the country she loved so much appealed to Annemieke, but she soon learned no birth is without pain.

'When the island of Krakatau off Java's west coast exploded in 1883, it caused a tidal wave that swept around the world. More than thirty-five thousand people were killed on Java alone. That's the eruption everyone knows about. But there have been much bigger and worse.'

If Jan had seen the effect he was having on Annemieke he would have stopped the lesson there. But eyes closed, and head back on the edge of the pool, totally relaxed and at peace with the world, he was oblivious to her feelings. Annemieke could not explain why she felt suddenly cold despite the warm, soothing waters. She listened with growing dread.

'Mt Tambora on Sumbawa killed ninety thousand people when it erupted in 1815, and sent eighty cubic kilometres of ash high into the atmosphere. The following year was known as the year without summer. Ash filled the sky in clouds so thick the rays of the sun could not penetrate. Imagine that, Annemieke.'

And Annemieke did. The thought terrified her. She thought about how she'd casually strolled around the rim of Tengkuban Prahu, and shivered. A shadow settled upon her and would not go away.

'They've stopped exploding now though, haven't they?' she asked hopefully.

'No way,' said Jan emphatically, enjoying his role of tutor. 'As recently as 1963, Gunung Agung erupted in Bali during the Eka Dasa Rudra rite, the most sacred of all Balinese festivals. It is so sacred, it is only held once each century. More than two thousand Balinese were killed and thousands more left homeless. Many Balinese died because they refused to leave their homes, even though they were in the path of the lava. They are a devout people and they believed they had somehow offended their god, and this was their punishment. They just lay down and the lava swallowed them up.'

A tight band of fear wrapped itself around Annemieke's chest. Her breath came in shallow gasps. She didn't know why she was frightened and that made it worse. There was a terror, a nameless terror, and it had found a home in her young mind.

'When we visit your grandparents we'll take you to see Mt Galunggung. It's not too far away. It's been playing up and letting off steam since April. Come on, sleepy head, let's go dry off.'

But Annemieke had never been more awake in her life. Nor more frightened.

Second Thursday

* * *

The following day Annemieke was quiet and uncommunicative. She didn't go down to the village to see her friends, and she didn't want to go with Jan as he went about the estate's business. Lita noticed the change in her but thought she was just wearying of the novelty and becoming bored.

'Tomorrow we will go to see my parents,' she said. 'It will be a nice change for you. We will stay at the Savoy Homann in Bandung, the hotel where your father and I first met.'

She hugged Annemieke to her, kissed her and held her close. Annemieke wanted to tell Lita of her fears, but couldn't find the words to express a feeling she didn't understand herself.

'It's a very happy place for me,' her mother continued. 'Then we'll go on to Pengalengan. It's hard to get your grandparents to leave their home any more. Tomorrow you'll see why.'

They left after breakfast. Jan chose to drive himself. He'd been to Bandung and Pengalengan often enough to know the way. Besides, as he freely admitted, he was not a good passenger and the local drivers frightened the life out of him.

'They're Muslims with the fatalism of Buddhists,' he claimed. And the fact that cars in Indonesia rarely have rear seatbelts fitted also concerned him.

As soon as they reached the vegetable growing district of Lembang they struck traffic. Roads where cars were once so rare that workers in the fields would down tools to watch their passing, were now crowded with cars, buses and trucks.

Jan had warned Annemieke of the changes but she hadn't believed him, preferring to remember things as they had been. The sight depressed her further. Bandung was even worse. They crawled along at a snail's pace through air thick and sluggish with exhaust fumes. When they finally reached the Savoy Homann, Annemieke pleaded a headache and went straight to bed.

She lay awake in the darkness wondering why things had gone so wrong. She'd known that Bandung had changed and the drive down from Jakarta had been worse if anything. Why hadn't it worried her then? Everything had changed in the hot pool at Ciater, but why? She drifted off into troubled sleep.

The following day they battled the tourist buses and sightseers on the way to Pengalengan and its endless rolling hills. Lita pointed out landmarks but Annemieke showed little interest. Lita tried to guess what could possibly be troubling her daughter. Finally she asked.

'Annemieke, we're going to arrive at your grandparents' house any minute now. You must cheer up. Tell me what's worrying you.'

'Nothing.'

'You've hardly said a word to anyone in the past two days.'

To Lita's surprise, Annemieke began to cry quietly.

'Annemieke, for heaven's sake, what's wrong?'

'Nothing.'

'Then cheer up. If you've got a problem, we can talk about it later.'

And Annemieke did cheer up. How could she not? There is a bond between children and grandparents based on love unfettered by parental or filial responsibilities. Lita's parents descended on the child they had not seen for eight years and fussed over her. With the intuition grandparents so often display, Neneng, her Sundanese grandmother and Barnaby, her British grandfather, gave her a gift which was guaranteed to win her heart and drag her out of her gloom.

It was a four month old monkey.

Annemieke squealed with delight.

'What is his name? What's his name?' she demanded, as the tiny creature nestled into the crook of her elbow.

'Osh,' said her grandfather. 'He's a foundling. When he was tiny and fretting for his mother that was the only sound that soothed him. We'd give him the corner of a piece of cloth dipped in milk and sugar, and whisper "osh . . . osh . . . osh" in his ear. Now he thinks it's his name. That's all he'll answer to.'

'Ossshhhhh,' said Annemieke. 'Osh . . . Osh . . . Osh.'

Osh turned his big limpid eyes upon her and began to suckle on her little finger. Barnaby bent down so that he and Annemieke were the same height and he had her absolute attention.

'You realise when you leave here you will have to leave Osh behind with us. But he will always be your pet. He will always be here when you visit.'

Annemieke and Osh became inseparable. She took Osh with her on a brass chain wherever she went, and carried a woven basket for him to sleep in.

She was forbidden to let Osh into her bedroom at night, but she always smuggled him in, and let him sleep on her bed, snuggled up in the hollow between her knees and stomach. They'd comfort each other when, off in the distance, Mt Galunggung rumbled and grumbled as pressure built up within its core.

For three days and three nights Annemieke forgot the thoughts that had troubled her. She regained her appetite and her tinkling laugh. She ignored Mt Galunggung and its billowing, grey plume. She had better things to think about.

On the fourth night Osh woke her, pulling on her arm and chattering in fright. She pulled him under her blankets and held him close but he still wouldn't settle.

'Ossshhh . . .' she whispered. 'Ossshhh . . . Ossshhh . . .'

Then she felt the bed move. The windows began to rattle. Then came a sound she'd never heard before but recognised instantly. It was more hollow and mechanical than her dreams had led her to believe. And so much louder. She turned to her window. The sky burned red. Molten white streaks slowly rose and arced back to earth. She screamed. The terror returned to her and this time it had a name. Mt Galunggung had erupted once more.

Fear numbed her brain and robbed her of the use of her legs. Osh clung even tighter as her fears lent weight to his. His nails bit into her but she was oblivious of the pain. Her screams brought Jan. He burst into her room, picked her up and hugged her tightly, not realising until Osh howled what the lump was squashed between them.

'Hush, little one. It's okay. Everything's all right. There's nothing to be frightened of.' His voice soothed while his eyes took in the tormented sky through her window. The room shook once more and Annemieke screamed.

'Hush, Mieke, hush. We're safe here,' he told the sobbing child. Jan had never seen her this way before. 'Hush, hush,' he soothed, 'we're quite safe here.'

But then he was interrupted by a sound like hailstones on a corrugated iron roof. Annemieke screamed again. The noise softened off to a pitter-patter, punctuated by occasional thumps as larger pieces of ejecta thundered onto the roof.

Jan looked out of Annemieke's window once more. The flaming sky seemed to have dulled and lost its threat.

'Look, Mieke,' he said, and made her look at the window. 'See? Already the fires are dying away.'

But Jan was wrong. Mt Galunggung thundered and the house shook to prove it. More ejecta arced through the sky towards their home. The eruptions hadn't diminished. Clouds of ash had merely obscured the fiery cone.

'The village people tell me this will go on for months yet. Jolly nuisance.' Barnaby and Neneng had come to help calm Annemieke. Her grandfather was his normal unflappable self and Annemieke drew comfort from this.

'We'll be all right here,' he confirmed. 'Wouldn't want to be any closer though, by Jove. Come on, let's all go and have a cup of tea. There's nothing we can do until morning.'

'Osh,' said Annemieke between sobs. The little monkey clung to her for dear life.

If Annemieke thought the end of the world had come, the first light of dawn only confirmed her suspicions. Ash like a dusting of snow coated the palms and tea bushes. It carpeted the gardens, lawns and driveway. It lay along windowsills and clung to the pitch of the roof. It coated the water lilies and even the surface of the pond. Grey ash coated the world as far as the eye could see.

They looked at a world without shadows, for the morning sun found the dense clouds of ash almost impenetrable. Even as they watched, the light grew dimmer and their range of vision decreased. Away to the east Mt Galunggung still thundered and vomited although it had long since disappeared from sight.

They sealed the house as best they could, but Javanese houses are built to allow air to circulate freely. They have tall ceilings with large open vents at the top, protected only by mosquito screens and security bars. Verandahs and long overhanging eaves protected the vents from the monsoonal rains. No one ever intended that the vents should close.

Soot and ash wafted in, penetrating every room, coating furniture, clothing, crockery, and the people who lived there. Lita and Neneng fussed around with cloths and covers but there was little they could do.

For Annemieke there was no escape. The volcano followed her everywhere. She hid from the ash by burrowing under her bed linen but the foul odours pursued her. Pungent, nauseating and sulphurous, they caught in her throat and made her eyes sting. There was no escape.

They sat around the radio as overexcited voices relayed exaggerated estimates of damage and casualties. Two thousand people had lost their lives, it claimed, and over forty thousand were left homeless. But Lita's father knew the real toll would come from people fleeing the eruption. And later, after the rains had come, from mud slides. That was the way it was in Java.

'Good will come of this, Annemieke,' her grandfather said.

Annemieke, who had withdrawn into herself and clung resolutely to an equally frightened Osh, raised her eyes. She could not imagine anything good coming from something so terrifying.

'The ash will replenish the soil,' her grandfather said. 'Make it richer. The stuff our mountains spit out is basic, not acidic as it is from lots of other volcanoes. That's why the soils in Java are so fertile, and why this tiny island has always been able to feed so many people. It may be hard for you to see it now, but our volcanoes are our blessing.'

'I want to go home,' said Annemieke suddenly. And then insistently as the idea blossomed in her mind. 'I want to go home. I want to go away from here. I want to go back to Tengkuban Prahu.'

She began to cry again, her breath coming in great heaving sobs. Lita put her arm around Annemieke, and she buried her head on her mother's shoulder. Lita looked over to Jan perplexed. They were not in any danger. The eruption had acted as a safety valve, releasing the pressure building inside. If it hadn't, they'd have had cause to worry.

'Let me talk to her,' said Jan quietly to Lita. 'Perhaps you can get us all some more tea.'

He sat down alongside Annemieke.

'Look at me, Mieke,' he said, taking out his handkerchief and gently wiping her eyes. 'The volcano can't hurt us now. We're too far away and it's growing weaker. The next few days won't be very comfortable with the ash—'

'Daddy! I want to go home now!'

Jan was stunned. Annemieke was not the sort of child to stamp her feet and insist on her own way. He'd never seen her so adamant before. But then, he'd never seen her scared before either.

'But why, pet? I've told you. We're safe here. Grandma and Grandpa have waited a long time to see you. They'll be upset if we suddenly run off for no good reason. Besides, the roads will be blocked by people trying to get away to Bandung and Jakarta. You remember all those tourists and buses? And anyway, even if the roads were clear, can you imagine what it would be like trying to drive through those clouds of ash? It's far too dangerous.'

Silent tears flowed once more down Annemieke's cheeks. How could she explain the darkness that gripped her? She threw her arms around her father's neck and pulled him fiercely to her. 'Oh, Daddy, something bad is going to happen! I just know it.'

'Shhh . . . you'll frighten Osh. Nothing bad is going to happen. You know I won't let anything bad happen to you or Mummy.'

'It is, Dad! Something bad is going to happen. I know it is! I can feel it.'

Her desperation unnerved him. This was so unlike his daughter. Then he remembered how quiet Annemieke had been. Since when? The day before they left? Since Ciater, since the hot springs. Then he remembered, and with a sickening certainty, realised he was the cause of Annemieke's distress.

'Oh, pet, I'm sorry. When I told you about Krakatau and Tambora I didn't mean to frighten you.'

'There's something else, Dad, there's something else and I just don't know what it is!'

The anguish in her voice was plain. Again Jan felt a ripple of unease.

'Please Dad, can't we go?'

Jan would do anything for Annemieke. But it was clear to him that it would be madness to try to leave now.

'We'll see,' he said, trying to buy time. 'We'll wait until evening. Then we'll see how it is.'

'Thank you, Daddy,' she cried and kissed him.

By evening, Jan thought, he could turn Annemieke around and make her see reason. But Annemieke had made up her mind that they would leave for home. Nothing would change it.

'I don't know what to do,' said Jan. 'This is so unlike her. She's never been like this before.'

Neneng smiled.

'It's her age,' she said. 'She is at the age where children discover they are not immortal and neither are their parents. It is something we all face in our own way. Perhaps this is her way.'

'Perhaps. Lita thinks she's had a premonition of some sort.'

'That is always what women think,' scoffed Barnaby. 'Give them something that can't be proved, some metaphysical nonsense, and they grab hold of it in a flash. Stuff and nonsense.' He began to laugh and Jan laughed along with him.

The women were unimpressed.

* * *

Late in the afternoon a westerly breeze blew up, pushing the ash clouds back towards their source. At times the visibility improved markedly, and then a gust would pick up the fallen ash and carry it in swirling clouds. Driving under such conditions was still patently dangerous, and Jan stooped to desperate tactics to convince Annemieke to stay.

'What about Osh?' he said to her. 'How can you just go and leave Osh? That's not fair. He's only just got to know you. He's begun to depend on you and now you want to just walk away and leave him.'

'Of course I'll miss him, Daddy,' she said. 'But I'll have to leave him sooner or later. Perhaps it's better if he doesn't become too attached to me. Besides, he'll be here when I come back. Grandpa promised.'

What could Jan say? He resigned himself to the inevitable.

'Get some sleep now. We'll leave at midnight.' In his heart Jan knew it was the wrong decision, but it had an immediate effect upon Annemieke. The girl who had sat around so listlessly now raced about the house getting ready for their departure.

Osh sensed the change in her mood and decided to join in this new game. As soon as Annemieke put things in her bag Osh pulled them out again. Annemieke pretended to scold him but he was back to his tricks as soon as she took her eyes off him.

'See? Even Osh wants you to stay,' said Jan. It was a last ditch attempt to make her change her mind but it didn't work. Jan went to his bedroom and lay down. He could hear Annemieke singing as he dozed off, preparing himself for the nightmare drive ahead.

Chapter Seventeen

Jan waited until the car was packed and they were ready to leave before washing the windows. To his dismay the ash turned into mud that streaked and clung stubbornly to the glass. He realised that he could never carry enough water to keep the windscreen clear for the duration of their journey.

'What on earth are we doing?' he complained.

'It's not too late to change your mind,' Barnaby replied.

'It's not my mind that needs changing.' Jan could not disappoint Annemieke now. The old man shrugged.

'Take my hand pump. A bit of pressure might help.' Barnaby stumped off to fetch it.

'Okay, Lita, Annemieke, into the car. Say goodbye to Osh.'

The farewells were subdued, tinged with disappointment and apprehension of the journey ahead. Jan took the pump from Barnaby and stowed it in the footwell on Lita's side. No point putting away something they were going to need before much longer.

The roads were not deserted as Jan had hoped. But neither were they blocked. The traffic crawled along at the pace of the slowest, gasping, wheezing truck. Jan was unwilling to risk overtaking, knowing with absolute certainty that there'd always be another truck in front.

Ash built up around the windshield and clogged the wipers. It penetrated the air vents and blocked the filters of the air-conditioning. Jan had no choice but to switch it off and suffer the heat. The beams from the headlights became ineffectual columns of grey which reflected back at them every time the wind gusted.

They passed countless cars and trucks which had been abandoned by the roadside. Too many, Jan thought, and puzzled over the cause. He checked his instruments and realised his own engine was beginning to overheat. The ash was clogging the fins of his radiator. He would have to stop and hose it down although this would rob him of all his remaining water. But what choice did he have?

The traffic slowed to a halt. Through breaks in the swirling ash Jan could see a glowing red snake of tail-lights winding through the hills ahead. Everywhere drivers honked their horns oblivious to the futility of the gesture. Jan smiled despite their predicament. It was such an Indonesian thing to do.

Jan saw his chance to check his radiator. He got out and raised the bonnet. Immediately the horn of the car behind howled in protest. He took out the polythene jerry can he'd filled with water and his father-in-law's pump. But his earlier experience with the windscreen made him cautious. He propped his torch up so that its beam shone on the bottom third of the radiator. He covered the nozzle of the outlet hose while he pumped up some pressure, then fired at the part of the radiator he'd illuminated. The force of the jet pushed the ash into the gaps between the fins where it settled like wet cement. As he'd suspected, the cure was worse than the problem. He put the pump aside. He had an idea.

'Annemieke, did you bring your hairbrush?'

Annemieke rummaged around in her little carry bag and passed the brush to her father. He ran it across the radiator in short sharp movements. A cloud of ash rose, blotting out the flashlight and snapping Jan's breath. He gagged. He made a desperate lunge for the pump and forced water into his mouth. He rinsed as quickly as he could and, with lungs near bursting, allowed the water to tumble from his mouth. He inhaled. And immediately collapsed in a fit of coughing. But enough air got into his lungs each time to enable him to catch his breath. His temples pounded and his eyes watered. He looked up and found Lita standing over him. She had every right to look panic stricken.

'I'm okay,' he gasped. 'It's just taking me time to learn the rules.'

He covered his mouth and nose with a handkerchief and began to brush once more. He brushed for as long as he could, then stepped out of the cloud of ash to breathe and clear his eyes. The dry ash came away easily. But the wet ash was a lost cause.

The traffic began to move once more. For half an hour they stuttered along behind the glowing tail-light in front of them until they reached the cause of the delay. A bus had gone off the road and overturned, scattering its human cargo among the underbrush. People called out in pain and distress, but there were plenty of others to look after them. Emergency services would be virtually nonexistent under the strain of the past few days. But the local people would improvise, Jan knew. They always did.

It was one-thirty, and they'd covered little more than twenty kilometres. But they were leaving the hills and the pace began to quicken. Jan had never liked travelling in a line of vehicles, and allowed a gap to grow between himself and the car in front. Immediately a car came from behind and filled it. He stabbed down hard on the brakes and hit his horn in a long angry blast. He need not have bothered. Once more he allowed a gap to develop so that if the car in front was forced to stop suddenly, he could avoid it and have time to warn the car behind him. But this time he was careful not to let the gap open too far. He didn't want to tempt anyone else to overtake.

But a gap is a gap. And just as nature abhors a vacuum, so too do Indonesian drivers feel the need to fill a gap, no matter how small. Before Jan knew it, another car squeezed in front of him and immediately braked. Jan did likewise. He glanced into his rear vision mirror but couldn't see anything. He could see only the glow not the shape of the headlights behind him. He was searching for them when the car behind hit them. Jan see-sawed the steering wheel as the pendulum effect pushed the rear of the car first this way then that. Their lack of speed worked for them and Jan brought the car to a sliding halt. He was badly shaken.

'You both all right?' he asked.

'What happened?' asked Annemieke, her eyes out on stalks. Lita's eyes were closed. She was praying to whichever god cared to listen.

Jan was surprised to see how little damage was done. The bumper was bent and the off-side rear mudguard. But both tail-light assemblies still functioned.

The driver who'd run into them was conciliatory. He'd lost a headlight and most of his grille. Clearly, he thought Jan was in the wrong for braking so suddenly. Jan was less forgiving and told him so.

'But,' his adversary claimed indignantly, 'everybody drives like this in Indonesia. You are in the wrong for not following closely enough behind the car in front of you. That is what caused the accident. If there had been no gap, you would not have been overtaken. If you had not been overtaken, you would not have needed to brake. If you had not braked, you would not have forced me to bump into you.'

He was right, Jan realised. The Indonesians were a nation of tail-gaters. He'd have to drive like them or not at all. They shook hands and a wary Jan drove on.

The wind had picked up and often Jan found himself driving blind, unwilling to brake in case the car behind ran into them again. Annemieke began to sing, softly, soothingly. She was the reason they were heading back to Tengkuban Prahu, and she was trying to help. She could see how tense Jan was. Under normal circumstances Jan would be touched. But tonight it interrupted his concentration and grated on him.

'Can't we stop?' Lita pleaded. She was scared and her voice showed it.

'Where?' asked Jan helplessly. 'If we stop on the side of the road there's a good chance a truck or bus will run into us. Besides, if we wait for daylight the traffic will only get worse. We're committed. We have to keep going. We have no other choice.'

'We'll be all right, Mummy,' whispered Annemieke from the dark of the rear seat. But she'd stopped singing and doubts had crept into her voice.

They crept onwards towards Bandung. Every time the car stopped in the queue for any length of time, Jan cleared the ash from the radiator. Other drivers did the same, faces swaddled in whatever cloth came to hand. Jan hadn't been the only one to inhale ash that night.

'Let's stop at the Savoy Homann,' Lita pleaded. But Jan had reached the stage where he just wanted to get home.

They drove through the centre of Bandung and began to ascend the hills towards Tengkuban Prahu. The traffic had thinned out a little. With a bit of luck, Jan thought, they'd arrive home around six or seven. He regretted leaving the lights of Bandung behind. Ash had irritated his eyes and made them sore. Now he had to peer once more into the gloom, tucked in behind the tail-light of the car in front. He could feel the tensions build up in him once more and waves of tiredness swept over him. He ached to rub his eyes but knew that would only irritate them.

As they got closer to Lembang, Jan let a gap grow in front of him. Cars streamed past at will till Jan found himself on stretches of road without another car in sight. Ash and dust swirled around them. Maybe the crater of Mount Tengkuban Prahu had come out in sympathy, Jan thought morosely. He could picture his tea bushes snowed under with ash. Tension eased with the traffic, and his attention began to wander. Then an oncoming or passing car would snap him back to reality, and he would start painfully, willing himself to remain alert. But his mind had found a warm, friendly place in his reveries, where it could relax.

His car started to wander as his concentration waned. He found himself looking for the roadside trees to guide the way, their trunks daubed with rectangles of reflective white paint. He began to greet them as friends and let them show him the shape of each curve. He adopted the habit of long-haul truckies who doggedly track the white lines on the road. There are no white lines on the road to Tengkuban Prahu, however, just white splashes of paint on the trees that mark most of the corners. But not all of them . . . Jan's dulled mind had not even begun to react when his car slammed head-on into one of those trees that had not been marked, and Annemieke hurtled past him taking the windscreen with her as she went.

Jan knew he'd crashed. But his brain was slow to acknowledge anything else. He heard a car horn blaring and realised it was his. The funny thing was he couldn't do anything about it. His right arm was jammed in front of him, and the steering wheel had moulded itself around his hips. Someone was pressing the back of his seat. It hurt. Who could possibly be doing that to him? Couldn't they see that it must hurt . . .

'Annemieke!' he screamed. 'Annemieke!' His mind recoiled at the horror it remembered. The fleeting impression of his precious daughter hurtling past him. 'Annemieke!'

'Be calm, Pak Jan, we are helping.'

For the first time he became aware of the presence of others. He could feel hands trying to free him. Why didn't they disconnect the horn? It would wake up Lita. Oh God! His shoulder exploded in pain.

'Very sorry, Pak Jan.'

Why couldn't he see properly? They were pushing his seat again and the pain raged through him. What was he trying to remember? It was something important. He turned to his left. There were more people huddled over something. Someone. Lita. Oh dear God!

'Lita!'

'Please stay calm, Pak Jan. We are doing all we can.'

His seat finally gave way to the efforts of his rescuers. The horn stopped. The pain in his shoulder eased marginally. He could hear soft voices and urgent whispers. He turned towards his wife as hands reached under him to lift him from the wreck.

'How is she?'

'She is unconscious, Pak. Her face is also cut and like you she has lost much blood. But her heart beats strong.'

So that was why he couldn't see. He tried to lift his hand to wipe the blood from his eyes but his shoulder shrieked a warning.

'Please move this leg, Pak. This leg. Yes! This leg. Now slide your backside, Pak, towards me, Pak. That is good, very good.'

Jan relaxed. Someone was in control. The quiet firm voice was in control. Somebody was taking care of everything. He would do as he was told. His mind sought a place of sanctuary but stumbled across a disturbing vision of his daughter disappearing through a million stars. The windscreen. Oh God. He began to sob.

'Are we hurting you, Pak? Perhaps there is another way.'

'No! Get me out! Get me out! Take me to Annemieke!'

'Gently, Pak, this way, gently.'

They reached under his arms and began to lift him gently from the wreck. The pain from his broken shoulder flared intolerably and he lost consciousness. When he came to, he was lying on the grass verge, his head cradled in someone's lap.

'Annemieke. Where is Annemieke?'

'She is gone through the windscreen, Pak Jan.'

'Take me to her.'

'That is not wise.'

'Take me to her. Please! I beg you! Take me to her.'

'If that is your wish, Pak.'

They helped him to his feet, over the grassy verge and storm ditch. In the beam from his broken, fading headlights, he could see shapes huddled over something where the grass gave way to the battalions of tea bushes. Tea. So close to home. So very close. His knees went and he nearly fell.

'Annemieke?' His voice was weak with the fear of what he might see. Strong hands steadied him. He edged towards her, legs rubbery, driven on only by a father's love.

'How is she?' he begged. And someone obligingly pointed the beam of their torch onto the shattered remnants of what had been Annemieke's face.

'Oh God, no!' he moaned. He sank to his knees, oblivious to his own pain. 'Oh dear God, no!'

'It is God's will,' someone soothed. 'His name be praised.'

'Is she . . . is she . . . ?'

'She lives, Pak. We have a van. I will drive you to hospital. My son will inform your staff.'

'You know me?'

'Of course, Pak. I am Djembar. My father worked for your father. My sisters pick your tea.'

Two women lifted Annemieke and carried her tenderly to the van. Jan followed, supported by his helpers. Lita was already in the van. She slumped unconscious in the back, supported by an old, grim faced woman who would not meet his eye.

She's blaming me, Jan thought. And why not? Why not? It's my fault. I have done this! The realisation hit him with numbing force. He cried out loud.

'Dear God, what have I done?'

They lay Annemieke down alongside Lita on cushions they'd stripped from the seats. Jan was helped in to the front seat alongside Djembar, and they began the trip back to Bandung.

Tears mingled with the blood and stung Jan's eyes and his head lolled forward on his chest. He'd killed his daughter. He'd killed his darling Annemieke. His heart broke and he fainted away.

'We must pray to God,' someone said in the darkness. 'Merciful God will decide.'

Ramon's voice faded away as it had on the Thursday before, and not even Neil was anxious to break the silence. Gancio rose quietly from his seat in the shadows where he'd been eavesdropping, anxious not to break the spell. His other lunchtime customers had left long ago. His afternoon staff had left soon after and his evening staff had not yet arrived. There was nobody to disturb the four friends. Gancio was careful as he prepared the tray but the smell of fresh coffee is seductive and the clink of cup on saucer irresistible to those in need.

'Well,' said Milos at length. 'You've earned your coffee. We all have. You tell a sad story, my friend. Once more you send us home with the weight of tragedy on our shoulders.'

'It is the story,' said Ramon. 'I cannot change that. Though God knows, there have been many times when I've wished I could.'

'Why do you keep doing this?' pleaded Lucio. 'You give us these beautiful women then you destroy them.'

'What would you have me do, Lucio, change my story? Pretend such things do not happen?'

'A storyteller always has the right to vary his story provided the changes aren't at odds with what has gone before.'

'I am aware of that, Neil, I have done that many times before with stories I've created. But this is different. There is no invention.' Ramon ran his fingers wearily through his hair. 'What do I have to do to convince you, Neil? This is a true story. This is how things happened.'

'Yeah,' said Neil thoughtfully. 'I'm beginning to suspect it is.'

THIRD THURSDAY

'What are you doing to your friends?' asked Gancio as he met Ramon at the door. 'Already they are on their second glass of Pinot Grigio. They were all seated by twelve o'clock.'

Ramon smiled.

'Ah, here is our storyteller,' said Lucio. 'We are all here, Ramon, eager for more.'

'Eager, yes,' Ramon said, as he shook hands with each of his friends, 'but for Gancio's creations and the Pinot Grigio. You have never arrived so early for my stories before. Why would you start now?'

'You kept us so late last Thursday we didn't have the opportunity for our usual post-mortem. So we came early today. That's all.'

'My apologies, Milos. I promise not to keep you so late today.'

'We didn't realise you were so familiar with Indonesia,' said Neil, upfront as always. 'You have lived there?'

'Did I say I had?'

'No, but it's a question of detail. How could you have come by all the detail if you haven't spent time there?'

'I am only repeating what was told to me. The gaps in my knowledge I have filled in myself. Do you think I have no access to books? I read prodigiously. Slowly, but perhaps more thoroughly than any of you.'

'You obviously have a great affection for Java.' Milos looked at Ramon with his half-smile that made him seem so innocent and harmless. 'Can anyone acquire such affection from books?'

'Shakespeare did.'

'Detail, yes . . . affection, perhaps not.'

Ramon shrugged.

'You picked an interesting place to build into your story.' Neil was in possession of a few facts and they burned to be aired. Given another life and greater opportunity he would have loved to be a public prosecutor. 'I looked it up in my atlas and got some information from Garuda. In a land of great volcanoes Tengkuban Prahu hardly rates a mention. And as far as I can make out there's not much reason to go to Bandung either. I'll take your word for the fact that you read more thoroughly than I, but you'd have to read a great number of books to find mention of either place. I'm convinced you've been there, maybe even lived there, and I don't understand why you're reluctant to admit it. What are you trying to hide?'

'Neil, there is no reason for you or I to go to Bandung or Tengkuban Prahu. Indonesia has so many other places which are much more interesting. But some people, like the Van der Meers, have every reason to go there. I told you this story is true. Could I tell it if I did not know the parties concerned and know them well? Could I know them well, without having spoken to them at some length? Really, what are you trying to prove? What is the point of this inquisition?'

Ramon had kept a smile on his face but the edge in his voice gave lie to it. People at other tables had turned to look at the men who seemed on the verge of quarrel.

'You should apologise to Ramon, Neil.' Milos spoke quietly but with the authority of the eldest. 'He hasn't even had time to sip his wine and already we've bombarded him with questions.'

Neil looked away, then back at Ramon.

'I am sorry, Ramon. But it's your fault I get so involved in your stories. And the stories that lurk behind your stories.'

'Neil's mouth sometimes works faster than his brain. That is his fault.' Lucio was anxious to placate Ramon and probably didn't intend to insult Neil quite the way he had. They all turned towards him, speechless.

'What'd I say?' asked Lucio.

Ramon began to laugh and Milos joined him, grateful for the diversion.

'Lucio, I think it is your turn now to apologise to Neil,' said Ramon. 'Then, when we have all apologised to each other, perhaps we can get back to the story.'

'No apology is necessary. Lucio was right. My brain's in neutral, my mouth in overdrive. The point is, Ramon, if your story is true – as you insist it is – and it trespasses on your life, then to what degree? What was the extent of your involvement? You must admit you've invited our speculation.'

'On the contrary. You are free to speculate but it is not at my invitation. Nor will I be drawn on the subject of my involvement or otherwise. I thought I'd made that quite clear at the beginning.' Ramon was delighted though his voice gave no hint. He could not have scripted things better. Clearly they had risen to his bait.

'That's true,' said Milos. 'But you often say one thing and mean precisely the opposite, no?'

'Do I?'

'You do and you know you do. But enough! It's time to just top up our glasses and let you get back to your story. Now, where are you going to take us today?'

'To Sydney airport to meet a man you probably feel you already know. His name is Eduardo Gallegos. Yes, I think you will recognise this man.'

'Intriguing. Will you find time to tell us about the boy Roberto?'

'Perhaps. I suggest we enjoy lunch. Signal Gancio so that he can tell us what delights he has in store.'

All in all, thought Ramon, the lunch had begun perfectly.

Chapter Eighteen

Eduardo arrived at Sydney airport on January 13, 1978, on a Qantas flight from Europe, relieved to have passed through immigration without hitch. He was now officially a resident of Australia, a new country with no burden of history to speak of, and a beckoning future.

He arrived with enough money to buy a small printing company needing only an infusion of capital, and the single-minded hunger of ambition. He also bought an apartment in a tower block, on the slopes of Rose Bay.

The two-bedroom layout was conventional, and the kitchen, bathroom and laundry were functional. The apartment was neither big enough to be large, nor small enough to imprison. Its single, overwhelming feature was its view. True, the aspect did not take in the Opera House or the Harbour Bridge, but these are mere adornments, jewels about the neck of the most beautiful harbour in the world. The view filled every centimetre of Eduardo's plate glass windows.

'Unsurpassed views of harbour to Manly,' said the estate agent's flyer, which was, for once, faultlessly accurate.

Eduardo was pleased with his new home, his eyrie as he liked to call it, and he was pleased with the potential of the company he had bought. But Eduardo was especially pleased with his adopted country. He loved the climate, and the easy-going attitude of the Australians. He thought they were the most likeable and commercially vulnerable people he had ever encountered – rather like Americans who hadn't lost their innocence and, at the same time, also rather British. This appealed to him, this expatriot *porteño*. *Porteños* have often been described as Italians who speak Spanish but think they're English. Eduardo liked to think he had a bit of the English in him.

On all counts, Eduardo should have been well-satisfied with the change in his life. But only amnesiacs can rule a line across their lives and deny all that has gone before.

In the stillness between the close of eyes and sleep, thoughts from his past returned unbidden to prick and twist and torment him. When sleep came, it would often bring Rosa.

He was in prison, along with hundreds of other victims of the regime. They stood in a line, pressed up against a stone wall. Men in bloody aprons waited behind marble slabs. The floor was awash with blood, and the drains were blocked with human organs. Rosa and Carlos walked along in front of the line selecting prisoners for execution. They were dragged to the marble slabs and disembowelled while their screams still rang from their throats.

He came to understand that Rosa held the power of life and death. She decided who would die, and who would be set free. He did not know why Rosa had been chosen for this job but suspected she had come to an arrangement with Carlos. She had condemned herself to a living hell in order to set free those she loved.

He watched her as she walked slowly towards him choosing her victims. She always bypassed Victor, Roberto and the girl Lydia. She freed six others he half recognised before she came to him. Then she would stand in front of him. Slowly she would raise her hand, and her unwavering finger would point at him. Eduardo would feel the arms grab him, arms that would drag him away to his death. He would scream and beg, but she was deaf to his voice. She never looked back.

He would wake up as they laid him on the marble slab, his sweat drenching the bed. Sometimes he would get up and lose himself in the distraction of late night television, with a large glass of whisky for company. Given time, he knew, the thoughts would fade and come no more. Given time.

The takeover of Leichhardt Printing was not the immediate success Eduardo had expected. Indeed, business took a sudden downturn. Quotes they would normally expect to win, went elsewhere. Clients who had been loyal for years sought alternatives. Presses lay idle, and those men with jobs dragged them out, and tried to make them fill the hours of their day.

Eduardo had been a fool. He readily conceded this. He had overestimated his ability and underestimated the task. He had not done his homework, had not taken the trouble to find out how either the city or the industry worked. He had made assumptions based on experiences in another country, in another life. They were mistakes his father would not have made.

When he purchased the business he did not feel it necessary to retain the services of the previous owners. In truth, he could not wait to get them out of the door. He made them agree to a no-compete clause, then sent them on their way.

That was his biggest mistake. The previous owners were brothers who had started the business and had built it up through the strength of their contacts. When the bond of mateship was severed, obligations ceased.

Eduardo also fired the foreman, a man who had worked with the company for more than thirty years and was hostile to change. Yet he knew every machine as intimately as other men know their mistresses. And he knew every job for every client that went through the shop. He was the man clients turned to when they needed priority or some other favour. He was the one they trusted to solve the thousands of problems that attach themselves to print jobs like ink to a page.

Eduardo had no choice but to dismiss him because he was an

obstacle to the changes Eduardo needed to make. Eduardo wanted new blood, but only a fool fires without a replacement in the wings. And he had been foolish.

He moved desperately to cover his errors. He wined and dined his way through the client list. But promises aren't bankable, and old bridges not easy to rebuild. He courted his plate-makers and the people who made his separations. Their fortunes, he reasoned, would rise or fall with his. But at the time, demand outstripped supply. They still made the plates and separations, but now they made them for his competitors. Their suggestion, meant kindly, for they had no dislike of this personable Argentinian, was to replace the man he'd fired with someone similar, poached from another printing company. That's how it worked, they said. People didn't lose their jobs, they simply changed desks. And took a salary increase along the way for the inconvenience.

The inertia in the industry began to wear Eduardo down. He needed a new entry point, a service nobody else offered, but was at a loss to know what it might be.

With little to do in the office, he began to walk the streets looking for ideas. He was taken aback by the number of bookshops and newsagents and began to count them. Then he began counting the titles of the magazines that crowded the racks, vying for space.

He had come from a country with a voracious appetite for magazines. The eleven million people of Buenos Aires could enjoy reading a phone book, if nothing else was available. Yet it seemed to Eduardo that the habits of his compatriots paled before the avid consumption of the Australians.

There were magazines on every conceivable subject of interest. Not one per subject, but competing titles, each helping to create a market and their own niche within it. He flicked through the magazines with mounting excitement. There were a few skinny publications, but most were plump and padded with glossy advertisements.

He bought women's magazines, men's magazines, cooking, gardening, sporting, electronic, computer and automotive magazines. He took them all home and pored over them. The most attractive pages were those that carried advertisements. Their layout was more adventurous, the thoughts more challenging and the use of type more tasteful and creative. Considerable amounts of money had been spent on their production and that fact was not lost on Eduardo.

He made a number of decisions that night, while the Manly ferries plied back and forth outside his plate glass windows.

Leichhardt Printing would change direction. He would still handle the institutional business and the packaging, but the company would now shift its focus to serving advertising agencies and, later perhaps, to publishing magazines.

He renamed his company the Hot Ink Press. He changed his hiring strategy. Instead of searching the printing industry for rising stars he now thought it incapable of producing, he turned his attention to advertising agencies. He wanted a man his potential customers would respect, who understood their needs and who had the courage to give up a secure job for the uncertain opportunities with an unknown Argentinian.

After more wining and dining, he unearthed one name that commanded both respect and genuine affection.

Phil Breedlaw was production manager of a multinational agency, and was responsible for all print production from artwork on. He was one of a proud but strangely masochistic band, who submitted their technical skills to the whim of art directors half their age. These art directors often had only a speculative idea of the result they wanted, and no idea at all about how to get it. That Phil was liked and respected by these high flyers with their fey talents was a tribute to his easy-going nature, and the long thankless hours he was prepared to put in.

When Eduardo finally convinced Phil to come and have a chat with him, his first reaction was one of disappointment. Eduardo was expecting a dynamo, but instead saw a tall gangling man in his late forties, wearing trousers that suggested prior ownership by someone considerably shorter. His hands and feet were disconcertingly large, and his haircut could only have pleased a sergeant major.

Eduardo tried hard to hide his dismay and disappointment. He reacted by being overly polite and considerate. But looks can deceive and hide depths that are not initially apparent. Eduardo found himself being interviewed. Thoughts he'd intended to keep to himself were dragged out for inspection and analysis. He found his ideas being enlarged and refined, and his elaborate courtesies gave way to excited discussion.

In years to come, they would debate whether Eduardo found the man he was looking for, or Phil the company. If marriages can be made in heaven then perhaps partnerships can as well, for that is how it seemed.

Through Phil's contacts, Hot Ink Press began to flourish. Phil knew where the money was and encouraged Eduardo to invest in the new computer technology and set up an art studio. He worked tirelessly and Eduardo would later concede that it was Phil who saved the business.

They offered advertising agencies quality and convenience and, most precious of all in an industry that always struggled to meet deadlines, they offered speed. The type and art studio worked around the clock in shifts. The roughs the agencies sent them by evening courier were returned fully comped by morning, always immaculately mounted and framed. They charged a fearsome price for these services, but agencies paid and paid willingly, as Phil had known they would.

Hot Ink Press became trendy and trendy people sought out Eduardo. They entertained him lavishly and he entertained them in turn. That was how he met Anders Peterson, creative director of one of the biggest agencies in town. Ridiculously good looking and ridiculously overpaid, Anders was almost half as talented as his personal PR machine made him out to be.

Meeting Anders was a direct consequence of Eduardo's decision to focus on advertising agencies. He understood clearly what a friendship with Anders could do for his business. But he could not begin to imagine the impact this man would have on his life, or how he would come to loathe him and blame him for the events that later took place. Eduardo did not know it, but he had set his course towards the point at which destiny turns and mocks those foolish enough to believe they are in control.

Chapter Nineteen

Although they did not see each other socially, Phil Breedlaw became the first good friend Eduardo made in Australia. Anders Peterson was the third. The second was a call girl.

Eduardo was not cut out for a life of denial. Yet he was scarred in his relationships with women and shied away from any emotional dependence.

He played with women the way sports fishermen play with fish, sometimes reeling them in, sometimes letting them run. The women who did not like this sport could get away easily enough, for light line suited his purpose and was easily broken. Those who stayed were the kind attracted to men with money or power, trading their bodies for dinner at Kables and the passenger seat in a Porsche. Some were clever enough to catch the fisherman, which was the ultimate prize, but none were clever enough to catch Eduardo.

Only once did he ever spend the whole night with a woman. It taught him a lesson. The nightmares had come and he'd cried out in his sleep. He'd woken in a cold sweat, the bedside light on, and this woman, not much more than a stranger, asking questions she had no right to ask. Doubtless she meant well, but Eduardo's response was to send her home in a taxi without explanation.

He was shallow and callous, though not without good reason. But who could possibly know those reasons, to understand and maybe even forgive?

There was one woman whom Eduardo genuinely liked and with whom he could relax, though he never confided in her. Her name was Estelle, and he met her at an advertising party. She was one of Anders Peterson's little pranks. She'd been hired along with others of her profession to take care of guests, should their sort of care be required. They came incognito, forbidden to disclose their true occupation, and were paid in advance. They were there to be picked up.

Eduardo saw through the charade the instant he stepped from the elevator. Knowing the game, he cheated. The girls were for the clients, not the suppliers, but Eduardo was sufficiently confident of his standing to steal Estelle.

His manners, as always, were impeccable, and he flattered Estelle with his attention and elaborate compliments. He set out to seduce Estelle as if she were a prized jewel of society.

Estelle was overwhelmed and, ignoring her training, allowed herself to be seduced into believing she was somebody else, the person Eduardo was creating. Ultimately, of course, she felt compelled to confess, but not before they had made love tenderly and thoughtfully, balcony doors open to the night, before that magnificent view.

Eduardo affected surprise at her revelation, and gave her no cause to feel shame. He graciously accepted the truth of it, and made her coffee. She was overcome by his worldliness and his tact. She thought he was the most remarkable man she had ever met.

He was probably the most cynical. In Estelle, Eduardo had found a solution to his problem. It didn't matter if he cried out in the night, for he knew she would ask no questions. It didn't matter if they saw each other often, because no emotions were involved other than the genuine affections friends might feel for one another. It helped immensely that they enjoyed each other's company.

Eduardo took her to the movies and to dinner, always paying for her companionship. She would argue about payment, but in the end would always accept his money gracefully.

The truth is, Estelle loved the way Eduardo made her feel, and the way he flirted with her. When she was with him, her self-esteem soared. She was beautiful, she was fun and above all she was worth something that had nothing at all to do with money. She liked to think of herself as his girlfriend. She took to wearing little or no make-up when they went out together, and wearing girlish clothes.

She became depressed when a week passed and Eduardo had not phoned her. She realised she needed him more than he needed her. But there were those times in the small hours when he would cry out and weep into his pillow. Then he would cling to her so tightly she could not move, and she would wonder what could possibly cause so much grief.

Estelle would probably have been happy to let their relationship drift along forever, but in fact the death knell was already sounding. As the friendship between Eduardo and Anders grew, Eduardo moved further into Anders' world. Anders knew all the right people and Eduardo was well aware of the importance of knowing the right people. So he courted Anders and his friends.

Anders was a show pony. At his advertising agency, he was regarded as a good strategist and a good thinker, a great presenter but creatively suspect. He knew what a great ad should be like, but was incapable of actually producing it. He stole ideas from his staff without a qualm. Yet invite him to a society function, and Anders went into hyper-drive.

His clothes were always the most outrageous, and his conduct the most extravagant. His male model looks never failed to grace the society pages, his arm in the firm safe-keeping of one heiress or another. It was as if Anders saved all his creativity and energies for his social life.

Society loved him, as much as it could love anyone, and he was always in demand. But few were more impressed with Anders' performance than Eduardo. Wherever Anders went, Eduardo was sure to go. They made a good team. Anders flashy and Eduardo urbane. They were eminently eligible targets, and targeted they were, by mothers who eagerly presented their daughters, ripe for the plundering.

As Eduardo's face became more widely recognised, his arrangement with Estelle became untenable. At first she had laughed at Eduardo's stories of foolish little rich girls, and she giggled when she saw his picture on the social pages. She was slow to realise the implications.

Eduardo was as gentle as he could be. He gradually extended the intervals between their meetings. The fact was, he could no longer afford to be seen with her, and she slowly came to realise this. Despite herself, she had surrounded their attachment with little myths and fantasies, some childish, but all of them precious. Their destruction brought heartbreak.

Eduardo was fond of her and her distress touched him deeply. But what choice was there? They each had lives to lead and their paths no longer converged.

'Will you still call me?' she asked.

'Of course,' he replied, and to his credit he did.

Some claim Eduardo's rise in Sydney society was as inevitable as the dawn. He was wealthy enough, or at least gave that appearance. He was sophisticated, heterosexual, and single.

He tiptoed lightly through attachments, artfully dodging entanglements, all the while putting on hold the sort of questions prospective parents-in-law with money feel entitled to ask. What else could a man with no past do?

Naturally there was speculation.

'He's a remittance man,' claimed the romantics, 'banished to Australia for some amorous indiscretion.'

'He's an opportunist, a johnny-come-lately from Leichhardt with ink under his fingers,' claimed others, 'trading on old world manners and an exotic accent.'

Anders would often be questioned about his friend, and asked to confirm or deny the latest rumours.

'He's just a good friend and a business colleague,' Anders would reply and laugh. Later he would relay the latest gossip to Eduardo, in the patently transparent hope that he would be forthcoming about his past. But Eduardo would only grin and shake his head.

'Such a big city. Such a small town,' he'd say.

Eventually Anders could no longer cope with the questions and Eduardo's continual evasions.

'For Christ's sake,' he said, 'what have you got to hide? This thing is getting bigger than Ben Hur. Everybody likes a mystery, Eduardo, but sooner or later the mystery has to be solved or everybody gets pissed off.'

Eduardo would no more take Anders into his confidence than run a full page confession in the *Sydney Morning Herald*. Yet he recognised the need to quell speculation because his silence only served to encourage it. He was not the only expatriate Argentinian in Australia and who knows whose ears might prick up and take notice? The time had come for the man with no past to acquire one.

'I will tell you this, Anders, and I ask you as my nearest and dearest friend not to betray my confidence. I do not speak of my past for only one reason. The memories are bitter and no useful purpose is served by reviving them. I do not want your pity nor the pity of our friends. I could not bear that. Some may see my story as heroic and me the tragic figure of misfortune, but that is a pathetic role which I'm anxious to avoid.'

Anders listened avidly, hanging on every word. Why is it that people whose stock in trade is the lie and the half-truth are themselves so easily gulled?

'You see, Anders, I come from a country where nothing is secure. Not property, nor reputation, nor life itself. Under the Generals, we have three choices. Side with the Generals or take no side at all, which amounts to the same thing, or align yourself with those who oppose them. It is easy to oppose the Generals. There is much to oppose, and there are many groups to join. But if you are caught you risk being hauled out of your bed in the middle of the night by the death squads. There is a name for people who oppose the Generals. They are *los desaparecidos* or the disappeared ones. Because once they catch you, you disappear. For ever. And so does your family's wealth. That is "redistributed".

'My family were wealthy. In Argentina the rich are very, very rich. They owned the controlling interest in an import-export business dealing in commodities, where the players were few and the prices easy to rig. Naturally, many palms had to be greased. Many large donations were made. To this day I am not sure what went wrong. I'm not sure whether it was my parents who became greedy or their beneficiaries.

'Whatever happened, my parents chose to align themselves with a group of liberal businessmen who were very vocal in their opposition to the Generals. They believed that they were wealthy enough to protect themselves from retaliation. They believed they had between them enough power to influence government and curb its excesses. To this day, I cannot believe the ease with which their egos overcame their intelligence.

'Of course it was foolhardy bravado. It was a scenario orchestrated by the Generals and their operatives. My entire family – my parents, brothers and sisters – were all swallowed up when the Generals cracked down.

'I know only the barest details. The soldiers came and my family ceased to exist. All our property and holdings were confiscated. I alone escaped because I was in America on business at the time. My uncle managed to phone me before he too was taken.

'I know my parents both had bank accounts in America and Switzerland because that is the practice in my country. But they never told me the details. Perhaps they left details with our lawyers, in a sealed envelope, addressed to their children in the event of their deaths. I would be surprised if they hadn't. But our lawyers never tried to contact me, and when I contacted them, they denied the existence of any such envelope. Obviously, I could not return to Argentina to challenge them.

'All I had left was my own bank account with the Chase

Manhattan, which my father had insisted I open. Without it I would have been left penniless, a pauper with no family and no country. It did not mean I was wealthy however. What little there was in the account brought me to Australia, and allowed me to purchase my apartment and the Hot Ink Press.

'That, Anders, is my story. You see why I choose not to repeat it, and why I must demand your discretion.'

'I'm sorry,' said Anders, genuinely moved, and for the moment convinced he would never tell a soul. But what value is there in a secret consigned forever to distant cells in a dull brain, its currency depreciating, its brightness dimming with each passing day? Within twenty-four hours, Eduardo's secret had burst the bounds of trust and friendship, and wormed its irresistible way onto Anders' tongue. The story spread from pillow to pillow, in whispers framed by promises of confidentiality, growing in detail and conviction, till all the curious were satisfied.

Eduardo caught the glances and the sympathetic smiles that blossomed around him, and milked the part, bearing his tragedy with an heroic stoicism. Yet his place in society was still very much that of the guest. He still had to supply the component that assured him of acceptance. He now knew what he had to give them, and began to contemplate ways of going about it.

Australia rushed headlong into the excesses of the mid-eighties. The entire population went on a spending spree as banks and other lending institutions fought with one another for the privilege of providing credit. Advertising agencies boomed as their clients spent big to grab as many of the consumers' borrowed dollars as they could. Their favoured suppliers boomed along with them.

The Hot Ink Press flourished, fronted by the stylish Eduardo, and backed by Phil's expertise. There seemed no limit to the possibilities. Money poured in the door, which they used to lease more equipment which could do things, faster, better and more cost efficiently. Their leasing commitments soared and their wages bill along with it. But they only had eyes for their turnover. How could they have problems when they were obviously doing so well? They had competition, powerful competition, but it seemed for the moment, at least, that they had them on the run.

Burton Simmons was their main competitor. They had dominated the profitable agency market until Eduardo had come along. Many of Eduardo's gains had been at their expense, but they were fighting back and more than matching Hot Ink Press' investment in new technology. For all that, Eduardo and Phil disparaged them as competition. As yesterday's heroes. Phil should have known better.

Burton Simmons had always been profitable and it caught the eye of the accountants. They saw the potential for even greater profits, and delegated the task of bringing them in to one of their whiz kids. The trade journals were full of the story as Burton Simmons announced the extent of their investment, and the services they would soon provide.

Eduardo and Phil were too successful to take much notice. Besides, the trade journals were only as accurate as the information they received. Nobody lied exactly, but you'd need extrasensory powers to discern the truth.

Another factor in the success of Hot Ink Press was undoubtedly the easy relationship that existed between Eduardo and Phil. They trusted each other and respected each other's special abilities. And beneath it all was genuine affection. They were two soldiers on the same side, fighting the same battle with different though entirely complementary weapons.

They rarely met socially, for outside work they had little in common. Nevertheless they enjoyed a meal together whenever they could and, through Phil, Eduardo was introduced to the delights of Asian cooking.

Eduardo became a devotee, and displayed all the zeal of a convert. He insisted all their business meetings took place in the evening over a meal, and they would agonise over their choice of venue. Eduardo had been raised on beef, yet he took to Sydney's prodigious choice of fresh seafood with the enthusiasm of a seagull. He loved sashimi, and whole snapper cooked Thai style. He loved oysters, lightly steamed with ginger and lime. He loved the fiery Szechuan dishes, the Malay prawn laksas, and fish balls with noodles in soup.

Through 1985, they continued to win clients from Burton Simmons and their success begat more success. They had the name and the reputation, and in the fickle world of advertising, that's usually enough to get the business. They were still a distant number two to Burton Simmons, but they dreamed of being number one.

The rude awakening came not long before Christmas. In the space of one week, they lost their two largest clients to Burton Simmons. Eduardo was aghast. He couldn't think what had gone wrong. Phil couldn't help. Phil showed him a note of thanks he'd received for the last job they'd done. The agency could hardly have been more effusive in its praise.

Eduardo rang both agencies asking why they'd taken their business away. In both cases, he got the same answer. Burton Simmons had made them a proposition which they could not refuse. As Phil sniffed around the trade, the details became clear. Burton Simmons were discounting. They had bought the business back at a price that could never return a profit.

'What's going on?' Eduardo asked Phil.

'I'm not sure. We've hurt them a bit, but not so much that they have to start giving their services away. The business we've taken off them means a lot to us. But it's not much more than a drop in a bucket to them.'

'How badly will it hurt us?'

'Don't know.' Phil thought for a second. 'We're going to have to replace it or lay off people, I guess. We'll have to check with Don.'

Don was their accountant. He was a fussy little man, precise in his habits and his dress. He had an overinflated sense of self-importance and an over-elaborate moustache. He wore both blatantly.

The obvious step was to invite him to meet over dinner. After all, Christmas was just weeks away, and it was their custom to take their accountant to a celebratory meal. Besides, in the scheme of things, this setback could only be temporary. Business was just too good.

They met the following night. Don listened politely as Phil and Eduardo discussed various ways in which they could maintain their technical advantage. They discussed the merits of yielding their pre-eminence to Burton Simmons and other competitors.

'Let others bear the cost of introducing agencies to the new technology,' Eduardo argued. 'We should sit back and see which system proves most popular, then come in with second generation equipment. That is how we will regain the advantage.'

'If you're intending to lease more new equipment, I would advise against it,' Don cut in quietly.

Eduardo and Phil were stopped in their tracks. They turned to their accountant, clearly concerned. Don was a plain talking man. That was one of the qualities they most admired about him. He never hid behind the jargon of his profession nor was he one to equivocate. But, while plain talking and straight dealing are admirable qualities, truth untempered by tact can have a rude, bludgeoning bluntness. And that night Don bludgeoned them.

'You're running very close to the wind.' he said. 'The fact is, you're too highly geared. You're in danger of losing it all. You've been paying too high a price for your success.'

Eduardo choked. Colour drained from his cheeks. 'Please explain,' he managed, in a voice stripped of all confidence. 'We were under the impression that we're doing rather well.'

'You're overextended. You've tried to run too far, too fast, too soon.' The accountant's thin voice took on a headmasterly quality. It almost seemed as though he took a perverse pleasure in delivering the bad news to his clients.

'You're updating equipment faster than you're paying for it. You need a twenty percent increase in turnover, beyond projections, just to service your debt.'

'But we are ahead of projections,' said Phil defensively.

'So you should be,' replied the accountant, with irritating confidence, 'to allow for the Christmas lull and January. All you need is a slow February or a default on a major bill, and you'll struggle to meet your lease commitments. Of course the banks will help, but that will only compound the problem. If the advertising industry takes a downturn, you're gone. If you lose one of your direct clients you're gone. If they take their packaging or catalogues elsewhere, well, you don't need me to tell you the impact that would have. And there's one other thing beyond your control or mine. Word's about that interest rates are set for a hike. Any idea what effect a one percent increase would have on your overdraft?'

'God help us,' said Eduardo. 'Phil, are you going to tell him or shall I?'

'It's your business, Eduardo.'

'Tell me what?' asked Don.

'We have a small problem.' Eduardo explained the loss of their two biggest accounts on the typesetting and studio side of their business.

'Well, you're in serious trouble. But before I suggest a scenario to you, what other exposure do you have that I don't know about?'

'I've talked to all my clients,' said Phil. 'Some have knocked back the Burton Simmons deal because they feel we do demonstrably better work. Of course, we've had to renegotiate rates, but really they're just token concessions. Ass protectors, if you like. Eduardo knows more about the printing side.'

'Only one potential problem I know about,' said Eduardo after some thought. 'We've been asked to quote on the new packaging for our biscuit-making friends. We do this each year. It keeps us honest and sets a benchmark whereby we do all subsequent packaging without requoting.'

'Who are we up against?' asked Phil.

'Lavenders and Alexander Printing.'

'Jesus.' Phil had turned pale.

'What's the matter?'

'The same people who own Burton Simmons' own Alexander Printing. They're both part of Austral Corp.'

'If I were you, gentlemen, I would not count on winning that account. Let me try out this scenario on you. If you were Austral Corp and you'd just purchased Burton Simmons, and invested who knows how many millions in new equipment, how would you protect your investment?'

'Please continue,' said Eduardo, though he could see clearly where Don was headed.

'First step, crush your competition. Or if the competition is highly profitable, absorb them. Gentlemen, they've chosen their moment to strike very well. Christmas-New Year is the worst possible time for cash flow. Staff move around so they know what equipment you have and what your commitments are likely to be. They know your vulnerabilities. They've stolen two of your biggest clients and are all set to steal a third. What does it matter if they lose money on the deal? If you go bad they'll swoop in and pick you up for next to nothing.'

'What do you propose?' asked Eduardo. He could not believe they could be so successful yet still go under.

'Usual solutions apply, I suppose. You could sell. I'm sure you could find a buyer other than Burton Simmons. But Burton Simmons may be happy for a quick resolution. They may agree to a price which rewards you reasonably for what you've put into the business. They'd want to lock you in on service contracts though. Again, another option, they may even settle for a minority interest. However, it seems a pity to give someone else the benefit of all your hard work. You could take on a partner. That would give you the injection of capital you need, but also lumber you with a partner not of your choosing. And you'd still be vulnerable to price cutting by Burton Simmons.'

'There must be some other way,' said Eduardo grimly. 'Please keep talking. It helps me look for ideas.'

'If your business was more broadly based, provided you could broaden it without adding to your debts, you could solve the problem. At least, it would provide a cushioning effect. The difficulty is, you'd have to move very quickly.'

'Why don't we all have another beer?' suggested Phil.

'Ah, Phil, I can always count on you in a crisis.' Eduardo began to laugh. The accountant was nonplussed, but his high pitched laugh joined theirs.

'I have an idea,' said Eduardo. He could see a possible solution to their problem which would secure his business and his place in the social life of Sydney.

'We're going to expand,' he said. 'We're going to broaden our base, and I'm going to take on partners.'

'Who?' asked Phil.

'You for a start. Come on, Phil, it's time you owned a part of the action. Profit share is just fence-sitting. Mortgage your house, sell your children, do whatever you have to do. Our friend here will make sure the price is right, for he too is now invited to become part of our business.'

He turned to his accountant.

'You know so much about our business, Don, why don't you run it? Leave Phil and I free to do what we do best. Your job will be to keep the business on a secure and profitable footing. Sell your business. Use the money to buy into ours. In ten years time you will be able to retire a rich man.'

'I would like time to think about this,' said Don.

'What have you got to lose?' Eduardo was persistent. 'If it doesn't work out, we'll sell. Try and tell me you won't do very nicely out of that. Besides, it's time you had a job that added value to the community, you've said so yourself. It's time you did something more than just look at the books of other people who are out there doing something. Making something. Come on, you are living vicariously. What is your expression? Yes, it's time to piss or get off the potty.'

'Burton Simmons will make things very difficult for us.'

'Yes. And we will make things bloody difficult for them!'

'Count me in.' Phil took a long pull on his beer and wiped his hand across his mouth 'God help me when the wife finds out.'

'Tell her you're going into the publishing business,' said Eduardo. 'Phil, you and I and our fiscal friend here are going to publish magazines. Tell me, Phil, what do you know about Indonesia?'

'They make bloody good satays. What do you know about Indonesia?'

'A booming economy and fledgling advertising industry. I've been talking to a creative director who has just come back from Jakarta. I suspect our old equipment would be quite useful up there. It could provide cash flow while we set up our main interest which will be publishing. Labour costs there are minimal. We can set up the publishing operation in a bonded area and serve Singapore, Australia, New Zealand and all south-east Asia from there.'

The detail would follow, Phil knew. Eduardo would need time to think it all through. He also knew Eduardo well enough to know this idea must have been maturing in his brain for some time. He felt euphoric. Eduardo had returned to his normal confident self and Phil would back him with every cent he had. So would the accountant. He'd hinted at it more than once. They'd be a good team. And Phil could not help but feel flattered whenever Eduardo displayed his confidence in him so publicly.

He forgot Eduardo's brief moment of panic and the weakness he had glimpsed. Confidence is contagious. Isn't that what had almost brought them undone?

Of course, it would take time. And in the meanwhile they would come under increasing pressure from Burton Simmons and their associated companies. But they would hang in. Now that they knew the nature of the game, they would take appropriate action. God damn it! They were just too good to go under. Weren't they?

Ramon eased slowly back into his seat to indicate intermission.

'I have told you enough for now about this man Eduardo Remigio Gallegos. Last week we all went home exhausted. Today I will pace myself.' He wondered who would be first to speak.

'You've done it again,' said Neil, and Ramon knew instantly that the seeds he'd sown had taken root. 'You've given this Eduardo your mannerisms. Or have you just lent them to him?'

'They are his mannerisms. But there is no reason why they should be dissimilar to mine.'

'Neil's right,' said Milos. 'The man you describe is also about your vintage, no? And of course you would have similar backgrounds.'

'The memories are bitter and no useful purpose is served in reviving them.' Neil caught Ramon's accent and inflections to perfection. 'You obviously learned to speak English by studying classical English. Your sentence structure, if you don't mind my saying so, is archaic, though your grammar is probably better than mine. Where did you learn your English? Where did Eduardo learn his? Or have you just given him the benefit of your education? Lent that to him as well, perhaps?'

Ramon was pleased by the continual reference to Eduardo. Nobody mentioned Jorge. And Neil always left the gate open, offering him a chance to distance himself from his double in the story. Unquestionably, they all wanted him to dispel their nagging suspicions. Ha! The game had only just begun.

'I learned my English in school and I graduated in English with honours at the University of Buenos Aires. I told you that *porteños* are Italians who speak Spanish but think they are English. There are parts of Buenos Aires where only English is spoken. Parts of Belgrano and Ranelagh. I had many friends there.'

'And Eduardo?' asked Neil.

'Eduardo also learned his English this way. That is not surprising. It is a very popular course. Some students, however, adopt Americanisms. Eduardo was not one of them.'

'You still maintain this is a true story?' asked Lucio, who had been uncharacteristically silent.

'Yes.'

'For once I think he's telling the truth,' said Neil quietly. 'I guess time will tell. Gancio's kindly brought our coffees. May as well drink them while they're hot.'

They sipped their coffees and cognacs in reflective silence.

'What will you tell us next?' asked Milos eventually. 'Will you tell us what happened to the boy Roberto? My wife also would like to know. She believes Roberto is the key to the story.'

Ramon smiled. Milos claimed he always went straight home and brought his wife up to date with whatever story was being told while it was fresh in his memory. Ramon suspected, however, that he also used her name to make observations which, if proved incorrect, would not reflect upon him.

'Perhaps. I thought you'd be more interested to hear what happened to Annemieke. I thought I would give the rest of the afternoon to her, though you complain that I always send you home with the weight of tragedy upon you. Perhaps I should continue with the story of Eduardo Remigio Gallegos. You tell me, which one would you like to hear more about?'

'I would like you to tell us more about Eduardo,' said Neil without hesitation.

'No!' cut in Lucio. 'I would like to know what happened to Annemieke. She did not die, you have already indicated that she did not die. You said death may have been a greater kindness. I think you should explain that.'

'I am surrounded by children.' Milos pretended to pull out what little hair he had left in frustration. 'Can you simpletons not see that Roberto may be the key to the story? Why do you think Ramon began with Roberto? Tell us more about Roberto. If that does not answer our questions, at least our questions will be more clearly defined.'

'It seems I have the casting vote. That is how it should be. The storyteller should never surrender control of his story.' Ramon smiled but inside he was furious with himself. Hadn't he just put control of his story up for auction? He could not think what had possessed him to do so. What if they had persisted with Roberto? It wasn't yet time to pursue Roberto's story. Milos was right. Roberto was the key, but the key was not yet ready to be cut. He would have to be more careful.

'I cast my vote. I give it to Lucio.'

'I will warn Gancio,' snorted Milos. 'He can reset the table. We will need handkerchiefs instead of tissues, no?'

Chapter Twenty

Bromeus Hospital is the best in Bandung, though there are many who dispute the claim in favour of Rajawali. Its theatres are well equipped and it is staffed by the elite of the medical profession. But that night, as Annemieke lay on the operating table, its resources were sorely tested by the casualties of Mt Galunggung.

Besides the horrific lacerations to Annemieke's face, broken ribs had punctured a lung, she had multiple fractures to both arms, and her nose and right cheek were so badly smashed, the sight of her right eye was threatened. She had lost a lot of blood, some of which pooled dangerously in her damaged lung, and she was badly concussed.

The surgeons who operated on her worked zealously to save her life. They put the broken child together again, set the broken bones, stitched the torn flesh, inflated the collapsed lung, and replenished her dwindling blood. They did a good job. But they were not, nor would they ever claim to be, cosmetic surgeons.

Lita's injuries although considerable, were less severe. Her seatbelt tore rib cartilages, and the buckle ruptured her spleen. Her hip was broken. She was also concussed and badly lacerated where the dashboard had buckled inwards and met her forehead.

Jan, too, was knocked out, but on doctor's orders. He wanted to be with Annemieke. He wanted to be with Lita. He wanted to hold them and tell them he was sorry, and beg for forgiveness. He was distraught with guilt. He was judge and jury, convicting himself without representation by the defence, or acknowledgement of mitigating circumstance. He fought the nurses and their aides until their numbers and the searing pain of his broken shoulder took its toll. He never felt the needle that brought temporary peace to his troubled mind. They kept him under heavy sedation for three days.

It didn't matter. They would not have let him in to see Annemieke or Lita and, even if they had, there was little to see of either beneath the swaddling of their bandages.

They took him to see Lita on the fourth day. The drugs that relieved her of her pain also held her in the twilight between sleep and reality. Her face, but for her eyes and mouth, was still mercifully hidden by dressings. Jan looked at her bare arms, swollen where they should be so slender and splashed purple with bruising where they should glow with coppery translucence.

'I'm sorry,' he whispered as tears filled his eyes. Tears for her suffering. Tears for his regrets. Tears because he couldn't take her in his arms and find the comfort he needed – the comfort she'd always provided him. He could not even bend down to kiss her. The rigid cast holding his arm and shoulders prevented him.

'I'm so sorry,' he whispered again.

Lita reached out and took his good hand in hers and squeezed as hard as her diminished strength would allow. She locked her eyes on his and Jan drew comfort as he had so often in the past. But Jan had misread the signals.

'Annemieke,' she gasped, and clawed at his hand. She desperately wanted reassurance that Annemieke was all right in this brief moment of clarity before the sodium amytal once more reclaimed her. But Jan interpreted her desperation as accusation and pulled away from her. His worst suspicions were confirmed. She blamed him! She blamed him! She had turned from him when he needed her most. He was bewildered and hurt, like a wronged child.

Fortunately for Lita, the effort took its toll and her eyes closed. She drifted off into troubled sleep. Does the mind heal during sleep, retaining what information it has need of, and discharging the rest? Possibly. For when she awoke Lita had no recollection at all of Jan's visit.

Jan left Lita's ward feeling damned. He needed absolution. Perhaps Barnaby and Neneng could have provided it. But they'd broken their vigil and returned to the Savoy Homann to sleep. There was only one person he could turn to. Once more reason fell victim to emotion, and he stomped the corridors demanding to see Annemieke. Once more nurses had to abandon their tasks and rush to pacify him.

'She is unconscious still, Bapak,' they said. 'She will not recognise you. Your visit will serve no purpose.'

'Where is she?' he bellowed. 'Take me to her. Now!'

'She is still in intensive care, Bapak. We do not allow visitors there. Please, Bapak, let us take you back to your ward.'

Jan's grief and despair was there for all to see, and the nurses and orderlies were not immune to it. He was the girl's father, she his daughter, and her life may yet be lost. They said they would take him to her ward. They would let him peep through the doorway. But they cautioned him that if he set one foot inside the door they would hit him with a needle.

They were good people and Jan had used his size and strength unfairly. He suddenly felt ashamed as his unanchored emotions swung with this latest change in breeze. His shame extinguished the fires of his rage and his strength left him.

'Take me in a wheelchair,' he mumbled, and they gratefully raced to fetch one.

They let him peep through the door but he never saw her. All he saw was a child's form swathed in bandages and plaster, and hooked up to nightmarish machines. Jan's guilt flooded back and unbearable remorse bore down upon him. He buried his face in his good hand. They sedated him then and there as an act of kindness.

Annemieke did not regain full consciousness for another two days, and drugs held her in her own never-never land for another three. Young bodies are fast healers, but healing and recovery are always a matter of degree. She was out of danger, there was that to be grateful for. But she was unrecognisable, even to her parents, when her dressings were being changed.

'It is too early to judge the outcome,' insisted her doctors. 'See how her face is swollen? But we are optimistic.'

They were right, of course. Her face was grossly swollen, her right eye closed over, her nose a shapeless lump, and everywhere, like the streetmap of a madman's town, there were angry red lines of lacerations and the cross-hatching of sutures.

Jan was stricken. He couldn't bear to visit Annemieke alone. He would no longer look upon the sleeping child unless all her bandages were in place. He would visit her with Lita when she was able, and Barnaby or Neneng when she was not. He would wait anxiously for them to arrive at the hospital, but once they were there he'd procrastinate. He could feel himself withdrawing from Annemieke and was powerless to stop. When he was with her he would take hold of her foot, seemingly the only part free of injury, only to release it in anguish before taking it up again, and releasing it, endlessly, unthinkingly.

Lita knew the agonies he was going through. Hadn't she recognised his vulnerability from the time they'd met? She used to call him a softie and a big sook as she soothed him, but these words were inappropriate now. Annemieke was his special weakness, and many times she had envied the relationship between them. She realised that she would need all her skills to comfort Jan, and make him realise that what had happened was an accident, that he was free from blame. Jan would listen to her words and want to believe them, but deny them all the same. She soothed him and when that didn't work, she berated him.

'How can you be so heartless?' she accused. 'How can you wallow in your own self-pity when she needs you? Go to her. Sit with her. Talk to her. Tell her stories. Tell her everything will be all right. Don't abandon her. Don't think that because her eyes are closed she cannot hear. The words are not important. It's your presence that matters. You must be there whenever she opens her eyes.'

'She'll never forgive me,' he pleaded. 'What I've done to her, she'll never forgive me.'

'Jan, it was an accident. There is nothing to forgive. Go to her. Don't abandon her. She will think she has done something wrong.'

Their words chased each other endlessly, and resolution was as elusive as last night's dreams. Mercifully, Annemieke was still under the spell of her medication. She sensed something was amiss as she drifted in and out of the fog. Something she had grown up with and taken for granted had changed. Something she had built her faith upon. But she could not yet work out what it was.

Annemieke awoke on the morning of her tenth day in hospital and knew immediately that this day was different. The medication had worn off and not been replaced. The clouds and fog lifted, and she began to string thoughts together once more. She knew she'd been in an accident. That much had penetrated her fog-bound mind. And she knew both her parents were all right because she was aware that they'd come to see her. She'd wanted to hug them, but there was a savage weight upon her chest and she could not move her arms. That was a funny thing. Where were her arms? She tried to open her eyes. One obliged, one didn't. And the one that did was blurred. She wanted to rub it awake but there was the problem with her arms again. Where were they? Where were her arms? She tried to sit up but warning pains in her chest stopped her. She became aware of other pain. Her face hurt a bit as well, and there was a dull ache in her head. What had happened to her? She began to feel afraid. She sobbed. A strange sound she hardly recognised as her own. She felt imprisoned. Not imprisoned. What was it? Paralysed! She was paralysed! Again she heard that strange sound that began as a sob. Then a voice, a kind, gentle voice, and a white shape appeared in her blurred and limited vision.

'Hello,' it said cheerily. 'I am Tin. I see you have decided to wake up. How do you feel?'

Annemieke clutched at the salvation the kind voice seemed to offer.

'Goo . . .' she said.

'Good?' asked the nurse. 'Excellent. I'll go and call the doctor. He'll want to see you while you're feeling so good.'

'Don't go!' cried Annemieke quickly. She was scared. There were things she didn't understand, things she wanted to know and she wasn't ready to be left alone. She wanted to know if she was paralysed but, in the end, the prospect was so terrifying she was too afraid to ask. Desperately she sought another reason to stop her nurse leaving.

'I can't thee clearry.'

'One moment,' her new friend said, and disappeared from view. Then Annemieke could feel warm, wet cottonwool wipe across her good eye and then a tissue. She opened her eye and looked into the face of her Sundanese nurse, hovering over her. She saw something else which both reassured her and frightened her at the same time. She found her arms, white columns reaching up in front of her. She'd seen enough school friends with plastered limbs to know what that meant, but at least it solved one mystery.

'Better?' asked Tin, her nurse.

'Yeth.' Then as an afterthought. 'My armth are broken.'

'Yes. And three ribs. And your nose. And your cheekbone. Oh, you should have seen the mess you were in when they brought you here. You are a very lucky girl, Annemieke.'

Annemieke couldn't possibly imagine how anyone could think she was lucky.

'Enough talking now. The doctor will want to see you before your parents come. Now don't go away.'

There it was. Confirmation. Her parents were all right and better than that, they were nearby. She could feel tears welling up and when she tried to stop them by scrunching up her good eye, someone set fire to her face. It was so unexpected and so sudden. The tears came in a flood she didn't dare stop. She barely dared to breathe in case the pain returned.

'Oh dear,' the kind voice said again, and she felt a tissue wipe across her eye. 'It's all right, Annemieke. Just lay still. The doctor is here.'

Annemieke opened her eye once more to see a dark, friendly face staring down at her.

'Well, well, how are we feeling this morning? A fine day for recuperation, I am thinking.'

His accent was strange, and to Annemieke's ears, almost comical. She wondered if she was dreaming. But Dr Ganguly was real enough, and his lapse into his native Indian accent was deliberate. He used it often as part of his bedside patter. It usually brought a smile to the face of patients who otherwise had no reason for smiling.

'My face hurtth. Thon fire,' said Annemieke.

'Well, we shall just have to put out the fire. Let me see.' The doctor shone a light into Annemieke's eye.

'Very good,' he said and then began to remove bandages. Annemieke had not been aware that her head was bandaged, but now when she thought of it, vague half memories drifted by. Of course! The doctor took his time. In fact he seemed to take an extraordinary amount of time.

He looked at her closed eye.

'Soon we'll be having it as good as new,' he said.

Then gently, ever so gently, he began to touch different parts of her face.

'Can you feel this?' he asked.

'Yeth. Yeth. Yeth. No. No.'

The examination continued. Annemieke concentrated, but she

couldn't always feel the doctor's touch, no matter how hard she tried. She didn't want to disappoint him, but the doctor didn't seem to mind in the least.

'Very good,' is what he said.

He turned his attention to her ribs.

'Ouchth,' she said.

'Very good, very, very good,' he said.

He tickled the soles of her feet and tapped her knees. It hadn't occurred to her to move her legs till now, and she was greatly relieved to feel them respond. But raising them hurt her ribs and her hips felt tender and bruised. Any lingering thoughts of paralysis evaporated.

'Very good,' said the doctor once more, looking extremely pleased with himself. 'Who would believe this is the same young woman they are bringing in ten days ago? Bloody marvellous.'

Tin laughed. Dr Ganguly's performance wasn't entirely wasted.

Annemieke wanted to smile. It seemed she was making everybody around her happy, and she wanted desperately to please for the reassurance it brought. But the effort had made her weary, and the pain had returned. She licked her lips so she could speak and thank the doctor.

Conscious now of every little movement, she became aware of how swollen her tongue was, and how lethargic. And something else. Teeth were missing. How many she couldn't guess, because her swollen tongue made detailed exploration difficult.

The nurse began to paint antiseptic onto her face and Annemieke concentrated once more on the touch of the swab she used. But it proved elusive no matter how hard she concentrated. Sometimes she could feel it so much it tickled. Other times she could feel nothing at all.

'Hello,' said the nurse unexpectedly. 'I think you'll find your daughter a lot brighter today. Right, Annemieke?'

Annemieke tried to turn in the direction of the voices she heard. The voices she longed with all her heart to hear. Her mum and dad had come to see her. Her spirits soared, but the sudden movement brought her back down to earth with a thump. Her face once more caught fire as if somebody had thrown petrol on it and struck a match. She fought back the tears. She wasn't going to cry, not now, not in front of her parents.

Annemieke turned her head as far as the pain would allow. She saw her mother first. She was sitting. No! She was in a wheelchair. And her face was also bandaged. Annemieke's mind reeled. Her good eye searched for her father and found him. He only had one arm! Alarm flashed across her face. Lita quickly reached across and stroked her hair.

'Shhhh,' she soothed. 'We're all right, little one. Don't be upset. I'll be out of this wheelchair soon enough, long before you and your father come out of your casts.'

Annemieke looked again at her father, and saw the cast about his shoulder and his missing arm strapped across his chest.

'I thought you'd lotht your arm,' she said and smiled.

To her horror, her father reeled back. She couldn't know what effect her attempt at a smile would have on him. Jan was already distressed. He'd steeled himself to look once more on the sight he tried so hard to avoid. He wasn't prepared for her mouth to open, lopsidedly, and reveal a gaping black hole where once her perfect white teeth had been. Now his worst fears flooded back. He had destroyed his daughter's face. He had robbed her of her beauty. He had taken a young face, so beautiful the angels would weep to gaze upon it, and turned it into something grotesque. A travesty. He could not help himself. In his horror and his shame, he reeled back and turned from her. He fled from the room.

'Dad! Dad! Come back!' Annemieke turned to her mother, imploring her to do something. To bring him back. To tell her what she had done wrong.

But on her mother's face she saw a look of such pain and hurt, she couldn't bear it. What had happened? What had she done wrong? Annemieke's mind whirled helplessly and she began to sob. And each sob added fuel to the blaze that now raged across her face, and twisted the knife in her side where her ribs had barely begun to heal.

'Mieke ... Mieke ... stop!' she heard her mother cry. But nothing would stop her.

'Nurse!' called her mother. 'Oh Mieke, Mieke ... please don't cry. Please, baby.'

Tin was quickly by Annemieke's side, plunging a hypodermic into her drip. Slowly Annemieke calmed as the sedative went about its task. Her breathing evened and the pain in her side faded away.

'What did I do wrong?' she asked her mother, eyes pleading.

'Nothing, pet, nothing. It's all right. Everything will be all right. Your father is just upset to see you, that's all. You know what he's like when you're sick. You know what a softie he is. He can't stand it when anything happens to his little angel. You know that, don't you? He loves you more than any one in this world.'

'Yeth,' said Annemieke.

'We'll just have to be brave, Mieke. We'll have to give him time to get over it.'

Her mother's voice had grown distant and she seemed a long way away.

'Osshhh,' her mother said, stroking her hair.

'Osshhh ...' Annemieke echoed, and thoughts of the tiny monkey filled her head as sleep stole her away.

Chapter Twenty-One

The big man sat like a small boy on Lita's bed as she quietly, and without anger, told him how much he had hurt Annemieke and how much he had frightened her. Jan had no defence other than his sense of guilt, which Lita would not accept.

'There can be no guilt because there was no fault,' she insisted. 'It was an accident. That is fate, that is the way things are. It was our fate to have that accident, to leave Pengalengan when we did, though both of us knew it was foolish to do so. No one can change their fate. And only a fool dwells on the past because that cannot be changed either. But if you are convinced you have done wrong, then make good your mistake. Go to her. Give her all the love you can find in your heart. Be her friend. Be her strength. Be her father!' Her voice had risen but she checked herself. She hadn't finished with him. She would stand over him to make sure he performed all his duties faultlessly. If he insisted on behaving like a child, she would treat him like one.

When she is well enough to ask for a mirror,' she said quietly, 'you will hold it for her.'

'No!'

'Yes, Jan, you will. You will hold the mirror for her and tell her how well she is progressing. You will tell her that everything will soon be back to normal. And if she is upset, you will wipe away her tears and comfort her. She needs you, Jan. She looks to you for her strength. You cannot fail her. You must not let her down.'

Jan could not meet Lita's eyes. When he finally did, he saw a face that could have been carved from stone.

'I've arranged for an orthodontist from Jakarta,' he mumbled. 'She has lost some teeth, but others were just snapped off. We can cap some and perhaps replace the missing ones with ceramic teeth. It would be much better than a plate.'

'Did you ask them to send for a new father as well?' Lita asked bitterly. 'A real father. Mieke can do without teeth for now, she can't do without her father.'

'I'm doing my best. I'm doing my best for her.' His voice lacked conviction. Wearily, he ran his hand over his brow. 'Oh dear God, I don't know what to do.' He turned to Lita for help, but it was not forthcoming. Lita had hardened herself against his agony.

'I have spoken to Qantas. Mieke will be able to fly in two weeks. Maybe things will be better when we get home.'

'Things will have to get better here first,' said Lita pointedly, 'or we're not going.'

Jan was taken aback. Did she really mean what she said? She did. Her eyes were hard and her jaw was set.

'Go to her, Jan. And when she asks to look in a mirror, you make sure you hold it. Not the nurse, not the doctor, not me. You hold the mirror. You are not responsible for the accident, but you are responsible for her. Only you can help her come to terms with what has happened to her, and how her life has changed. Only you.'

Jan was big. But he found he didn't have the strength to defy the tiny, determined woman who sat before him.

'Okay,' he whispered. 'I'll do it.'

If he had just volunteered to test a hangman's noose, his face would not have been more grim.

But Lita did not see his face. She had turned her wheelchair away from him. She had turned her back to him, isolating him, shunning him. As he had done to Annemieke.

* * *

Jan was as good as his word. He left Lita and went straight back to Annemieke. He sat with her while she slept and he was the first thing she saw when she woke up.

'Oh, Daddy' she said and wept great tears. Jan dabbed them away with cottonwool. He apologised. He promised he would never walk away from her again. He sat with her all the rest of that day. He stroked her hair and read to her. They played 'I Spy' knowing full well that all Annemieke could see laying flat on her back was the ceiling and the ropes and pulleys that held her plaster-encased arms. It became their private joke as Jan consistently failed to call 'ceiling' for something beginning with 'C'. She did not notice that Jan would always excuse himself when her bandages needed changing. If she thought about it at all, she would have thought Jan was just making room for her nurse.

When she returned from the operating theatre, her gums swollen and throbbing from the implantation of her new teeth, Jan was there when she woke up. They'd also taken the opportunity to rebuild her shattered nose, so her face was once more puffy and sore and new dressings covered both eyes.

'Love you, Daddy,' she slurred, from her drug induced depths.

'Love you too, Mieke,' he replied. But his soft voice belied his mood.

Annemieke never complained, even when pain caused her to cry out. And though she dreaded being wheeled off to theatre, she never voiced her fears to her father. Perhaps she should have. Then Jan could have helped, and in the act of helping, begun to assuage his guilt. But her courage stood solidly by her. And she did not want to risk upsetting Jan and losing him again.

Each time they took her to theatre and each time they brought her back in pain, Jan's heart went out to her. He sat with her, and he read to her, but he could not take away her pain nor make her better again. Nor could he promise there would be no more operations. He could do nothing. His frustration metamorphosed into anger, which built by the hour and by the day. And his anger made him careless.

'When we get back to Australia,' he said to her one day, 'I'm going to get you the best plastic surgeon in the country. I don't care what it costs.'

Annemieke knew what a plastic surgeon was, but why did she need the best one in the country? The truth slowly began to dawn on her.

'I want to look in the mirror,' she said.

Jan talked her out of it. Never in his life had he been more persuasive or more desperate.

'Your bandages aren't ready to come off,' he reasoned. 'Your face is still too swollen. It won't mean a thing. Wait until your nose is fixed properly. Wait till we get home.'

Good reasons and good excuses tumbled from his lips. There was nothing he would not say, no promise he would not make to delay the inevitable. And he succeeded. Annemieke agreed to wait until they arrived back in Australia.

She began to count off the days, eager to board the plane that would take her home. Then, it seemed, her nemesis had returned to haunt her.

On June 24, 1982, just three days before they were due to leave for Sydney, Mt Galunggung struck again and nearly claimed another two hundred and forty lives. A British Airways 747, on a night flight from Kuala Lumpur to Perth, ran headlong into an ash cloud thrown up by Mt Galunggung. Within seconds, ash and debris penetrated, blocked and extinguished all four engines. The crew had no choice but to put the aircraft into a shallow dive and begin restart procedures.

For ten terrifying minutes, passengers and crew hurtled through the darkness towards the ocean until, within three and a half thousand metres of disaster, they encountered clean air and the damaged jet engines reignited. But their ordeal was not yet over. As the Boeing struggled to regain altitude, it encountered a second cloud of ash and, again, all four engines were lost. But the crew were nothing if not fast learners and turned back towards clean air. The pilot detoured two hundred and fifty kilometres back to Jakarta, where the stricken aircraft landed safely. It was a miracle it landed at all.

As soon as Jan heard about the near disaster, he rushed to Annemieke's bedside. He was lucky. The news had not yet reached her. So he told her all about flight BA 9, praising the skill and courage of the flight crew and the bravery of the passengers. He built it into a story, all the better for its happy ending.

'Could it happen again?' Annemieke asked, her fear obvious despite the bandages. In her mind, the volcano had caused their car to crash. If it had caused their car to crash, could it not also do the same with their plane?

'No,' said Jan firmly. He did not want a repeat of her performance at Pengalengen. 'Now that the authorities are aware of the problem, the ash clouds are being plotted. All flights will be directed around them. So there's nothing to worry about. There's no way it could happen again.'

Annemieke was not entirely convinced, but now Jan had a new focus for his energies. He sat with her, talked with her and reassured her. Yet he still left the room whenever her bandages were being changed.

His cowardice hadn't escaped Lita and she challenged him.

'If you can't face up to her injuries,' she accused, 'how can she? What will you do when the bandages come off for the last time? Spend the rest of your life in the toilet? She needs your love and she needs your strength. But what do you give her? Play-acting. You are just going through the motions. Lose her trust and her faith in you now, Jan, and you lose it forever. She will never forgive you. Neither will I.'

Their arguments always ended the same way, with Lita defiant and Jan storming off down the corridor. Jan knew Lita was right, but what could he do? Anger is a convenient emotion when the only alternative is guilt.

'When we get back to Australia, everything will be all right,' he promised himself, though he had absolutely no grounds for his belief.

When the day came for their return to Australia, the people of Tengkuban Prahu came in their hundreds to farewell them. They came by whatever means they could. Whole families clinging to one another on motorbikes. Others packed in perilously over-loaded vans or crammed three to a seat on buses. They lined the hospital exit while the Council presented flowers and their formal best wishes to Jan and Lita.

Jan was touched to the core. He took Lita's hand in his good hand, as he had in the old days, and she let him. She hoped the simple therapy of an open, honest, uncomplicated people would bring him to his senses. He accepted the best wishes of the Council and thanked them for their thoughtfulness. He walked alongside her wheelchair as the orderly pushed her towards the hundreds of village people, all holding bouquets of flowers. He thanked them for coming on Annemieke's behalf, explaining that she was still confined to bed and would be taken directly to the waiting ambulance. He regretted that they would not be able to see her.

But then a murmur swept through the crowd and he heard a voice cry 'Annemieke!'. He turned to see her propped up on a mobile bed, being wheeled, doubtless at her insistence, down the driveway towards them. Her friends broke ranks and rushed to be by her side.

Jan was stricken. He didn't want them to see his daughter this way, to see what he had done to her, not before he'd had a chance to repair the damage. He imagined them recoiling in horror when they reached her, and a strangled 'No!' escaped his lips.

Lita dropped his hand as if it burned, and spun around to face him with a look of fury. Jan ignored her. He couldn't take his eyes off the village girls. They reached Annemieke. But they didn't recoil in horror.

They laughed and smiled, and rejoiced to see their friend again, even though the bandages left little to be seen. They laid their bouquets upon her bed and presented her with a book of prayers and best wishes that every living soul in Tengkuban Prahu who could write had gladly signed.

'What's wrong with me?' Jan asked, but there was no one there to answer him. Lita had gone.

For the first time since the accident, Annemieke felt like laughing, really laughing. She was engulfed by waves of happiness, and realised then what had been missing all along. Her eyes, for the other had at last deigned to open, saw relief and joy in the faces that surrounded her. They had come close to losing her, but she had survived. That was cause enough for celebration. She longed to throw her useless arms around them, around each one in turn, to hug and to hold, and to feel the simple comfort of being held tightly by another warm, loving, human being. She saw her mother at the foot of her bed smiling broadly, Levi by her side. Lita winked at her and Annemieke's spirits soared. She began to believe that this was the beginning of the end of her ordeal. She wanted somehow to tell her mother this, but she could no longer see her as more bouquets piled up on her bed, as those behind passed their gift over those closest. It seemed now that everyone from the villages surrounded her. She looked for her father. He must be so pleased, she thought, but she couldn't find him. It didn't matter. Life had begun again for Annemieke.

Hospital orderlies cleared the path for the ambulance, and she and Lita and the nurse Tin, who would accompany them to Australia, were taken on board.

'*Salamat jalan!*' the smiling faces chorused as the doors closed.

'Mum,' said Annemieke, still bubbling with excitement, 'everything is going to be all right. Like Dad said. Everything will be all right when we get home.' Then a thought crossed her mind. 'Do you think the boys will tease me?'

'Of course they will. That would be normal, wouldn't it?'

Normal. How Annemieke yearned for things to be normal once more. When she wouldn't have to wear bandages. And she wouldn't be afraid to look at her face in the mirror.

* * *

'Didn't those ash clouds come close to bringing down a Singapore Airlines flight as well?'

'Yes that's right, Neil, but that was about a week or so after the British Airways flight and, mercifully, some days after the Van der Meers had arrived safely back in Australia. Otherwise it's doubtful if Annemieke would ever have stepped aboard any plane. Now let me ask you a question. Do you still find Jan van der Meer too perfect?'

Milos laughed.

'No. You warned us that he was flawed and he certainly is. Let me compliment you on the skill with which you changed his character.

'Milos, that is grossly unfair. I changed nothing. I told you the story of a man who had not been tested. Then I told you the story of the same man after he had been tested. Where is the inconsistency?'

'I suppose you are right,' Milos grudgingly conceded. 'His behaviour is consistent with the time he found the baby Annemieke in the monkey forest. But to answer your original question . . . yes, I find the flawed Jan infinitely more interesting. Why would this be? Perhaps this is your underlying theme?' Milos' eyes flicked on to high beam and his voice bored into Ramon. 'Have you also been tested, Ramon? Are you also flawed?'

Ramon was taken aback. There was no ready response and his silence, though brief, spoke volumes.

'Irredeemably,' he said finally, laughing openly and altogether too obviously. 'Please, is it also my responsibility to order coffee?'

'Coffee is coming,' said Neil matter of factly.

The audience of three stared at their storyteller. Milos had caught him by surprise. Ramon had been ambushed by a question bristling with implications and he had faltered. Where lay the truth now?

FOURTH THURSDAY

'Today I will finish the first part of my story,' Ramon began. 'I have introduced you to the man you know as Eduardo, and to the girl Annemieke who will soon become a woman and then his wife. That will be the second part of my story. But first I must bring the beginning to its conclusion and tie up the loose ends.'

'What's this?' interrupted Milos. 'Is this another game? Or has the master storyteller changed his mind? Truth does not have the convenience of fiction – you said that yourself, no? Yet now you are going to tie up all the loose ends. Suddenly your true story smacks of fiction. Life is made up of loose ends, you of all people know that. It is a jigsaw puzzle with pieces missing and others that don't fit.'

'Yes, Ramon, why the change of heart?' There were times when Neil gave the impression that he would gladly delight in plucking the wings off butterflies. 'Last week we came around to your point of view and accepted that your story was probably true. You're not going to double-cross us now, are you?'

Ramon smiled patiently.

'I see I shall have to choose my words more carefully. Of course life is as you describe it, Milos. It has more loose ends than a bowl of Gancio's spaghetti. My story is true and I will remain faithful to the truth. I have not changed my story and if I have given you an impression to the contrary, then it is only through carelessness.

'I was a touch simplistic. I will not be tying up any loose ends. It is simply a question of bringing time frames together, of merging stories and of completing the sketches of the main characters so that you can better understand the inevitability of what ultimately transpires. But life is not all loose ends. If it were, there would be no stories, for stories need coincidence and the intervention of fate to become stories.

'We are all victims of fate but fate does not play a lone hand. It has an ally in our flaws and weaknesses and only occasionally in our strengths. When fate combines with strengths men and women go on to greatness. But for most of us, it is our weaknesses that shape the course of our lives; the things we do in haste and regret for ever; the sins that come back to haunt us. So it is with Eduardo and Annemieke.'

'Don't tell me your little angel Annemieke is also flawed?'

'That is for each of you to judge, Neil. She will be tested as her father was tested and as her husband-to-be was tested. You must make up your own mind about each of them. Is Jan a bad father because he was not born with the usual restraints on his emotions? He is a man unafraid to love, to give all his love without reservation and to show his feelings without inhibition. Surely this is a quality to be admired. You can condemn him as immature and irrational, but I say, there is a man whose faults I would willingly exchange for mine.

'And what of Eduardo? What was his crime? He was manipulated by his own father. He was used and betrayed by Carlos. He lost the woman he loved – the wonderful Rosa – for no better reason than that he was young and foolish and slow to realise the value of what he had. And had she been less impetuous and spoilt, perhaps the two of them would have married sooner or later and there would be no story to tell. No crosses to bear. You can condemn Eduardo for his shallowness and his arrogance and for his cynical betrayal of Victor, but I look upon him as one of life's – and fate's – victims.'

'Ramon has a point.' They turned to Lucio. 'When Eduardo

speaks I hear Ramon's voice. His mannerisms and his sophistication are Ramon's. And his kindness and thoughtfulness, particularly to the prostitute Estelle, that is what I would expect from Ramon. There is a lot of Ramon in Eduardo and so I must say this also. There is a lot to like about him and a lot I am prepared to forgive.'

Lucio was plainly embarrassed, probably no less than the other three. His declaration of support had caught them all by surprise. But it was also a plea for caution, from one friend to another.

'Thank you, Lucio,' said Ramon. 'Whether he speaks with my voice or not, there is much about him to like and admire. And forgive. Where fate gives most of us a loving family it gave him wealth instead. Where fate gives most of us street wisdom it imprisoned him in privilege.'

'Do I hear violins?'

'No, Neil, that's just Gancio making cappuccinos.'

'What about Roberto?' asked Milos. 'Are you going to tell us what happened to him?'

'Yes, I will tell you what happened to the boy Roberto but later perhaps.'

'Today?'

'I promise.' Ramon had not anticipated that the day would begin so well. He was exultant. All good storytellers are part author, part actor and past masters of manipulating their audience. That is food and drink to them, nourishment for their egos. And Ramon's ego was hungrier and healthier than most. Nevertheless Lucio's caution rang loud and clear. 'There is a lot of Ramon in Eduardo.' He would have to be more careful.

Chapter Twenty-Two

'Her arms are healing well,' Dr Ryan said, 'but her face causes us concern.' He knew he would have to tread gently. It was never easy dealing with parents of children injured in automobile accidents, and while the mother was calm and stoic in her acceptance, her husband was something else altogether. He had suggested trauma counselling, and the emphatic manner in which he had been rebuffed only served to underscore the need.

Now he watched the big man, as he had since their arrival at Sydney's Royal North Shore Hospital a week earlier, struggling to suppress the volatile emotions within him. His wife either pointedly ignored him or spoke to him as if he were her son, and young son at that. The scenario was not new to the doctor, but that didn't make it any the less painful or frustrating to witness. She blamed him or he blamed himself, it didn't matter. They were both victims of post-accident trauma, which society had not yet come to accept and did little to treat.

'There's nothing more I can tell you about her arms. We'll take the pin out of her left arm in eight to ten weeks, but after what she's been through, that's hardly a major operation. Her ribs are healing well, though like yours, Mrs Van der Meer, they'll be tender for some time yet.'

'Her face, Doctor,' said Jan grimly.

'Basically the surgeons at Bromeus did a good job, a commendable job in fact, given the nature of her injuries. Fortunately faces also tend to heal very well, particularly when the patient is Annemieke's age. As you've seen, her skin is nonkeloid forming which is not always the case with people with Asian blood. So in time, we expect her scars will fade away to almost nothing. Where tissue has been lost and where lacerations are irregular, a little cosmetic surgery is called for. That should take care of that. But we'll wait a while to see how well she heals.' Dr Ryan hesitated as he considered ways of delivering his next piece of news, where the prognosis was not quite as rosy.

'There is a complication,' he began. 'This is the area of most concern.' He saw Jan stiffen in his seat and his jaw clench. He decided to turn his attention to the small woman in the wheelchair. In times of doubt, head for the strength.

'As you can imagine, the nerves in her face took a savage beating. In particular the fifth and seventh cranial nerves. The fifth nerve, or trigeminal, is responsible for the general sensibility of facial skin and anterior scalp. This is just one aspect of its function. The numbness Annemieke feels on the right side of her face is a result of damage to this nerve. Now the good news here is that sensory nerves are very good at repairing themselves, and the surrounding nerves also tend to grow in and help. It will take a little time but the numbness will gradually contract and in all probability disappear altogether.' He smiled a smile full of warmth and optimism and was gratified to see Lita respond. But Jan may just as well have been made of stone.

'Now we come to the seventh nerve, or facial nerve. It is a motor nerve which controls among other things the muscles of the scalp, face and neck. There is considerable damage and you have probably already seen how this has manifested itself without realising it. Annemieke herself hasn't realised what the problem is, possibly because of the surrounding numbness. She has a condition known as Bell's palsy. It is not uncommon and not necessarily disfiguring. Indeed there are some personalities on television who have the same problem to some degree.'

'What do you mean "not necessarily disfiguring"?' Jan's voice was controlled, but his hands shook. Dr Ryan turned to him.

'Exactly what I said. The condition exists but it may not necessarily be an inhibition on your daughter.' He turned back to Lita who watched him carefully, measuring his words. What price would Annemieke have to pay? And Jan? She wanted badly to take Jan's hand in hers but it was no time for weakness.

'Annemieke has little or no use of her facial muscles below her right eye. The miracle, one that you should be eternally grateful for, is that she didn't lose the sight of her right eye. In fact, we have not been able to detect any nerve damage there at all.' They were unimpressed with that particular miracle. His attempt at good news had only served to amplify the bad news. The temptation was to be blunt and not pull his punches. To stun the big man and send him on his way. But Dr Ryan was a good doctor, and caring for the parents of his patients was as much a part of his job as caring for the patients themselves. He continued.

'The problem will show itself in lack of expression on the right hand side and a slackness in that side of her mouth. Now, sometimes the nerve recovers, in which case your daughter will regain all or partial control. But I would be irresponsible if I suggested to you that this was a probability. Let me say this, however. Nerves are very complex and frequently do the unexpected. Some of the peripheral nerves were also injured but these too, like the sensory nerves, tend to regenerate. They may restore some mobility. Her best chance, though perhaps not as good as we'd like, lies with microsurgery, and the sooner we get on with that the better. Once nerves tangle and scar tissue forms, things become much more difficult.'

'You say the chances of success are not good. Could you be a little clearer?' The tone of Lita's voice was matter of fact, but inside she was like jelly. Yet she wanted the truth laid on the table before them, plainly, so that Jan could recognise it, confront it and accept it. Or explode. Either way, she wasn't prepared to spend the next few days or weeks worrying what his reaction would be. Let him get it over with now, so she knew what she had to deal with.

'Microsurgery is our only hope, but it's a slim hope. It's a delicate business at the best of times. If, for example, the nerve had been cut with a scalpel and repaired immediately, the chances would be very good indeed that full mobility would be restored. Now the further you move away from that ideal, the less your chances become. In Annemieke's case, the nerves were not severed cleanly by a scalpel, nor were they only severed in one place. Nor were we able to operate on them immediately. So already some scar tissue has formed. All this reduces our chances, but we can't say to what extent until the specialists have had a look and had a chance to assess the results of their handiwork.'

'Don't beat around the bush, Doctor.' Jan's voice was hostile. 'What you're saying is that half of my daughter's face is frozen like a dummy's, unable to smile, unable to frown, unable to do anything. And it's likely to stay that way, because you can't do anything about it.'

Jan rose to his feet, his fists clenched.

'Well thank you very much! It's my daughter you're condemning, my Annemieke you've given up on. I'm going to find somebody who can do something, who isn't going to give up!'

Jan stood there shaking, frustrated and impotent as the words tumbled from his lips. But the words faltered in their flow, and so did Jan. He crumpled, and slumped down into his chair, covering his face with his hands.

Dr Ryan had expected this outburst. What appalled him was that the wife ignored her husband entirely. She offered no words of comfort, she didn't spare him a glance.

'You were saying that microsurgery gave us a chance of partial improvement,' she said coolly. 'Of course we will take it. Do you have anything else to tell us?'

'Unhappily, yes.' Why don't these people take counselling, Dr Ryan thought savagely. Nothing else will save this marriage.

'Her nose. At the same time, we would recommend some repair work. Her sinuses and nasal passage are obstructed, and we'd also like to reset her nose. There is some nerve damage there as well. It seems she has lost her sense of smell but I'm not sure there is much we can do about that.'

'Thank you, Doctor,' Lita said. 'Just do your best.'

'You can rest assured of that.' Dr Ryan got up to show them to the door.

'One moment, Doctor.' Jan's voice seemed to come from a place far away. 'Your best. Is there anyone better?'

'Not that I know of. Not in this country. And none that I know of in any other. Science is our shackle. Until somebody comes up with new knowledge, a new procedure, or finds a bionic solution, all we can do, all any of us can do, is what we do now. Our people are as skilled at doing that as anyone. I'm sorry, Mr Van der Meer, I have no miracle for you. I wish I had. We'll do what we can, as best we can.' He put a sympathetic hand on Jan's shoulder.

'I'm not sure you realise how lucky you are, Mr Van der Meer. Whatever god watches over you and your family was on duty the night of your accident. You still have a beautiful daughter and, yes, she will be beautiful once more once she recovers and gets away from us. And she will come to terms with her disability far better than you could ever suspect, given your love and support. She is young and strong, and the young are enviable in their resilience. She will bounce back and all this will be forgotten. This is your first time in this situation but I have witnessed it many times. She will bounce back. Just give her lots of love and support. She is a lucky girl. God only knows how lucky! It's a miracle she's still alive. You want a miracle, Mr Van der Meer? There's your miracle. Cherish it.'

Chapter Twenty-Three

Annemieke was resilient. She amazed the doctors and staff with the speed with which she recovered from her latest bout of surgery. Of course, she had help. It seemed whenever she awoke from sleep her father was by her side, watching over her. Sometimes he played with her or told her stories, but on other occasions he was silent and moody. Annemieke learned to accept his mood changes, when she would simply draw comfort from his presence.

Her mother and brothers were also constant visitors. The twins bubbled with energy and good humour. They teased her endlessly. They wrote rude limericks on her casts and stuck 'No standing' stickers on her feet, and 'No junk mail' above her mouth. One day they brought in a mask with the face of a hideous old man and stuck it over the bandages on her face.

Then they held a mirror up for her so she could see how she looked. Jan was aghast but Annemieke could not stop laughing. They hid behind the curtains as a practical joke, and she called the nurse. Her scream would have woken the dead. The boys took polaroids of Annemieke with the mask on, and sent them to her boyfriends at school.

They bought her icecreams which she couldn't possibly eat by herself, and drip fed them into her mouth. Often the icecream fell out of the cone onto her face, but that just made it funnier.

But the day she both looked forward to and feared was fast approaching. The day when they would remove her bandages and let her look at herself in the mirror. She knew there was still a long way to go. That her face was still swollen and discoloured by bruising. But she would be able to see how much she'd changed. She'd know whether she'd still have her good looks. Or not. It was enough to terrify any woman, let alone one no more than a child.

Jan dreaded the moment when he would hold the mirror up for her. He'd seen how much Annemieke's face had improved and how well she was healing. But she was not the girl she had been, and he found it hard to believe she would ever be as beautiful again. She'd been told about the palsy. But hearing is one thing and seeing another. She would not know what it was until she saw it. How would she react then? What could he say to her? What comfort could he possibly offer her?

When the day came, Jan slipped the smallest mirror he could find into the bag they were taking to the hospital. Lita made him take it out and put in a big one. They met Dr Ryan and went together to Annemieke's bedside. Dr Ryan patiently explained what she would see.

'There's still a lot of bruising,' he said, 'and your lovely face is still very swollen. Some of your scars are still a touch livid. But all of these things will go away, Annemieke, and you'll be the beautiful girl you were before. You remember I spoke to you about Bell's palsy? That will take a bit of getting used to, but you'll quickly learn to work around it. Now let's see, where did they put the zip?'

He always said this whenever he removed her bandages and she always laughed.

'There,' he said. 'I bet that feels lovely and cool. Now let's see if your father remembered to bring a mirror.'

'Jan,' Lita said, 'it's time to show Annemieke what a good job her doctors are doing. Come on. Don't tease her.'

Slowly Jan took the mirror from his bag and sat down beside her. He held the mirror in front of her eyes, barely able to watch her reaction.

There was none. Not for a long while. Not for what seemed a long while. Her eyes worked back and forth over the mirror, scanning her face, taking in every blemish.

'Not bad,' she said finally, still looking at her reflection. 'I thought it would be a mess.'

But the quaver in her voice betrayed her, and when she smiled only half the face in front of her smiled back. She tried again and got the same result. She knew her parents and Dr Ryan were watching her, fearful of her reaction. She fought back her tears because she had already determined she wasn't going to cry. Not in front of everybody. There'd be plenty of time for tears later, when it was dark and nobody was there. She needed time to think about it, to get used to what she'd just learned about Bell's palsy.

'Oh, Mieke . . .' she heard her mother say. She turned away from the mirror to face Dr Ryan.

'Come on,' she said. 'Take your polaroid.'

Jan and Lita turned to Dr Ryan.

'It's part of the therapy,' he said weakly. 'My idea. Patients can see how much they improve from day to day and week to week. It's proved very popular and successful.'

When Dr Ryan lined up the camera, Annemieke dutifully smiled as he clicked the shutter. It was too much for Jan.

'I'm sorry, Annemieke, I'm so sorry. I'm sorry I've done this terrible thing to you.' Jan had turned white. He twisted and turned the mirror in his hands until opposing stresses caused it to shatter. He seemed unaware of it. And he seemed not to hear Lita when she yelled at him. And he never heard the gigantic sob that racked Annemieke's body, nor did he see the tears that flowed. He left the room heartbroken.

Poor Annemieke. Strength begets strength, and weakness begets weakness. Annemieke was strong, but not strong enough for both of them.

A charade began that morning which was to continue for many

years, until Eduardo came into their lives and answered their prayers. Jan returned to Annemieke's bedside that afternoon contrite and apologetic. He pretended well enough, for not only was his child's well-being at stake, but his marriage also. Lita had made that perfectly clear. He told Annemieke again that he loved her and that he felt responsible for what had happened to her. This made things appear worse to him than they really were, he said. He told her how much she had improved since he first saw her with her bandages off. He took her step by step along the process of recovery.

'Bell's palsy is not as bad as it first might seem,' he said. 'You'll adjust to it and you'll learn ways around it. A lot of famous people have Bell's palsy, even some Hollywood actors.'

Jan was as persuasive as he could be, and he spoke with conviction. But the conviction was not his, it was Dr Ryan's. He had gone to the doctor's office before seeing Annemieke, and Dr Ryan had coached him on the appropriate words to say. He had been delighted that Jan had come to him and did all he could to help.

For her part, Annemieke pretended to be greatly relieved and encouraged by what Jan said to her. She put on a brave front. She laughed and she joked and she told Jan not to be a big sook, as she'd heard her mother say countless times before. It was a family joke.

But Annemieke had been deeply hurt. Her father's reaction when she tried to smile for the camera had convinced her that her disability was truly grotesque. She would be a freak. She had once been beautiful and popular. Now she'd be someone other kids felt sorry for, or joked about behind her back. Worst of all, she knew she would have to carry the pain of her hurt alone, for to tell anyone would risk revealing its source, and driving her father further away from her.

A gap not of her making now existed between her father and herself. This, too, hurt her deeply. But was the gap so wide it could never be bridged? Annemieke hoped not. She decided she would do everything in her power to build that bridge. She had her father's capacity to love and her mother's strength. She could have no better tools. So she began to pretend, and she hid her hurt beneath the elaborate fabric of that pretence.

Her brothers were magnificent. They visited her every day. They brought their friends to see her and they brought her school friends. They weren't ashamed of the way she looked and they were determined she wouldn't be either. They brought their camera and began their own gallery of photos beneath Dr Ryan's.

They discovered that if they rubbed the back of the polaroid with the blunt end of a biro while it was developing, colours would bleed into each other and lines distort. So they took photos of her, mutilated them so they looked like something Picasso might have painted, and pinned them on her wall, well beyond the reach of her plaster bound arms.

When Dr Ryan was visiting he would sometimes pick up the wrong set of photos to show her how well she was healing. He would discuss the wrong photos at length with student doctors, while Annemieke howled in mock protest. Dr Ryan was no fool. He knew what Annemieke had been through and he knew the value of laughter. He also suspected that the least of Annemieke's problems were physical.

She never complained. She listened with keen interest to everything Dr Ryan said and, with the help of his polaroids, became an expert on the progress she was making. She'd point out which scars were healing best, and show where swelling had subsided. Her beauty, which she had once taken completely for granted, was slowly returning. One morning Dr Ryan took a polaroid which could have been taken before the accident.

Everyone remarked on it. Even Jan was genuinely impressed. But a still photo is exactly as its description suggests. And despite all the encouragement and support she received, Annemieke was acutely aware of the disconcerting effect her palsy had on others.

In the lonely hours at night, when sleep eluded her, she'd practice frowning and smiling and squinting, hoping to reactivate her shattered nerves. But all her efforts were in vain. The right side of her face remained stubbornly inert. She would weep silent tears into her pillow for her lost perfection, and for what the world would think of her now.

Chapter Twenty-Four

Annemieke was released from hospital thirteen weeks after her return from Indonesia. Her left arm was still protected by plaster, following surgery to remove the pin, but she had full use of her right arm. As Dr Ryan had predicted, her face had healed remarkably well. The scars had faded and blended easily with her pale olive skin. But the microsurgery had met with only modest success, and the right side of her face still failed to obey her wishes.

Superficially at least, the Annemieke of old returned to her family and friends, and her home in Mosman. But she was a very different girl to the one who had begun the year so optimistically. More and more, her affliction began to shape her personality and influence the way she lived.

The palsy made her appear slow and dull-witted. One side of her face would be vibrant with animation, the other frozen in limbo. Her friends had trouble interpreting her signals.

'We don't know whether you're being funny or serious,' they said. And she found them staring at her in morbid fascination when she spoke.

She could relax with her mother and her brothers, but even with Jan she was always on guard. She'd find him staring at her, but when she smiled and tried to catch his eye, he'd look away. She learned the trick of warning him before looking at him, so that he could better prepare himself. She would begin a sentence and then look up at him and he would respond by being overly attentive. Everybody knew the game they were playing and everybody pretended they weren't.

Sometimes when they were out together, and ran into acquaintances of Jan's who had never met Annemieke, he would fail to introduce her, as if ashamed of her. Annemieke learned to be bold at these times, to step forward and introduce herself, though sometimes it took all her courage. She would silently pray that Jan's friends would not stare at her or ask embarrassing questions. Occasionally a curious or sharper eye would dwell on her face for a moment or two longer than was polite, but for the most part, people had the good taste not to comment. But Annemieke knew it was only a matter of time before somebody innocently tore the scab from the wound. She could not keep exposing herself and her father to that risk.

She began to retreat into the shadows. She learned that no expression was better than half of any other kind. She became withdrawn and defensive, and avoided doing anything that would turn the spotlight on her. She began to decline her father's invitations to accompany him and he never once pressed her to change her mind. The gap widened between them.

Her friends began to drift away. She was once the centre of their social activity. Now she was a satellite on an ever more distant orbit. Some friends remained loyal, motivated as much by kindness or a sense of obligation as by friendship. But when the new year began, Annemieke was obliged to repeat the previous year's study because of all the lessons she'd missed. Annemieke found the demotion humiliating. Worse, she was now in a class whose interests lagged a year behind her own and with whom she had no rapport. She found the girls silly and the boys juvenile. And her old friends tended to forget her when they planned parties and expeditions to the movies. It probably wasn't deliberate on their part. She was simply out of sight, out of their orbit, and therefore out of mind.

Annemieke withdrew further and further. She'd come home from school and bury herself in her homework. Or she'd practise piano for hours on end, playing the same pieces over and over as she struggled to master the more difficult passages. Lita warned the family against objecting, pointing out that it was the best possible therapy for her wasted arms. So she played and she played until she could play no more. Even then, she'd immerse herself in her music theory.

She sat and passed her grade seven theory and practical without bothering with levels five and six. Her music teacher encouraged her to play in the school orchestra, and to play solos at school concerts, hoping it would help to draw her out of her shell. She obliged and played without a trace of nervousness or excitement. All her expression was in her fingertips and the music she played. She acknowledged applause with a quick bob of her head and an even quicker exit.

Music became her love, but it was also a legitimate retreat from the world. Sometimes she'd play for so long that her arms would ache unbearably, and she could scarcely hold them out in front of her. But she now had her dream. Music, she decided, would be her life and her career. She would be a concert pianist. But if, as it proved, her injuries denied her the dexterity to make the grade as a performer, then she'd happily teach.

She worked hard on her music and on her school work. She also worked hard on what she secretly called her 'expression'. Her facial muscles atrophied from lack of use, and their slackness was becoming apparent. Her nightmare was that she would lose control over the right side of her mouth, and she'd unwittingly dribble. Or she'd be drinking and liquid would spill out. It had never happened but the possibility terrified her.

She developed a habit of dabbing her lips with a handkerchief or serviette after every sip or mouthful of food, until it became an unconscious act which recurred regularly throughout her waking hours. Her 'no-expression', which had served her well, had taken on a different aspect. She now looked sullen and sulky even when she was happy. Sometimes it seemed she looked ashamed.

One day she overheard Jan and Lita discussing her, and vowed to do something about it. She realised it would eventually wear down her family and the few close friends who still found time for her. She changed. She adopted a look of detached serenity. It was within the scope of expressions she could manage without her palsy being obvious.

For the first time she began to observe her mother critically to discover what made her appear so regal. She was amazed to see how Lita made her tiny frame seem so much taller. She came to realise that expression was only a part of impression, and that impression was founded on deportment and attitude.

She kept her back straight and her chin high, like her mother did, and she slowed down the pace of her movements until she achieved the same fluid grace. She taught herself to meditate from a book, and learned to carry herself with the same sense of calm and inner strength that she saw in her mother.

Sundanese women mature early, and already her hormones were hard at work in her body. Her family noticed the change in her and put it down to her coming of age. The boys at school couldn't help but notice either. They watched her glide past them, weak-kneed in their admiration. Yet they hesitated to approach her. Ironically, it was not her palsy that put them off, but the results of the regime she had adopted because of it. She topped her year in every subject she studied, and her academic achievements made them feel insecure. But even more formidable was her mask of 'detached serenity', which made her seem infinitely more mature and sophisticated than they, and strato-spherically remote.

The girls in her school admired her apparent sophistication and told her so. Once more Annemieke found herself the envy of her peers. It was a wonderful feeling, redolent with echoes from her past. She worked even harder on her 'expression' as a result. At the age of fifteen, Annemieke appeared to have moved into woman-hood without ever having been a teenager.

The omission would prove catastrophic.

* * *

For two years Jan pestered Dr Ryan, but the doctor could offer nothing that he had not already tried. He was genuinely sorry. But the reality was that the damage to Annemieke's facial nerve was irreparable and irreversible, at least by any known techniques. He said it was time Jan accepted that.

He arranged a last meeting with neurologists and neurosurgeons, and once more they patiently explained the limitations of their capabilities. They pointed to their success in limiting the disability and, all in all, concluded that Annemieke, given the nature of her injuries, had been a very fortunate young lady indeed. They could offer no more hope, other than that nature may yet work a miracle and restore partial mobility. It was a faint possibility, but one that couldn't entirely be discounted.

Jan went home from this last meeting with Dr Ryan, and gave up. He'd done all he could. He would now try to learn to live with what he'd done to his child. As usual she was playing piano. He sat down quietly to watch her unobserved.

She was playing Beethoven's *Moonlight Sonata*. In the afternoon light filtering through the lace curtains she looked exquisite. He took stock of her beauty, the strength she'd inherited from her mother, and the calm and serenity that seemed to radiate from her. The *Moonlight Sonata* rose and fell with its sweet sad beauty, and Jan was drawn into reverie, contemplating what might have been. Her beauty, he suddenly realised, was like the beauty of a nun, and he longed for the radiant and gregarious little girl he'd lost forever on the slopes of Tengkuban Prahu. He felt the melody sweep over him and carry him off in its flow to the sweet land of his memories.

Annemieke played on until, sensing his presence, she turned and saw him watching her, tears flowing down his cheeks. This time, at least, he didn't turn away. She stopped playing and threw her arms around his neck.

'The Moonlight Sonata has the same effect on me,' she said, and smiled her lop-sided smile. Immediately her right hand produced a handkerchief to dab the side of her mouth.

Ramon finished speaking and his audience was loath to break the spell. They were, each of them, in Jan's shoes. His tears were familiar to them. They were the tears of every man who has ever lost something precious. A wife, a child, a country or even the promise of his own youth. They were reminders of their own vulnerability.

'Coffee and grappa,' said Gancio theatrically. 'You'll like this grappa. Very special. Brings tears to your eyes.'

The four men burst out laughing.

'What's the matter? What did I say?' Gancio replayed his words in his mind, wondering if he'd accidentally made a joke or said something rude. English was a tricky language sometimes.

'Nothing at all,' said Ramon, solicitous to his friend. 'It was all a question of timing.'

'Ah! Okay. No matter.' Gancio returned to his kitchen shaking his head.

'You see how you waste your breath and our time, Ramon?' Milos took a sip of his grappa. 'If it's tears you want, just order the special grappa.'

'What's the point?' moaned Ramon. 'Why do I bother? I take my time and build a mood, patiently drawing you into my web, then . . . whammo! The spell is broken and it's all one huge joke.'

'Don't worry, you got us where you wanted to take us. You did well.'

'Thank you, Neil. A rare compliment.'

'You were fishing for it hard enough.'

'I think it was a very beautiful moment.' Lucio looked around at his friends. 'Sad and beautiful. Soon my daughter gets married. It made me think of how I will feel when I have to give her away to another man.'

They thought about this. Until now they hadn't even known

Lucio had a daughter. They still weren't convinced that he had.

'I didn't know you had a daughter,' said Neil.

'Why should you? As Ramon said at the start of this story, we know so little about each other. Perhaps it is best this way.'

Ramon smiled inwardly. Once again Lucio had issued a warning. Had the others detected it? Why wouldn't they? They shared the same suspicion.

'How about we get back to business?' It was Neil. Nobody would ever accuse him of sentimentality. 'You've tied up that loose end beautifully. The next few years of Annemieke's life are clear to us all. She'll glide along skilfully avoiding the world without appearing to do so. She'll become a silent beauty, a wraith that flits among the shadows. She'll continue with her solitary pursuits. Everybody will compliment her on the food she cooks, her manners and bearing, and say what a fine young lady she is. But nobody will get remotely near to her, outside her family and small circle of friends. She won't have regular boyfriends because her defence systems won't allow it. She'll become aloof, serene and unreachable. She may even begin to feel superior to other mortals, as if she were on a higher plane than everyone else. In other words she'll spend the next few years of her life like a sleeping beauty waiting for her prince to come along. Do we all agree?' He looked around the table. Milos and Lucio murmured their agreement. His eyes settled on Ramon.

'Please tell me,' Ramon said, 'if you've heard this story before. Yes, Neil, that is exactly what happened to Annemieke. You tell it so well, why don't you finish the rest of the story.'

'How can I? I'm not Eduardo. And it is Eduardo's story, isn't it, Ramon? You've told us at length about Annemieke but, at the end of the day, it is Eduardo's story. How can I tell you how that bastard would act?'

'No, it is not Eduardo's story. It is the story of Eduardo, Annemieke and the gift he gave to her. I told you that at the very beginning. Now let me ask you something. Do you still think Eduardo is a bastard?'

'Yes, he still thinks Eduardo is a bastard. He just said so.' Milos was like a father stepping between two warring kids. 'The question is, has Neil's intrusion jeopardised the rest of the story you intended to tell us today?'

'Truncated . . . not jeopardised.'

'Good. Then can we continue? I would like to hear what happened to Roberto.'

Ramon sank into deep thought. At least that's the impression he gave.

'I have not yet finished with Eduardo,' he said finally. 'There is more to tell before this first part of my story concludes. But since you have been so patient, Milos, I promise I will tell you about Roberto before the day is out.'

Chapter Twenty-Five

At the beginning of September 1986, Burton Simmons made their move. It was not the move Eduardo had expected and it momentarily gave him cause to regret the partnership proposal he had made to Phil and Don. He could not go back on his word now even though the partnership had not been finalised and no money exchanged. But Phil had mortgaged his house, and Don was in the final stages of selling his business. He was morally bound. Besides, their confidence in him had moved him more than he would ever admit.

Still, the offer from Burton Simmons, made through their high-flying parent company Austral Corp, was astonishingly generous. It would make him a rich man. But the five-year service contract he'd have to sign would also make him someone else's servant, a role with which he would never be comfortable. The 'no-compete' clause also meant he'd have to abandon his dream to enter the publishing business – the business he'd been trained for and in which his heart lay. It was also the business his social life demanded he enter.

He called a meeting with Phil and Don and told them of Burton Simmons' proposal. Both men turned pale. Eduardo would be a fool to refuse such an offer, and where did that leave them?

'I have two choices,' Eduardo began earnestly. 'I can accept or refuse. If I accept I will compensate you both for your dislocation. They may wish to retain Phil, but either way, I cannot compensate either of you for the loss of opportunity. But if I refuse their offer you will think me a fool.'

The two men looked grim as they listened to Eduardo, and watched their hopes and plans disintegrate.

'The question is,' continued Eduardo, 'are you two still prepared to go into partnership with a fool?'

'You bastard!' cut in Phil. 'You're going to tell them to get stuffed, aren't you?'

'You're a bloody fool, Eduardo!' Don tried to maintain the detachment of his profession and failed miserably. His moustache bobbed up and down as he fought to control his grin. 'You could coast for the rest of your life.'

'That is the problem. I'm not yet ready to rack my cue, as Phil puts it. If we are successful in the publishing business, and I am determined we will be, we will make far more money than this. Besides we have a good business, and we have the skills to survive the tough times ahead. Surely this Austral Corp have bigger fish to fry?'

'Perhaps, but don't count on it, Eduardo.' Don was thoughtful for a moment. 'Don't get me wrong, I'm not trying to be negative. I'm more than delighted we're going ahead with our plans. I'm not convinced that, if our positions were reversed, I would have been so loyal. But we shouldn't get carried away in the euphoria.'

'This is euphoria?'

'Shut up, Phil. Go on, Don.'

'Well you've met the new brains behind Burton Simmons. Burton Simmons is just a stepping stone on his pathway to corporate glory. His fortunes, for the moment, are inextricably linked to the success of Burton Simmons and we're in his way. There is the problem.'

Eduardo knew Don was right. Cam Kambourian was a Harvard-educated whizz kid. He had impressed Eduardo with his mental agility, his immense confidence and his persuasiveness. He would be a powerful adversary.

'We'll just have to bunker down.'

'No way, Eduardo,' said Phil who still hadn't stopped smiling. 'That's how your lot lost the Falklands War and how we lost in Vietnam. No, mate, we've got to be guerrillas and use guerrilla tactics. Advertising is a disorganised business. All we have to do is make sure we're there when they need help. Sooner or later they'll get embarrassed by the build-up of favours they owe us, or simply take the line of least resistance. Either way we'll be back in business. But it we wait for business to come to us, Burton Simmons will knock off our clients one after the other. What do you reckon?'

'Makes sense to me,' said Eduardo.

'Good, let's go have a beer.'

Cam Kambourian was speechless when Eduardo refused his offer and defied the mighty Austral Corp. When he regained the use of words he had little control over them, and they spewed from his mouth in insults and threats which demeaned them both. His grim advisors led their superstar out of Eduardo's office.

Eduardo was appalled. The encounter brought home to him the enormity of the decision he had made.

The opening engagements were one-sided. Hot Ink Press took a pounding. More advertising agencies gave their work to Burton Simmons while their sister company, Alexander Press, walked away with the biscuit-packaging business and were actively submitting for more of Eduardo's accounts.

Phil and Eduardo wined and dined their contacts endlessly. They got sympathy and moral support, but they didn't get their business. As Phil had predicted, they managed to pick up lots of one-off jobs, but the cost of winning each job barely made the exercise worthwhile. Some agencies stood by them, resolute in their insistence that quality and service take priority over price, but they were in the minority. The Hot Ink Press struggled to meet its overheads.

Whenever they had to let staff go they were snapped up by Burton Simmons, who used them to replicate Hot Ink Press' superior systems and procedures. The edge that Eduardo and Phil had always maintained was all but eroded. Phil was forced to seek work at the bottom end of the market, in sales promotion and direct response, where margins were tighter and quality less of a consideration.

Eduardo and Phil were on the slide and they knew it. The problem was there was no second string to their bow. Because of the desperate situation at Hot Ink Press, Eduardo had not had time to even begin setting up the publishing business. All the while, their capital was disappearing into the black hole of lease repayments and overdraft rates. Something had to give or they would lose it all.

'We're in trouble,' said Don. 'Our revenue and margins are down, and the cost of servicing the remaining business is up by around fifteen percent. I suggest we forget about our guerrilla tactics and consolidate with those clients who have stood by us and service the Christ out of them. Lose them and we're history. We won't actually make any money by doing this, but we'll substantially reduce our losses.

'Eduardo has also taken a hammering with the printing business but less so. And I think there's a good reason for this. I happen to know that the management of Alexander Printing are less than impressed with being used by Burton Simmons to undermine us. They have their own whizz kid who's just as keen as Mr Kambourian to climb the corporate stairway. Word is they're getting tired of taking a loss just to make Burton Simmons look good. That may explain why we won the last pitch against them.

'My strategy is that we should repitch the clients we've lost. If we're guilty of anything here, it's petulance. Eduardo, you put such a premium on loyalty, but giving us the flick wasn't an act of disloyalty on our client's part, just good sound business. You got miffed so you've ignored people who are our prime prospects. People who know us, trust us, and with whom we've had a valued relationship. So swallow your pride and get off your arse. Go see them and resubmit. We can afford to cut a few points off the last quote we gave them. Fact is, we can't afford not to. And don't assume, by the way, that their relationship with Alexander Printing has been all peaches and cream. You didn't have a great deal of respect for their work before, and I've heard nothing to suggest things have changed.

'So come on, guys. Think positive. What was, is gone. What is, is just a temporary setback. Think only of what's going to be. Now get out of here and get on your bikes.'

'Now I know why we pay you,' said Phil. But Eduardo just looked at the little man with the outsized moustache in awe and admiration.

They adopted Don's strategies and applied them with vigour. Eduardo's old clients were pleased to hear from him again, and happy to give him the opportunity to re-pitch. There was no overnight miracle but the fightback had begun. People could see the advantage of having two strong companies competing keenly for their business. Where they could they gave him projects. It was a start.

Phil consolidated their position with their major agency clients by providing a service Burton Simmons couldn't match. He was always available. Nothing was too much trouble. No demand too great. He put in hours that made a widow of his wife and strangers of his children. With family and mortgages Phil, more than either Eduardo or Don, could ill afford to lose.

Don guided their fortunes with skill. He collected monies owing with sensitivity, so as not to alienate their clients, but he wouldn't allow their terms of business to be abused. He was strong but fair. He handled the banks and creditors with aplomb. He knew the game well and played it to perfection, being truthful with those who responded best to truth, and elusive wherever he sensed weakness or poor accounting practice. And so they survived until, four months down the track, they began to make a profit.

Unfortunately, the banks chose this moment to further increase overdraft rates and the profit evaporated.

'Not to worry,' said Don. 'The good news is that at least we have the money to pay the banks.'

Chapter Twenty-Six

Fate intervened, with the stockmarket crash of October '87. The high flying entrepreneurs and corporate raiders now found their shares marked down to a fraction of their previous value and their assets along with them. Panic set in.

To Eduardo and Phil, the crash was little more than a subject of wonder and lunchtime distraction. They had no shares other than their holding in Hot Ink Press, and the crash had no bearing on those that they could see. Rumours abounded about which multinational agencies would fall and which would merge, but that didn't affect Eduardo or Phil either. They were too busy on their treadmill keeping Don, the bank and their creditors happy.

They were caught by surprise when Burton Simmons began laying off people and increased their prices. They rushed to tell Don but he seemed only mildly interested.

But Eduardo and Phil, hardened in their role as frontline foot soldiers, now saw the opportunity to win back the initiative. Business began to pour back through their doors. Rumours began to fly that Burton Simmons were in trouble. Staff that had left Hot Ink Press for Burton Simmons returned to the fold and confirmed that all was not well within that company. They spoke of savage cost cutting, of company cars sacrificed to reduce overheads, of executives stripped of their mobile phones and of grim-faced management suddenly vacating their offices.

Eduardo and Phil were savage in their retribution. They had worked hard when they were going broke but they worked harder now. They reported each success to Don but his delight always fell well below the level they had expected. It began to worry them, but before they could take any action Don called a meeting.

'I think you guys should back off on your attacks on Burton Simmons' business,' he said.

'For God's sake why?' Phil exploded. 'Those bastards put us through the wringer. We're just returning the compliment.'

'Yes, why?' Eduardo asked quietly. He could not imagine why Don should make such a request. His first thought was that his friend and partner was in some kind of trouble.

'I want you to back off Burton Simmons for one very good reason,' Don said coolly. 'By this time next week we'll own them.'

'What!' Eduardo and Phil's voices exploded as one. Don began to laugh, high pitched and squeaky. Tears rolled down his cheeks. There had never been a moment as sweet as this in his life. It was revenge for all the times he'd been left on the outer while he struggled to understand the trade banter and jokes between Eduardo and Phil. He tried to focus on the stunned faces of his partners who looked as bemused as he normally did. That only made him laugh more. And the more he laughed, the more the tensions of the past twelve months washed away. He would happily have laughed forever.

'What are you up to, you bastard?' shrieked Phil, but Don's laughter was infectious, and in it, both Phil and Eduardo could hear the dark clouds roll away.

'Tell us!' Phil grabbed hold of Don, and twisted his arm painfully behind his back.

'Okay, okay. Let me go. Okay. Let me get my breath back. With the banks blessing, I've put in a bid for Burton Simmons which has been accepted, subject of course to your approval. We're picking them up for peanuts, not much more than asset value.'

'How long has this been going on?' asked Eduardo.

'Since October.'

'Since October and you never thought to mention this to your partners?' There was a chill in Eduardo's voice.

'I thought about it plenty of times but it all began as a long shot. You would have laughed and told me not to waste my time. But then it became increasingly clear to me that Austral Corp was in trouble, and the improbable began to look decidedly possible. I thought then that I should tell you.' Don began to laugh again. 'But you two guys were so hell-bent on revenge, I figured that our best interests lay in allowing – no, encouraging – you to exact it. You ripped their business to pieces, far better than I could have ever orchestrated. What did you want me to do? Take away your incentive? Tell you we're going to buy them, so you could slack off? No way. Our greatest weapon was your hunger for revenge. So I took a calculated risk. I withheld information from you. I used my judgement. You tell me, was I right?'

Eduardo thought about it. He realised he was a touch jealous because the coup was not of his making. But wasn't this precisely why he'd asked the fussy little man to be their partner? To manage the business, while he and Phil toiled at the coalface? If so, then logically this triumph was also his because it came about because of his foresight.

'We were all right. You for pulling off this extraordinary coup. Phil and I for taking you on as our partner. I am a lucky man to have two such partners. Now, you bastards, when can I start our publishing business?'

'Let's talk about it over a beer.'

'Beer, be buggered, Phil,' said Don. 'French champagne.'

'Champagne! What is this?' demanded Milos.

'A surprise. I arranged it with Gancio earlier. It's my shout to celebrate the conclusion of the first part of my story.' Ramon smiled at his three companions. 'Surely you don't object?'

'I most certainly do.' Milos was up on the edge of his seat, almost standing as his anger built. 'You have not concluded anything. You have yet to tell us about the boy Roberto. You promised.'

'Yeah, you did. Ramon.'

'So I did, Neil, and so I shall. I shall tell you about Roberto over the champagne. It's still early and we have plenty of time. It is not the champagne you object to is it, Milos? If so, Gancio will be delighted . . .'

'Thank you, champagne is fine. Why do you do this to me, Ramon? Why must you tease?'

'It's a failing in my character. But you see, Milos, I have kept the story of Roberto till last for a good reason. I began this section of my story with the boy Roberto. Now I conclude with him. It has a symmetry you must admit.'

Lucio and Neil were laughing quietly, enjoying Milos' discomfort. But it was time for Lucio to help Milos off the hook.

'Ramon, I think you better tell your story now. There's more pressure building up inside our friend here than in this Pol Roger. Tell us about Roberto. Put Milos out of his misery.'

'And his wife,' chipped in Neil mischievously.

Chapter Twenty-Seven

Carlos was careless. Heady with his triumph, he forgot about the boy. He did not even look for him. He was long gone from the house when he remembered his oversight. He sent men back, but he knew they would find nothing. It was a pity. It would take some of the gloss from his achievement. Besides, the boy might have been useful when they interrogated Victor. Better still, he could have used the boy to ingratiate himself with people who might one day be useful to him. Or, at very least, collect a handsome gratuity. Among Argentina's childless couples of wealth and importance there was a ready adoption market. Many children and babies were stolen from among the Generals' victims to satisfy this need. Carlos cursed his missed opportunity.

The following Thursday, copies of *Argentina Libre* appeared as usual in bars and cafeterias and public places. *La Voz del Pueblo* was again strident in its protest, as it named the Generals' latest victims and the man who had betrayed them. The style had changed but the message was the same. *La Voz del Pueblo* is not one man, it proclaimed, but many men. *La Voz* would not be silenced.

* * *

Roberto did not see the soldiers drag his parents away. His eyes refused to accept any more horror. He shrank back into the tube of carpet where the heavy layers could deaden the sounds he did not want to hear. He wept copiously, silently so that he wouldn't be heard, or so softly no sound could escape. He cried until he could cry no more. He didn't even hear the urgent, familiar voices calling his name.

He was found by a neighbour who was aware of the game the boy played with Victor and thought to look inside the rolled carpet. Roberto screamed in fear, his eyes wide but unseeing. He had fouled himself. He needed to be picked up gently and carried to a quiet place. He needed to be cuddled and soothed and comforted by people with faces he knew and trusted. He needed someone to take the place of the mother and father he had just lost, and ease away the unbearable pain. But there was no time for such sympathies. The soldiers could return any minute to make good their colossal blunder.

They bundled up the screaming boy, and ran with him from one house to another until they felt they were safe. They hid him at his best friend's home, but he would not recognise them, and his screams threatened that family's safety as well. So they hid him in a dark basement with his friend's mother, and stuffed blankets around the doorway to block out his screams. In that pitch blackness, in arms that were strange to him, Roberto screamed out in terror, oblivious to the tender ministrations of the brave, heartbroken woman who sheltered him. Finally, merciful sleep took him into its shadow.

They kept him in the basement for three days, until they felt it was safe for Rosa's eldest sister, Bibiana Gimenes, to come and collect him. In all that time, he never spoke a word, and clung fiercely to the kind woman who nursed him.

Bibiana's heart opened to the tiny tragic figure, but the last thing the boy needed was more tears. Bibiana had some of the look of

Roberto's mother, and she was the favourite among his aunts. He let her take him from his mother of three days without protest.

Bibiana wanted to take him straight into her family, and counter his nightmare with tidal waves of love. Her schoolteacher husband agreed that would be best for the boy, but he could not allow it. Certainly Victor's family would come under surveillance, he argued, perhaps theirs would too. Her husband's wise counsel prevailed.

So for three months Roberto was kept on the move, shunted between family friends. He never knew where he'd be from one day to the next, where he would sleep or who would kiss him good night, or come to him when he cried out. He was not allowed to attend school, nor was he allowed to play with other children. Life on the run became the only life he knew.

The first flood of pity and sympathy receded, and the boy became a burden on those who sheltered him. He never spoke and he never smiled. He had long ceased to cry except in the loneliness of his sleep. He had become a chronic bed wetter and, as patience ran out, his hosts began to berate him. Who could blame them? They took risks for this boy who never showed any gratitude nor returned any affection, who cocooned himself within walls of silence. They began to regard him as an idiot. Finally, Bibiana came to his rescue.

'Enough!' she cried to her husband. 'You think the Generals care any more about this small boy who cannot speak? They probably care even less than those who shelter him. If we don't do something now the boy really will go crazy.'

She took Roberto home with her and that night he slept in her bed. Her husband Domingo, a good and kindly man, was not impressed but he was not prepared to argue. It was a small sacrifice to make, he reasoned, for a boy who had so big a need.

'If that will help the boy,' he said, 'then that is what we must do.'

For two months Roberto slept in their bed, and for two months Domingo put up with the disruptions of his bed-wetting. Slowly Roberto began to relax. He felt safe in this house where nobody hurt him even when he wet the bed. He began to play with

Bibiana's three children, a boy his age and two daughters who were older. But still he steadfastly refused to speak, communicating by nodding or shaking his head, by pointing, and sometimes when he was playing a game he particularly liked, by giggling.

At the end of two months, Bibiana made up a bed for him in the same room as her son Julio. She didn't ask Roberto, she didn't cajole him, she just did it. Roberto's trust in Bibiana was so complete, he went along with the change.

He stopped wetting his bed at night, and he stopped running for cover whenever anyone came to the door. He was slowly returning to normal, but still he would not speak.

'Until he speaks, I cannot send him to school,' Bibiana argued. 'The other children will crucify him, and he's been through enough.' She turned to her husband.

'You will have to teach him in the evenings. He may not answer, but he listens. When the time comes for him to go back to school, we cannot send a child the others will think is stupid.'

So Roberto became Bibiana's shadow and devoted helper. He went with her when she did her shopping, and he helped her with her cleaning and cooking. She loved him like her own children, and talked to him constantly, asking questions but never seemingly concerned that he didn't reply.

'He will reply when he is ready,' she told Domingo. 'We must be patient.'

The breakthrough came in a way nobody could have foreseen. Bibiana needed food for dinner, so she and Roberto went shopping, just as they always did. He would stand quietly by while she haggled over her purchases, never taking his eyes off her. She would consult him on the meat she was buying, or the vegetables, or the fruit. He would smile at some suggestions, frown at others, and in this way communicate his choice.

They would call into a *bonbonería* as a treat, because Roberto loved candy. It was the one thing he got genuinely excited about.

He would examine all the jars, read the labels as best he could, study the wrappers, and deliberate in trembling excitement before he made his choice. Bibiana thought they were the only times Roberto seemed truly happy. She felt that when Roberto was ready to speak again, it would be in a *bonbonería*, and he would ask for a candy that he hadn't found on display.

But once more as they headed home, with Roberto concentrating on making a boiled sweet last far longer than the makers ever intended, he kept his silence. Bibiana couldn't help but feel a little disappointed, but her patience was bottomless. She knew one day he would speak to her. It was only a matter of time, of faith, and the healing power of love.

She took no notice of the dog walker coming towards them, his pack of thoroughbreds keeping an orderly formation on their leashes. Why should she? Tourists might find novelty in it but it was a sight Bibiana saw every day. She felt the tiny hand that held hers tighten its grip which caused her to glance once more at the approaching pack, but she saw nothing to concern her. The dogs seemed to strut with the arrogance of their rich owners, showing no interest in them whatsoever.

But another pair of eyes were watching, and they looked upon the pampered thoroughbreds with loathing and hatred. The dog pack trotted onwards, oblivious to the Rottweiler guard dog on duty in the cab of the delivery van parked at the kerbside. The dog walker guided his charges closer to the roadside to allow Bibiana and Roberto to pass. Perhaps he was going to exchange greetings with them, for he certainly wasn't watching his dogs when the Rottweiler chose to strike.

The Rottweiler threw itself against the half-opened window, snapping and cursing and threatening to rip the throats out of each of the dogs which had dared stray onto his territory. The pack reacted instantly, like a bomb burst, motivated entirely by self-preservation.

Bibiana and Roberto were as badly frightened and surprised as the dogs. But they were slower to react. Before Bibiana realised what was happening, dogs crossed in front of her, behind her, and one even got jammed between her legs. She fell and was immediately engulfed by the panicstricken canines. Their claws tore at her back and arms. She tried to get up, but she was caught in a cat's cradle of leashes. She called out for Roberto, but her voice was lost amid the cacophony of howling, yelping, snarling dogs, the screams of the dog handler and another voice, shrill with fear.

'Get back! Get back!' it cried. She could feel somebody hauling dogs off her and wresting with the leashes. She was aware of somebody crouching over her, protecting her. She could hear other voices as passers-by rushed to help. But there was only one voice that interested her, a voice she'd waited so long to hear.

'Mama?' it begged. 'Mama?'

It was all over, almost as quickly as it happened. Concerned hands helped her to her feet. Her arms and legs were scratched and bruised, and scrabbling claws had gouged her back. She ignored the pain and she dismissed the hapless dog handler and his effusive apologies. She thanked the people who had come to her rescue. She could not get rid of them fast enough. This was her moment of triumph and she did not want to lose it. She took Roberto's small hands in hers and gazed down into the anxious face that stared up at her.

'Mama,' he asked, 'are you all right?'

'Yes, Roberto, I am. Thanks to you. You were very brave.' She looked at him shyly and his face flushed crimson. 'Roberto, I can't begin to tell you how happy I am to hear your voice again. Now take me home.'

'I lost all my sweets,' he said.

Life changed abruptly for Roberto. Having spoken, he could no longer retreat into his old silent ways. He was enrolled in school as Roberto Gimenes, eldest son of Domingo's brother from the province of Tucuman, and he sat at a table next to his cousin Julio. Nobody queried why the boy was sent to Buenos Aires to stay with his uncle. There could be any number of reasons. Poverty, sickness, politics. It was better not to ask. By any measure, Roberto's disguise was thin and would not bear close inspection. But Bibiana was right. The Generals had long since lost all interest in the boy.

Roberto never became like other boys his age. He was quiet and moody, and preferred books and music to football and the rough and tumble of being a boy among boys. After school, he would race home to Bibiana and hang off her apron, helping her to prepare dinner, just like before. He'd beg to go shopping with her, so they could pass by a *bonbonería* and he could get his ration of sweets. This was fine for a seven-year-old boy, but he still behaved the same way when he was ten.

In 1982, the Generals shot themselves in the foot. In a bid to deflect attention away from their crimes and gross mismanagement of the country and its economy, they provoked the war with Great Britain over the Falkland Islands. Such is the insanity of Argentine politics that the people went along with it.

Yet Britain and Argentina had always enjoyed a close and valued relationship. Britons introduced the first shorthorn and the first Aberdeen Angus, upon which the beef industry was founded. British capital and engineers gave Argentina banks, railways, tramways, telephones, telegraph, wireless, gas, electric light, and industrial machinery – the foundation stones of modern Argentina. Now Britain was about to give them a hiding.

In the aftermath of the war a return to democracy was inevitable. The Generals hastily passed legislation granting themselves and their agents immunity for crimes committed during the 'dirty war'. But they'd gone too far to be forgiven.

In 1983, the Radical Civic Union led by Raul Alfonsin was swept into power in the country's first democratic election in seven years. It was a time for accounting, time for a fresh start. *Les Madres de Mayo*, the mothers of the Plaza de Mayo, marched every Thursday, parading photos of their lost ones and the agony of their grief. The people cried out for justice. President Alfonsin reversed the Generals' hastily passed legislation, and lifted their immunity.

Officers turned against their comrades. The papers filled with details of mass graves, secret detention centres, and horrific tortures. Some spoke of prisoners being bound hand and foot, and thrown into the ocean from helicopters. Victims of torture revealed their mutilations to an outraged populace. A picture of a man was flashed around the world. He had been robbed of his sight, his hearing, his tongue, his hands, his feet and his manhood. Yet a brain still sparked inside this wreck of a human being, a brain that was very much alive though horribly deprived. The irony was that the man was not the victim of the Generals at all, but of a vengeful father. The man was none other than Carlos.

The country cried out for revenge. General Jorge Videla and Admiral Emilio Massera were jailed for life, and more than six hundred officers were charged. Former President Galtieri, Brigadier General Dozo and Admiral Anaya were cleared of charges relating to the 'dirty war', but served short terms in prison for their part in the war over the Falklands.

For many Argentinians, retribution was just another sad chapter in their country's sad history. The awful truth was, despite its enormous mineral and agricultural wealth, Argentina was bankrupt. For years the Generals had diverted massive funds to build their military machine, and wise Argentinians had sent more than thirty billion US dollars out of the country to safe havens. There seemed no way Argentina could possibly service its debts to foreign banks.

For Domingo and Bibiana, it was all too much. They were determined their children and their adopted son would have a better life, away from violence and turmoil, and sought sanctuary in another country. They arrived in Sydney in late September, 1984.

FIFTH THURSDAY

'So? How you like my *spaghetti al limone*?'

'Gancio, it was superb.' Ramon gestured around the table. There were no dissenters. 'That is one thing we always agree on even when we can't agree on anything else. Your pasta is superb. Why don't you make us pasta more often?'

'Anyone can make pasta. Perhaps not like my pasta. But you are not big eaters. Maybe Lucio because he likes to eat. The rest of you, no. You like to pick at things. You like the little delicacies. That is why I make you antipasto. That is why I make you many small dishes. Simple.'

'I've got to tell you, Gancio, it's not a pasta I would have ordered. But it was great.'

'Thank you, Neil. But do you know why you wouldn't order my *spaghetti al limone*? It is because you are Australian, Neil, that is why.'

'That is discriminatory and inflammatory, Gancio. I thought we were all Australians now.'

'Let me finish. Maybe none of you would order my *spaghetti al limone*. That's why I don't put it on the menu. You've all lived in Australia too long. Your tastes are corrupted.'

'This better be good, Gancio,' cut in Lucio, 'speaking as one Italian to another.'

'You forget you are also Australian and Australians like protein on their plate. If I put it on the menu at the same price as my blue swimmer crab *linguini* or *marinara*, who would order it? Where is the value? Why pay for blue swimmer crabs and just buy lemon? But my lemon spaghetti costs just as much to make. Tell you what I'll do. I'll tell everyone that *spaghetti al limone* is the special of the day. If anyone orders it I'll bring you my special aged grappa. Free.'

'You're on. What's the main course?'

'Garfish. I remove the bones and pan-fry them in butter and a little olive oil and garlic. With fried parsley and *patate fritte*. For you, Neil, fish and chips.'

'Don't forget the lemon.' Neil watched Gancio retreat to his kitchen then turned to Ramon.

'So where are you going to start today? Are you going to start with Roberto and keep your symmetry? Obviously he is going to meet up with Eduardo and confront him. That will be the climax. End of story.'

'Ah, Neil, if only life were as simple as you draw it.' Ramon could not be provoked that easily. The second part of his story would be the hardest to tell, and he would have to be careful not to get caught up in the telling like an actor lost in the character he plays. Often, in order to generate the right emotions among his audience, Ramon had to assume them himself. Still it was worth the risk. This was by far the most audacious game he'd played with them. This was the ultimate test of his storytelling skills.

'No, I will not begin with Roberto, and, Neil, would you please stop trying to tell my story. If you think you know how it ends, leave now. Don't spoil it for the others. What are you going to do?'

'I've come so I'll stay. I promise to behave.'

'Thank you. Today I intend to begin with the young lady Lucio would doubtless like to hear more about.'

'Rosa?'

'No The lovely, lonely lady of the night. Eduardo never lost touch with Estelle. He was true to his word. Sometimes they dined together where the chance of anyone recognising either of them was remote. Do you think she might have been ashamed of Eduardo's caution? Not at all. She saw the wisdom of it. Besides, Eduardo was her only true friend and she believed they had no secrets. Eduardo would not do anything that would hurt her, but they could not close their eyes and pretend they were not the people they were.

'It's difficult to believe that anyone would want to hurt Estelle, though the risk of physical abuse is something all the women in her profession have to live with. Perhaps I should begin by telling you what happened to Estelle while we wait for our garfish to arrive.'

Chapter Twenty-Eight

Estelle was a working girl but she didn't work the streets and she no longer cruised the hotels. She now worked through an escort agency, whose strict rules protected her and her clients. They would not accept anyone as a client, neither man nor woman, unless they had a personal introduction from one of their existing clients. Estelle thought that made them very exclusive and gave them class.

She had reached the top of her profession. Sometimes she was hired for an evening and she would be wined and dined in style. She gave her companions the benefit of her charm, her wit, and her intelligence, as well as her body. Sometimes she was hired for days at a time, and sometimes for a week or more, as an escort for a visitor. She was always discreet, even when her clients weren't, and she was always in demand. She had her favourites, of course, but was careful not to give any indication as to who they might be. The agency was quick to suppress any possibilities of an extracurricular relationship. They had their reputation to think of.

Estelle was as happy as she'd ever been. She could now pick and choose her assignations, though she rarely refused any, because she genuinely enjoyed her work. Her agency never had a more conscientious nor delightful employee.

She had her own apartment off Victoria Street, Kings Cross, which she furnished herself, in a style which suggested the guiding hand of Eduardo. A lot of chrome and glass, modern mixed with art deco. She enjoyed doing her own shopping, and the little delis around the Cross came to know her well. She adored King Island ham and Canadian smoked salmon, especially with a freshly baked baguette.

On this particular day, the decision to have ham or salmon for her lunch occupied her thoughts. She stood on the corner of McLeay Street, waiting for the traffic lights to acknowledge the existence of pedestrians. There was nothing about her make-up or clothing to suggest she was anything but a well-dressed, wholesome young woman going about her legitimate business. She was no more aware of the motorcycle gliding towards her than she was of the endless cars and taxis that passed by. She didn't see the gloved hand that reached out towards her, and she certainly didn't see the open razor that it held. But she felt its sting as raked across the top of her breasts and upper arm, and she heard the sudden blast from the exhaust as the motorcycle accelerated away around the corner.

She was puzzled by the strange sensation and the sudden wetness. She was wondering if she'd been splashed by a puddle when the people around her began to scream. She looked down in bewilderment and saw the spreading crimson stain. She watched uncomprehending as her dress turned red, and little rivers formed around her shoes before rushing over the falls into the gutter. She fainted.

The Kings Cross slasher had claimed his first victim. On and off over the next few months there were more attacks. Nobody was really sure if they were the work of one person or of copycats. There was no pattern and no apparent motive. The randomness of the attacks made them doubly terrifying. Nobody was ever arrested or charged.

* * *

'Your garfish,' said Gancio proudly, presenting each plate momentarily before placing it on the table.

'Ramon, you bastard!' Lucio was outraged. 'How can you do this to us? How can you do this and then expect us to eat our lunch?'

'Garfish is a particular favourite of mine. If you can't eat yours I will be more than happy to help out.'

Milos and Neil broke up laughing. Ramon – whether by luck or cunning – had judged things to perfection.

'But what happened to Estelle? Is she dead?'

'Now, Lucio, we have a rule, no?' cut in Milos with mock severity. 'We do not tell our stories while we are eating. Otherwise we do not do justice to the meal or the story.'

'Thank you, Milos. The garfish really are superb. Lucio, you would be a fool to leave them.'

'Sometimes you worry me, Ramon. I wonder what really goes on inside your head. If this is a true story then Estelle deserves our sympathy and our pity. Yet you turn her misfortune into a big joke.'

'I apologise, Lucio. You are quite right. I was wrong to try and sandwich her between courses.'

Once more Milos and Neil choked back their laughter.

'You are a bastard, Ramon. Sometimes I think you have no heart.' He turned to Neil and Milos. 'You are right. He's a calculating bastard.'

Chapter Twenty-Nine

By the age of eighteen, Annemieke probably knew more about camouflage than any military expert. Her looks drew men's eyes irresistibly to her. Then she'd find them staring, not at her, but at the immobility in her right cheek, the slackness about her mouth, and the downturn of her lips. Sometimes she would read pity in their faces. But mostly she would see their interest check and die, as if her affliction was a communicable disease.

On the few occasions she allowed boys to take her out, they'd make excuses for her to their friends, pointing out that she'd been in a bad car accident. There'd be murmurs of sympathy and, inevitably, there'd be somebody thick-skinned enough to want to know all the details.

So she learned. She learned to look for the location of lights so she could turn the right side of her face away from the brightness. She cocked her head to the right when engaged in conversation, and her long hair would fall forward and throw that side of her face further into shadow. At dinner she would always take the last chair on the right facing in. When she went to the movies she always timed her entrance with the dimming of the lights. She became a chameleon. She learned how to hide in public places.

When she ventured outdoors during the day she clung to her old ways and wore a broad-brimmed hat. She also wore over-size sunglasses, which she allowed to rest on the lower part of her nose. Her brothers used to joke that they needed a torch to find her.

Annemieke believed she had disguised her disability to the point where she was rarely vulnerable. But, in effect, she was shutting herself off from the rest of the world. She'd erected barriers and discouraged people from trying to break through. She seemed cool, detached and serene but, in fact, she was always on her guard. She created her own little world and locked herself into it, not realising that by doing so, she'd locked everyone else out.

Her girlfriends had a succession of regular boyfriends yet Annemieke had none. They went out together in boisterous groups yet Annemieke always held back, never quite part of the inner circle. She wanted the intimacies that close friends bring to one another, yet she wasn't prepared to let herself go and pay the price demanded of her. She didn't understand the temporal nature of curiosity. She couldn't see that, within the space of a week, all her friends would not only cease to show interest in her affliction, they wouldn't even notice it.

So Annemieke played the part of the happy teenager for her family's benefit, but daily her loneliness grew. Her friends spoke of their sexual encounters and the gap between them and the virginal Annemieke widened alarmingly. She needed somebody who was more worldly and mature, somebody she could respect and trust enough to put aside her self-consciousness. At night she fantasised about meeting such a man, but she had to wait another four years before her father brought him home to dinner.

Chapter Thirty

When Eduardo boarded the Garuda Airbus to Jakarta, he was dismayed to find the business section fully booked. Normally he could count on at least three seats to himself, at least as far as Bali. Now only one seat remained, his, on the aisle next to the biggest man on the aircraft.

He groaned inwardly. He recognised the man from previous trips and knew exactly how broad those shoulders were. However, he suppressed his apprehensions and, with his usual impeccable good manners, sat and introduced himself.

'Good morning. I believe we have seen each other before on these trips. My name is Eduardo, Eduardo Gallegos.'

'Jan Van der Meer, pleased to meet you at last.' He extended his giant hand towards Eduardo. 'You are right, I have observed you many times. I have often wondered what it is you do that keeps you so busy.'

'My work keeps me busy.' Like most frequent flyers, Eduardo dreaded being trapped by talkative strangers and held captive to conversation in which he had not the slightest interest. His portable computer was his escape route. But until the aircraft was safely in the air, it had to remain stowed under the seat in front of him. He had no choice but to give the man alongside his full attention.

'I know you are a creature of habit,' the big man continued, 'so you can relax. I won't be the one to break your routine.'

Eduardo relaxed immediately. His companion understood. His relief was palpable.

'Let me tell you what you do. The first thing you do is reach for your paper or a magazine. Not today, because this rude stranger has interrupted you. Sometimes the magazine you read is one in which I advertise – *The Collector*. Perhaps we have a common interest? Once airborne you plug straight into your computer. You skip breakfast. You work through the movie. You drink only coffee. You stop working for lunch. You drink red wine with soda water with your meal. I tried it myself out of interest but I cannot recommend it.'

Despite his reservations Eduardo laughed.

'Then you work until the plane touches down in Bali. You stay aboard during refuelling and sometimes you doze off. I have dozed off watching you so I'm not entirely sure what you do next.'

Again, Eduardo found himself smiling. The big man continued, obviously enjoying himself.

'You skip the meal on the Jakarta leg and keep tapping away on your computer. Half an hour out of Jakarta you go to the toilet to freshen up. You always take around ten minutes so I make a point of going before you in case a woman occupies the other toilet to do her make up. Ten minutes is a long time for a man my age to hold his water, particularly on an aeroplane. Something to do with the altitude. You smile, but it's true. I know I only look thirty, but in fact I am nearly twice that age. What are you? Forty? Forty-two?'

'Forty-four, pushing forty-five.'

'Huh! You are still a child. One day you will find out what it is like to grow old. But I am digressing. You are always one of the first off the plane and you always thank the crew in Bahasa. Let me tell you, they appreciate that. Too many people never bother to learn the host country's language. Then while I wait for a blue taxi, your driver picks you up in a Mercedes.'

The Airbus began its lumbering run down the runway, striving for the speed necessary to defy gravity.

'I must say I am impressed.' The big man amused Eduardo, and for once he was not automatically counting down the seconds before the red light went off and he could reach for his computer. 'You are very observant.'

'Not at all!' Jan roared. 'Just bored. So bored that you are the most exciting thing I can find to keep myself entertained until the movie comes on. Not true. I read a little. I sleep a little. But I cannot work on these things. Perhaps it is the airconditioning. Perhaps it is just that I don't have your discipline.'

'Perhaps the issue is not one of discipline, but lack of organisation. I have to work on the plane because I can never seem to finish my work before I leave.'

'No, I cannot believe that. You are far too methodical. But tell me, what is your interest in antiques?'

'Largely commercial, but not entirely. I collect French glass. Late nineteenth century and early twentieth. However my main interest is that of publisher of *The Collector*. You say you advertise in it. I am always delighted to meet a client. What is your specialisation?'

'Primitive art from Indonesia. I deal in Indonesian art and antiquities. Not as a retailer, you understand, but as an importer. A lot of my customers also advertise in your magazine.'

'Have you ever thought of opening a retail outlet yourself?' Eduardo's mind began to tick over with possibilities. After all, given his connections, it could turn out to be a very lucrative little business.

'Of course. Every time I see the mark-up my clients put on my pieces.'

'Then perhaps one day we should discuss this.'

Jan turned around in his chair. He appraised Eduardo slowly.

'Perhaps, when we have known each other for longer than ten minutes.'

'Why?' asked Eduardo, not put off in the least. 'You already know all about me. You have told me so yourself.'

'Ah.'

'Perhaps there are one or two things you don't know about me.'

Eduardo smiled at his bland understatement. 'My business is printing and related industries. I have two partners but I am the senior partner and major shareholder. Our latest venture is publishing. We have set up an operation in the Pulogadung Industrial Estate. We print magazines for Singapore, Europe and Australasia. We have two titles of our own: *The Collector*, which you know about, and a glossy society rag, called *Fashion House*. It seems that Australia's finest like nothing better than to have their faces or their homes splashed around the pages of magazines, and so I oblige. It makes me popular, provides me with priceless contacts, and we make a little money out of it as well. The reason for my earlier comment is that I feel these people are just waiting for an opportunity to divert some of their enormous wealth towards the purchase of primitive art, provided it is suitably expensive of course.'

This time it was Jan's turn to laugh, and the chairs shook and his voice bounced around the tiny cabin. People turned to look for the source of the disturbance but Jan seemed not to notice.

Their rapport was established. The computer lay idle beneath the seat for the duration of the journey. They tripped over one another in their eagerness to reveal their interests. Jan told Eduardo about his little shop in Amsterdam and his life among the tea bushes on Tengkuban Prahu.

'Once I made my living selling tea and a little on the side selling antiques. Now I sell my tea exclusively to the two major Australian tea packagers. I grow exactly what they want and only need to meet them twice a year. They are happy to deal with an Australian who is the major partner in an Indonesian tea plantation. So now I spend my time selling antiques.'

Eduardo was intrigued by Jan, and impressed with his knowledge of Indonesia and his fluency in the language. He realised that Jan could be valuable to him, not just in Sydney, but in Jakarta as well. So he sat back, happy to listen to Jan talk. They talked through lunch and they talked through the in-flight movie, and they ignored the passengers who objected. In turn, Eduardo told Jan of his plans to open a typesetting studio to service advertising agencies and clients in Jakarta.

By the time they landed in Jakarta, they'd talked for nine hours. But still that wasn't enough. Eduardo offered Jan a lift in his company Mercedes and persuaded him to forsake the Hilton for the Hyatt Aryaduta. They checked in and arranged to meet for dinner.

'When do you leave for Kalimantan?' Eduardo asked over the spicy soup Madura.

'Day after tomorrow,' Jan replied. 'First I must have words with my shipping agent. His fees have become outrageous. He has an exaggerated opinion of my willingness to pay.'

'Will you fire him?'

'No. That is not the way things are done here. Face is also important in Indonesia. We will sit down together like old friends and we will negotiate. We will lie to one another and he will soften me up with little delicacies, and we will try to understand each other's position. Finally, we will agree on a price neither of us is happy with which, as you know, is the only fair result.'

Eduardo laughed. This man obviously knew his way around in negotiations with Indonesians. Where Eduardo had struggled, Jan would glide. Eduardo needed his knowledge and acumen. Once more he backed his intuition. Jan was a man he could trust, and Eduardo was never one to let an opportunity slip by.

'I have two propositions to put to you,' he said. 'We can work the details out later. But in my experience, where there is willingness on the part of both parties to make something work, the details become insignificant. I mentioned to you that we intended to set up a type studio and print shop within Jakarta proper. You have the knowledge to help me do this properly. I will need a local partner, and I will need staff. I will also need to import equipment. I would like you to be our consultant, for a suitable fee, naturally.

'Secondly, I would like the opportunity to become the sole outlet for your antiquities in Sydney or, to be more precise, I would like us to be partners in a sole outlet. We should have a formal partnership. You know yourself that retail is where the serious money is, and money doesn't come more serious than it does among my contacts. Why, the purchase of a piece or two virtually guarantees the new owners a double-page spread in *Fashion House*. Who could resist? Both propositions need some thought. But I believe we could prosper, both of us.'

It was Jan's turn to laugh.

'I'm flattered, of course, but you hardly know me.'

'I have spent the past twelve hours getting to know you. When did you last devote twelve hours to getting to know someone?'

'You have a point,' Jan conceded. 'In principle, I agree. I am more conservative, however. My Dutch heritage perhaps. I will need references.'

'Of course,' said Eduardo smoothly. 'Now let us celebrate. We are about to become Siamese twins, joined in the most binding place possible. At the wallet. Now, where is our waiter? Even in this Muslim country, a good Burgundy cannot be too expensive.'

It was, but they bought a bottle anyway.

Chapter Thirty-One

Eduardo arrived home from Jakarta at seven-thirty on a bleak Monday morning. He went directly to his apartment in Rose Bay, as was his custom. It didn't matter how much he travelled, he never tired of coming home to his view, and not even a grey day could entirely dull its welcome. He showered, then lay down on his bed. He had never cracked the secret to sleeping on an aircraft, and the night flight from Jakarta was definitely best spent asleep.

He pressed the playback button on his answerphone and smiled when he recognised his first caller. He hadn't spoken to Estelle for nearly three weeks. He'd rung and she'd rung, but they'd missed each other. Estelle liked to leave teasing messages for him. But this time her message gave him nothing to smile about. There was an edge to her voice, a distress she was trying hard to conceal. She gave a new number to ring and hung up. Eduardo was about to jot down the number when he heard Estelle's voice leaving a second message. Once again it gave the number. He listened to his tape right through. Estelle had rung three more times. And each time her voice grew in urgency. He listed his callers and rang Estelle first.

As soon as Estelle heard Eduardo's voice she became tearful. She began to apologise, but Eduardo wouldn't hear of it.

'Get in a cab,' he said. 'I'll put on the coffee.'

At that time of the morning, it is difficult to get a cab going in to the city, but easy to get one going out. Estelle was ringing Eduardo's doorbell before the coffee was properly brewed. He met her at the door, and she immediately burst into tears again. Eduardo took her in his arms and let her cry herself out. Despite his curiosity, he wouldn't press her to speak until she had calmed down and was ready.

He sat her on the sofa and brought her coffee and microwaved croissants. He mentally prepared himself for a tale of lost love. What else could it be? What else could possibly upset her this way?

'Now tell me,' he said gently, as if he didn't know.

To his surprise she simply stood and began to undress before him. She removed her jacket and began to take off her blouse. She unbuttoned it slowly but not in a way calculated to arouse. Eduardo was caught off guard. She pulled her blouse open wide. She wasn't wearing a bra. Eduardo saw the angry red line that ran like an equator around her breasts. He looked up at her face in horror. She wouldn't meet his look. She gazed past him at a spot halfway up the wall.

'Who did this to you?' His voice was still soft but menace had usurped sympathy. Whoever had done this terrible thing would not be allowed to get away with it.

'I don't know.' Slowly she began to button up her blouse. 'I really don't know. That's the trouble.'

'Tell me what happened.'

So she told him and she told him about the police afterwards.

'At first they were very nice. It didn't matter when I told them I was a prostitute. But then they questioned me about who I worked for. When I didn't tell them, they got angry. They thought I knew who had attacked me, or who had sent the man on the bike to attack me. They wanted a reason. They didn't want to believe that there was a maniac out there with a razor attacking women at random. They asked about my clients, if one of them might have a grudge against me. I told them that was impossible. Then they said that it was likely a weirdo had an obsession with me. That he was probably watching me. And he'd try to attack me again. They said they weren't prepared to keep an eye on me unless I helped them more with their enquiries to eliminate other possibilities. They're convinced someone I know is responsible. But I know that's impossible. So either the attack really was random, or there is a madman out there somewhere watching me.'

She began to sob again.

'I went to the agency and told them what had happened. I told them how I'd kept their name out of it, and also my clients. They were so sympathetic and appreciative. When they asked to see what the razor had done, I showed them without any hesitation. That's when they told me I couldn't work for them any more. I was damaged goods. Their clients wouldn't like it. I was bad for the image of the agency. Oh, Eduardo! I can't go back to freelancing. I can't go back to being a five-minute fuck!'

Tears flowed and there was no stopping them. Eduardo held her close while his mind went to work on her problem. She needed his help and he would not let her down.

'Where are you staying?' he asked.

'The agency has an apartment which they are letting me use for two weeks. I won't go back to mine. After that I don't know.'

'I do. You will stay here. With me. I'll move my work things out of the second bedroom and it can be your room.'

'Oh, Eduardo!' She threw her arms around him and held him tight.

'We will sell your apartment and buy you another. You can stay here till then. Now, there is another issue. Your career. It is time you had a change of career anyway. Always quit at the top, right?'

'Right,' she said hesitantly, not knowing what else she was qualified to do.

'Now tell me, because I need to know. What do you know about primitive art and artifacts?'

Estelle looked at him blankly.

'It doesn't matter. We have plenty of time and we will teach you. In the meantime, I'd like you to get your hands dirty. Like mine. I'm sure my partner Phil Breedlaw has a place for you at Hot Ink

Press. The pay will not be quite what you're used to, but it's only temporary, and meanwhile the rent is free.'

'Eduardo, you are the best friend anyone could ever have. I don't know how to thank you.'

She made a movement as if she intended to thank him anyway, in the best way she knew how. Eduardo laughed and stood up.

'No thanks are necessary between friends. You make yourself some breakfast. These croissants have died on us. I must get some sleep. We can discuss these things later. Oh, perhaps this will get you started.'

He pulled the large, glossy book which he had bought in Jakarta out of his cabin bag. It touched on everything there was to know about Indonesian art and artifacts, and was as good an introduction as anyone was ever likely to find. He'd studied it himself during the flight home.

Estelle was speechless. She was down and out and he'd picked her up. She was homeless and he'd given her a home, jobless and he'd found her a job. She was lonely and alone, and he'd enveloped her in the warmth of true friendship. Once more her life had point, purpose and security. He'd done all this for her in less than an hour. She watched him close his bedroom door behind him, then picked up the book and did exactly as she was told.

Chapter Thirty-Two

It was six weeks before Jan returned from his travels around the Indonesian archipelago. He visited the Dayaks in Kalimantan, remote villages in Irian Jaya, the Minangkabau and Bataks in Sumatra, bargained and haggled with dealers throughout the length and breadth of Java, spent a small fortune on the Portuguese influenced artifacts on the island of Flores, and bought Balinese paintings from Ubud and Batuan. He worked hard, sniffing out ancient objects and bargains. He also pushed his contacts for the special pieces they held back to sell to others with more willing wallets and surprised them by paying their price.

Eduardo's proposition had intrigued him, yet he was still reluctant to accept it. He wrestled with his innate conservatism. In truth, he didn't need the hassle or risk of starting up a shop. He was well enough off, and there had been times when he and Lita had talked about his retirement. Also, he hardly knew this man Eduardo. He might be a conman or he may have lost interest. Despite the conflict within him, Jan drove himself to the point of exhaustion, on the off chance that it all might come together.

Nevertheless, he still found time to visit his old friend in Ujung Pandang. Andi Sose, the old Bugis captain, had given up the sea and returned to his home port. Jan had met up with him once more on a buying expedition to Sulawesi eight years earlier. Jan's driver had taken him to Prahu Harbour and Pantere Anchorage in the hope of finding him. There, he had seen the old sea captain sitting patiently on an ancient wooden seat, watching the pinisi sail off to Kalimantan. Andi had not recognised him until he sat alongside him and slyly introduced himself.

'Do you still carry my knife, captain?' Jan asked.

A slow, incredulous smile of recognition spread over the old man's face They had exchanged stories and rolled back the years, but it had not taken Jan long to come to the sad realisation that Andi no longer had anything to live for. He had returned to captain another pinisi but once more the owners had sold his ship from beneath him. At his age, he had little hope of finding another.

Jan saw him infrequently, but every visit gladdened the old captain's heart and caused great celebration. Andi lived comfortably enough, but there were few luxuries. Every time Jan visited him, he brought a small suitcase crammed with chocolate, cream biscuits and cartons of cigarettes. And he always gave money, in secret, to the woman who looked after Andi.

They would sit together at the dockside, and Andi would fill Jan's head with the comings and goings of the Bugis fleet. How many ships went down in the last typhoon. Who had got caught smuggling contraband or drugs. How many pinisi had been superseded by the big Japanese-built freighters which had moved in on their monopoly. In this, way, Jan learned of the fate of One-Eye.

'He was too old to still be sailing,' said Andi matter of factly. 'But the sea was his home. Dry land was the only thing that man feared in this world. He was a good man, and there was always a pinisi that would find a place for him. He worked only for his bed and food, for he was no longer worthy of wages. He was swept overboard in a storm. We were all happy that he died at sea.'

There was sadness in the old man's voice, not for his lost comrade, Jan realised, but because he had been denied the same opportunity. Andi's face hid his age well, but his eighty year old body had lost its strength.

'It is a bad thing,' he said finally, with resignation rather than bitterness, 'to force a man to give up the sea before he is ready.' He took hold of both of Jan's hands.

'Promise me this,' he said. 'Promise me you will never give up the sea.'

'I promise.' Any lingering doubts Jan had of starting up a new business at this stage of his life now vanished. 'I promise I will never give up the sea. In fact when I get back to Australia, I think I will build myself a new boat.'

The old man beamed and for a brief instant he was a young man again. The two friends sat together and watched the sun arc towards the horizon.

'You never told me how Daeng came to be so badly scarred and lost his eye.'

'It was nothing out of the ordinary.' Andi's eyes glazed over as he thought of the time so long ago. 'We sailed into a typhoon. The mast split. The top half fell and struck his face. He must have heard it splitting and looked up. He should have known better. His face split wide open and we could see inside his head. We each of us took turns to sit behind him, to rest his body up against ours so that we could hold the two parts of his head together. We did this all the way to Singapore. We thought he would die but he didn't.'

'He never spoke?'

'He couldn't. When the mast hit him, he bit off his own tongue. But when we sang our songs he would join in. The noises he made were nonsense, of course, but it didn't matter. His friends understood him.'

'Dear God. It's a hard life you chose to lead, Andi.'

'Yes, my friend, very hard. But also a good life.'

Jan's driver returned to pick him up. Both men knew they would never see each other again.

Chapter Thirty-Three

'Hello, Eduardo, it's Jan. I am back.'

'Welcome home. I hope you are not too tired.'

'How do you know I only got back this morning?'

Eduardo laughed.

'Easy. Do you think I am not also anxious to continue our conversation? Besides, the last plane arrived two days ago, and I did not think you would wait two days before you contacted me.'

It all sounded so obvious coming from that leap-frogging mind. Eduardo was easily the most stimulating person Jan had encountered in a long while. He would have been devastated if Eduardo had had a change of heart. But Eduardo positively bubbled with warmth and enthusiasm. Jan's biggest problem would be to slow Eduardo down to a pace he was more comfortable with.

'I may have some good news,' Eduardo continued. 'We may have our first employee. But we can discuss this when we meet. How about lunch tomorrow? Bathers Pavilion at Balmoral Beach. It must be near your home, and there is not a single Asian dish on the menu.'

Jan laughed at Eduardo's thoughtfulness. After six weeks in Indonesia, another Asian meal was the last thing he wanted.

'What time?'

'Twelve-forty-five. The table will be in my name.'

Eduardo rang off and Jan could barely contain his happiness. He'd only been back a few hours, yet they already had staff! He could hardly wait to meet up with Eduardo again.

'It's good to see you like this, Jan,' Lita said. 'Whatever that man does for you, I hope it doesn't stop.'

'You will meet him soon,' Jan promised. 'I will bring him home to meet you and we will have one of your wonderful dinners.'

Lita knew exactly what that meant.

'I hope he's worth the effort,' she said dryly, though she was more than happy to oblige. 'I will invite the boys over, if they can drag themselves away from their girlfriends.'

Jan in this mood was the nicest man in the world.

Eduardo arrived at Jan's Mosman home at precisely eight p.m. He carried a bottle of Veuve Clicquot Brut champagne, a basket of hand-made chocolates and a bouquet of red roses and baby's breath. If it was all a little too much, it was because Eduardo, for once, was not familiar with the protocol. He simply had no experience of dining at other people's homes. He ate in restaurants, either as host or guest, and only rarely at the homes of Sydney's elite, where he was just one of a number of guests, and the occasions formal. He was out of his territory.

He wore a cream linen suit, a pale open necked shirt, and light, woven leather shoes without socks. If he was striving to appear casual, he failed dismally. He would not have been more formal in black tie.

'Eduardo! Come in, come in.' Jan's welcome was so boisterous, Eduardo felt slightly embarrassed. He wondered what Jan had said about him, what he had to live up to.

'Lita! Come. Eduardo is here.'

A tiny woman bustled out of the kitchen. She appeared shy and self-conscious, but Eduardo could see the strength in her bearing.

She seemed much younger than he had expected, and more beautiful. She was delighted with the flowers and the chocolates.

'Jan never brings me flowers any more. And certainly not roses. My goodness! Just look at them. Excuse me, I must find a vase for them. I want them to last as long as possible.'

'These are my two sons, Tom and Pieter.'

Eduardo turned at Jan's words, prepared to meet two boys. Instead he was confronted by two men, both towering giants, taller even than their father.

'Pleased to meet you.' Their voices rumbled like thunder but they had their father's gentleness in their eyes.

'How can Lita possibly be their mother?' Eduardo asked Jan in mock surprise. 'One, she is not big enough. Two, she is not old enough.'

The boys smiled politely. They had heard it all before. Jan took Eduardo's jacket and they moved into the lounge. Eduardo felt strangely out of place. He allowed Jan to dominate the conversation, adopting the role of polite listener all through the pre-dinner drinks. He discovered that both boys worked as waiters in exclusive restaurants, despite the fact that Pieter had a degree in engineering and Tom a degree in business administration.

'University taught them to use their brains,' Jan said. 'Now their brains tell them to open their own restaurant. Who can argue? High-class Asian, that's what it's going to be. There are enough bad ones already.'

Eduardo smiled and logged this information for future reference. He was glad to take his seat at the table.

He watched the casual, relaxed way the family took their places, the easy rapport and lack of fuss. Small talk abandoned him and he felt oddly adrift. For the first time in his life, he found himself among a normal family in a normal family home. It was a new experience for him, and he couldn't help comparing it with his own upbringing. He was fascinated by the Van der Meers, and envious of them, and the realisation of what he had missed out on saddened him.

'You are very quiet, Eduardo. Are you feeling all right?'

Eduardo snapped out of his reverie to see Jan, Lita and the boys looking at him with obvious concern.

'Forgive me.' He searched for words, a witty response, before deciding on the truth. 'It is a long time since I have been part of a family. Even if I am only part of a family for one night. I had no idea what my life has been missing.'

'Don't you have any family?' Lita asked, appalled.

'Sadly no. That is part of the price of being a refugee. But my family was never close. Not like this. If I am honest with you, I must tell you I was raised by servants.'

'How awful!'

'It s pretty awful around here sometimes,' said Tom, lightening the mood. 'You should be here when we fight. My sister throws a mean punch.'

'Aha!' said Jan. 'Eduardo, it is time you met the fifth member of our family. My daughter Annemieke.'

Eduardo had hardly been aware of the figure gliding soundlessly past with a large plate piled high with samosas. The wraith-like figure was now at the opposite side of the table, her left profile towards him as she served. Eduardo was not a religious man, but he honestly believed right then that he had seen an angel.

'Annemieke,' he heard Jan say, 'this is our new partner, Mr Gallegos.'

Eduardo could not take his eyes off her. He was unaware that he was staring, or that he was being closely watched by her two brothers.

'Mr Gallegos.'

'Eduardo, please.' He struggled to his feet. 'I am delighted to meet you, Annemieke.'

She smiled a strange sad smile that was somehow wrong, then glided effortlessly away. Eduardo stood staring at the doorway to the kitchen through which she had departed. Jan coughed discreetly.

'I'm sorry,' Eduardo said, feeling guilty without quite knowing why. He settled back in his chair, an unaccustomed tingling in his cheeks. 'Argentine men are children where beautiful women are concerned. And this is the second time tonight you have returned me to my childhood.'

'All men are children before beautiful women,' Jan said grinning. 'Even their fathers. Now, Annemieke will not forgive us if we don't eat her samosas. Come, they are getting cold.'

Eduardo noticed the two boys relax, but what had made them tense? He was confused. But his brain, already overloaded, pushed his confusion to one side. The family attacked the samosas and ate them with their fingers. So did he.

The dinner was superb. Lita had prepared her own version of a rijstaffel, serving each dish individually, from the curry puffs to noodles and sates, and finally the fiery Padung dishes. Eduardo combined pickles and chutneys and relishes with the different dishes as directed, and asked about every dish, enquiring as to its origins and the composition of its flavours. Through a supreme act of will, he managed to drag his attention from Annemieke, who effortlessly played the part of attentive listener, waiter and assistant chef. Through it all, she somehow managed to elude his close scrutiny. He talked about his contacts in Sydney society, and exaggerated the lengths to which they'd go in order to have their faces grace the social pages of his magazine.

'They have enough money,' he said. 'All they want is recognition. After all, what pleasure is there in being rich if one is not also famous? So I give them that. I trade faces for favours.'

They laughed at his self-deprecating cynicism.

'My partner, Phil Breedlaw, has had the best idea. We feature homes in the magazine. Of course, it has become a status symbol to have your home featured this way, and we have people queueing up for the privilege. Naturally, the presence of a few authentic Indonesian artifacts could only help their chances.' He gave Jan a sly look which everybody was intended to see.

'But won't that cause problems?' Tom asked. 'What about security? Your magazine would be like a catalogue for burglars.'

'That's the beauty of the whole scheme,' Eduardo said. 'Phil has signed up a security company to sponsor the series. We're even running a feature on security systems. The advertising revenue is formidable.'

Eduardo began to laugh and found he could hardly stop. He couldn't remember ever feeling so relaxed and happy.

'I'm almost ashamed to take the money,' he said.

Annemieke brought in the final dish, a cake of coconut icecream with lychees and mangoes. She seemed to be laughing along with everybody else. But like a silver fish turning and twisting in the water, her brightness would appear and disappear in the twinkling of an eye, as her head turned in the process of serving. Then he understood the enormity of her tragedy.

'Thank you,' he said looking into her eyes with a warmth which gave no hint of his discovery. 'You are a very special young woman.'

It was after two when the taxi came to take him back to Rose Bay. He felt intoxicated, not so much by alcohol, but by the company, the laughter, and the extraordinary vision called Annemieke. He resolved to see more of her, but he knew he would have to tread warily.

At forty-five, he was twice her age, and she the daughter of his new partner in business. He would have to be patient. He knew he would first have to win the family completely, before he could ever win her. He began to plan his campaign. He would ask Jan, discreetly of course, about her paralysis. He did not believe nature could have been so cruel.

That night he slept through until nine a.m. It had been a long time since he'd slept so well and without interruption.

'Without interruption,' he thought, and wondered if the sins of his past life had finally loosened their hold.

Annemieke also slept late, but it was because her excitement had drawn her in and out of sleep as thoughts tumbled over each other. Eduardo was the most stylish and elegant man she had ever met. He oozed confidence and charm, yet none of it seemed contrived. Moreover, her father liked him enormously. Could anyone ask for a better reference? Not in her eyes. She was certain he was the man she had dreamed about meeting. And now an odd thing struck her. In all the years she had indulged her fantasy, her Prince Charming did not have a face. Of course he had a face, but she could not bring to mind his precise features and realised she never had. Now when she closed her eyes, she saw Eduardo, and there was nothing about his face, his voice or his mannerisms that she had missed.

She'd noticed him watching her, but she was practised in this game, and used her craft to deny him all but fleeting glimpses. How would he react, she'd wondered, when he saw what she so skilfully hid? She watched him as he told his stories. He was so self-assured, so quick to laugh, and so appreciative and interested in each dish he was served.

When the time came for dessert, Annemieke took the tray from her mother. She'd decided to reveal her other side It was a risk, but she had to know. Her mother gave her a smile of complicity, and sent her on her way.

Annemieke knew exactly what she was doing. She served Eduardo first, then moved clockwise around the table. She served her father, allowing her long hair to fall forward so Eduardo could not see her face. As she moved on to her brothers, she angled her head so that her hair stayed behind her shoulders. She smiled, turned, bowed her head and raised it in a smooth but unending sequence, revealing her secret in carefully calculated moments. She knew the instant he spotted her sagging cheek, yet he gave no obvious sign. He did not turn away from her. His eyes locked onto hers and his smile radiated a warmth and affection she hadn't felt since she had sat, as a child, on her father's knee.

'Thank you,' he said to her. 'You are a very special young woman.'

Eduardo tactfully drew attention to himself while Annemieke

finished serving. It's as well he did, for her hands shook, and she would have been mortally embarrassed had anyone noticed.

'He's passed the test,' Annemieke thought to herself with mounting excitement. 'And so have I.'

Chapter Thirty-Four

The opening of their new shop gave Eduardo the opportunity to set the first phase of his plan in motion. To win over the Van der Meers.

They called their shop 'Java Man', and it opened in exclusive Double Bay. The glitterati turned out in force in support of Eduardo, and for the free champagne and press coverage the event promised.

Jan had been shocked by the amount of money budgeted for the opening, but even more so by the prices Eduardo was charging. They were outrageous, though Jan had to admit, many of the items for sale were among the best he had ever brought back.

'Don't worry,' Eduardo said. 'People love to pay, and these people more than most.'

Jan watched as proof of this theory walked out of the door, and red 'sold' stickers blossomed.

'It won't always be like this,' Eduardo counselled. 'These people also like to be seen to be paying. We'll have to have an opening with each new shipment.'

'In that case,' said Jan, as Estelle walked past with bottles of Moët in each hand, 'perhaps we should also import our own champagne.'

Together they watched Estelle. She was the perfect hostess. Tom and Pieter had taught her how to pour champagne without filling the glasses full of bubbles. She was a good student, but few students have such attentive teachers.

At ten p.m., Eduardo escorted Anders Peterson and the last of the guests to the door. Anders didn't leave empty handed either, Jan noted. In fact he thought Anders had a particularly good eye and appreciation of primitive art. Estelle opened a fresh bottle of Moët and brought out a tray of canapés she'd withheld.

'Well, we should just about have covered costs,' Eduardo said smugly as he collapsed into his chair.

'Oh, I think we've done a bit better than that,' Estelle chimed in. 'We've taken cash and deposits on items worth just over a hundred and fifty thousand dollars.'

Jan and Lita looked at each other in amazement, and began to laugh. The whole thing was beyond their comprehension, another world entirely.

'It's a pity Annemieke could not come,' Eduardo observed innocently. 'Is it because she is uncomfortable in crowds?'

There was an awkward silence, but Eduardo was a good judge of timing and occasion. He knew it was a good time to ask, while they were still high on their success.

'It is the legacy of a car accident. In Indonesia. Near our home at Tengkuban Prahu.' Jan's voice was steady as he told the story, but Eduardo was struck by the silence that surrounded it. Nobody dared draw breath. Each sentence was punctuated by an extended pause. It was as if somebody had rolled a hand grenade among them and everybody had tensed for the explosion. He had not anticipated the extent of the wound he had opened.

'There is nothing more the doctors can do for her,' Jan concluded. 'Perhaps in the future, somebody will come up with something that will help. Who knows?'

Lita took Jan's hand in hers. She had never heard him tell the story to anyone before, other than their doctors. Now, here he was, opening up to this man they barely knew. He had not resented Eduardo's question nor, it seemed, did he regret answering it. She wished her husband had met Eduardo sooner.

'Annemieke wanted to come, but she knew she would not be comfortable here.' Lita smiled warmly at Eduardo. 'Too many cameras. Too much publicity.'

'What about you, Lita? Are you comfortable here?' Eduardo was puzzled by Lita's smile. He couldn't dwell on its implications, because he felt it was his responsibility to move the conversation on. Besides, there was another item on his agenda. Another idea which would bring him a step closer to Annemieke.

'Yes, I am comfortable here. Why do you ask?'

'Then would you be prepared to help us, to work here with Estelle, and teach her about Indonesia until she is able to speak confidently to our clients?'

'Yes, I think so.'

'Excellent! Pieter, see if you can find another bottle of Moët. We now have a staff of two.'

Pieter obliged, but he too had his price.

'Now that you have conscripted both my father and my mother, perhaps you will do something for Tom and me?' Pieter paused for effect. 'When we open our restaurant, will you promise to handle the opening? You seem to have an extraordinary talent for it.'

Eduardo agreed without hesitation. He laughed and made facetious suggestions about the things they could do. He was happy to oblige Pieter and Tom. In fact, he was elated. The first part of his plan was in place and taking effect. He was winning the family. They loved him. And that helped clear the path to Annemieke. Still, he knew there was a long way to go, and a precipitous move would ruin everything. He would not make his move until he was certain it would be welcomed. The impatience of old stirred within him. He ached to see Annemieke again. Rosa had returned to stalk him in his sleep and he knew only Annemieke could drive her away.

An idea began to form, one so childishly hopeful that he almost dismissed it. But ideas, even those born of wishful thinking, never entirely go away without first being explored.

'I know it is a long shot,' Eduardo said, 'but do you think you can help?'

'I'll see what I can do,' his doctor replied. 'It's really a question of researching back issues of every reputable medical journal to see if anyone has published a paper. Then scan all the current issues as they come out. I know some medical students who will be glad of the opportunity to earn some pocket money.'

Eduardo went straight from the doctor's surgery to his office at the Hot Ink Press. Between their new interests in Indonesia and Java Man, he had lost touch. Phil and Don both did a good job, but it never hurt to keep them on their toes. Moreover, he had been neglecting his contacts. He had clients to woo and friendships to reinforce.

Anders had continued his inevitable rise. If it is true, as it is often said in the advertising business, that those with the most hot air go furthest, then Anders would go further than most. Probably to the top, for he had hot air to spare. Still, he was influential and Eduardo had been rather cavalier with their friendship.

They resumed their partying. Indeed, Anders had never left off. But Eduardo could not help comparing the butterflies who were their prey with Annemieke. He found he no longer had much appetite for casual affairs. Daily Eduardo became more disgruntled. He wanted to see Annemieke again, but he couldn't find any justification. Not one that wouldn't risk exposing his motives.

Each morning he rose early and went into his office. He reviewed the finances, workflow and projections with Don and Phil. The meetings became increasingly acrimonious and, inevitably, Eduardo and Phil would end up shouting at each other. Eduardo disputed decisions they had made in his absence, even though he had previously made it perfectly clear they had every right to make them. He nitpicked over detail and railed over the slackness he perceived to be creeping into their operation.

Phil took the brunt of Eduardo's ill humour because they shared the same expertise. He blamed Phil for the business they had lost, and for quotes they had failed to win. Don acted as peacemaker between the two, but it wasn't long before his sense of justice was sufficiently aroused for him to take Eduardo aside, and tell him the facts of life.

'It is the nature of our business to win and lose accounts,' he said. 'Every day we hold on to an account brings us closer to the day we lose it. Who gave me this wisdom? No clues, but he is an arrogant, insensitive Argentinian. Who is first in every morning and last out at night? No clues, but he has big feet and an even bigger heart. Who has kept our profit margins up despite the cost-cutting in the industry? Let me tell you, he's the same bloke who wears his lunch on his tie and did more than either of us to ease the Burton Simmons people into our operation – and motivate them to work their butts off for us! You owe Phil an apology. God in heaven! How do you think we've been funding your Indonesian operations and the bloody take-over? The business has never run better. Of course there have been some slip-ups. But what do you expect? Phil's had to do your job as well as his. You snap at him over minor issues when you should compliment him on the big picture. I don't know who's put the prickle up your arse, but if it's a girl I hope you screw her or marry her or whatever it is you want to do to her, and do it soon.'

Don's face had flushed red with anger and his moustache bristled with indignation.

'I'm sorry, Don.' Eduardo looked down at his feet like a scolded child. 'I accept that I have been unreasonable. I am, as you implied, distracted. Sometimes I behave like an arsehole.'

'Sometimes you are an arsehole. Gold-plated.'

'Grab Phil. Let me take you both to lunch so I can apologise.'

Eduardo took them to lunch at the Malaya, where the forgiving Phil solved another of Eduardo's problems.

'One day,' he said, 'I'm going to book into six different

restaurants on the same night, and have my favourite dish in each.'

The potential of the idea hit Eduardo immediately.

'That is a fantastic idea. Brilliant! May I borrow it?'

'Feel free,' said Phil, in a voice heavy with irony. 'I have my dreams, and they stay dreams. You have my dreams and they become reality. I think I'll get drunk.'

Chapter Thirty-Five

Eduardo arranged everything for Saturday night. He spoke to all the restaurants, and arranged a table in each at staggered times. He paid in advance with a generous tip, though the restaurateurs he spoke to were intrigued by the idea and flattered to be involved. Each was determined to produce the finest dish. Eduardo was well known to them, and hadn't he promised to write about the night, and run the story in his magazine, *Fashion House*?

Eduardo booked a stretch limo, and picked up the Van der Meers promptly at seven. Pieter volunteered to sit with the driver, while Tom and Eduardo occupied the fold-down seats. Annemieke sat diagonally opposite him so that her best side was towards him. She wore a simple black dress, high at the neck and virtually absent at the back. She wore no jewellery apart from French jet drop earrings, studded with tiny rhinestones. If she wore make-up, it went unannounced. It appeared she had gone to no trouble at all, which guaranteed that she had gone to a great deal of trouble indeed.

Eduardo was overwhelmed. He switched his charm onto automatic and talked non-stop in the hope that it wouldn't show.

They began with sushi made with toro, the prized, fatty, underbelly of tuna, before crossing the road to a second Japanese restaurant for California roll, and the tiny dim simlike, gyoza.

Eduardo summoned the limo with his portable phone, and they were off to a Vietnamese restaurant for warm pork julienne rolls, and cubed beef dipped in lemon juice and ground white pepper. At each stop, the manager made a point of having their photograph taken with himself in a prominent position.

The next stop was Eduardo's favourite Chinese restaurant, for lamb pancakes, followed by chilli lobster. In each case, Eduardo as host would allow his guests to take their seats first. Yet each time, they left a space for him with Lita on his right, and Annemieke on his left.

Annemieke told him about her studies at the Conservatorium and he hung on every word. The boys took discreet notes for their restaurant-to-be, and their observations often reduced them to laughter. Conversation never flagged, for the limo came to collect them as soon as they had finished their plates. Eduardo's favourite Malay restaurant was next, where the chef greeted them with a plate of fried anchovies, liberally dusted with chilli. Eduardo had prepared the Van der Meers for their final dish, a beef rendang so hot and fiery it could eat its way through armour plate in less than half an hour. But the chef had not prepared Eduardo for what he had done.

He had gone beyond instruction, and produced his own mini rijstaffel, which included beef rendang, but five other dishes as well. Obviously, he had an eye on top billing when Eduardo published his story.

The Van der Meers gasped at the quantity of food placed before them. Eduardo just laughed.

'Eat what you can,' he said. 'Perhaps a little of each. But not so much that you spoil your appetite for dessert. Just enough so that we can show due appreciation for the effort my friend here has gone to.'

The photographer appeared magically, to capture the smiling faces, the magnificent platter of food, and Eduardo with his arm around the chef. Jan had already eaten more than enough, but he could not resist the rijstaffel.

'This takes me back to the Savoy Homann,' he said. 'Like this restaurant, they use chillies without fear. Lita and Annemieke are too timid. They never use enough chilli for my taste.'

'Oh?' said Annemieke. 'I think our dishes are at least as hot as these. Taste.' She reached across the table to offer her father a piece of beef which she had impaled on her fork. Jan opened his mouth and took the offering. He should have known better.

He gasped, and gulped for air as the inside of his mouth ignited. His face flushed and tears came to his eyes.

'What did you do to it?' he gasped.

'I didn't think it was hot enough for you,' said Annemieke innocently. 'So I slipped in a couple of these.' She pointed to a side dish of small, red cluster chillies.

The boys howled with laughter, and Eduardo looked at Annemieke anew. He saw a young woman who could hold her own in this family of giants. He glimpsed the spark which her poise hid well but did not extinguish. It reminded him briefly of someone he'd known in his earlier life. If he had been attracted to Annemieke before, he was now irresistibly drawn.

The last stop was the Regent Hotel for dessert, coffee and cognac. Annemieke radiated happiness and her happiness seemed to infect everyone, especially Jan.

'I have never seen you so happy, Annemieke,' he said. He turned to Eduardo. 'It was so kind of you to also invite my children.'

Annemieke flushed with embarrassment. She excused herself and went with Lita to the ladies' room. There is the problem, Eduardo thought to himself. He smiled at Jan, but his heart sank. He was Jan's friend. That is how Jan saw him. That is how the family saw him. Yet he had a feeling that Annemieke saw things differently. Was she aware of his interest? He looked at Jan and the two boys as they chatted to each other. How would he ever get past their guard?

Eduardo began to ring Jan at home under the pretext of learning more about doing business in Jakarta. Sometimes Annemieke would answer the phone and they'd chat. At times he would forget that he had rung to speak to Jan, and would hang up before being passed on. He gradually learned Annemieke's routine. When she would be home, when she would be at the Conservatorium, and when she was the one most likely to answer the phone.

One day he casually mentioned that they should have lunch together. He knew that she finished at the Conservatorium at noon on Wednesdays. He proposed that they meet at the southern entrance to the Queen Victoria Building at twelve-forty-five the following Wednesday. He said he would be in town that day. He made it sound like the most natural thing in the world, then held his breath for her reaction. She said she would look forward to it, then made her farewells.

Eduardo hung up. He was surprised to find himself shaking with tension. She had accepted. Lunch was an appointment, he'd rationalised, dinner was a date. He judged that her guards would accept an appointment, where they might baulk at the other. Lunch was innocent. And, after all, was he not now a family friend?

The next step was to make the appointments a regular event, so that Jan and the boys would come to realise the true basis of their friendship. By then, he judged, there would be an acceptance of the fact that Annemieke also had a claim on him, rather than the other way around. From that perspective Eduardo knew that Jan would have no option but to give his blessing. All he required was patience. And the willing complicity of the angel called Annemieke.

Gancio brought them their coffee and free glasses of aged grappa. Three tables had ordered the *spaghetti al limone* and raved about it.

'They only ordered it because they saw me bring it to you,' Gancio complained. 'People are like that when they think they're missing out on something. It's not a fair test!'

'Tough luck, Gancio,' said Neil. 'It just goes to show we're not all troglodytes.'

'What are troglodytes?'

'People who wouldn't order *spaghetti al limone*. Cheers!' Neil raised his glass at Gancio's departing figure. 'So,' he continued, 'we've had the horror story, the adventure story, and now we have the gluey romance. What have you got planned for the ending? Farce maybe?'

'You are a cynic, Neil. Sometimes I wonder why we put up with you.' Milos took a sip from his coffee. 'I think the point Ramon is making is the one Lucio alluded to. There is much to like about Eduardo. Do you remember him saying that? Just as Eduardo set out to win over the Van der Meers, Ramon is trying to make us like Eduardo.

'Look what he did for Estelle. That was the act of a nice man, no? Look how he courts Annemieke. That is the act of a nice man. See how he gave up his womanising, his deflowering of rich virgins. He wants us to believe Eduardo has grown up and become a nice man. That's his not-so-well-hidden agenda. I think he's trying to tell us that Eduardo was a nice man all along and that fate and his youth were responsible for his earlier transgressions.'

'Do me a favour, Milos. I know exactly what Ramon's up to. I just don't buy it.'

'If you know what Ramon's up to, why do you insist on revealing your thoughts? How can we trap him in this game he's playing if you keep revealing your hand? He'll just change his story, no?'

'It's a true story.' Ramon laughed. 'How can I change it? If I did it would no longer be true.'

'Yes,' said Lucio thoughtfully. 'Neil can say what he likes because he won't change anything. I believe Ramon's story is true. The Kings Cross slasher is real. I've actually met a woman who was slashed by him. It was like Ramon said. She had this scar which ran right across here, across her breasts. She nearly died.'

'Lucio, excuse me for prying but if you know that kind of detail you probably also know this woman in the biblical sense. I don't want the grubby details, but doesn't your wife ever wonder what you do when you don't come home?'

'It's none of your business, Neil, but you are implying something I find offensive. I am not a man who cheats and lies to his wife. As a matter of fact we are very good friends and we love each other. But we are no longer intimate – for reasons that would make a story every bit as long and as involving as Ramon's. Perhaps one day I will tell it. But my wife does not insist that I share her celibacy nor does she want me to discuss my other women with her. She just asks me to be discreet. Besides, I am not young and fit and handsome like you, Neil. I'm not tall and distinguished like Ramon nor a rich sugar daddy like Milos. The opportunities for a short, fat, bald Italian are more limited. No, don't laugh.'

But of course they laughed and teased Lucio mercilessly. They'd inadvertently opened a wound and now had to pretend they hadn't. Lucio's admission had embarrassed them all.

'How did we get on to this?' asked Neil finally.

'We were discussing truth,' said Milos. 'Perhaps we've had enough truth for one day.'

'Does that mean you don't want me to continue with my story?'

'Nice one, Ramon, you never miss a beat.'

'I'll take that as a compliment, Neil.'

Chapter Thirty-Six

It began raining mid-morning on the day Eduardo was to meet Annemieke. Eduardo cursed his luck. He had neither raincoat nor umbrella. He'd chosen to wear his new Zegna double-breasted suit with the once-more fashionable button fly, and he took the prospect of it getting wet as a personal affront. All morning he hovered around his window checking the sky, hoping for the wind to change direction and blow the clouds away.

Phil and Don kept well away from him. They could see the mood he was in and knew there was more to it than a drop of rain. The fact is Eduardo was nervous. He'd slept badly and his unwelcome night visitor had come to torment him. He awoke with a feeling of dread and foreboding. The day hadn't improved.

His taxi was late arriving, as the city traffic bogged down in the rain. He realised with dismay that Annemieke would arrive before him. Unforgivable.

'Can't we go any faster?' he asked the driver.

'Sure, mate. No worries. We could both get out and walk.'

The taxi crept along Parramatta Road, into Broadway and down George Street. He was already ten minutes late. One hundred metres short of the rendezvous, the traffic ground to a halt as cars heading north towards the harbour bridge blocked the inter-section. Eduardo watched the traffic lights change from red to green and back again without a single vehicle budging. He realised the hopelessness of his situation. He checked the sky. It still looked threatening but the rain had eased. He decided to walk the rest of the way. He paid off the cabbie and got out.

Almost immediately, it began to rain again. He wanted to run to save his suit but his pride would not allow him such an undignified arrival. He walked faster. It rained harder. The traffic still hadn't moved, but even so, the pedestrian lights were in his favour. He saw Annemieke across Druitt Street and waved. She waved back.

The intersection of Druitt and George is one of the few where pedestrians are able to cross diagonally. Eduardo was slow to spot the young woman racing towards him from his right. Her umbrella had blown inside out, and she held it horizontally as she tried to control it. Eduardo stopped to let her pass in front of him.

As the young woman raced past the handle of her umbrella caught in his fly. He felt himself tugged forward and almost overbalanced. Then he heard the unmistakable sound of fly buttons hitting asphalt. Even above the noise of car engines and horns, he heard them hit the road, spin and roll. He closed his eyes in disbelief. He stood frozen and humiliated. Anger and embarrassment fought for ascendancy. The woman stopped, mortified.

'Go away!' Eduardo's brain screamed.

'I'm so sorry,' she said, and unthinkingly peered at his fly as she tried to unhook the handle of her umbrella.

'Allow me,' said Eduardo through gritted teeth. He could hear other pedestrians laughing. He could see them pointing. He handed the umbrella back, and began to move away.

'Wait! Wait!' the young woman screamed. And to Eduardo's horror she began picking up the wayward buttons, one by one, as taxis honked, onlookers whistled, and the traffic lights turned green.

'Here,' she said as she tipped the buttons into Eduardo's open palm. 'I'm so sorry. I really am.' She turned and fled.

Eduardo also wanted to turn and run. But Annemieke had seen him. Clutching his buttons in his hand, he moved zombie-like to the kerb. The rain intensified. It was the last straw. With no dignity left to lose, he sprinted for cover. Annemieke was smiling. Or was she laughing at him?

'You saw what happened?'

Annemieke's smile widened, and she nodded in sympathy.

'It seems our lunch is over before it has even begun. I must catch a taxi home and change.'

'Nonsense!' said Annemieke. 'Come with me.'

She took him by the hand and led him into the Queen Victoria Building. She led him straight to a menswear boutique.

'Could I borrow a needle and some cotton?' she asked, and explained the problem. Eduardo was dispatched to a changing booth by the sympathetic staff, to wait while Annemieke sewed his buttons back on. Eduardo sat, head in his hands. He could not conceive of a more ignominious beginning. He was late, wet and humiliated. He was in no fit state to charm anyone, let alone someone as beautiful, intelligent, and as important to him as Annemieke.

She passed his trousers back through the curtain. He put them on, buttoned his jacket and, summoning the remnants of his dignity, stepped out. The staff applauded. He looked shyly at Annemieke, inviting comment, hoping she wouldn't laugh. She rose up on her toes, put her hands on his shoulders and kissed him. Before he could react, she had moved a step back, but her hands still held his shoulders. She cocked her head on the side so that the expressive side faced him.

'How am I going to explain to Jan and my brothers,' she asked, 'when they discover I had your trousers off on our very first date?'

Eduardo began to laugh and Annemieke joined in. He took her hands in his.

'That's exactly how I feel,' he said. 'Like a boy on my first date.'

She squeezed his hands. Eduardo was back on the rails, and further down the track than he'd ever hoped to be.

* * *

The change in Annemieke was remarkable. Quite simply, she blossomed. The discreet, conservative clothes, so much a part of her camouflage, gave way to bold fashion. Her tinkling laugh, once a rare treat, now rang through the house at the slightest provocation. She brought an exuberance to everything she did, and her carefully stage-managed poise and serenity were relaxed, at least around home.

Lita knew the source of her happiness. Indeed, she'd known from the very first, from the night of the rijstaffel. But she kept her knowledge from Jan and the boys. She understood that they must come to see what was plainly before their very eyes, in their own good time. Why is it, she wondered, that men are so blind about things so obvious?

It was months before Jan made the connection between Annemieke's happiness and her Wednesday lunches with Eduardo. He'd thought Eduardo was being kind, the way an uncle might indulge a favourite niece. He finally twigged to the fact that Annemieke was having abnormally long conversations with Eduardo, before passing the phone on to him. He took his suspicions to Lita.

'They remind me of us,' Lita told him, 'when we met at the Savoy Homann. I was eighteen, four years younger than Annemieke, and you were a man of thirty. It may be hard for you to accept, but your little darling has grown up, and she has made her choice. You are going to have to share your friend with Annemieke.'

'I wonder if it is a good thing,' he said. 'I may have been thirty when I married you, but Eduardo is middle-aged. I think I will speak to him.'

'Over my dead body.'

Jan turned to his wife. He knew he was beaten.

'It's not easy, you know, when your daughter runs off with your best friend. I wonder if it is possible for Eduardo to be both my friend and my son-in-law?'

Lita threw her arms around her big, unhappy bear.

'Of course it is! Now you have Annemieke to think of, not yourself. When you see her, you give her a big hug. Just look at her, Jan. She is so much in love, and it has made her more beautiful than ever. Just look at her!'

Jan did as he was told. Lita was right.

Chapter Thirty-Seven

Eduardo should have left well alone. He'd fallen in love with Annemieke and she with him, and her family had given their blessing. Already they openly discussed marriage, and they were planning a party to formalise their engagement. Eduardo should have been content, but when the opportunity came to make the grand gesture, he could not resist it. If he had, then this story would be of no consequence.

When he found a message from his doctor on the answerphone, asking him to call, he was mystified. He rang the surgery and made an appointment.

'I've got some encouraging news,' his doctor told him. 'One of my student helpers has come up with this.' He passed a medical journal across his desk.

'It's what we've been looking for. It seems a Dr Tannen in California has published a paper on some rather extraordinary and innovative neurosurgery techniques. His specialisation is restoring and reuniting nerves which have been severely damaged and scarred. His particular preoccupation is with the facial nerves. Ring any bells with you?'

Eduardo was stunned. The long shot had come home. For one of the few times in his life, he was speechless.

'He claims a high success rate, but he also admits to being highly selective in accepting patients for surgery. Basically, this means there are those he can help, and those he can't. Now, before we get our hopes up on behalf of your young lady, we'd better find out in which camp she belongs. And, Eduardo, put that paper down now, unless you're prepared to spend more money than you can possibly imagine.'

Eduardo didn't put the paper down.

'What do I do next?'

'If you like, I will write to Dr Tannen. No doubt he will want a full medical history, so you'll have to clear that with the Royal North Shore Hospital. Then, if the description falls within the general ambit of his activities, he'll want to examine her. Then, and only then, if he's confident that your friend won't spoil his averages, he'll agree to operate. It's still a long shot, Eduardo. If you intend to discuss this with her, you'll be well advised to moderate your enthusiasm.'

'Good God, man! How am I supposed to do that? This is fantastic news.'

Eduardo was elated. He had already decided that this would be the ultimate engagement present. He would be the one to bring back the full glory of her beauty, the full radiance of her smile. She would adore him for it. The whole family would adore him. Already he basked in the glory. He did not consider for one second that she might not be eligible for surgery, or that the surgery might not be a success.

That night he took Annemieke to a little French restaurant near Crows Nest. He was excited and Annemieke tried to guess the reason.

'You're going to propose to me,' she said. 'On your knees in front of everybody.'

'No,' he said, 'but I will if you like.'

He kept her guessing all through the meal until she threatened to strangle him.

'Annemieke,' he began, 'months ago, when we first met, I went to see a doctor friend of mine. I told him about you and asked if he knew of anything that could give you back the missing part of your smile.'

He told her how the doctor put students onto the job of researching medical journals. As he spoke, he noticed Annemieke grow more and more tense with anticipation. She knew where he was leading, and couldn't wait for him to get there. But years of disappointment had taught her caution. Only now did he understand his doctor's words of advice, but already he'd gone too far. She clearly believed he was capable of miracles, even this most precious of miracles.

He told her about the doctor's unexpected call, and he told her about Dr Tannen and his new techniques. She wanted more, but he'd realised too late the trap he'd set for himself.

'My doctor believes you are precisely the sort of case Dr Tannen specialises in,' he lied. But for the table between them, she would have thrown her arms around the man she loved, and sobbed for joy.

'Oh, Eduardo,' she said. 'Please tell me I'm not dreaming. Please tell me this is happening.' She gripped his hands fiercely and tears began to flow.

For once, Eduardo had brought his car, and they drove down to Balmoral Beach. They sat on the sand watching the waves while Annemieke got over her initial excitement.

'Don't tell Jan or Lita yet,' cautioned Eduardo. Somehow he had to lower her expectations. 'First we must get the Royal North Shore Hospital to release your medical history to Dr Tannen, to confirm your suitability.'

'What do you mean?' she asked, suddenly aware of the implications.

'It is the procedure. It is boring and it is slow.' Eduardo could see the disappointment in Annemieke's eyes. She'd been let down

before and now it was happening again. No! He decided to commit
to the lie.

'My doctor says it is a formality, but it is the way things
are done. We send over your records, then Dr Tannen invites
us over to his clinic for an examination. That is how it works.
Don't worry. You have suffered too much to ever be disappointed
again. This time we will really have something to smile about.
Not half a smile, Annemieke. But a big smile, from ear to ear. So big
that the top of your head nearly falls off. Imagine that,
Annemieke.'

And Annemieke did. Eduardo's confidence was infectious. She
wanted so badly to believe. And so did Eduardo.

Over the next weeks he hounded his doctor's staff for a
response. At first they were understanding, then irritated by his
persistence. They finally convinced him that they would call the
instant they had any news, be it day or night. Eduardo was in a
meeting with clients when his doctor rang. His clients couldn't
help but smile when the smooth, cultured Argentinian suddenly
whooped and hollered like a cowboy gone mad. He poured
everybody a glass of champagne and abandoned the meeting.
What was the point of going on? They'd get no more sense out of
him that day.

'Pack your bags, Annemieke,' he said.

'What!' The joy and relief in her voice overwhelmed him, the
volume near deafened him. He pulled the phone away from his
ear.

'California here we come.'

He still urged her not tell her family. He'd seen what the
prospect of disappointment could do to Annemieke, and he
wanted to spare Jan and Lita. The last few weeks had been agony
for him, as they must also have been for Annemieke. He cursed
himself for not heeding his doctor's advice. He berated himself for
his impatience. He wondered if he'd ever learn.

'We'll tell them we're going on holiday to Los Angeles,' he said. 'To Disneyland. There is a possibility that Dr Tannen will decide against operating. I'm sure that won't happen, but it's a possibility we must face. If that happens, only two people will be hurt. Just you and I.'

'No,' said Annemieke. 'They are as much a part of this as I am.'

'Then let me tell them with you. I will come over tonight after dinner.'

Jan and Lita were stunned. It took a while for them to grasp what they were hearing. New techniques? New procedures? Lasers? California? They looked at Eduardo. Was there anything this man could not do?

Jan and Lita hugged them both and, not knowing what else to do, hugged each other.

'I pray to God your trip is successful,' Jan said. 'Yes, to God. If this miracle works, I swear I will become a believer.' He turned to Eduardo and hugged his friend once more.

'Eduardo, I don't know what to say. I gave up. You didn't.' His voice was near breaking.

'Open some wine,' Eduardo said. 'Let's celebrate. I simply took over the baton, Jan. It was time you let some one else carry it for a while.'

'It is Eduardo's engagement present to me,' said Annemieke. 'Isn't it the most wonderful present any woman ever had?'

The direct flight to Los Angeles takes a little over thirteen hours by 747 SP. Eduardo and Annemieke went straight from the airport to the hotel which had been recommended by the Feldman Clinic. It was small and elegant, and so expensive Eduardo wondered if it was not also owned by the Feldman Clinic. His suspicions grew stronger when he realised most of the guests were either patients or relatives of patients. Still, it was very comfortable, and virtually next door.

Annemieke's excitement on arriving in the United States for the first time in her life was overshadowed by her reason for being there. It was still early afternoon, and both of them wanted to lay down and sleep. But Eduardo insisted that they would be better off if they could stay awake, at least until evening. He knew the importance of adjusting to local time as quickly as possible.

Their appointment at the clinic was for ten the following morning. Eduardo didn't want Annemieke lying awake worrying all through the small hours. He suggested they go to Rodeo Drive but Annemieke wanted to leave that till last. Instead, they spent the afternoon around the hotel pool, playing at being tourists, but unable to shake their growing anxiety.

'I can't stand the wait,' Annemieke said in a way that reminded Eduardo of just how young she was. 'What will we do if they decide they can't do anything for me?'

'What do you want to do?'

'Go home.'

'Let's just see what tomorrow brings,' Eduardo said gently. 'We've come too far to be beaten now. We both know everything will work out fine. You know that. I know that.'

But of course neither of them did. Eduardo took her hand and led her back to her room. She was so tired he thought she might burst into tears. He made her take two Mogadons.

'Ring me when you wake up,' he said. 'It doesn't matter what the time is. Promise you'll ring me?'

'I promise.'

Tiredness and the Mogadons overcame her anxieties and she slipped into dreamless sleep.

Chapter Thirty-Eight

The Feldman Clinic encapsulated everything Eduardo disliked about America. The bland smiles, bland courtesies and endless platitudes got on his nerves. But Annemieke seemed not to mind. She'd withdrawn to her most serene, aloof and distant. She barely looked at Eduardo as she was escorted into the surgery.

The preliminary examination was inconclusive. Two neuro-surgeons examined her, comparing their findings with the reports from the Royal North Shore Hospital. One thought Annemieke would benefit from surgery, but wasn't sure to what extent. The other disagreed. He could see no point in going on. They asked Annemieke to return the following day when Dr Tannen would conduct a third examination. His decision would be final, they said. They apologised for the delay and inconvenience.

Annemieke was devastated. She didn't know how she'd get through the next twenty-four hours. She just wanted to return to the hotel and cry. Instead, Eduardo bundled her into a cab, and took her to Disneyland. It was precisely the distraction she needed, and they didn't return to their hotel until one in the morning.

Dr Tannen turned out to be a small man with big eyes, a sad face and very little conversation. He examined Annemieke and referred to his notes. He examined her again and again, reclining, and rotating her chair with his little remote control. Unexpectedly, he took her hand and she glimpsed the kind man behind the professional demeanour.

'You poor young lady,' he said. 'What you have been through?'

He patted her hand. Annemieke's heart sank. He sat down at his table, now seemingly oblivious to Annemieke's presence. He gazed into space, his mind reviewing data that only he could see. He stood and looked at Annemieke with his big, sad eyes. He pressed the intercom.

'Please send in Mr Gallegos.'

Eduardo was ushered in. He saw instantly the look of defeat in Annemieke's eyes. He wanted to rush over to her and comfort her. Instead, he shook hands with Dr Tannen and calmly exchanged formalities. Only then did he pull up a seat alongside Annemieke, and take her hand.

'The injuries happened too long ago,' Dr Tannen began. 'Perhaps if you had come to us sooner, we could be more optimistic. The nerve ends will be very tangled, you better believe, and buried beneath scar tissue. Full mobility is no longer possible. I rate my chances of restoring partial mobility at less than fifty percent. I am sorry. On this basis I cannot recommend surgery.'

'Just do your best.' Annemieke's face was contorted by her effort to retain control of herself. There was no doubting her determination.

'Young lady, I wish I could offer you more hope. But our techniques are still in their infancy. We are learning all the time.'

'You say you wish you could offer more hope. There is some hope, then?'

The doctor turned to Eduardo.

'I never said there was no hope. Yes, there is reason to hope. But not enough to justify surgery in my opinion.'

'Doctor, Annemieke has lived too long with no hope. We gladly accept the risks and the expense where there is some hope. Even a glimmer.'

'That is your decision?'

'Yes, Doctor.'

'Then I am glad. To be truthful, I do not feel as pessimistic as I sound. When I look inside, things are not always as hopeless as they appear on the outside.' He walked over to Annemieke's side and placed his hands either side of her head. He tilted it one way and then the other, as if assessing the job ahead.

'Yes, young lady, I can promise you some improvement. Just how much, well . . . that remains to be seen. But, since you have asked me, I will do my best. You better believe. I will do my very best.'

Annemieke went into surgery five days later, having spent the intervening time at Disneyland seeking total distraction. She loved Space Mountain and the Matterhorn. She loved the animatronic bears. Each night she stayed up late to watch the grand parade down Main Street. She let her hair down, which is to say, she pulled it back for the first time in public since her accident. She no longer cared if people stared. She didn't give a damn what they thought. She shut them out of her mind. What they saw now would soon no longer exist. She went from one ride to the next, with a determination to do them all as many times as possible. She ignored all of Eduardo's attempts to discuss the operation. He indulged her, and put her to bed at night, so late and so worn out, Mogadons were never a consideration. Annemieke was totally unprepared for failure.

Eduardo could do nothing but wait. He wasn't alone, though he might as well have been. Like him, the relatives of other trauma victims were not disposed to share their anxieties, and the encouraging smiles induced by occasional eye contact soon lost their currency.

There was a bar, a smokers' room, and a small cafe which also served meals. There was a TV and a library of magazines. Eduardo edged into the bar and poured himself a large scotch. Another man immediately did likewise, revealing without words the similar state of their minds. Eduardo gave him a brief nod of understanding. He sipped his drink and pondered his impetuosity.

In taking on the role of God, he had failed to appreciate the stakes he was playing with. If the operation failed, Annemieke would be shattered, and there was no telling how she would react in her distress. He suspected he would be the first casualty, for offering her a chance she never really had. She would withdraw from the world again, far beyond his reach.

And what of Jan? And Lita? He'd played his cards rashly and risked his whole stake. Would they still want him as a friend, partner, and permanent reminder of the distress he'd caused?

He poured another scotch. They'd trusted him, and he'd fed on their trust. They thought he could work miracles and he had fostered that notion. He cursed his arrogance and impatience. He cursed whatever it was in him that caused him to destroy the things he loved most. But he couldn't sustain his anger. He loved Annemieke deeply and, irrespective of the outcome, she was going to need him. At least, in the immediate future. He wouldn't let her down. He took another long pull from his scotch, and set himself to wait.

'Mr Gallegos?' He looked up into the nurse's plastic smile. 'Would you come with me, please.'

The operation had run nearly two hours over schedule. Eduardo could not decide if this was good news or bad. At first glance, Dr Tannen offered little encouragement. His face was drawn and lined with fatigue.

'I must apologise for keeping you waiting.' The doctor raised his big eyes to Eduardo. 'Sometimes I wonder who has the most difficult role. The patient, the surgeon or those who must wait.' His eyes crinkled in a tired smile. 'Today I think it is the surgeon. You better believe.'

'How is she, Doctor?' Sustained tension had reduced him to an artificial calm.

'She is well. Sleeping, of course. Probably in better shape than either of us.' Once more he gave Eduardo his tired smile.

'How did it go? The operation.'

Dr Tannen's shoulders slumped and he shook his head. Eduardo's spirits died. But a wry and unexpected smile lit the doctor's sad face.

'It is amazing. I wonder how many other patients I have turned away unnecessarily. To tell you the truth, I don't know why I accepted your young lady. Luck? Who knows? I can tell you this. We are very pleased with what we have accomplished today.'

'What?'

'It is too early, of course, but we are very optimistic.'

'Doctor, for heaven's sake, what are you saying?'

'We were able to rejoin the major nerve. This was an accomplishment we did not expect. Nature is amazing. Sometimes after accidents like your friend had, the nerves reconnect of their own accord. They grow back together. In Annemieke's case they made a damn good try. But there was too much scar tissue, some of it, I'm afraid, even caused by previous surgery. But it gave us a remote chance. It was the most difficult thing I have ever done.'

Eduardo was dumbstruck.

'We were also able to join up many secondaries and generally tidy things up. The potential is there for a near full recovery of mobility, but we won't know for sure for some time. However, the improvement will be considerable. I will write a paper on this one. You better believe.'

Eduardo reached over the table and grabbed the doctor's hand to shake it. But it wasn't enough. He embarrassed the doctor and surprised himself by throwing his arms around him and hugging him.

'Doctor, I don't know what to say. How can we ever thank you?'

'Perhaps you could put me down?'

'I'm sorry.'

'No need to apologise. I understand. Now, Annemieke should wake up in four to five hours. We will keep her under sedation, otherwise she will be in considerable pain. However, there is a chair by her bed. Go have a shower and something to eat, then sit with her. When she wakes up, just tell her everything went well. That should do until morning.'

'Thank you again, Doctor.'

'Let me tell you this. She is a very lucky young lady. You are a very lucky man. It was an enormous risk you took.'

'Doctor, you better believe!'

Annemieke remained in the clinic for another week while her face healed, and the doctors conducted further tests. Every day, the news was more encouraging as her long dormant facial muscles slowly reacted to stimuli. They showed her exercises to regain muscle tone and gave her a mirror so she could see what she was doing. She smiled, she grinned, she frowned, she rolled her jaw, she pursed her lips. She exercised until the sting from her incisions forced her to stop.

'It will take months,' Dr Tannen said, 'until the benefit of the surgery is fully apparent. Who knows? Seventy, eighty percent mobility, maybe more.'

The percentages didn't matter to Annemieke. The right hand side of her face had awoken from its slumber. She had a new smile which would only grow wider and more beautiful. She gazed at her reflection, as Narcissus had done before her.

She hugged Eduardo and she hugged Dr Tannen. She hugged every nurse in the clinic until their plastic smiles melted into genuine ones. Her happiness knew no bounds. She rang Jan and Lita, and just the sound of her voice confirmed their hopes. Eduardo had to talk vigorously to stop them boarding a plane and flying over. Jan embarrassed Eduardo with his thanks.

It was Dr Tannen who tempered the euphoria.

'You will continue to improve for some time,' he told Annemieke. 'Maybe for more than one year. Only then will we know the full extent of your recovery. I would like you to send me a video of you doing your facial exercises in three, six, nine and twelve months. If you come back to Los Angeles at any time, I would like to examine you.'

Annemieke and Eduardo assured him that they would do everything he asked.

'There is one more thing,' he said finally. 'You have been very lucky, Annemieke. You will not be lucky twice. You must always be on your guard. Any more damage to that nerve will be inoperable and therefore, I'm afraid, also permanent.'

Slowly the significance of what Dr Tannen was telling them sank in.

Chapter Thirty-Nine

Annemieke and Eduardo were married two months after their return from America, amid a barrage of flash and strobe lights. Society photographers vied with one another for the most beautiful photograph of the most beautiful bride they would ever see. They shot from the front and both sides, and every angle brought a dazzling reward. Young men who had been brought up with Annemieke and attended the same school, bit their bottom lips when they saw what they'd let slip away. Young women looked at her, and saw why they had never been able to catch the elusive Argentinian.

Guests at the wedding were enchanted by the fairytale element, the gift Eduardo had given his bride to restore her lost beauty. They wept to see a couple so much in love. Who could witness their happiness and not be moved? But there was one who found no joy in the occasion.

Anders Peterson, in his privileged position as best man, experienced nothing but envy. Eduardo had always played second fiddle to Anders when it came to women. Yet Eduardo had ultimately walked away with first prize, and Anders knew he would never find another woman to compare. He stared at Annemieke throughout the service, though it is doubtful anyone noticed. They only had eyes for the happy couple. On this day, Anders Peterson was thoroughly upstaged.

* * *

Ramon let the sentence hang, until his three comrades came to appreciate that the day's storytelling was over.

'So,' said Milos. 'Our friend Eduardo is about to discover what it feels like to be Victor, no?'

'Perhaps.'

'I've been wondering why you kept bringing Anders into the story. You said earlier, when Anders and Eduardo first met, that the meeting would somehow be catastrophic for Eduardo. At least, you implied that.' Neil paused for a moment. 'I must admit though, there were times when I thought you kept him in the story just to let Lucio Casanova here know he wasn't the only bloke on earth with an irresponsible willy.'

Ramon and Milos winced. Once Neil had found a scab to pick at he could never leave it alone. But Lucio ignored him.

'I can't believe that Annemieke would let a man like Anders touch her. She's a nice girl. He's rubbish.' Lucio was disgusted at the idea. 'He's not a real man.'

'What do you say to that, Ramon?' Neil was pushing again. 'I can't see the two of them getting at it either.'

'You'll find out next week.'

'I think I know how the story goes from here,' said Milos. 'But I won't be like Neil. I won't say anything and spoil your story. Unless, of course, you're going to cheat and introduce a new character right at the last minute.'

'No. The main players are all in place. I have no tricks up my sleeve.'

'Oh, I think you do, Ramon. I only hope you know what you're doing.'

Ramon wondered how much his friend had guessed.

Milos went straight home from the restaurant. His wife was

waiting for him, eager to hear the latest episode of Ramon's story. Milos told her, but his heart was not in it and his telling lacked lustre.

'What's the matter?' his wife asked.

'Don't you see?' Milos asked in a voice both sad and weary. 'Don't you see why he is making us like Eduardo? Can't you see the dangerous game he's playing? Ramon's conceit is putting our Thursday lunches in jeopardy. He has no right to gamble like this.'

His wife had rarely seen him so upset.

SIXTH THURSDAY

Eduardo and Annemieke set up home in Vaucluse, on the west facing slope, just south of Watson's Bay. They had the Pacific Ocean behind them and, before them, the full sweep of Sydney harbour. The house, built in the thirties and hardly touched since, was a 'renovator's dream'. But few properties bettered it for position. Annemieke looked at all the work ahead of them, and hesitated. Eduardo looked at the view, and acted.

'After Rose Bay, I cannot live without a view of my harbour,' Eduardo maintained. 'Now I can forgive myself for selling my apartment to Estelle.'

Annemieke entered the sort of life she'd only ever read about. She ate at the best restaurants and danced at the most exclusive nightclubs. She moved among the rich and mildly famous and was photographed almost as much. No butterfly ever emerged from its chrysalis into brighter lights. She became two people. The Annemieke Eduardo had married, and the girl finally liberated from the prison of her palsy.

Largely through their good friend Anders, she began to catch up on the pleasures she'd missed out on as a teenager. They dragged Eduardo to rock concerts and to pubs, to hear her favourite bands play. Afterwards, they often went back to Anders' apartment at Potts Point, just down from the Cross.

Anders was a vocal advocate of inner city living, though his income guaranteed his comfort wherever he chose to live. He had the entire top floor of a seven-storey apartment block, built in the thirties from sandstone and an unattractive brown brick. The street was narrow, and crowded with two-storey terrace houses, which leaned heavily against one another for support. The only open space was provided by concrete steps, opposite the apartment block, which led to the street above.

Annemieke loved the apartment. The architects had left the art deco facade with its tiny bottle glass windows intact. But the rear wall was floor to ceiling glass which opened out onto a rooftop patio, overlooking Rushcutters Bay and Darling Point. The interior was like a display room for modern, prohibitively expensive Italian furniture.

Annemieke loved to sit out on the patio, while Anders entertained them, and most of the eastern suburbs, with his latest CDs. No private home had a better – or louder – sound system. A recording studio had acquired the components for Anders and installed it for him. He never missed an opportunity to show it off.

When Eduardo wearied of playing the perennial teenager, or when his business interests took him away, Anders stepped in as Annemieke's willing escort. They played at flirting, for that amused Annemieke. But always, when Anders overstepped what she saw as the boundaries of their game, she would admonish him. He'd play the spurned lover, and ham it up to the full. She never suspected only part of him was acting.

But the teenager really only surfaced at night, and then only on the occasions that were appropriate. By day, she attended the Conservatorium and supported her studies with the hours of practice they demanded. She kept an eye on the tradesmen, who knocked down walls and moved the kitchen and dining-room from one end of the house to the other. They replaced small windows with big windows and French doors. They built a patio and surfaced it in Barbetti terracotta tiles. They turned the house around until it focused entirely on the view, and the view infiltrated every part of the house.

Annemieke chose paint for the walls and architraves, agonising over changes in shades. She chose what she called 'koala colours', the soft dusty colours of the bush. She also made their meals, laundered their clothes, and kept their home spotless between the fortnightly visits of her Korean cleaners. She had a gardener to help one day a month, and an ironing lady for one morning a week. With her piano practice, her housework, her supervising, and her shopping, her days were full.

Eduardo loved to watch Annemieke play piano. Her face mirrored both the mood and the complexity of the music. She would become so engrossed that she would be oblivious of Eduardo's attention until, when she finished, he'd applaud and she'd smile with sheepish embarrassment.

Once he even videotaped her playing and dubbed the result onto the tape she sent to Dr Tannen. He had replied with a brief note of appreciation. Eduardo and Annemieke revelled in each other's company, and they loved their new home. But, increasingly, Eduardo's business commitments kept them apart.

With Jan's assistance, Eduardo had managed to set up his type studio and printing shop in Jakarta. They were pressing agencies for business and making representations to Garuda Indonesia and Indonesia's department of tourism. But in this first critical year, Eduardo knew that the business would succeed or fail on the basis of his personality, and the degree of his involvement.

In Australia, the recession had begun to bite and they needed their Jakarta enterprises to help carry them through it. Clients had cut their spending and advertising agencies had their budgets slashed, all of which flowed through to the Hot Ink Press. Rather than lay people off in Sydney, they offered to transfer them to Jakarta to help train the local staff. Most were grateful for the opportunity.

At first, when Eduardo was away, he would ring Annemieke every day. But as the months passed and the shortcomings of the Indonesian telephone system took their toll, he'd skip a day and sometimes two. It didn't seem to matter. While Eduardo was away

Annemieke put special effort into her music, determined to sit and pass examination by a visiting Fellow of the Royal Acadamy of Music.

'Why?' Eduardo asked, when she told him of the hours of work she was putting in.

'Because I intend to teach piano,' she replied. 'I haven't the talent to perform, but I can teach. And I want the qualifications to teach at the highest levels.'

'Then you had better put an advertisement in the local paper,' Eduardo said, with a sigh of resignation. 'What use is a teacher with no pupils ?'

Her evenings when Eduardo was away were her time for recreation. When she wasn't out with Anders she often met up with her old girlfriends, the ones who had stuck by her during the dark years. Their non-stop talk of boyfriends and sexual encounters excited and discomforted her at the same time, and she was made very aware of what she'd missed out on, how easy it would be to make up for lost time.

Men were irresistibly attracted to her and, much to the disgust of her friends who had not yet married, they homed in on her and made her the centre of attention.

'I'm married,' she'd say. 'Don't waste your time. Talk to the others.'

But few men regarded her wedding ring as an impediment, and some became surly when she rejected their advances. It often put a damper on their enjoyment, and they'd have to move on. Annemieke loved Eduardo, wholeheartedly and unambiguously. Nevertheless, she envied her friends their freedom. She was only twenty-two, after all.

She mentioned this one night to Anders, while they were still high on music and buoyant with champagne. Anders, who had almost resigned himself to the role of trusted friend, drew renewed heart. Their flirting had become ritualised, a meaningless but entertaining game they were even happy to play in Eduardo's presence. Nevertheless, it provided him with the perfect vehicle with which to play upon her regrets, and chip away at her resolve.

'Monogamy has its strong points,' he'd say. 'But variety certainly isn't one of them.'

He took to referring to her as 'the nun', and would shake his head sorrowfully whenever she admired a good looking man or a well-muscled body.

'Do you know why nuns are nuns?' he'd say. 'Because they can't have none.'

'Have you ever been kissed?' he'd ask. 'Properly, roundly and hugely kissed by anyone other than Eduardo? No? That's not a shame, that's a monumental disaster!'

One night he told her all the different ways of being kissed, until she flushed from the vicarious pleasure and ordered him to stop. Anders preyed on her innocence and lack of experience. He preyed on her trust. He undermined her femininity and made her feel inadequate. And at last, one night, he persuaded her to let him give her 'a proper goodnight kiss', as he called it.

He kissed her with all the passion and expertise he had, and she was thrilled. Against her own will she found herself pressing tightly against him. She pulled away as she felt his arousal, and it went no further than that. But it was a start. It was the start Anders had patiently played for. He knew then that he would never give up. One day he would have her.

Poor Annemieke felt guilty, yet she could not forget what she had experienced. She was ashamed that she'd let it happen. She was even more ashamed that she'd enjoyed his kiss so intensely. And she was ashamed of the excitement that would not go away.

Sometimes in bed, or when playing the piano, or doing the housework, she would think back to that moment and wonder how it might be with another man. These thoughts tormented her. She'd dismiss them, but they came back unbidden. She decided she would never allow herself to be alone with Anders again.

When Eduardo came home from Jakarta, she roasted a piece of rump fillet and served it the way he loved it, red raw, and barely warm in the middle. She raided their wine cellar for a Show

Reserve 1970 Lindemans Hunter River Burgundy. Then, when she took him off to bed, she gave him a welcome home he would never forget. Eduardo believed he was the luckiest man alive.

Chapter Forty

Bibiana and Domingo did not find their new life in Australia easy, as Eduardo had done. At first they stayed with Domingo's brother, on a barren new housing estate at Campbelltown, in Sydney's far west. They experienced a side of Sydney tourists never see.

The dry months of winter and spring had burnt off what little vegetation there was. There were no trees to offer shade, they'd all fallen to the developers' bulldozers. One day it would be blindingly hot with temperatures up around forty degrees Celsius. Then, seemingly out of the blue, storm clouds such as they'd never experienced in Buenos Aires would rush in and pepper them with hailstones the size of billiard balls. Then the rain would attack the baked ground, and cut it up into rivulets and gullies as it washed away the precious topsoil and turned the subsoil into mud.

Still, they made the best of it. Whenever they could, they crammed into Domingo's brother's van and drove to the south coast, where the sea breezes brought blessed relief. They were disappointed with their start but not downhearted. This was a new country and it was only a matter of time and hard work before they established themselves.

But first they were to receive another setback. Domingo was contracted to the Department of Education, as a condition of being granted resident status. He had no choice but to go where he was assigned. And he and the family were sent to Collarenebri, a small country town in the north west of New South Wales.

Collarenebri's greatest asset is the thousand or so people who live there and on the stations that surround it. Like most country people, they are honest, open and forthright, and quick to lend a new family a helping hand. Especially the new school teacher's family. And especially when the family is new to Australia.

The Gimenes family did not know what had struck them. This was a far cry from the lush pampas. This was desert dotted with scrub and occasional blades of grass. The land was flat and featureless, except for the Barwon River which cut a deep ravine around one side of the town. Bibiana looked and wondered how such a placid and innocuous river could cut the land so deeply. They would soon learn.

The town had no cafes, no *confiterías*, *bonbonerías*, *whiskerías*, and no tangoes. It had an old pub, which would never make it onto the heritage listings for preservation, and an RSL club that offered snooker tables and table tennis for recreation. If you wanted more fun, you made it yourself.

They lived with dust through the drys, and roads that became slippery as ice at the first fall of rain. They learned to cope with the dust, the downpours and, if that wasn't enough, with other people's downpours. They learned that the rain that fell on them wasn't the problem. It was the rain that fell further north. Rain that gathered in gullies and streams hundreds of kilometres away, before tumbling into the Barwon River and swelling it to a raging torrent that rose above its steep ravine and burst its banks. The Gimenes family became expert in filling sandbags and baling out classrooms.

They got over the thrill of seeing kangaroos in the wild, and learned how to avoid crashing into them in their car. They became blind to the sight of emus dying slowly, their feet trapped in a twist between the top two stands of wire fences. And they became deaf to the dawn to dusk screeching of cockatoos and galahs in flocks of a thousand or more.

They were happy enough. The people of Collarenebri loved having fun as much as any others, and there was always a barbecue on somewhere, or a cricket or football match. Domingo became famous for his *parrillada*, and Bibiana for her laugh. One daughter played netball, and the other swam breaststroke faster than any other girl in her school. Her son Julio played football, cricket, and fished for giant cod from the banks of the Barwon. Everybody got by except Roberto.

Roberto's hand-eye coordination was sorely lacking. He came last at athletic carnivals and was no better in the swimming pool. He was a quiet, studious boy who would rather read than watch television, and rather play piano than football. And he was mortally shy.

Country kids are no different to any others. If you don't shape up, they're the first to tell you. And they told Roberto at every opportunity, until it became painful for him to venture outside. So he stayed indoors, played his piano and helped Bibiana, thereby confirming what every kid in town suspected. He was a sissy.

Bibiana felt for him, as did the rest of the family. But what could they do? They were stuck in Collarenebri for at least three years, and there is a limit to what anyone can do on another's behalf. This was one battle Roberto would have to fight on his own.

Towards the end of Domingo's three year tenure, he was given a choice. He could stay on at Collarenebri indefinitely, and ultimately become principal, or accept another rural posting at Gulargambone away to the south. They were bitterly disappointed. They'd hoped for a posting, back to Sydney or, at the very least, to Newcastle or Wollongong.

They sat up at night and discussed their limited options. They could either accept their posting or resign. They discussed staying. They had made many friends in Collarenebri, and the kids, with the exception of Roberto, were happy enough. But mostly they discussed leaving and living in Sydney.

It was like a magnet to them. A city not too dissimilar to the one they'd left behind in Argentina. A city with museums and galleries and theatres and cinemas. With a nightlife. With cafes and restaurants, clubs and bars and dancing. With crowds of people and all the trappings of civilisation. Inevitably, they talked themselves into giving up the security of the Education Department for the bright lights of Sydney.

'The children deserve no less,' Bibiana said in justification. 'They must learn that there is more to life than sport and weather maps. They have the right to be young in a city.'

Domingo agreed to stay on in Collarenebri while they planned their escape. He was adamant that they would not leave without first finding a job, so he combed the *Sydney Morning Herald*'s classified section. He applied for the job of Spanish teacher at a TAFE college. He applied on spec to every private school listed. He applied for storemen's jobs. He applied to manage petrol stations and shoe stores. Where he had no previous experience, he invented it. Who could check?

Sometimes his prospective employers didn't bother to respond, others sent their regrets. He was either unsuitable, the job had gone, or distance made him too hard to deal with. He kept sending off applications.

'It's like a lottery,' he said. 'One day something will come up.'

And it did. In the space of a single week, he was invited to attend interviews for the positions of booking clerk with Aerolineas Argentinas, service station manager in Campsie and, to their joy, teacher at a private school for boys in Sydney's eastern suburbs. He booked a seat on the bus to Sydney, and his family held their breath.

Domingo was the least academically qualified of all the applicants at the private school. But his fluency in Spanish, Italian and Latin saw him through. His English, he was told, would have to improve. Domingo took the plunge and moved the family to Sydney, even though he was made uncomfortably aware his appointment was subject to review. After Campbelltown and the dust of Collarenebri, there was only one place they wanted to live. Near the sea.

Of course, they could not afford a view, but they were happy enough with the square, featureless, brick house they bought in Dover Heights. It faced the morning sun, and was sheltered from the blustery southerlies. But its key attribute, as far as the Gimenes family was concerned, was that it was less than ten minutes from Bondi Beach by bike or bus one way, and ten minutes from Watson's Bay the other. It was exactly the home and the start they were looking for.

For Roberto, the move to Sydney was salvation. While his brothers and sisters went to the beach, he went to art galleries. He discovered trendy cafes where people went to look at one another just like they did in Buenos Aires. He discovered David Jones's Elizabeth Street store where a pianist entertained the shoppers with selections from the classics.

He was overcome. He'd never seen anyone play so beautifully. He couldn't tear himself away. He positioned himself so he could watch the pianist's hands as his fingers danced lightly over the keys. Nobody else stopped to watch and he began to wonder if he'd be moved on.

But the pianist had spotted the tall, thin lad with his shy manner and began to play to his audience of one. He played with verve and passion. Bemused shop assistants turned to see what was happening, as if they were hearing the piano for the first time. The pianist threw a smile at Roberto, then, via a timely decrescendo, brought his playing back to its former level.

'Thank you,' Roberto mouthed, and left the smiling pianist to see what other wonder Sydney held for him, around the next corner.

Bibiana set about turning their squat little house into a home. She would have dearly loved to strip away the dreary wallpaper, but they didn't even have enough spare money for paint. So she scrubbed and washed where she could, and covered up the cracks and the patches of damp with pictures and furniture. She would have to get a job, she realised. Her four children needed school uniforms and books. All but her eldest, Monica, needed bikes. And now Roberto was pleading for piano lessons. She needed a job. She knew Domingo would argue, but they had no choice.

Chapter Forty-One

Jakarta wasn't Sydney. Jan had warned him that things moved slower and took longer. But Eduardo had arrogantly ascribed some of that slowness to Jan. Now he was learning differently. Everywhere he went in Jakarta, he was warmly received. He made his presentations to enthusiastic audiences. If promises were bankable, the business would be booming. Yet each month it struggled to make costs and, without the patronage of expat Australians would have struggled to do that. Eduardo found it hard to reconcile the reception his presentations received with the lack of business.

'You have much to learn,' Jan counselled. 'Indonesians are rather like the Japanese in that they don't like to be the bearers of bad news. Nor do they like to disappoint. So when they smile and say yes, you cannot take this as an indication that work will automatically follow. What they are saying is, "Yes, we are interested and would like to enter negotiations both official and unofficial". Your presentations only win you the right to pursue the next step.

'You will find another variation on this when you finally produce work for them. Whatever you show them, they will admire and appear to accept. Even if they don't like it. Then, over the next few days, word will filter back and you will have to be receptive to this.

When you present your work you must learn to always leave the door open for a dignified and courteous rejection. It saves time.'

Eduardo realised that his publishing company in the Pulogadung Industrial Estate had actually taught him nothing about doing business with Indonesians. All his clients were off-shore. Fortunately, the East was booming, and they were picking up work hand over fist from Singapore and Kuala Lumpur. But the Jakarta based work was proving difficult to crack and demanded more and more of his time.

'Perhaps if you lived in Jakarta,' voices advised, often enough for Eduardo to feel the point was laboured. The simple truth was, his clients would be more comfortable with him if he actually lived there, played golf with them, dined with them. It would help him come to understand how the city worked.

Eduardo was not a flashy man and greatly preferred understatement in his dress. His one ostentation was an oversize Mont Blanc pen which Annemieke had given him as a wedding present. He had long admired the pens, and loved the weight and feel of it in his hand. He went nowhere without it. In Jakarta, he could not help but notice the effect it had on the Indonesians. Obvious wealth made a big impression. So he flashed his pen as much as he could, added a gold Rolex to his wrist, designer labels to his clothes, and purchased a Louis Vuitton executive case.

Gradually, Eduardo came to spend more and more of his time in Jakarta and less and less in Sydney. He tried taking Annemieke with him but that didn't work either. He would spend all day and half the night on his business dealings, leaving her captive in her hotel, more alone than she was in Sydney. Understandably, she was reluctant to risk the helter-skelter of Jakarta's traffic any more than she had to. One accident in Indonesia was enough. So Annemieke stayed home while Eduardo travelled.

Eduardo came home as often as he could but, frequently, he would be exhausted and reluctant to go out. Phil and Don would demand his daylight hours and, when they didn't, Jan or Estelle would claim him for Java Man.

'It is a temporary aberration,' Eduardo told Annemieke. 'Once

Jakarta is up and running smoothly, everything will settle down. I will be yours exclusively once more.'

Annemieke was patient, but she was also young. And she'd been patient and gone without for too much of her young life.

'If it wasn't for this blasted recession, I'd be tempted to let this Jakarta thing go,' Eduardo told her. 'But the fact is, we need it to work. It could prove our salvation over the next few years.'

Annemieke saw the sense of that and she understood. But she had her own problems, and she was lonely. She called her old friends for companionship and for expeditions to the bright lights. And she rang her mother every day or called into Java Man. But something was missing. Eduardo was missing. So she rang the next best thing.

Anders was delighted to hear from her, and seemed genuinely concerned at the despondency in her voice. He sent a car for her immediately, and took her to lunch at Beppi's. He poured wine into her, fed her whitebait fritters from New Zealand and scampi from Western Australia. He lent her a most sympathetic ear and made her laugh with outrageous stories. When they had finished, he put her back in the car and sent her home a little drunk, happy and feeling wonderfully feminine.

When Eduardo heard over the phone how happy she was, he faxed off a thank you note to Anders.

Chapter Forty-Two

'I thought you might be Argentinian,' said the voice on the phone. It was a boy's voice, high-pitched and uncertain, and given to breaking. Whether it was just his age, or nervousness, Annemieke couldn't tell. 'Gallegos is quite a common name in Argentina,' the boy continued. 'I thought a teacher who spoke Spanish could help me where my English is inadequate.'

'My husband is Argentinian,' Annemieke said, and laughed. 'If it helps, I'm very good at understanding English spoken with an Argentinian accent. Besides, I also speak Dutch and Bahasa, so one way or the other we will get by.'

'How much do you charge?' the boy asked.

'Twenty-four dollars an hour for students, or twelve dollars for half an hour.'

Annemieke heard some whispering taking place.

'I'm afraid I will only be able to afford half an hour a week.'

'That's fine,' said Annemieke. She only had three other students and was anxious not to let this one get away. 'If you come at four every Thursday afternoon, I'm free until five. We might be able to stretch your half hour a little. Provided you don't tell anyone . . .'

'Oh no, no, thank you. I won't tell anyone.'

His joy reached down the wire and touched Annemieke. She

could hear him whispering the good news to somebody else in a rush of Spanish.

'Good. Thank you. I will begin this Thursday. Thank you.'

'Excellent. Now are you going to tell me your name?'

'I am sorry. I got so excited. My name is Roberto. Roberto Gimenes.'

He arrived promptly at four o'clock. That is, he rang Annemieke's doorbell at four o'clock. He'd ridden his bike there straight from school and beaten the clock by more than fifteen minutes. He'd pedalled up and down her street until the appointed hour. Now he stood heart beating, head pounding, as he heard her footsteps approach the door.

'Hello, you must be Roberto. Come in.'

Roberto followed her through the door in awe. His music teacher at school was a dragon. The other music students spoke of their teachers in terms that suggested all music teachers were the same. Yet Mrs Gallegos was lovely. And not all that much older than himself.

'Sit down, Roberto. Now, tell me about yourself. How many years you have been playing piano, and what levels you've reached.'

He told her. She seemed pleased when he said grade four, and delighted when he told her his passion was classical music. She asked him to play for her and he played 'Song of India'. He chose it because it was a slow piece which gave his nervous fingers a chance to steady. It crescendoed and diminished with the slow regularity of waves washing up upon the shore. He concentrated with all his might. He wanted so much to please his new teacher. When he finished, he turned to her shyly. He was pleased with the way he had played.

'Very good,' she said. 'You have nice touch. But are you aware that you missed out a whole phrase? Two bars, in fact.'

Roberto was stunned. Where? Where?

'In future, when you play to me or just for yourself,' Annemieke continued, 'use your music and read the notes. Otherwise you won't improve.'

'I'm sorry,' mumbled Roberto. He could not believe he'd failed when he'd tried so hard.

'Don't be sorry,' Annemieke said. 'Play it again, this time with the music. You start while I get us both a cool drink.'

Annemieke realised the boy was highly strung, and saw how deeply he had felt her criticism. She needed to give him a chance to relax. He wasn't a bad player but neither was he gifted. And he'd developed a number of bad habits. Not using the music. Dropping his wrists. Lifting his elbows. And not using the pedals. The question was, how did she bring up these inadequacies without shattering his fragile confidence? Annemieke realised she needed the drinks break as much as the boy.

'That's better,' she said, and gave him a tall glass of lime juice. 'Do you know Beethoven's *Moonlight Sonata*? As far as he was concerned, it was the first movement of his *Sonata Quasi Una Fantasia*. But when it was first performed, a critic wrote that it reminded him of moonlight on Lake Lucerne, and so it became the *Moonlight Sonata*. It's actually grade seven, but I think you should be able to manage it. We'll also do some work on your theory. When you understand harmony better, you'll find you won't have to read note for note. Let's begin, shall we?'

Annemieke sat alongside Roberto on the piano stool and began to play the first two sheets of music to him. He watched transfixed. He could smell her perfume and feel her arm as it lightly brushed his. Her fingers barely touched the keys, yet the most beautiful music swirled around him. He could see the moonlight twinkling and dancing on Lake Lucerne as the critic had nearly two centuries earlier. And before she had finished the little she played, Roberto was in love with her. If there had been something lacking in his life, a reason for his existence, a sense of purpose, he found it now in Annemieke. All he wanted to do was please her. He decided he would dedicate his musical career to her. She would be his teacher and inspiration. He would practise every day, not for one hour but for two! He would do his theory, not four pages a week, but eight! He would be her star pupil. He would worship at her feet. He would worship the most perfect human being he could ever imagine.

'You play better than the man at David Jones,' he said.

Chapter Forty-Three

Eduardo flew home for Java Man's new showing. He shamelessly revived old contacts and renewed friendships grown cold. He was apprehensive about the showing given the recession, and Jan's excursion into primitive art from other areas of the South Pacific. Typically, he threw himself into organising the evening with all his enthusiasm.

'I see more of you when you're in Jakarta,' Annemieke complained.

'My apologies,' Eduardo replied in tones that were hardly apologetic. 'But it's your father's neck riding on this one too. We mustn't fail.'

'Then let me help,' she said. And she did.

She helped price and catalogue every new piece. Jan had been to the Solomons, Papua New Guinea and Fiji. He had discovered among his clientele a definite bent for tribal weaponry. He had spears and shields, missile clubs from Fiji, and greenstone Maori clubs from New Zealand. He brought back money rings from the Solomon Islands and tribal stools from New Guinea. Annemieke helped display them, tucking small and delicate pieces behind glass, away from the clumsy and the light-fingered.

She ordered the champagne and Canadian smoked salmon. Estelle told her where to go to get the best, and the price had shocked her. Eduardo only laughed. On the night, she worked tirelessly as both hostess and waitress, even though they'd hired waitresses. And the night had met with the success it deserved. Their takings were on par with their opening night. Annemieke was ecstatic. She turned to Eduardo.

'C'mon,' she said. 'You owe us all a magnificent dinner and whatever comes after. We'll tidy up tomorrow. Anders, you'll come too, won't you?'

Anders looked at Eduardo, willing him to put her off. Eduardo took a deep breath and summoned up his reserves of energy.

'Let's go,' he said. 'Estelle ring the Brasserie and warn them that we're coming. Oh, and you'd better ring Combined Taxis.'

Eduardo turned to his delighted wife and took her in his arms.

'I'm here until Monday,' he said. 'That's five nights. I give them all to you. You decide what you want to do, where you want to go, who you want to take, and we'll go do it. Stuff Jakarta. Stuff the Hot Ink Press. And stuff you too, Jan.'

Everybody laughed except Anders.

Eduardo was true to his word. The frustrations, boredom and loneliness Annemieke had experienced all evaporated in a whirlwind of socialising. It was a return to the early days of their marriage, and no honeymooners ever indulged each other more. Anders cried off and left the love birds to it, claiming prior commitment to a new business presentation.

The tonic worked for them both. When Eduardo flew back to Jakarta, he felt curiously refreshed and renewed despite the succession of late, late nights, rich foods and alcohol. Annemieke felt as if a burden had been lifted off her and a tension released. Her mind no longer wandered down forbidden pathways, and joy and vitality returned to her piano playing. She returned to her old friend and enemy, Chopin, and did credit to his mazurkas.

Roberto could not help noticing the change. She had him playing minuets and waltzes which he disliked, and loving every second of it. Whenever he mastered a difficult section, she'd jump up from her stool and hug him, or kiss his cheek. It made him try all the harder. He found himself laughing with her when he goofed and, whenever he played mistake free, he'd throw his arms in the air like a football supporter whose team had just scored a goal. He loved his half hour lessons which always stretched to an hour, but they were never long enough. Just long enough to send him home, inspired, motivated, and hopelessly devoted to his teacher.

But it could not last. Gradually everything settled back into the routine, with Eduardo spending more time in Jakarta than he did at home, and Annemieke getting progressively more lonely and dispirited. Nevertheless, she kept true to her promise, and avoided seeing Anders alone. When he rang to tell her he had four tickets to see Dire Straits, she saw no reason why she should not accept. She asked who else was coming, and he told her it was a writer from the office and his wife. She accepted with glee.

She met Anders at the Marble Bar. They had a couple of drinks while they waited for the other two to arrive.

'They may be late,' Anders said, 'so I've given their tickets to them. One of their kids isn't well. Nothing serious, but you know what parents are like.'

They waited half an hour, then went on ahead. The two seats alongside remained empty throughout the concert.

'You'd think one of them would have tried to make it,' Anders said. 'These seats cost a fortune.'

Annemieke let him drive her home. She'd enjoyed the concert and his company, and he seemed genuinely disappointed that the other couple had failed to appear. They didn't stop for drinks on the way. Annemieke felt obliged to invite him in for a nightcap. She knew it was wrong and that she'd left herself vulnerable. But Anders had done nothing that night to suggest his intentions were anything but honourable.

They sat on the sofa together and played music while they drank their coffee. Anders was indiscreet and told stories about his girlfriends which he probably shouldn't have. Annemieke laughed.

They played more music, drank more coffee, and gossiped shamelessly.

'A kiss,' Anders requested as he made to leave. 'A proper kiss, too, to end the night, if you don't mind.'

'Behave yourself,' she said in mock admonishment, but allowed him to take her hands in his, and kiss her. Again, she felt the thrill surge through her body. She knew it was wrong. She knew she should push him away, but she didn't want the delicious feeling to end. Then his head was on her chest and he was kissing the swell of her breasts, and he was slowly pushing his tongue as far down her cleavage as the front of her dress would allow. Her brain screamed 'No!', but her back arched and her hands reached inside his shirt.

'Just this once! Just this once!' her inner voice begged, and she shuddered as he slipped his hand gently up her thigh.

Anders took his time. He wanted her to want him, not just for one night but for as many nights as he chose, until he tired of her. He caressed her breasts and explored her body and her secrets with his tongue.

Her eyes were closed, her head bent back, her body straining towards her lover. Her breath came in short gasps. She moaned and twisted as her ecstasy grew. Then he entered her, and her orgasm was instantaneous. They made love in an orgy of pleasure that only ended, reluctantly, with the morning sun.

Anders left then, and Annemieke lay unmoving in a state of utter fulfilment. She was determined not to feel any guilt or remorse. After all, she had only taken what had been denied her as a teenager. It was purely a question of chronology, she argued to herself. Most girls do it before they marry. She was just a little late getting around to it. That's all. That's what she told herself. But it didn't work.

The phone rang. It was Eduardo. His voice brought home her betrayal.

'I love you and I miss you,' he said. 'I'm coming home tomorrow, no matter what. Love me?'

She assured him she did. But it was all she could do not to break down and confess over the phone. She hung up and cried. She vowed she would never betray Eduardo again. She would never so much as look at another man. She would love Eduardo, Eduardo only. But the taste of Anders' kisses lingered on her lips and she still felt light-headed from their love-making. When she showered, she only had to touch herself to be reminded.

She heaped promise of fidelity upon promise. But promises made under the duress of regret are often all too fragile and easily swept away in the floodtide of temptation.

Anders had done his job well.

Chapter Forty-Four

Annemieke sought a diversion while Eduardo shuttled back and forth to Indonesia. Roberto was almost ready to sit the grade six practical and theory exams, and she was determined that he would pass with flying colours. She began to give him extra tuition without charging him, and was relentless in strengthening his weaknesses.

Roberto responded with redoubled effort. He lapped up the extra attention and his playing improved appreciably with each passing week. He appreciated the effort Annemieke was putting in on his behalf, without ever suspecting her true motive. He romanced about what appeared to him as their special relationship. She was his goddess, a paragon of virtue, above all the dross of the world.

When her husband was away and he was there, Annemieke was safe. Safe from the man who phoned and stole the sunlight from her face. Safe from the man who turned her sad, desperate 'no' into a reluctant 'yes'. Safe from the man who cast a cloud over his lessons, and caused Annemieke to lose patience with him. She would apologise, throw her arm around him so that her breast pushed against his shoulder, and hold him tightly until he forgave her. Then she'd laugh, and Roberto's heart would melt, and he'd wonder what sort of a person would deliberately upset her.

As he rode his bike home to Dover Heights, he'd think of the poems he would write that night, alone in his room with his fantasies, as over and over he pledged his undying love. He made up his mind. After his grade six exam was over, he would be her protector. He would protect her whenever her husband was away. He would follow her and make sure she came to no harm.

On the Sunday before his exam, Annemieke arranged a final two-hour session, as much to instil confidence in her star pupil as polish the edges of his playing. Eduardo was home, and Lita and Jan had come over for dinner. Annemieke asked Roberto to stay and promptly made him play for his supper.

'It will help you overcome your nervousness in playing to strangers,' she said.

Roberto played, hesitantly at first, but Annemieke's smiles gave him confidence. He launched into his pieces with such elan that the audience had no choice but to sit up and take notice. Roberto glowed with the applause.

It was a mild spring evening so they sat outside for dinner.

'What brought your family to Australia?' Jan asked Roberto, trying to involve the boy in their conversation. He shrugged and was going to deflect the question with a trite answer, when he noticed that Annemieke was also interested in his response.

'Were you chased out like Eduardo?' Annemieke asked. 'Penniless and homeless? Tell your story, Eduardo.'

'I was never penniless,' Eduardo began, and told the story he had invented to quell the curious, some ten years earlier. He had expanded and developed it, so that it had a more convincing ring, and it was now his official history. He'd prepared his story well. But nothing had prepared him for Roberto's.

'My story is not pleasant,' Roberto began matter of factly. 'To begin with, my real name is not Gimenes. I was born Roberto Sanguineti.'

In the gathering gloom, nobody noticed Eduardo start, and the blood drain from his face. He looked at the thin, sensitive boy, stared at the eyes which had locked onto his from beneath the stairs. As Roberto continued to speak, all doubt vanished.

'My father was a brave man. He was a hero to all Argentina. They called him *La Voz del Pueblo*, the voice of the people, because he had the courage to speak out against the Generals. He was betrayed by a friend who wanted to steal my mother away.'

'Eduardo!' Annemieke called. 'Are you all right?'

Eduardo had slumped in his chair, his head in his hands. Annemieke rushed to his side as Jan turned on the lights. Eduardo was sweating, his face screwed up in a painful grimace, his eyes squeezed shut.

'Eduardo! What is it? What's the matter?'

'It's nothing. Nothing. Just something I picked up in Indonesia. I've had it before. Help me to the bedroom.'

But it was Jan who virtually carried him up the stairs and gently helped him to lie down. Annemieke fussed around him as Jan left the room.

'I'm all right,' Eduardo pleaded. 'Just a little headache and fever. It's nothing really.' He begged Annemieke to leave him to sleep, and go back to her guests.

She did as he bid, but Eduardo knew he would not sleep. His past had stalked him over ten thousand kilometres and caught up with him. The knife blade of his guilt twisted and turned mercilessly in his stomach, opening old wounds. He dared not sleep. He knew Rosa would be there, waiting, to condemn him to the death he deserved.

'I'm sorry, Annemieke,' Roberto said, standing as if to leave. 'Maybe my story has revived unpleasant memories.'

'Nothing of the kind. Please sit down, Roberto. Eduardo is very adventurous with his food, and sometimes he has to pay the price. Unfortunately, tonight is one of those times.'

'It is we who should be sorry,' said Lita, 'for intruding so rudely into your past. I'm sure you don't enjoy being reminded of it.'

'I was six years old,' Roberto said. 'I have grown up with the knowledge of what happened. To be honest with you, I remember little. The detail I gave you is the detail others gave to me. They said I should be proud of my real parents and didn't hide them from me. That is what happened. That is how I came to be adopted. That is how I came to live in Australia.'

Conversation flickered and faltered. They were all moved by the sad-faced boy. As soon as dinner was over, they wished him luck with his exams, and Jan and Lita dropped him home on their way back to Mosman.

The next morning, Eduardo was no better. Despite his protestations, Annemieke drove him to their doctor.

Chapter Forty-Five

Eduardo was furious with himself. The first time he had neglected to check whether his flight was departing as scheduled was the day he arrived at the airport to find the plane delayed for twenty-four hours because of an electrical fault. Naturally, any spare seats on the Qantas flight had already been filled by those who had taken the trouble to ring first.

He cursed his stupidity and returned straight home. Annemieke was out, probably shopping. He decided to spend the day with the editorial staff of his magazines. He was on his way out again when the phone rang. He tossed up whether to leave it or pick it up. Obviously, the call wasn't for him. But Eduardo wasn't the sort of man who could just let a phone ring. He picked it up.

'Annemieke . . .' sang a man's voice.

Eduardo was confused.

'Anders?'

The phone slammed down in his ear. Eduardo was stunned. At first, his mind refused to accept the implications. It had sounded like Anders' voice. But why would he hang up like that? Eduardo closed his eyes and desperately tried to think of an innocent reason for the call and its rude termination. His heart sank and his stomach churned. Suspicions nagged and taunted. He found it almost impossible to believe that his wife was seeing another man. But what other explanation could there be? There must be one, he thought, and once he heard it, it would be blindingly obvious to all but a suspicious mind.

He clung to this silly foolish hope. But the seeds of doubt were sown, and seemingly, on soil as fertile as Java's. Doubt, the great destroyer, blossomed in his mind.

He reached for the Yellow Pages and dialled a private investigation agency. He left a note for Annemieke explaining the circumstances of his aborted flight, and left to keep his appointment. He took with him as many recent photographs of his wife as he could find, and a videotape of her which they'd forgotten to send to Dr Tannen.

'It is better to know the truth,' he told himself, 'than to live with suspicions. I will not condemn her unjustly.'

When he arrived home that evening, Annemieke had cooked him a special meal.

'Why now?' he thought. 'What is she trying to make amends for?'

Then he dismissed his suspicions and cursed his impatience. He would know soon enough. In his heart, he still clung to the belief that there was an innocent explanation. In the meantime, she deserved his trust. Trust and love.

'It's a celebration,' she said happily. 'I've got you for an extra day.'

She seemed perfectly sincere. She was the open, honest, innocent, loving Annemieke he adored with every cell in his body. He was heartened, and felt guilty at what he now determined was a typical Argentinian over-reaction. He made a mental note to call off the watch dogs.

They finished dinner and made love like newly-weds. It was a very weary Eduardo who dragged himself to the airport the following morning, and onto the aircraft. He never needed his computer. For the first time he fell asleep. Even as the undercarriage retracted, his eyes closed and he forgot all about his mental memo to the private investigators. He would be gone for three weeks.

Anders never told Annemieke about the call Eduardo had intercepted. Perhaps he didn't consider the effect it might have had on Eduardo. Perhaps he realised the first hint of possible discovery would be enough to frighten Annemieke away, and he hadn't yet finished with her. Either way, he took the soft option and kept his mouth shut.

As soon as her last student had left, Annemieke went straight to Anders' apartment in Potts Point. Often as not, they no longer bothered with the pretext of a show or concert. She couldn't know, as Anders with his years of experience surely did, that their affair was fast approaching the terminal stage. Anders would not be sorry when it finished. He just hoped she'd be realistic when the time came, and wouldn't ruin it all with tears and hysteria.

Neither of them considered for a second that Annemieke might have been followed to her assignation, and certainly not by two people, each working independently of the other and for entirely different reasons. One was the boy Roberto, lurking miserably in the shadows beneath the concrete steps that led down from the street above, wishing he could somehow storm the castle and rescue his lady and her honour. Instead, he caught the bus, and went home to pour out his misery in his poetry.

The other sat with a thermos of coffee, a pack of cheese sandwiches, a transistor radio tuned into 2KY – the racing station – and an earplug screwed firmly into his ear. He'd removed the bulb from the interior light of his Honda so that he could open the car door occasionally to admit the breeze. He kept his log sheets and his form guide on the dash, in the spill from the overhead street light. He was an experienced agent. You pay for the best, you get the best.

* * *

In the three weeks that Eduardo was away, Roberto found himself outside the building that housed Anders' penthouse on four occasions. On his third visit he became aware that he was not alone. He saw the Honda. Saw the shadowy figure inside. Saw the eyes watching. His first instinct was to bolt, for it revived in him long suppressed fears. Fears of night raids by secret police. Of people being dragged from their beds to horrifying deaths in the blood house of the city morgue. His heart raced and his head pounded. He felt faint. He summoned up all his courage and stayed. Nothing happened. The longer he stayed, the calmer he felt. He stayed until the last bus was due, and sneaked off to catch it.

He had to warn Annemieke. But how could he, without exposing his own covert activities? Without revealing his own shy and furtive love? Instead he vowed to watch her even more closely. The man in the car intended to hurt her. He could not allow that to happen. He could not sit by and lose her as he had lost his own mother.

Ramon finished speaking, yet he refused to acknowledge the others. He appeared vacant and distant, as if focused on events that only he could see. His friends watched him, caught up in the tension of the story which Ramon's silence prolonged.

'Your coffee, Ramon. You deserve it.' Milos made room for Gancio to serve. 'You have earned a rest. Perhaps Lucio can dig out one of his stories.'

Ramon downed his espresso in one gulp and motioned for another.

'There is nothing I can say,' said Lucio. 'I don't like the way this story is heading and I've never felt less like laughing in my life. That Anders is a bastard. If this is a true story, you give me his address and I'll go punch his face. He won't be so handsome when I finish with him.'

'Alas, my friend, it is all too late.'

'Is Eduardo any better than Anders?' Neil asked. 'After all, he set out to seduce Rosa in much the same way for much the same reasons. And he did it twice.'

'No! It's not the same,' Lucio protested. 'Eduardo loved Rosa. What he did, he did for love. Love can drive a man and make him do things. But Anders is selfish and cruel. He is just a greedy spoilt child! You can't compare the two.'

'You can, as far as I'm concerned. In my book they're both bastards. What do you think, Milos?'

'I reserve my opinion. Ramon is not yet finished with Eduardo. I think by the end of the day we will know what kind of man Eduardo is. Am I right, Ramon?'

'As always,' Ramon replied, but without a trace of warmth or humour in his voice. 'Whatever you think of Eduardo or Anders, what does it matter now? It's all too late. Much, much too late.' Ramon finished his second espresso as he had the first, and sat back to complete his story.

'It is not too late, Ramon,' cautioned Milos. 'It is not too late. You know what I'm saying, no?'

'The story has to be told, Milos.'

Normally, at this stage, Ramon's audience would be on the edge of their seats, eager for the conclusion. But today was different and they all sensed it. There was an air of doom, of impending tragedy. It was hard to put a finger on, but it was there. They were still keen, of course, to hear how the story developed. The problem wasn't the story. It was the ending they were apprehensive about. How would it all end?

Chapter Forty-Six

Eduardo was devastated. His wife and his best friend! It took time for the double betrayal to sink in. He'd convinced himself that the call had been innocent, because that was what he wanted to believe. What stunned him most was that he knew that Annemieke loved him. She wasn't play-acting, stringing him along with cold, calculating deception. She loved him! He was sure of it. Yet he looked at the log the investigators had kept, and despaired over the photos.

Anders. He should have known better. A soft groan escaped his lips as he confronted his own stupidity. He winced when he thought of the fax he had sent to Anders. And the number of times he'd thanked him personally for taking care of Annemieke. But how could she let him con her? Seduce her? She knew what he was like. There was no sense to it.

The private investigators had learned from experience to let the evidence do the talking. They kept in the background, watching their client surreptitiously. This way, if he spat the dummy he'd just rip up the reports and photos rather than directing his anger and hostility towards them. They waited to see Eduardo's reaction.

'I must compliment you on your thoroughness,' he said. 'I wish there were some mistake. The evidence, unfortunately, is overwhelming.'

Their account was pinned to the log. He paid in cash. He left immediately, without shaking hands. That was something else they'd learned to expect.

Eduardo needed time to think. He couldn't face his office and he couldn't go home. He caught a taxi to Circular Quay and bought a return ticket on the Manly ferry. He travelled back and forth across the harbour, oblivious to its beauty, and to the other passengers. Strangely, he felt no anger, just an overwhelming sorrow and sense of loss.

It was inevitable he realised, that Anders would do what he had done. Anders had charm to burn, and was a formidable seducer of women. Adultery, like crime, is ninety percent opportunity, and Anders had never lacked for opportunity. Indeed, Eduardo had provided him with endless opportunity, gift wrapped it, and given it his blessing. Still, he had expected more of Annemieke. This is what troubled him the most. He knew that she would be no more than a passing fancy to Anders, a sop to his ego. But what was he to Annemieke? After Anders, would there be someone else? And someone else after that? Would they all simply be encounters? The gap between their ages yawned as wide as the entrance to Sydney Harbour.

Eduardo loved Annemieke more than ever now that he faced the prospect of one day losing her for good. The thought was too painful to contemplate, yet he had to consider the possibility. He could never let her go, no matter what. But how could he keep her when he was so often away from home? When his wife was so young and beautiful? The ferry bumped and bobbed as it tied up at Manly.

'Do you want me to order you dinner?' said the deckhand as he walked past him for the umpteenth time.

Eduardo ignored him, fascinated by a sudden thought. It hit him with the force of a sharp kick to the head. Yet he hesitated, unsure. Had the intervening years taught him nothing? But what choice did he have? What choice?

* * *

When Eduardo arrived home that night, Annemieke could see that something had upset him. He was depressed and unusually uncommunicative. She brought him a glass of wine, a 1980 St George. She'd opened it to cheer him up. She watched him absently take a sip. He knew what it was immediately. But before he could remonstrate with her for raiding his classic wines, she threw her arms around him and planted her lips over his so he couldn't speak. She giggled and wouldn't stop kissing him until he responded in kind.

'You deserve it,' she said, 'for working so hard and being such an adorable husband.'

She wriggled out of his grasp and walked away with an exaggerated sway of her hips. What she imagined was a street girl's walk.

The irony was not lost on Eduardo, yet still he smiled. Whatever the attraction was with Anders, Eduardo could not doubt her love for him. Clearly, Annemieke was not putting on an act.

'Damn you, Anders,' he said to himself. But despite his Argentinian blood, he could not contemplate revenge. He might just as well have said 'Damn you, Eduardo', for he knew where the blame really lay.

He resolved not to think about Anders, because the thought of him with Annemieke would deaden him in a way Annemieke couldn't help but notice. And it was important to the plan twisting and turning in his mind that she suspect nothing.

He watched as she brought him some French brie and biscuits, and duck pate. He watched as she knelt straightbacked, and placed the tray on the table in front of him. Her every movement spoke of grace and elegance. She was beautiful. So beautiful. Every man in the world would look at her and see her as he did. He had no choice, and the realisation brought a wave of such overwhelming sadness that he reached out and grasped her hand.

Annemieke was puzzled, but smiled in a way that only confirmed his conviction. His plan was as simple as it was terrible.

He would put Annemieke beyond the reach of other predators. He would send her back to the shadows. He would take back his engagement present.

Eduardo announced his intention to return to Jakarta the following week. This gave Annemieke five days' notice. The investigator's log suggested this would be sufficient time for her to arrange a meeting with Anders, even though he intended to limit their options.

'Just a lightning visit,' he said. 'One meeting, that's it. Up Thursday morning, back Saturday morning.'

Annemieke saw this as an opportunity to end her relationship with Anders. It had gone on too long. All she'd wanted was to experience another man. She hadn't expected to fall victim to Anders' charm. She hadn't expected Anders to fall in love with her. Oh, he'd told her often enough how desperately he loved her, and she felt guilty for leading him on. She couldn't tell him it was over on the phone because that would be cowardly, and she didn't know how badly he'd take it. No, she would go to his apartment, she would tell him of her decision in person, and then they would part. Still friends, for Eduardo's sake. She loved Eduardo and he loved and trusted her. She would never betray Eduardo again.

Eduardo rose early on the day of his departure, confirmed the status of his flight from the bedside phone, and gently kissed Annemieke goodbye. He picked up his Mont Blanc pen from her bedside table, screwed its top back on, and slipped it into his case. Annemieke was always borrowing his pen, but could never remember to put the top back on. Half awake, half asleep, she looked so beautiful and vulnerable, and so utterly desirable that he nearly aborted his plans right there. He considered confronting her, there and then, with his knowledge. They could talk it through. She would weep and beg his forgiveness, and she would be sincere in her pledges of fidelity. But she'd made that pledge once before, at their wedding, and Eduardo knew that the world was full of Anders Petersons. How could he ever completely trust again where his trust had been betrayed? He couldn't take the risk of losing her.

He took a last look at her sleepy face, so perfect, so content, so unsuspecting, and engraved it upon his memory. He thought of all that Annemieke had been through in Los Angeles. He closed his eyes for a moment at the thought of what he had to do. Then he turned and walked away.

His taxi was waiting but it didn't take him to the airport. It took him instead, to the Sebel Town House, a small and exclusive hotel favoured by visiting musicians and entertainers. It was less than a kilometre from Anders' apartment.

Eduardo began his preparations. He listed the things he would need. An open razor headed the list. He would not be foolish enough to buy that in the Cross. And cottonwool pads. A black tracksuit, cheap and nondescript, of a type he'd never wear. It must have pockets. He wrote down Old Spice aftershave and deodorant, a far cry from the Egoiste he normally wore. He added rubber gloves to the list, and sneakers. In each case, the darker the better.

Borer killer was last on his list. He wanted a particular brand which had long since disappeared off the shelves of most hardware stores. He knew one store that still stocked it, because Jan had found it there and bought it to treat the woodworm that attacked artifacts they held in storage. The label wisely cautioned against use in confined spaces. It was eighty percent chloroform.

Eduardo put his list in his pocket. He walked away from the hotel before hailing a cab to take him to Camperdown. Eduardo knew he'd picked the right man when the driver looked up Missenden Road in his street directory. Eduardo would walk the rest of the way to the shops in Newtown. He probably didn't need to be so careful, but he took a perverse pride in exercising the caution he'd learned in Buenos Aires.

* * *

Anders rang at four-fifteen to confirm their arrangements. Roberto watched Annemieke get up and walk to the phone. He watched her fingers tense and her lips draw tight. She barely mumbled into the phone, but he heard every word. His heart ached. She saw him watching as she hung up and smiled. But it was a shadow of a smile.

He began to play the piece again, his playing indifferent, but Annemieke didn't pick him up on it. She was distracted and inattentive.

'Perhaps I should come back another time,' Roberto said.

'What?'

Annemieke looked at Roberto in surprise. She'd forgotten all about him! She was startled by the expression on his face. As if he were reproaching her for something.

'I'm sorry, Roberto,' she said. 'I didn't mean to ignore you. Let's start again. Chopin demands that both of us concentrate.'

But both teacher and pupil were distracted, and Annemieke cut the lesson short. Roberto gathered his music books and sullenly stood to leave.

'Use the rest of the day for practice at home,' Annemieke said. 'I don't know what's got into you since you passed your exam. Your playing has gone backwards.'

'I'm sorry,' he mumbled. 'I've been busy with other things.'

He looked up at her as he left and Annemieke thought he was about to cry. She wondered if something at home was upsetting him. Maybe he'd found a girl who hadn't yet found him. He was the right age. She watched him pedal off down the street then forgot him.

Chapter Forty-Seven

Eduardo wondered if the Kings Cross slasher was as thorough in his preparations. Probably not, he reasoned, for the slasher had no set target, and just struck where opportunity presented itself. Where the risk of capture was least. The slasher was an amateur. He, Eduardo, would be the professional. He laid his purchases down on the hotel bed, and checked them.

There were one or two discrepancies in his plan that worried him. The slasher always went for the body. His trademark was the horizontal slash across the breasts. Eduardo would be aiming higher. Also, the slasher didn't anaesthetise his victims before he struck. Nevertheless, Eduardo was certain the slasher would be blamed. Besides, the papers had already hinted at the possibility of copycats. He would leave Annemieke's handbag and jewellery intact to rule out theft as a motive. No. He was confident the attack would be seen as just another senseless act of violence by a maniac with a grudge against women. Sydney had its share of them.

He knew from the investigator's logbook that Annemieke never met Anders before eight-thirty in the evening unless they were going to a show. He knew she would arrive by taxi, get out at the corner, and walk down the narrow street to Anders' apartment. She would walk on the lower side, the same side as the building.

She had each time before. He would be waiting for her, in the narrow lane between the apartment building and the first of the terraces. There was little risk of discovery. The lane was barely wide enough to accommodate the handlebars of a bike. And it had steps. He hoped she'd come. He couldn't bear to go through with it all again.

He showered. He used the hotel shampoo. He washed off every trace of the toiletries he normally used. Annemieke had little sense of smell but he took no chances. He shaved, then splashed on Old Spice. He hated it. He lay on the bed with a towel around his waist. He thought about what he had to do.

Two incisions, he reasoned, half a centimetre apart and parallel. That should be enough. It would only take seconds, and he'd be gone. The chloroform would keep Annemieke unconscious for about a minute. That would be enough. Then she'd come to, realise what had happened and scream. People would hear and come to her help. She wouldn't suffer long. If they didn't come, she could easily make it to Anders' apartment. The blood would be messy but, whichever way, she would not suffer long.

Her suffering would come later. She was all too aware of Dr Tannen's caution. She knew there was no second chance. But Eduardo would be there to comfort her, to cocoon her in his love and soften the blow. She would be devastated, of course, but he would help her through it. His devotion would only make her love him more.

That was his plan. He lay on his back and went over and over it in his mind. But other thoughts rose unbidden. He tried to concentrate on his plan but Rosa was insistent. She appeared before him demanding his attention, her bloody butchers waiting for a sign. He jumped up off the bed and stumbled into the bathroom. He ran the tap and repeatedly doused his face in cold water, banishing Rosa but not his guilt.

His guilt had not lessened over the years, it had merely been pushed aside. Now it flooded his senses bringing regrets and questions he'd desperately repressed. Hadn't he always known in his heart that his plan was doomed – that Carlos would never stand by and let him walk away with Rosa? His superiors would never have forgiven him. No, he had condemned Rosa to her fate as surely as he had condemned Victor. Why? Because he could not bear for another man to have her if he could not? Was that the reason? The parallel wasn't lost on Eduardo. Poor Annemieke. There was nothing he could do. He could no more allow anyone to steal Annemieke from him than cut his own throat. He sank back onto the toilet seat and held his head in his hands, the heartless young man in an older man's body. The years had changed nothing.

Roberto bore all the agonies of those helpless individuals who love without hope. Added to his pain was the burden of her infidelity and his fears for her safety. His fear of the shadow in the unlit car.

'Once more,' he said to himself, 'then I will confront her.'

He knew where she would go and decided to get there before her. To stand guard under the stairs, and warn her if the man in the car made any move. But what could he do then? What could he do? This question tormented him. He had too long to think about the answer.

Eduardo left the Sebel at a brisk jog. He jogged down towards Rushcutters Bay, before winding his way back uphill towards Anders' apartment. His route dog-legged back and forth through laneways and quiet back streets. He approached the narrow lane between the two buildings from the opposite end. His nervousness had made him run faster than he intended. He paused to catch his breath, then slipped invisibly into the lane.

There were gateways into people's gardens. Of course there were! Why hadn't he considered this? People used the lane to carry their garbage out onto the street. Was it collection night? He looked up and down the narrow pavement. Nobody had put their bin out.

His heart rate slowed. He took a deep breath. And another. And another.

He prayed that Annemieke would come soon. He could barely stand the tension. Sweat stung his eyes. He wiped it away. Somebody walked past the lower end of the lane. Silhouetted! As he would be. Yes! The street was lighter than the lane. But wait! His mind replayed what his eyes had seen. He'd only seen the top half of the silhouette, probably less, because of the way the lane arced downwards. All he had to do was crouch. So he crouched, as low as he could.

He checked his watch. Eight-thirty. Come on! Come on! He put his hand in his pockets, checked the items he'd checked a hundred times before. All there, as he knew they would be. He heard footsteps. His heart turned cold. He crept silently towards the street. He heard laughter, and a door open. He waited. The door closed. Once more he glanced up and down the street. Deserted.

He shrank back into the shadows, blood charged with adrenalin, heart pumping.

'Good Christ,' he said. 'Sweet Jesus.'

Nine o'clock came and went. A man shouted and a woman wept somewhere in one of the houses further down. A drunk pissed on the wall opposite, before staggering up the stairs to the street above. Just before ten, a cab pulled up outside the apartment building. A man got out. Eduardo recognised his voice. It was Anders. It was Anders, with a voice amplified and distorted by alcohol, telling the cab to wait. It was Anders telling Eduardo to go. Annemieke would not be coming that night.

'Dear God,' Eduardo thought, 'I have to do it all again tomorrow!' He didn't think he could.

Chapter Forty-Eight

Annemieke showered and changed. Now that she had made up her mind to break with Anders, she felt strangely righteous. She had the foolish notion that Eduardo would be proud of her, proud of the sacrifice she was making for him. She dressed conservatively, in a suit with a blouse that buttoned to the neck. She even wore a bra. On top of it all, she wore the cloak of her newfound morality.

She would give Anders no chance to sweet-talk her. No chance to plead and soften her resolve. She would sit him down and, as kindly as she could, let him know that whatever had been between them was now finished. She hoped he'd be adult about it. They might even have dinner together afterwards.

The last, pale glow of departing day faded and died in the course of the taxi ride to Potts Point. The air was hot and sticky as she paid her driver off on the corner.

'Have a good weekend,' he said.

'You too,' she replied, making the effort to smile

She regretted wearing her suit. She wished she'd worn something cooler. To compound her problems, the tension which she'd largely held at bay through the day, now began to manifest itself.

'That's all I need,' she thought, 'puddles of perspiration under my arms.'

She groaned at the image. She knew she would handle Anders once she got over the first part. Starting was always hardest. As she walked the short distance to Anders' apartment, her mind rehearsed her opening sentences. They all sounded pathetically corny, like something from a television soapie. She was totally preoccupied as she passed the alley, and a pad of chloroform was clamped over her mouth and nose, and a strong arm dragged her into the alley. Her first instinct was to draw breath and scream. She lost consciousness.

Roberto jumped with fright. His breath came in fear-stricken sobs. It was happening again! His mind flashed back to another night under a different set of stairs. He wanted to rush to Annemieke, to save her. He wanted to cry out. But his fear let him do neither. He watched, unable to help, unable to tear his eyes away. The man had his head down as he dragged Annemieke into the alley. Then he looked up. He looked both ways up the tiny street. It only took an instant, but in that instant he was caught in the spill from the street light.

Roberto reeled back in shock. It was him! It was the man he'd locked eyes with from beneath the stairs in La Boca. The man was older, and he had changed, but he recognised the look. The look of fear, panic, repugnance. Shock overwhelmed him as his brain released locked away memories. Images, unspeakable images, flooded back. He saw Carlos advance on his mother. He saw his cock, hard and evil. He heard his laugh. He heard his mother struggle and the soldiers laughing. His pounding heart threatened to burst, and the six-year-old boy inside his body cried out in anguish. But no sound escaped his lips any more than it had ten years earlier. In fear, his voice once more abandoned him.

* * *

Eduardo dragged his razor out from the pocket of his tracksuit. He snapped it open. He had to be quick. He didn't dare look upon her face, for if he did, he knew his courage would fail. But how else could he be sure of severing the nerve? He didn't want to hack at her face. He didn't want to disfigure her. He just wanted to return her to the way she was when he met her.

When he had lain on the bed planning his every move, it had all been so simple. He'd visualised how he would do it. How he would slide the razor across her face. Now he realised his colossal blunder. He was right-handed. He had to strike the right side of her face. He would have to do it backhanded. Or move behind her. There wasn't time! There wasn't room. Dear God! He looked down at her to line up the razor. Her sleeping face was innocent, pure as an angel's.

'Do it!' the voice inside him screamed. 'Do it!'

But he hesitated, the razor poised centimetres from her cheek. He closed his eyes.

'Now!' screamed the voice. 'Do it now.'

Chapter Forty-Nine

Roberto hit Eduardo with all the force he could muster. It was a clumsy attack, but it was enough to knock Eduardo off balance. They faced each other, on their knees, the unarmed, tearful boy and the wild-eyed madman with the razor.

'Why?' Roberto screamed at him.

Her throat burned and she wanted to throw up. She was waking up. But where? She couldn't remember going to bed. What was happening to her?

'Why?' a voice screamed nearby. 'Why? Why?'

The fog swirled in her brain but slowly she began to remember. She was on her way to see Anders. Something had happened. What was it? She struggled to remember. She heard somebody sobbing. Eduardo?

'Because I love her. Because I love her.' Tension drained from Eduardo and he couldn't help himself.

'No! Why did you betray my mother and my father?'

Mother? Father? Eduardo? She opened her eyes. There was a thin slit of darkness paler than the rest . . . the sky? . . . and people moving within it.

'Why did you bring the soldiers?'

Her head ached and suddenly she vomited. The voices stopped. Her head cleared and she remembered. The hand over her face and the strong arm. She lay still and listened.

'Why did you betray us?'

Roberto?

'What are you talking about?'

Eduardo?

'It was you. I recognised you. Don't deny it. It was you!' The boy began to sob.

'Eduardo?'

He turned and found himself looking into Annemieke's frightened, wondering eyes. It was too much for him. The boy's accusations. Now Annemieke's. The razor dropped to the ground. It bounced and skidded. Annemieke picked it up. He cupped his head in his hands.

'Eduardo, what is this? What are you doing here?'

Tears streamed down Eduardo's face.

'I love you,' he said. 'I could not lose you to Anders. Or to anyone else.'

'But, Eduardo,' she begged, holding the razor in her fingers, horror in her eyes. 'What were you going to do with this?'

'Dr Tannen said . . .'

He stopped. He didn't need to say more. Annemieke looked at the distraught figure of her husband and understood exactly what he had intended to do.

'I couldn't do it,' he sobbed. 'I tried to close my eyes, but I looked at you. I couldn't do it.'

She dropped the razor and took him in her arms, the unfaithful wife made to face her husband's desperation. And the bottomless pit of her shame.

'I saved you,' said Roberto. 'He killed my mother and my father. He tried to kill you.'

'Thank you, Roberto,' she said softly. 'Now I think you should go. We'll talk later.'

The boy began to cry, silently, pitifully. But Annemieke had no comfort to give him. She gave him twenty dollars for a taxi instead.

Ramon finished speaking and sat motionless, head lowered.

'Is that it?' asked Milos bluntly.

Ramon nodded.

'Why did you change your story? That ending is preposterous. You did not tell us the story of Rosa and Victor, of their betrayal by Eduardo, only to have Roberto's accusations dismissed with a single sentence and a twenty dollar cab fare! That is preposterous!'

'A crock of shit.'

Ramon turned away from Milos and Neil.

'And you Lucio, what do you think?'

'I think it's bullshit too. I think you changed your story.'

'Why, Ramon?' asked Milos again. 'Are you going to tell us? Or shall I?'

Ramon stayed silent, head bowed.

'Then allow me. You have gambled with our friendships, my friend, and you have lost. We have all lost. And why? Because of your arrogance. The arrogance of Jorge Luis Masot alias Eduardo Remigio Gallegos alias Ramon Basilio Pereira. You think we didn't suspect this was your confession? We – each of us! – suspected this. We tried to warn you. But no! You are too smart. You think you can tell us fiction and convince us that it is truth. Sometimes you almost succeed. But this time you told a true story thinking you could trick us into believing it was fiction like all your other stories.

'That was unbelievable arrogance. You were right when you said "truth does not have the convenience of fiction". You know that. We know that. And, Ramon, we are not so stupid that we can't tell the difference! I'm not certain when you realised this, when you realised you had lost control of your little game. So you changed your story. You gave us this trite ending.

'Ramon, you have done a terrible thing. We did not ask to know your sorry history. We did not want to know. We were happy taking each other at face value and enjoying each other's stories. But I for one will not sit at the same table as Jorge Luis Masot.'

'Me neither. If you're not Eduardo . . . Jorge – call him what you like – why did you change the ending? If you are, then you're not somebody I want to know.' Neil looked contemptuously at Ramon. 'Jesus Christ, you're an arsehole.'

'Is it true, Ramon? Is it true what Milos says? Are you this man Eduardo?'

Ramon ignored Lucio's plea. He sat, face expressionless, saying nothing.

'I am sorry, Ramon, sorry that you felt you had to do this thing. I will miss our Thursday lunches.' Lucio was almost in tears.

Gancio approached the table with coffees and cognac. He took one look at their faces and hesitated.

'You owe us the truth, Ramon.' Milos now sounded more resigned than angry. 'For old time's sake, you owe us the real ending. Eduardo took back his gift, didn't he? The most precious gift any man can give to a woman – that is how you described it. That is how I expected the story to end. And I expected retribution. If not, why bring Roberto back into your story? You owe us, Ramon, in the name of all the lunches we have had together. You owe us the truth.'

Ramon played with the crumbs on the tablecloth before him. He absently picked up the pepper mill and, using it as a pestle, began to grind the crumbs to dust. They stared at him, waiting for his reply.

'Do not judge me yet,' he said in a voice so small they strained to hear him. 'You are quite right, my friends, that is not how the story ended. In truth, the story still awaits its final chapter. But the events did not occur in the way I just told you. That is not what happened. I will backtrack but, please, first some coffee.'

'Fuck the coffee.'

'Fuck you, Neil! Fuck you! Fuck you! Let him have his coffee. We'll all have some coffee! If this is our last lunch together let's do it properly.' Lucio glared at Neil daring him to argue.

'I agree with Lucio,' said Milos. 'What harm can it do to have a coffee? Let's all have a coffee, then let Ramon finish his story. Gancio, please serve.'

They drank their coffee and sipped their cognacs in silence. There was nothing left to do but preside over the ashes of their lunches, and of a story that had gone horribly wrong.

Chapter Fifty

Roberto was a coward. Not by choice. All of us want to be heroes and Roberto was no exception. But violence terrified him. It immobilised him. It stole his breath and denied him the use of his limbs. Just as he had been unable, as a small boy, to come to his mother's defence, so he was now unable to defend Annemieke. Twice the boy was tested, albeit in the most cruel of circumstances, and twice he was found wanting.

So he didn't rush headlong into that dark, narrow lane unarmed to tackle a man who could pick him up and snap him like a twig. He stayed hidden in the shadows of the stairway while Eduardo's razor raked Annemieke's face, not in delicate incisions half a centimetre apart, but in frenzied, panic-driven slashes.

Roberto watched as the man in the black tracksuit reappeared. Watched as he snatched quick looks up and down the narrow street. The man began to jog towards him. He jogged across the street. He jogged directly under the street light. He jogged briskly up the concrete steps, and away.

Roberto didn't run to her. He thought she was dead. He couldn't bear to look at her dead. Then he heard a muffled cry. Then sobs. Then the sound of somebody being sick. Then a scream. Of fright? Pain? Then he heard a cry of such pain and agony, his heart stopped and his blood froze in his veins.

'No!' she cried. 'Oh God! No!'

He saw Annemieke stagger out of the alley. Her hands covered her face. Even in the dark he could see the blood. He saw her stagger to the apartment block. Saw her press the intercom. Heard the buzzer. Saw the door open. She staggered inside. He heard people's voices. Lights went on down the street.

Later, witnesses said they saw a tall, thin young man run away.

Annemieke staggered sobbing into Anders' apartment. She needed him to take her in his arms. Hold her. Comfort her. Share her tragedy. Instead, she saw Anders recoil in horror. When he finally put his arm around her, it was only to guide her to the bathroom. He poured water into the basin and gave her a towel.

'Jesus Christ!' he said. 'Jesus Christ!'

He dialled emergency. He went back into the bathroom sickened by all the blood. Especially blood tainted by scandal. Annemieke fainted and he caught her as she fell. He lay her down on the bathroom floor and turned her head to the side. He didn't want her to drown in her own blood. Not in his bathroom.

The ambulance arrived, and the police. He asked what hospital she'd be taken to. No, he wasn't going with her. The one kind thing he did was ring the father of an ex-girlfriend. He was one of Australia's leading neurosurgeons and he remembered meeting Annemieke. She had told him all about the Los Angeles clinic and Dr Tannen. Peter Metcalf was a good man. Of course he would attend her.

Then Anders busied himself sprinkling stain-removing powder over the blood on his carpet, before the police trod it all through the apartment.

Annemieke was taken to St Vincent's where a theatre was already being prepared for her.

Eduardo jogged back to the Sebel Town House. Just another jogger dodging dog shit and syringes. In his black tracksuit, in the hot evening air, it wasn't hard to work up a solid sweat. Besides, tension had given him a good base to build on. He disposed of the razor and gloves through an iron grille over a storm drain. He buried the bottle of borer killer and the cottonwool pads under rubble in a mini-skip.

He collected his key from the desk. The night clerk put his shaking hands down to exhaustion. Why did people jog? He couldn't see the point.

Eduardo poured himself a large scotch, and drank it so quickly it hurt. He poured another. He stripped off his tracksuit and checked it for blood spots. There were several. But he'd chosen his tracksuit well. The fleecy-lined cotton had absorbed the blood like blotting paper and, against the black, the blood spots looked no different to sweat.

He put the tracksuit back into the plastic bag it had come in. He did the same with his shoes and socks. He packed the lot into a carton and taped it up. Tomorrow he would send it by courier to Jakarta. He'd dispose of it there.

He showered. He took his time and scrubbed himself from head to toe. He towelled himself dry, then splashed on his familiar Egoiste. He lay down on the bed, naked and exhausted, a glass by his side, and a bottle by the glass.

Returning to the alley for the second time had taken more nerve than he had thought he possessed. Now that it was over, he was glad Annemieke hadn't turned up on the first night. The police or Jan would have spent all day Friday trying to track him down in Indonesia. He smiled. Phil and Don had tried to find him often enough, and never succeeded. Still, they might have checked with the airline, and that could have proved embarrassing.

Then it was time to face his thoughts, to consider what he'd done. To let remorse wash over him, to purge his regrets. He had to be over doubt and self-recriminations by morning. He let the bitter tears flow, and wallowed in whisky and self-pity.

He got up at five, not having slept, and phoned the airport. Garuda flight GA 899 was due in at six forty-five a.m. He dressed without showering and caught a taxi to the airport. He arrived at the airport as dishevelled as any incoming businessman. He knew from previous experience that it takes roughly twenty minutes to clear immigration and customs, when you don't have to stand around the carousel waiting for bags.

He bought the *Sydney Morning Herald* and the *Telegraph*, and sat down to wait out the time. The *Telegraph* carried the story on the third page, with a front page banner leading the way. 'Kings Cross Slasher Claims Fourth Victim!' Not bad, he thought. But the sub-head grabbed his full attention. 'Police hunt tall youth.' He raced through the story. Two witnesses had seen the youth running from the crime scene. He was tall, he was thin, and he might have had long hair. They saw him run up the same steps he had.

Eduardo felt the onset of panic. Who was he? What had he seen? What was he doing there? Why hadn't he spotted him? If he'd seen anything, wouldn't he have done something? Yelled out? Come to help Annemieke? Eduardo calmed his mind and began to think. There was a lot of crime and illicit activity in the Cross. The kid might have been there to buy or sell drugs. Or sell his arse.

He could be a runaway. Or already wanted by the police. There could be any number of reasons why he hadn't cried out, why he wanted to be somewhere else when the cops came. That's if he saw anything. But he did, didn't he?

It didn't matter. The kid wasn't going to say anything. And if he did, could he recognise him? Eduardo doubted it. At least the kid had served a purpose. He was the prime suspect.

He turned his attention to other matters. The story identified Annemieke as 'the wife of businessman and socialite, Eduardo Gallegos'. He noted that she had been taken to St Vincent's. It spoke of multiple lacerations, yet he had planned only two. Exaggeration? He tried to think, to take his mind back to the blind panic of those fateful few seconds. What had he done? He had a dreadful feeling that he'd done a lot more damage than he'd intended. He felt sickened. His control was badly shaken. Dear God. Poor Annemieke!

He read on. Her family had been notified. Police believed her husband was away on business in Indonesia. That much of his plan was still in place. It reassured him. He checked his watch. Five past seven. Time to make his way down the escalator to the arrivals hall. Time to mingle with the tired travellers from flight GA 899, and join the queue for a cab.

He went directly to St Vincent's, arriving shortly after eight. They took care of his overnight bag, and escorted him to his wife's bedside. They said they'd notify the police.

They'd put Annemieke in a four-person ward and tightly curtained off her bed. She was asleep, still feeling the effects of her post-op sedation. Eduardo sat by her side and he took her hand.

The lower part of her face was swathed in bandages though none covered her eyes. He could see she was pale, deathly pale, but what did he expect? His heart went out to her. Tears filled his eyes. But he knew that what he had done he'd done for love. There was honour in his motive. It was necessary. It would never be necessary again.

He rubbed her hand and kissed it. He sat there, unmoving, for an hour and a half while she slept. He never took his eyes off her. Her eyes flickered. He squeezed her hand. Her eyes met his. She tried to speak and couldn't, but it didn't matter. What could she say that the distress in her eyes hadn't already made obvious?

'You're all right, Annemieke. You're safe now.'

Annemieke looked into his face, looking desperately for a sign of hope. She hung on his words.

'I love you,' he said. 'No matter what, I love you. You will always be beautiful to me.'

Annemieke closed her eyes. Tears slid onto the pillow. Her body heaved with sobs.

Eduardo collected his bag from reception, and a message to phone Detective Sergeant Lenehan at Kings Cross police station. He rang from the hospital.

Lenehan extended his regrets, admitted that they had little to go on, and added nothing to what Eduardo had already read in the paper. He promised to keep Eduardo informed the minute there were any new developments. Eduardo thanked him sincerely, gave him some contact numbers, and went home. He didn't expect to hear from him again. After he had showered, he rang Jan and Lita. They were devastated. Eduardo gave them what comfort he could.

He returned to visit Annemieke in the afternoon. Jan and Lita were there. They hugged and consoled each other. They stayed by Annemieke's side for two hours but she didn't wake up.

Eduardo asked to speak to the surgeon and was given Peter Metcalf's number. He rang immediately. 'Please God,' he thought to himself. 'Don't let it all have been in vain!' He knew how skilled Metcalf was.

The receptionist put him through.

'Hello, Peter?'

'Eduardo, my dear fellow. What can one say? What a tragedy.'

'I'm relieved that it was you who operated on Annemieke. I don't know how that came about, but I sincerely appreciate it. If anyone can help her, you can.'

Peter Metcalf was a good doctor and no fool. He didn't know what Annemieke was doing in Anders' apartment while Eduardo was away and he wasn't going to be the one who raised it with Eduardo. He would comment only in his professional capacity.

'We've done all we can. You appreciate we're not playing on a level pitch here. Normally, a clean cut with a razor wouldn't present too many problems. There were five major lacerations. Only three cut across her right cheek. Her nose took the impact of the other two. The nose is not a problem. Her right cheek is another matter.

'Two of the lacerations cut right across Dr Tannen's work. There was not a lot we could do there. I've spoken to Dr Tannen and he would like to examine Annemieke as soon as she is fit to travel. He is not optimistic, and from now on, time is your greatest enemy. If I were you, Eduardo, I'd get her on a plane bandages and all. Dr

Tannen can do things we're not yet equipped to do. I'm very sorry that I can't be more encouraging, Eduardo. That poor girl, your poor wife, she doesn't deserve this.'

'Thanks, Peter. Thanks for all you've done.' Eduardo was silent for a moment. 'Let me know when you think Annemieke can fly. We'll grab whatever chance we can.'

Eduardo knew there was little cause for hope. Dr Tannen had made that clear. But it would give Annemieke something to hang on to, something to help her over the initial shock. He would give her his full encouragement. He went to a florist and ordered a huge bouquet of cornflowers and freesias. He found a card with a baby monkey on it. The monkey had a bandage around its head as if it had toothache. He signed it 'From Osh', and framed the signature with little x's.

He returned to St Vincent's that evening. He was the perfect husband, the adoring lover, and her best friend.

By the following morning, Annemieke had begun to come to terms with her new injury. She clung desperately to the hope that Dr Tannen could help her as he had before. Eduardo was a tower of strength and she bitterly regretted having deceived him. Time and again she thought of confessing. But what would it accomplish? It was all over. Why cause him more pain?

He came to see her on the way to his office. It was Sunday, but he had a lot of work to catch up on. He held her hand and filled her with optimism. He'd already booked their flight to Los Angeles. Peter Metcalf thought she could travel in two days. She'd be uncomfortable, but she'd have pain killers and sedatives. He kissed her again, told her how much he loved her, and went to his office.

Her brothers came at noon and, then at six o'clock, Roberto came to visit her.

Roberto looked terrible, as if he hadn't slept for weeks. He seemed unable to look at her. She couldn't smile to put him at ease, so she held out her hand. To her surprise, he took her hand and kissed it, and clutched it to his chest.

'Annemieke,' he said, his voice shaking. 'I have something to tell you.'

Chapter Fifty-One

Eduardo was surprised to see Annemieke's visitor, the boy Roberto. Eduardo had not thought to ring him. His presence irritated him.

Eduardo stood awkwardly at the foot of her bed with yet another bouquet of flowers, not knowing whether he should intrude. Roberto seemed embarrassed, but then, he always did.

'I was just going,' he said.

'No hurry, Roberto. You are welcome to stay.' Eduardo smiled. 'Annemieke is probably getting tired of my company anyway.'

The boy just looked at him as if he'd never seen him before, then turned to Annemieke.

'I'm sorry,' he said. And left.

'Strange boy,' said Eduardo.

Annemieke's bandages had been replaced. Thin pads were taped to her cheeks and across her nose. Eduardo bent over and kissed her. Her response was listless.

'Soon you will be able to open your own florist shop,' he said, not knowing where to put his latest offering. 'Soon the hospital will run out of vases, and they'll have to put your flowers in the bottles people pee in.'

But she didn't react to his attempts at humour. She seemed far away, distracted. She didn't avoid contact with his eyes so much as make no effort to establish it. He took her hand gently.

'What's the matter, sweetheart? Eh? I know this must be difficult for you. It's unfair. And it's cruel. But don't give up hope.' He squeezed her hand gently, but she still looked away.

'I stayed back late at the office so I could ring the Feldman Clinic. You are booked into surgery on Wednesday. Dr Tannen is delighted that we can move so quickly. That's good news, isn't it.'

She nodded.

'I spoke to Peter Metcalf again. He said you're healing very well, and there won't be any scars. None that other people will notice.'

Annemieke turned her head to look at him. She looked pale and drawn.

'I'm tired,' she said. 'Too much has happened. Would you mind . . .'

Eduardo was being dismissed. It took a moment or two for it to register.

'You want me to leave?'

She squeezed his hand, an instinctive reaction to the childlike incredulity in his voice.

'Please, darling. I'm very tired.'

'I'll come back later.'

'Tomorrow will be fine.'

Eduardo wandered down the corridor towards the elevator. What's gone wrong, he wondered? How could she be so tired? She'd slept most of the day. Then he realised that what seemed past history to him was only forty-eight hours to her. What he was shutting out of his mind, she was reliving.

He could imagine the thoughts going through her head. If she hadn't been unfaithful to him, none of this would have happened. She wouldn't have been outside Anders' apartment to fall victim to the Slasher.

'She has a lot to come to terms with,' he thought. 'No wonder she's tired. Poor Annemieke.'

These were his thoughts as he stepped out onto the pavement, paused to adjust his eyes to the darkness, and began walking towards his car.

'How do you feel now, Jorge Luis Masot?'

Eduardo froze. The surprise was so complete he was caught totally off-guard.

'You killed my mother and father. Now you have mutilated your wife.'

Sickened, he turned. It was Roberto. He stood in the pathway of a rundown terrace house, in the shadow of its overgrown garden.

'Roberto . . . I . . .'

Roberto came up to him, eyes blazing, walking slightly sideways as if fearing he'd get struck at any second.

'Don't try to deny it,' he said. 'I saw your reaction.'

'What? You startled me, that's all. What are you saying?'

'I saw your reaction, Jorge Luis Masot.' The boy crabbed around him as if he were an exhibit in a gallery, never taking his wild eyes off him. 'And I saw you two nights ago. In the alley.'

The boy seen running away. Tall. Thin. Dear God! It was Roberto! Eduardo fought hard to control his panic. It seemed like forever, but only milliseconds had passed. Anger reared up inside him. This boy, this snivelling, pathetic wimp was going to destroy him. He couldn't let it happen. He had to think, take control.

'What nonsense are you talking, Roberto? God knows what's going on inside your childish brain. I am not listening to any more of this.'

Eduardo began to walk away, but the boy walked with him.

'Oh you'll listen to me, Jorge Luis Masot. If you don't, I'm sure the police will.'

Eduardo stiffened. He kept walking, thinking. The police would check with immigration and the airline and he'd be history. The boy had him. He had to listen. But he could still argue.

'If you wish to continue this insane conversation, we shall do so in my car. Look! See how people are staring.'

They walked in silence to his car. Eduardo needed the time to think. To plan. He unlocked the car. Roberto climbed into the front passenger seat. His hands were shaking. The boy was so immature.

'Now tell me, Roberto,' Eduardo said gently. 'You are obviously upset. Look at you! You are shaking. And you're not thinking clearly. I don't know how you came to see the terrible thing that happened to Annemieke, but if you were there, why didn't you get help?'

The fire had gone from the boy. His store of courage was exhausted. Now he again had to face his cowardice.

'I know what I saw, Eduardo. I saw you. I knew Annemieke was going to see that man who upset her. I got there before her and hid under the concrete steps.'

So that's where the little wimp had been! Why hadn't he seen him arrive? He thought back. He couldn't see the steps from inside the alley. It was too narrow.

'I thought she was in danger. There was another man. In a car. He'd been watching her.'

Jesus Christ! How long had he been following her? The pup was in love with her!

'I saw Annemieke walk up to the building. I saw you jump out of the alley and put something over her mouth. You looked up and down the street and the light shone on your face. I saw you clearly.'

Roberto's voice had begun to rise and he fought to hold down the sobs that were building up inside him.

'I saw then who you really are.'

'What do you mean?'

'How could I forget the face of the man who betrayed my parents? You are the man who saw me hiding in the rug beneath the stairs. You are Jorge Luis Masot!'

Roberto began to sob uncontrollably.

'You are Jorge Luis Masot. That is why you were sick the night I came to your house, and told you my real name.'

'That was fever. The doctor confirmed it next day.'

'No!'

'Yes, Roberto.' Eduardo waited until the boy had calmed down. 'You poor boy.' The tide had turned for Eduardo. With a softness and tenderness he did not feel, he began to reason with the boy.

'God knows you have had an unfortunate life, Roberto. What happened to you is unspeakable. But things like that can scar you for ever, Roberto. It can distort your mind. Make you believe you see things which aren't true. This is what happened to you.'

'No!'

'Yes, Roberto. You followed Annemieke because you love her. No, don't deny it. It is not hard to love Annemieke. You say you saw the man attack her. Come out of the alley and grab her.'

'It was you!'

Eduardo ignored him.

'Tell me, Roberto, why didn't you go to Annemieke's help? Even if you had just rushed out and stood in the middle of the street shouting, the man would have run away.'

Roberto couldn't look at him.

'Don't you realise what happened to you? Your mind played tricks on you. The terror you felt unlocked the terror of your past. Suddenly you were back in La Boca, a petrified six year old. You became confused. You confused what you were seeing in your mind with what was happening in front of you. You saw a face, and you thought it was the face of the man called Jorge who betrayed your parents.'

'No! It was the same man. It was your face.'

'Roberto, you were only six years old.' Eduardo's eyes bored into him. His words came unrelentingly, pummelling and chipping away at Roberto's conviction. 'You would have trouble now recognising your own parents. You have admitted as much.'

The boy wept, face in his hands.

'You saw a man, Roberto, and your mind saw another. I have been to Anders Peterson's apartment many times. I know the street. I know the alleyway. I know the steps. It is not possible to recognise anyone from where you were hiding. The street lights are not bright enough.'

'No! I saw you! I saw you clearly. You ran past me up the steps.'

'Roberto, you saw a man run up the steps. Why you insist on giving him my face I don't know.' Eduardo was angry now, exasperated. 'I didn't run up any steps. I was on a plane coming back from Jakarta.'

'No! You were there.'

'No, Roberto. Now you are wrong and you must accept it. I am prepared to forget this conversation ever took place. But if you persist I will get angry. Besides, why on earth would I ever hurt Annemieke? She is my wife. We love each other.'

'You wanted to punish her.'

'Why?'

'Because she was seeing another man.'

'Was she?'

'Yes. You know she was. The man Anders.'

'Roberto, you must stop this nonsense. Anders is a good friend. I asked Anders to look after Annemieke while I am away. That is all.'

'No! That's not how it is!'

'Yes, Roberto, it is. Come, let me drive you home. It is time you stopped all this nonsense.'

Eduardo looked at the boy beside him. He was crumpled against the seat, sobbing softly. He looked pathetic.

Eduardo started the car.

'One thing, Roberto. I must warn you. I will forgive your ramblings. But I don't want you to say a word of this to anyone. To anyone, you hear? Particularly Annemieke.'

'It's too late.'

Eduardo's heart stopped.

'What do you mean?'

'I told Annemieke everything. Tonight . . . at the hospital.'

Eduardo felt his body grow cold.

'Did she believe you?' he asked quietly.

'Maybe.' A note of triumph crept back into Roberto's voice. 'I know what I saw, Eduardo. Now you will have to live with her suspicions for the rest of your life. Every time she looks at you she will wonder. Every time she looks at her face in the mirror. Every time you get into bed together. Doubt will nag at her for the rest of her life. She will never be sure of you again. And you, you will never be sure either. You will never know what she believes. And every time you look at her, you will be reminded of what you have done to her, and what you did to my mother and father. For the rest of your life you will be reminded. For the rest of your life. That is your punishment, Eduardo Gallegos. That is your punishment, Jorge Luis Masot.'

Eduardo pulled up outside the boy's house. Roberto opened the car door and fled into the night.

'Yes,' said Milos thoughtfully. 'That is what happened. Revenge is a terrible thing, but who can argue that it wasn't deserved?'

'Revenge!' Neil turned on Milos. 'What sort of revenge is that? You think that is punishment enough? You think that fits the crime? That's no punishment to a bastard like Eduardo. If that man could live with the knowledge of what he did to Rosa and Victor, then he can live with what he did to Annemieke. Why not? That's not punishment! That's not revenge! Do you think Rosa would be satisfied? Imagine if Rosa was looking down from the heavens. Would she now rest in peace, satisfied that Eduardo had finally got what was coming to him? Satisfied that justice was done? No! Would you? Would I? No! She would want more! Her soul would cry out for justice and justice demands more! Roberto was a wimp and his revenge was wimpish. Justice demands more!'

'Neil is quite right, Milos. Justice demands more. Justice demands that Eduardo pay for his crimes, and pay in full.' Ramon groped for his glass. 'Some more wine, perhaps? My throat is dry and, Milos, you interrupted before I had concluded my story.'

'There is more?'

'Yes, my friend, there is more.'

Chapter Fifty-Two

Annemieke and Eduardo once again made the long anxious journey to the Feldman Clinic. That first time Annemieke had known in her heart that the trip would be successful. This time there were no such feelings, and she was prepared for the worst.

Yet Dr Tannen saw things differently. The incisions were clean, almost as if they had been done by a scalpel, and that helped. He claimed a seventy percent success where they had expected none. It was not joy Annemieke felt, but relief. Relief that she would not be banished once more to the shadows. Certainly, the spark had gone from her smile forever and, with it, a degree of her self-confidence. But at least she could still smile. She could still smile.

They never discussed Roberto's revelations. Annemieke did not dare, because in doing so she would have to admit to her infidelity, and perhaps she would also have to face the horrible truth that the man she had married was a monster. Suspicions and doubts lingered. But Annemieke found it hard to reconcile Roberto's accusations with the man who was her husband. Eduardo did nothing to give substance to Roberto's claims. No husband was ever more supportive or understanding or loving. Yet Roberto had spoken with conviction, and revealed his pain and humiliation when he had no need to speak at all. Unless . . . unless . . . he was telling her the truth.

Annemieke lived two lives, one which she shared with her husband, and one which she shared with the dark suspicions which inhabited her lonely hours. Sometimes, with the passage of time, doubts and suspicions can wither for lack of sustenance, and perhaps this would have been the case with Annemieke and Eduardo. But for Rosa.

Rosa returned. And she demanded retribution. She came to Eduardo as his head lay on the pillow alongside Annemieke's. She walked along the line of prisoners towards him while her butchers waited for her to choose their victims. But this day, as the butchers stropped and sharpened their blades, Rosa had only one victim in mind. She stopped in front of him. She smiled, a sad bitter smile. And, this time, she spoke to him.

'Was it not enough to betray and destroy me? Did you learn nothing? Is there no room in your heart for anyone but yourself?'

'Forgive me, Rosa,' Eduardo pleaded. 'Rosa, I beg you! Forgive me! Rosa!'

She turned towards the men in their bloody aprons.

'A heart so selfish does not deserve to live,' she snapped. 'Take it from him!'

'No, Rosa, no!' he called after her as they dragged him away. 'Rosa! Rosa! No! Rosa!'

Annemieke heard the words clearly. How could she not? Eduardo was shouting, screaming.

'No, Rosa! Please! *Ten piedad! Ten compasión!* Forgive me! Have mercy, Rosa! No! Rosa!'

'Rosa!' . . . the name she had never wanted to hear from her husband's lips. 'Rosa!' . . . the name that confirmed Roberto's story. 'Rosa!' . . . the name that brought home the truth about her husband and that night outside Anders' apartment.

She reached over to her bedside table. For what? Something! Anything! Her hand closed around Eduardo's Mont Blanc pen, which she'd borrowed and left as usual uncapped. She clutched it in her hand like a weapon.

'No!' she screamed. Then stabbed it into the face of the monster beside her. He screamed, but she ignored him. He fought her, but she fought back, stabbing, stabbing, stabbing, until he fought no more, and the blood from his sightless eyes splashed over her. She fled the house.

She thought she'd killed Eduardo, but she'd sent him to live in hell instead, tormented by the belief that Rosa had reached back from the grave and through Annemieke exacted her revenge. His nightmare became reality, his reality his nightmare. He was trapped forever in the dungeon of his blindness, trapped forever in his worst fears. There was no escaping Rosa now. Never again could he open his eyes and admit the light that would drive away her shadow.

'My God! Oh my God!' Milos could not look at the man who was his friend, even though he knew Ramon could never see him. Then none could speak. Tears ran down Lucio's cheeks but he was oblivious to them.

'Is this the justice you wanted, Neil?' It was too much for Lucio. He could not bear his grief in silence. He blamed Neil. It was Neil who had pushed for this final, terrible chapter. 'Look at this man before you! Is this the justice you wanted? You tell me to my face. Is this what you wanted? Does our friendship of the last four years mean nothing to you?'

But Neil was unrepentant.

'So,' he said finally. 'So that is what happened. That is how you lost your sight. I can't pity you, Ramon. You deserve all you got. Probably more.'

'The pity,' said Milos sadly, 'is that you told this story. That you chose to tell this story at all.'

'Yes why, Ramon?' pleaded Lucio. 'Why did you tell this story?'

'It's all right, Lucio, it's all right,' Ramon said soothingly. 'I asked you all not to judge me too harshly, yet to a man you have. Do you honestly believe I could be this monster Eduardo Remigio Gallegos? Do you think so little of me?'

'Are you saying this story is not true, that you invented the whole thing? If so, then I don't believe you!'

'No, Neil, I am saying no such thing. I am only saying that I am not Eduardo or Jorge, and never was.'

'Bullshit! You're a lying bastard!'

'Enough! Enough, Neil.' Milos adopted the manner of their unofficial chairman. 'Think for a change. Over the past four years there have been many occasions when we have fallen prey to Ramon's tricks and games, no? Does it not occur to you that this whole sorry affair might just be another of his tricks? Think! Let me ask you this, Ramon. Are you such a good storyteller that you can confess your terrible past and have us doubt the truth of it? Or invent a story and have us question the fiction? Are you, Ramon?'

'Yes, Milos, if you believe this story to be fiction, then apparently I am. However, I maintain it is a true story. But maintaining it is true does not implicate me in a confession.'

'Then why did you change the ending? If you had not changed the ending I could convince myself that you were not this man Eduardo. But you changed the ending. Why did you do this if you did not have something to hide?'

Ramon reached towards Lucio and felt for his shoulder. He let his hand rest there.

'Lucio, my friend, I did not change the ending. That is precisely the ending I intended. It was a fine embellishment, I think. And I should thank you all for your help in making it work.'

'This is preposterous, Ramon. You are preposterous.' Once more Neil raised his voice, and it echoed around the empty restaurant. 'You went too far and you trapped yourself. You can sweet-talk as much as you like, but you can't talk your way out of this. You are Eduardo, Ramon, and you will never convince me otherwise.'

'Oh?' said Ramon evenly. 'You have evidence for this assertion? Would you care to share it with us?'

'Why did you not deny it when we first accused you of being Eduardo?'

'Why spoil a good story?'

'Oh, you laugh, Ramon, you can play the funny man. But the truth is, right from the very beginning, in describing Eduardo you described yourself.'

'I have explained that. We are about the same age, we share similar origins, mine somewhat more humble, of course and we both went to university and studied English. On this basis, I am not just Eduardo but a million other Argentinians.'

'And the printing?'

'Argentinians are as addicted to newspapers and magazines as Australians. Again, I have told you this. Millions read them, thousands work on their production.'

'What about the way you behaved? Your words can deceive but your body language tells us otherwise.'

'Oh really, Neil. Are you suggesting that storytellers may not use actions or gestures to underscore their story? Would you strip me of this most fundamental of devices? Really!'

'There is the matter of your blindness.'

'Ah, Neil, you are as blunt as ever. Still, it has taken you four years to ask. A car accident, Neil, a car accident. If I can be accused of anything, it is in having the poor taste to weave my disability into my story. But the choice was not mine. As I have told you more times than I can recall, my story is true.'

'You are preposterous!'

'Yes, Neil,' cut in Milos. 'He is preposterous. He has always been preposterous, no? He uses his blindness as a weapon. You're the one who pointed that out. He always maintains his stories are true, yet we cannot look into his eyes to see if this is so. Perhaps this story is no more true than the others, in which case we have no right to accuse Ramon of anything. On the other hand, if his story is true, we should take our time and consider all the evidence before we make accusations. It seems to me Ramon has deliberately led us down pathways we were too eager to pursue. Perhaps it is we who were blinded. Perhaps it is we who should be embarrassed.'

'I hear many "perhapses", Milos. Let me add another. Perhaps I should leave you now so that you can sort through the "evidence".

What was it your beloved Goethe wrote? "Truth like God does not exist, only the search for it"?' Ramon stood to leave. Milos handed him his cane.

'Truly, you are impossible!'

'Would you have it any other way, Milos?' Ramon chuckled. His back was straight, his head high. He appeared victorious, not defeated, and they could not help but notice. But was this more play acting? 'Gancio will see me to the door. I'm sure he will have no difficulty finding me a taxi. Till next Thursday, then?'

He bent forward and extended his hand. All three men hesitated, but finally each took his hand in turn.

'Till next Thursday,' they chorused.